W9-CES-369

A PIECE
OF THE
ACTION

ALSO BY STEPHEN SOLOMITA

A Twist of the Knife
Force of Nature
Forced Entry
Bad to the Bone

NEW HANOVER COUNTY
PUBLIC LIBRARY
201 CHESTNUT STREET
WILMINGTON, N C 28401

A PIECE
OF THE
ACTION

Stephen Solomita

G. P. Putnam's Sons
New York

G. P. Putnam's Sons
Publishers Since 1838
200 Madison Avenue
New York, NY 10016

Copyright © 1992 by Stephen Solomita
All rights reserved. This book, or parts thereof,
may not be reproduced in any form without permission.
Published simultaneously in Canada

Library of Congress Cataloging-in-Publication Data

Solomita, Stephen.
    A piece of the action / Stephen Solomita.
        p.   cm.
    ISBN 0-399-13730-0
    I. Title.
PS3569.0587P54   1992   91-43155 CIP
813'.54—dc20

Printed in the United States of America

1   2   3   4   5   6   7   8   9   10

This book is for Kathy.

I would like to thank Mrs. Kathleen Roche of the Hagstrom Map Company, Inc., for supplying me with a vintage N.Y.C. 5-Boro Atlas. The Hagstrom 5-Boro has been the cab driver's bible for as long as anyone can remember. I also have to thank my researcher, Judy Appello. Someday, back issues of publications like the *Daily News, Billboard, Variety,* and *Vogue* will be nicely stored in computers attached to laser printers. But, for now, access means hours of peering at microfilm that looks like it was printed in the nineteenth century and lost rolls of dimes poured into copiers that don't (or *won't*) work.

This is a work of fiction. Despite the well-documented (by the Knapp Commission) existence of the pad. Example: The pad was almost exclusively controlled by the patrol division of the NYPD. When it came to corruption, detectives, like Sal Patero, were strictly on their own. A word to the wiseguy.

One

DECEMBER 26, 1957

JAKE LEIBOWITZ stood in front of the bathroom mirror, trimming his tiny mustache and cursing his eyesight. He was all of thirty-seven years old and already his eyes were going bad. Walter Winchell's column in the *Mirror* was nothing more than a gray blur. If he wanted to read, to keep up with the fast crowd, he was going to have to get glasses.

"With the Jews, it's always the eyes," he said to himself. "If I don't watch it, I'll end up with coke-bottle glasses and a gray beard." He shook his head in disgust. "Now I'm talkin' to myself, again."

But he couldn't be angry with himself. Not on the brink of a New Year's which had the promise of ushering in a really *new* year. He'd been waiting a long time to get his big break, long enough to know there might not be another one coming. He intended to make the most of it.

"I got lost for a while," he muttered, lifting the scissors to the edge of his upper lip. "But I ain't lost now."

The jet-black hairs of his mustache were no more than an eighth of an inch long. When he stepped far enough away to bring the mirror into focus, they melted into one another like a dark smudge on a piece of paper.

He tossed the scissors into the bathtub. "I shoulda gone to the barber this afternoon. Gotta look good for the wops." He picked up a hairbrush and began to tear at the tight curls on his head. Jake kept his hair short, but he couldn't keep it down. His curls, especially in wet weather, stood out in every direction. Even in a suit, he looked more like a shaggy-headed beatnik than a nice Jewish gangster. That's why he never left his apartment without wearing a hat.

Jake loved hats the way some men love shoes, kept a dozen in his closet (his *mother's* closet, he reminded himself, mustn't forget that little fact) and usually tried on most of them before leaving the apartment.

"I never met a hat I didn't like," he said, chuckling at his own joke.

Soon, *very* soon, he'd have enough hats to fill a dozen closets. And he'd shop for his suits at Brooks Brothers instead of Robert Hall. Maybe he'd even have a tailor make one up by hand. But not a Jew tailor with glasses so thick they looked more like binoculars. He'd go to Chinatown and find a tailor from Hong Kong. Let the chink make him a gray sharkskin suit, then buy a pair of Italian shoes and a matching tie and, of course, a snap-brim fedora.

"It shoulda happened long ago, Jake," he told himself. "If life was fair. Which it ain't."

The bitch about it was that you could control a lot of things in your life, but you couldn't control everything. For instance, you couldn't control wars. He'd been a twenty-year-old kid when the war broke out, and he'd been coming up in the world. The Depression (they called it the *Great* Depression though he couldn't see anything great about it) had hit the packed immigrant neighborhoods of the Lower East Side with the wallop of a Colt .45. Even the gangsters had suffered. He should know, his father had been a gangster. At least until they found him floating in the East River.

That was in '33 and life for the Leibowitz family had been harder than hard after Poppa made the mistake of challenging the wops. The wops had a genius for organization. They based it on their families and the villages they'd come from in Sicily. Jews didn't do that. There was no Pinsk gang, no Bialystoker mob. Jewish gangsters wanted their kids to be doctors (or, at least, to *marry* doctors). And there were a lot more Italians than Jews in the good old U.S.A. All the Jews had come to New York (most of them to the Lower East Side which, in the 20's and 30's, seemed more like the Warsaw Ghetto than Manhattan) while the Italians had spread out. A wop who wanted to kill a Jew could call in a button man from Boston or Providence or Chicago. A Jew who wanted to kill a wop usually did it himself.

Still, even considering all that, even considering his poppa's big mistake, Jake Leibowitz had done okay. He'd begun by shoplifting his way through the middle of the Depression, working with several other boys, including an Italian. Then, in the natural course of things as he understood them, he'd graduated to commercial burglary, shimmying through unlocked bathroom windows until he'd outgrown his specialty. Until he was old enough to pick up a rod and take what he wanted.

It was too bad about the war. Too bad, because he'd understood the essential lesson. The wops didn't really care what you did to put bread in your mouth as long as you took care of them, as long as you gave them a piece of your bread. What was that old saying? The only sure things are death and taxes? For Jake, the wops were the government and the tribute he paid them was the gangster version of the graduated income tax.

Jake took another step backward and the face in the mirror jumped into focus. It wasn't a bad face, all in all. True, his eyes were set too close and his thin nose had a definite hook. But those eyes were a mild blue and the nose was small. Meanwhile, his cleft chin (as formidable as Robert Mitchum's) dominated his beak, just as high, prominent cheekbones dominated those narrow eyes.

"A regular Tony Curtis," he observed. "Only bigger." He tightened his chest muscles until the individual bands of tissue criss-crossing his ribs stood out like leather straps. He'd always been strong and the war had made him stronger. Not that he'd spent any time fighting the Germans or the Japanese. Jake's career in the regular army had ended ten minutes after he arrived in Fort Dix to begin his basic training. Sergeant T. Blair Johnson, in the manner of drill sergeants everywhere, had put his face within two inches of Jake's, and screamed out a series of obscenities, most of which concerned Jake's mother. Two days later, when Sergeant Johnson finally woke up, he was lying in the base hospital, recovering from a fractured skull.

"It was the war," Jake muttered. "The war put me in a bad mood. It wasn't fair."

Jake had first reported to the induction center on Whitehall Street in the spring of 1939. The army had evaluated him thoroughly, then declared him 4F, which was supposed to mean *permanently* unfit for duty. So why, in 1942, even though millions of schmucks were volunteering, had they called him back, re-examined him, overlooked his extensive criminal record, and re-classified him 1A? He'd stopped asking himself the question three weeks later when he got a telegram: *Greetings*, it began.

What had bothered him most, as the packed bus drove through New Jersey on its way to Fort Dix, was how happy the other recruits were. They'd laughed and joked, bragging about what they would do to the Krauts and the Japs, a bunch of *schmucks* eager to get their brains blown out. And for what? There was nothing in it for *them*. Nothing but crumby food, aching bones and an early death.

"A man's gotta do what a man's gotta do." Jake tossed several punches at the face in the mirror. His hands were very fast. Always had been. The redneck sergeant unlucky enough to greet the bus carrying Jake Leibowitz had been out before he knew what was happening. That was part of what Jake called "Plan B."

Plan A had been just to disappear, stretch it out until he was caught, then do his time. But there was no way for him to operate if he was on the run. He was just getting started with the wops, doing them little favors, hoping for a piece of the gambling east of Canal Street. If he spent the rest of the war (and the damn thing could last for ten years the way it was going) in Toronto with Uncle Bernard, his career would be up shit's creek. Permanently.

Better to step right up and take your medicine. Better to pound on some officer, do a year in the joint and get back to work. The wops were being drafted, too. If he got out before they did, there'd be plenty of action.

By the time the bus had arrived at Fort Dix, Jake was too crazy to wait for an officer. Which was just as well, because they ended up giving him eighteen months for what he'd done to the sergeant, six months more than he expected. If he'd beaten an officer, they probably would have given him five years.

But even the extra six months would have been okay. As long as he behaved himself, he'd be out in a little over a year. He was going to a joint called Leavenworth, in Kansas. How bad could a joint in *Kansas* be?

"Leeeeee-bow-witz," Deputy Warden Blackstone had drawled. "What kind of name is that, boy? Is that a Jewish name? Are you a Jewwwww-boy?"

Standing in front of the Dep, flanked by a pair of massive, blond, crewcut sergeants, Jake finally understood that the earth did not end at the far side of the Hudson River.

"Yessir," he answered.

"Leeeeee-bow-witz, are you from Newwww Yawk City?"

"Yessir."

His fellow convicts had been no more accepting than Dep Blackstone. They thought all Jews were soft, flabby tailors. Hiding behind thick glasses, cringing over their prayers. Jake had had to prove himself again and again. Each time he did, a court-martial added a few years to his sentence. The end result was the opposite of what he'd intended. By the time he'd gotten out, WWII *and* the Korean War were over. The wops didn't even remember him.

On the other hand, twelve years in the slammer had given him a confidence and maturity he might otherwise have never achieved. After a time, somewhere in the spring of '45, the names had stopped. No more "kike" or "sheeny." But that didn't mean his fellow cons had seen him as one of the boys. They'd held their tongues because they were afraid of him, not because they'd liked him.

Jake had begun to talk to himself on the day he'd realized that he couldn't fight his way to acceptance. He would never be one of them. It was like the Italians, in a way. A Jew could work with the Italians, but he would never be equal to the lowest Sicilian. Meyer Lansky, whose name was in the papers almost every day, was a good example. He'd created his own gang because he could *never* get in with the wops, could never become an ordinary soldier, much less a Don.

"Them old Jews was tough," Jake said. "Hymie Weiss? Bugsy Siegel? Louis Lepke? Hell, Arnold Rothstein was king of New York when Al Capone was still suckin' on his mother's tit." Stepping into his bedroom, Jake began to dress. "But they musta not had kids or somethin'. The kids I come up with're movin' outta the neighborhood. Goin' ta bullshit Queens or Brooklyn. Can't wait to get away."

He pulled a silk undershirt over his head, then stepped into silk boxer shorts. It was kind of depressing—the only luxury he could afford went on the inside where no one could see it. But that was all going to change. He'd put a lot of effort into attracting the wops' attention. Doing a warehouse here, hijacking a truck there—fencing the loot to a Jew with a loose mouth. He and the only two pals he could dredge up—Izzy Stein and Abe Weinberg.

One day, two gorillas had arrived on his doorstep. He'd known them right away. They worked for Antonio "Steppy" Accacio. Steppy Accacio, if he wasn't exactly Sam Trafficante, was an up and comer, a connected man with a finger in half a dozen Lower East Side pies.

"We only just heard about ya," one of the gorillas, Joe Faci, had said politely.

"I understand," Jake had responded, just as politely. "Whatta ya gotta get?"

"Ten percent. And it would be good if you would fence ya merchandise with our guy on West Street."

"I got the money upstairs."

"We'll go with ya."

"Nah, it's my mother's apartment. She's home."

Faci had thought about it for a minute, searching Jake's face. "That would be all right," he'd responded. "Ya won't be long, I hope?"

"Two minutes."

Jake had made it in one and a half, emerging with a stuffed envelope he'd been saving for months.

"How come we didn't know about ya before this?" Faci had asked, accepting the envelope. "You ain't such a young guy."

Jake had explained about the army and Leavenworth and Faci had listened with respect. He would go back to his boss and pass the information over with the envelope. Jake Leibowitz had done twelve years of very hard time. He was a man you could work with. A man you could trust. He wouldn't open up the first time the cops slapped him around.

Fifteen minutes later, his mustache as good as he was going to get it, Jake Leibowitz sat in the front seat of his mother's 1951 Packard Clipper and studied his two companions intently. The both of them, Izzy Stein and Abe Weinberg, were top-notch in his book. Loyal and bright, they were everything good Jewish boys were supposed to be. Except, he had to admit, for the "good" part. And they weren't boys, either, but hardened ex-cons who'd somehow failed to take advantage of the G.I. Bill.

"Ya know what to do, *right*?" Jake looked hard at Izzy who looked away. "Ya know who I'm talkin' to, *right*?"

Izzy shrugged. "Whatta ya worried about, Jake? Ain't I been doin' it all along?"

What bothered Jake was that Izzy, though he'd done two short bits up in Elmira, had never worked with a gun before Jake recruited him. Not that Izzy was soft. Izzy's prior criminal career had been characterized by a very practical truth: you could get yourself pinned for a hundred burglaries and not do as much time as an eighteen-year-old kid who ripped off the local gas station with his father's .38.

"It's one thing to hold a piece on some truck driver who's crappin' his pants," Jake said calmly. "What we're gonna do here is entirely different."

The set-up was pretty simple, really. The whorehouse was run by a married couple, Al and Betty O'Neill, who'd fallen behind on their payments to Steppy

Accacio. Al and Betty were making noises like they didn't see any reason why they should pay the cops *and* the mob. Accacio wanted to teach the loving couple a lesson they should have learned before they went into the whore business. Namely, he wanted Jake and his boys to pistol-whip the crap out of the pair of them. Jake could keep whatever he found on the premises for his trouble.

"What it is, Jake," Faci had explained, "is Steppy wants that you should put ya hearts inta ya work."

"I get too enthusiastic," Jake had replied, "it might be they won't wake up. I ain't a doctor, Mr. Faci. I can't tell the difference between almost and dead."

"Findin' that line," Faci had flatly declared, "is the difference between being an artist and a mug."

Izzy finally raised his head. He met Jake's eyes and held them. "You got nothin' to worry about, Jake. I already decided to do it. I ain't some fairy who's gonna chicken out at the last minute."

"How 'bout you, Abe? You hot to trot?" Jake turned his attention to a grinning Abe Weinberg.

"Ready, ready, Teddy, to rock and roll." Abe held up a six-inch sap. "I brought my pal, Elvis, along for the ride." He dumped the sap in his coat pocket and dragged out his .45, the one he'd taken off an MP in 1944. "I don't wanna mess up Little Richard doin' balop-bam-boom on some pimp's head."

Jake, unable to keep a straight face, broke into a smile. He wanted to ruffle Abe's hair the way you'd rub the head of a smartass kid, but he was afraid that he'd never get his hand back out. Abe was crazy into rock music—Buddy Holly, Gene Vincent, Jerry Lee Lewis, Ricky Nelson and, of course, the King, Elvis Presley. To Jake, they looked like a bunch of greasy-haired punks, the kind that hung out on the corner and never went anywhere, but Abe worshiped them, even the niggers. He sang all day (except when Jake told him to shut up) and combed his long straight hair into a greasy four-inch pompadour. His favorite outfit was a black leather jacket, black denim trousers and black motorcycle boots. He would have been wearing them right now, if Jake hadn't ordered him to put on an overcoat.

Izzy was Abe's exact opposite in every respect but the most important one, his relationship with the law. Izzy was small and wiry, whereas Abe was tall and broad. Izzy's beak was so big it almost covered his thin mouth and receding chin, while Abe looked like a damned Irishman. Tall and raw-boned, Abe's tiny, upturned nose and the spray of freckles across his cheekbones were almost ridiculous on a man named Abe Weinberg.

"Look here, Abe, I want ya should calm yourself down a little bit," Jake said.

"Ya know somethin, Daddy-O, you got a way of takin' all the fun outta life. Like, don't be cruel, okay?"

"Cut the crap, Abe. I don't want them people unconscious before they tell us where the money's hid. You don't hit nobody. Ya wave that friggin' forty-five and keep ya distance. Understand?"

Jake's temper was legendary. Abe understood *that*. When Jake lost his temper, it stayed lost.

"Don't be so nervous, Jake." Abe's voice was soft and soothing. "It's gonna go all right."

"It better." He took a second to look into the eyes of both men. "C'mon, let's get it over with."

They made no effort to hide themselves as they crossed the street and approached the red door marking 800 Pitt Street. This was a lesson for the whole neighborhood, a lesson from the wops to any fool who believed he could operate independently. Not that there was anyone out on the street. The light rain was mixed with ice, now. It was more than enough to discourage the locals.

Jake knocked twice, paused, then knocked twice again. The door opened immediately and the trio stepped inside. The fat man standing in the hallway, Al O'Neill, began to back up as soon as he saw them.

"Where ya goin', pal?" Jake asked, his .45 rising until it pointed directly at Al O'Neill's mouth. "You got a hot date or somethin'?"

"What, what, what . . ."

"Where's the bitch? She in the back?"

"You want a woman?"

"I'm talkin' about your old lady," Jake said. He stepped forward and jammed the barrel of his .45 into the fat man's mouth. "Don't fuck with me."

O'Neill brought his hand to his mouth. Blood ran down along his fingers, soaking into the cuff of his shirt. "Don't kill me," he whispered. "Please, don't kill me."

"I want the bitch," Jake repeated. "I want the bitch right now."

"Please, please, please."

"Shit." Jake drove his foot into the fat man's crotch. "I know the bitch is in here somewheres. Take us to her or I'll blow ya friggin' head off."

Jake knew exactly where Betty O'Neill was, but now that he'd demanded obedience, he couldn't very well back down. He cocked the .45 and the sharp click of the hammer settling into place had a sobering effect on the retching Al O'Neill. The fat man pushed himself to his feet and led Jake down a narrow hallway to a door at the rear of the building.

"It's me," he called, pushing his way inside.

The thin, almost haggard woman sitting behind the desk was every bit as shocked by the appearance of Jake, Izzy and Abe as her husband had been. Her reaction, on the other hand, was far different.

"You coward," she screamed at her husband. "You just *let* the bastards in."

"I didn't," Al protested. "They used the signal. If you weren't so god-damned cheap, we woulda had a peephole and I wouldn't have to let people in without knowin' who they are."

Betty O'Neill rose to her feet, her eyes riveted to her husband's. "Ya coulda *asked*," she screamed. "Ya coulda asked who it was."

"What're you, a moron?" Al was spitting pieces of white enamel each time he spoke, but he didn't seem to notice. "You wanna ask guys comin' to a whorehouse to shout their names out? If ya didn't squeeze every nickel until it bleeds, you woulda listened to me and paid Accacio his vig." He suddenly turned to Jake. "Look, I tried to make her pay up. I swear. But ya can't make this bitch do nothin'.."

"Shut the fuck up." Jake swung the .45 in a long arc, bringing the barrel down on the pimp's bald skull. He put so much force into it that he was sure the .45 was bent and he made a mental note to check the automatic before he fired it again. The blow, he noted with satisfaction, had split Al's forehead, from the hairline to the bridge of his nose. The flow of blood was astonishing.

"Where's the money?" Jake asked calmly.

"You talkin' to me?" Betty said. Despite everything, she was still defiant.

Jake nudged her unconscious husband with the toe of his shoe. There was no response. "Where's the money?"

"What money?"

"Whatever you got. And it better be plenty."

"It's only nine o'clock. We're just gettin' started. I didn't take in more than fifty bucks the whole night."

"Izzy," Jake said, "would you talk to the woman?"

Izzy nodded solemnly. He handed his .38 to Abe and moved behind the desk. Betty, her anger suddenly transformed, put her hands up defensively.

"Hey, look at this," Izzy said, grabbing the woman's left arm. "She's a dope addict."

Jake looked at the dark scars running up the woman's arms and shook his head in disgust. Now it made sense. Betty O'Neill was putting Steppy Accacio's piece of the pie in her arm. It was pretty amazing. Before the war ended, nobody Jake knew had even *heard* of heroin. Sure, there were hopheads around, but they were getting opium from the chinks or morphine from the crooked doctors. The heroin had started coming into New York with the returning G.I.'s. Now, it was everywhere and the profits were unbelievable, like Prohibition all over again. Convincing the wops to give him a piece of the dope action had become Jake's major goal in life.

"See if ya could find her stash," Jake said.

"Right."

It didn't take long. Most junkies couldn't stand being more than a few feet from their scag and Betty O'Neill was no exception. Izzy pulled twenty bags of heroin out of the center desk drawer and held them up for Jake's inspection.

"Take 'em in the toilet," Jake instructed. "And flush 'em down."

"No," Betty said. "It's not mine. I mean it's not *all* mine. It's for the girls, the ones that use."

Cute, Jake thought. The O'Neills were dealin' dope on the side. And not givin' Steppy his piece. Jake took the heroin from Izzy and cradled it in his palm.

"What it is," he said, "is that you should tell us where the money is if ya wanna keep your dope. And I'm talkin' about *all* the money, not just what you got in the drawer. I want what you got under the floorboards. Or behind the wall. Or in the ceiling. Now, what you should consider is that I'm gonna find it anyway. If I can't beat it outta *you*, I'll wake up your old man and get it from him. Ya can't protect the money, but ya *could* keep ya dope. I know you Irish got potatoes instead of brains between your ears, but I think even a spud-head, like yourself, could figure this one out."

Jake was right. Betty O'Neill, after considering his proposition for a moment, crossed the room and pulled up a section of the floorboard to reveal a small pile of banded fives, tens and twenties. Jake estimated the take at close to six hundred dollars. He put the money into his pockets, filling his jacket and his overcoat, then nodded to Izzy.

"Do what ya gotta do," he said.

Izzy, perhaps to impress his boss, approached the job enthusiastically. He used his fists and the leg of a chair instead of his .38, but the only drawback to this approach was that he had to hit Betty O'Neill thirty times to produce the desired effect. Each time he drove his fist into her ribs, he received two rewards: the sharp crack of splintering cartilage and Betty O'Neill's equally sharp scream.

"He hits pretty hard for a little guy," Jake observed.

"Gotta rip it up," Abe sang, "gotta tear it up."

Izzy kept at his work until Betty stopped screaming. Then he let her drop and all three men turned to leave. When they saw the small brown man standing in the doorway, they did a double-take worthy of the Three Stooges.

"*Que pasa?*" Luis Melenguez asked as the three men stared at him, wide-eyed. "*Que pasa,*" he repeated, as Abe Weinberg pulled Little Richard out of his coat pocket. "*Que pasa, que pasa, que pasa,*" as the hammer drew back and the automatic exploded and a .45 caliber slug blew the back of his head off.

"What'd ya do that for?" Jake asked, wondering if he should be angry or not. "It was just a friggin' spic."

"I hadda make my contribution, didn't I?"

Two

JANUARY 2, 1958

NYPD PATROLMAN Stanley Moodrow sat before a full length mirror in the boys' locker room of Robert Lehman High School and watched while his trainer,

Sergeant Allen Epstein, wrapped his huge hands with a narrow strip of white gauze.

"Tighter, Sarge," he hissed. "A little tighter."

"You sure?" Epstein answered, dropping the gauze bandage to reach for a roll of white surgical tape.

"I gotta go six tonight. I don't wanna hurt my hands in the first round."

"You can't hurt your hands punching air, Stanley. This guy's fast."

Moodrow tried to frown, but found himself grinning instead. Punching air? The phrase summed up his whole career. "Punching air" and "too damned big." It was funny, in a way. The last fight of a boxer's career wasn't supposed to be held in a Brooklyn high school. And it wasn't supposed to be the most important fight of that career. The last fight was supposed to come after a career filled with main events in Madison Square Garden, with championship belts held aloft, with popping flashbulbs and crowds of reporters.

Moodrow turned away from Epstein and curled his hands into fists. Satisfied, he studied himself in the mirror. Or, at least, he studied that portion of himself visible in the narrow glass. If he wanted to see the whole of his six foot six, 245-pound frame, he'd have to stand on the other side of the locker room. But he didn't want to see his chest or his shoulders. Stanley Moodrow was looking into his own eyes, looking for any sign of indecision.

"Too damned big," he thought. That's what his first serious trainer, Sammy Turro, had told him. "You're too damned big, Stanley. Ya stay in the fight game, ya gonna get your ass kicked."

Moodrow had begun his fighting career in 1948, when he was fifteen years old. Most kids take up boxing because they're afraid, but not Stanley Moodrow. He was always the biggest kid in his class, always a head taller than the tallest student. Maybe that was why, despite his good grades, he was cast as a dummy, a dope. The other kids made fun of him and he reacted, as kids will, by beating the crap out of them. That ended the teasing, but it hadn't made him popular.

No, the end result of his schoolyard victories was that the losers, the hoods and the dummies, came to admire him, while the rest of the school left him entirely alone. Stanley Moodrow knew all about losers—growing up on the Lower East Side of Manhattan, there was no way to avoid them—and he wanted no part of their lives. Lost in arrogance, they hung out on every street corner, sucking on bottles of beer, dreaming of easy scores and easier sex. Right up until the day a judge sent them up the river.

"These are bums, Stanley," his father, Max, had explained again and again. "All of them. They don't want to work, so they take what they need from the people. Better to be a dog than a bum. God willing, I'll live long enough to spit on their graves."

God, apparently, *hadn't* been willing. Max Moodrow fell off a ladder at a Bronx construction site four days before his son's fifteenth birthday and died on the way to the hospital.

But that didn't end the lectures. Moodrow's Uncle Pavlov took up the theme before his brother was in his grave. "I hear you're fightin' in school, Stanley," he counseled. "It's okay to be tough. Ya gotta be tough to survive down here. But don't be stupid, all right? Don't be a bum. Ya wanna fight, go in the ring where it'll do ya some good."

Uncle Pavlov, a ten-year veteran of the NYPD, just happened to be in charge of the P.A.L.'s Lower East Side boxing program. He also just happened to be smart enough to act surprised when his brother's kid turned up a month later.

"Hey, Stanley, fancy meetin' you here."

"I thought I'd give it a shot, Uncle Pavlov. I mean boxing. I wanna try it out."

Try it out? The truth was that fifteen-year-old Stanley Moodrow wanted to be a champion. Like every other kid who put on the gloves. And his first twenty fights did nothing to discourage him. It wasn't just the power in his right hand. Stanley Moodrow, like all good fighters in the early stages of a career, simply refused to lose. He found a way to win, even when overmatched, to eat the pain and keep on coming. If his fists weren't good enough, he beat his opponent into submission with the sheer force of his will. The pain—and there was *plenty* of pain—was a badge of honor.

"Ya mind's not where it belongs, Stanley."

"Huh?" Moodrow turned to his trainer. "What'd you say, Sarge?"

"The fight, *schmuck*. The one you're gonna have tonight. Get your mind on the goddamned fight."

Moodrow stood up and kicked the stool away. He set himself in front of the mirror and began to shadowbox with his reflection. Fights, he knew, don't begin with the opening bell. They begin the day the match is made and progress through a number of stages. Training, first, then a layoff two days before the bout, then the weigh-in, the taping of the hands, the ritual of working up a sweat, the long walk to the ring, the introductions. You could lose your edge anywhere along the way. The will to win could be sucked out of you like a malted through a straw.

"I'm gonna take this guy tonight," he said without stopping. "It's six rounds, not three. I'm gonna catch him and take him out."

The thing about it was that you could control a lot of things in your life, but you couldn't control everything. You couldn't control the fact that you were seventeen years old and six foot five inches tall and maybe you'd kicked the hell out of YMCA competition, but now you were in the Golden Gloves and your opponents were faster and more experienced. Very few kids are full-blown heavyweights at the tender age of seventeen.

Moodrow made it to the semi-finals, despite the fact that his opponents were all in their twenties, but that was the end of it. Bobby Brown was a three-time Golden Gloves national champion. Four inches shorter and thirty pounds lighter than Moodrow, he used his speed to every advantage, darting in to throw four-punch combinations, then moving back and away before Moodrow could respond. The blood began to flow halfway through the second round and the referee stopped it fifteen seconds into the third. Moodrow, back in the dressing room, tried to make an excuse.

"It was a butt," he told the doctor sewing his eyelid back together. "A butt," he insisted to his trainer.

Sammy Turro was kind enough to wait until the doctor finished, until there were no witnesses, before he enlightened his fighter.

"Ya too big, Stanley. Too fuckin' big. There ain't no champions big as you. And don't give me Jack Johnson, neither. Guys today are scientific. They know how to stay away. You get in against one of the good ones? Eddie Machen? Zora Folley? Cleveland Williams? I don't care how hard ya work, they're gonna use ya for a punching bag. Lotta guys big as you, guys with your heart, they go into boxing anyway. Fifteen years later they're sparrin' partners for two bucks a round. They hear bells whenever they close their eyes."

"Sammy," Moodrow insisted, "he *butted* me."

"Yeah, well I didn't see no butt, Stanley. But if he *did* put his head in your eye, you oughta send him a thank-you note. Another two minutes and he prob'ly would'a killed ya."

Moodrow, eyes riveted to his reflection in the mirror, stopped throwing punches and assumed a defensive posture, fists alongside the jaw, elbows tight against the ribs. It was the "peek-a-boo" defense used by the current champion, Floyd Patterson, who should have been quick enough to do without it. For Moodrow, on the other hand, it amounted to an acceptance of punishment. He wasn't fast enough to slip punches, to move out of harm's way. He was going to have to take one to give one. Or take two. Or three. Or four.

"All right, Stanley, don't overdo it. You're supposed to warm up, not leave your fight in the dressing room."

Moodrow ignored him. Allen Epstein didn't know squat about the fine art of bringing a fighter to his peak on the night of a big bout. Epstein was in it for the same reason as Moodrow, though he wasn't dumb enough actually to be the one in the ring.

Moodrow had never seen his desire to be a world champion as simple ambition until his third week at the Police Academy. He'd looked at the freshly scrubbed faces of the other recruits, then raised a finger to the still-pink scar on his brow. He knew things they didn't know, things you learn by going into the ring and winning your first twenty fights. He knew, for instance, that he could have turned pro and worked himself into contention for a championship. Maybe he would never *be* a champion, but white boxing fans were always scouting the horizon for another Rocky Marciano, another Great White Hope. Hadn't they taken a rank amateur like Pete Rademacher and bet him down to even money against Floyd Patterson? He, Moodrow, big as he was, could have played the part, maybe even gotten a title fight against a champion looking for an easy payday. Maybe, if he'd been *real* lucky . . .

The kids sitting alongside him didn't understand any of it, the victories or the defeats. They couldn't know what it felt like to give up the dream when you'd already come halfway. There were twenty-four thousand cops in the NYPD and twenty-one thousand were out there pounding a beat. Most of them would spend their entire careers on the street. Checking the backs of closed hardware stores. Directing traffic in the rain. Hoofing it from one call box to another. It would pay the rent, but it was a long way from heavyweight champion of the world.

Thank God for civil service exams. There was a way to move up in the job without the direct approval of the brass. You pass the sergeant's exam, you're a sergeant, the lieutenant's exam, you're a lieutenant, the captain's exam, you're a captain. That wasn't the way Stanley Moodrow wanted to do it, but if Plan A failed, he'd go that route. Plan A was to be appointed to the detectives, to carry the Gold Shield, to spend his workdays in a suit instead of a uniform.

It was a nice dream, but there was no detective's exam to take. Detectives were appointed by other detectives and, according to his Uncle Pavlov, there was more politics in that Gold Shield than in the rest of the Department put together. In order even to be considered for the detectives, you had to catch the attention of someone already *in* the detectives. Which was almost impossible, because beat cops rarely came into contact with the suits. Meanwhile, there were dozens of cops out there whose fathers, brothers and uncles already carried the Gold Shield.

"If you wanna get the attention of the suits," Uncle Pavlov explained, "the best way to do it is by making a big collar. The kind that gets your name in the papers. But you have to be careful not to step on any toes. The rule is that detectives detect and patrolmen patrol. If you stumble onto a robbery in progress and blow the scum away, you're a hero. If you follow a burglar for a month, waiting to catch him inside a warehouse, you're a hotdog."

"I understand, Uncle Pavlov," Moodrow replied. "But what I'm hearing is that I'm never gonna get an appointment unless I get lucky. You should pardon me when I tell you that I don't see myself as a lucky guy."

Pavlov Moodrow tapped his nephew on the forehead. "Then why don't you be a *smart* guy, Stanley. You got good grades all the way through high school. You didn't fall down, even when your father passed over. Do yourself a favor, go up to City College and take some classes. Study for the sergeant's exam in your spare time. If the detectives call you up, that's great, but if they don't, you got something to fall back on. And there's no luck involved in it."

Moodrow took the advice to heart. Twice a week, in addition to his duties as a beat cop on the Lower East Side, he rode the subway up to City College and sat through a boring lecture. He managed to accumulate eighteen credits in three years, a long way from the hundred and thirty he needed to graduate. But graduation wasn't the point. The point was to make his ambition known and to memorize the Patrol Guide.

He'd been given his copy of the Patrol Guide on the day he entered the Academy. All six hundred looseleaf pages of it. The Patrol Guide was supposed to provide a step-by-step procedural guide to every situation ever encountered by any cop anywhere. Most patrolmen, on the advice of the older cops who shepherded them through their first months on the job, dumped the Patrol Guide in a closet and learned the shortcuts offered by the veterans. Stanley Moodrow, on the other hand, took sections of the Guide to work with him, studying the mechanics (and the paperwork) of police procedure. The sergeant's exam was based almost entirely on the Patrol Guide.

Moodrow, his career on course, was just finishing his third year on the job when Sergeant Allen Epstein, newly transferred from Midtown North, found him on the corner of Clinton and Houston Streets.

"Patrolman Moodrow?"

"What's up, Sarge?"

"Get in for a minute. I wanna talk to you."

The minute turned into twenty as Epstein explained that he knew all about Moodrow's amateur boxing career. He pronounced that career glorious, then went on to proclaim the glories of the Manhattan South Police Boxing Club, which, under his expert guidance, would become the finest in the Department.

Moodrow listened politely—Epstein was, after all, a sergeant—but he had less than no interest in the glory derived from beating some cop into submission. Glory was a world title, not a sweaty dance in a high school gym.

"The thing about it," Moodrow explained, "is that I'm taking classes uptown and I'm studying for the sergeant's exam. I don't have the time to train."

"How much time does it take? We're not talking about the pros here. These guys are all in the same boat as you."

Moodrow, hoping to end the discussion, had looked Epstein in the eye. "You go into the ring unprepared, you're gonna lose. And you're gonna get hurt. I don't need that in my life. What's the point? To prove that I'm tough? I already know I'm tough. Take a look at this." He'd waved section fifteen of the Patrol Guide in Epstein's face. "The only thing I'm interested in proving is that I can pass the sergeant's exam."

"You won't be eligible to take the sergeant's exam for two years. What's the rush?"

"I wanna be ready when the time comes."

And that, as far as Stanley Moodrow was concerned, should have been that. But a week later, Epstein was back.

"I see you're an ambitious cop," Epstein argued. "You wanna move up in the job. I didn't know this last week, but I know it now. Ambition is fine with me. I understand it because I also wanna move up in the job. So, lemme ask you one question. You answer it right and I won't bother you again. The

Manhattan South boxing squad competes against other police squads and usually we get a crowd of around three hundred. Who do you think comes to watch?"

"It's gotta be other cops, right?"

"Yeah, but what *kind* of cops?"

"Maybe you could just tell me what's on your mind, Sarge. I'm supposed to report in five minutes."

"The cops who come to the regular matches aren't on foot patrol. Foot patrolmen are mostly young. They've got families to raise. It's the older cops who show up. Lieutenants, captains, deputy inspectors. These are cops who can help you, Stanley. Who can put you into squads where you'll make decent collars. The goddamned chief of detectives is a boxing maniac. The . . ."

"The chief of detectives?"

"That's right. Matthew Halloran, himself. He fought in the amateurs twenty-five years ago. Now, he gets his kicks watching cops beat the hell out of each other. You want a gold shield, Stanley? That what you're lookin' for?"

"I wouldn't complain," Moodrow admitted.

"If you fight and win, especially when we're up against squads from the firemen or sanitation, the chief of all the detectives in New York City will come to the locker room and shake your hand. My squad's fighting in Brooklyn next Tuesday. Come and see for yourself."

Moodrow *did* go to see for himself and while the *chief* of detectives was nowhere to be found, Moodrow recognized several dicks from his home precinct, the 7th. The captain of the 7th was there too, screaming for blood or victory, whichever came first.

The essential message was obvious—even if there was no glory, no thrill of victory for Stanley Moodrow, that didn't mean there was no glory for the spectators. They reacted like they were at Yankee Stadium instead of Saint Regis High School.

Three days later, Moodrow began to train. A month later, he had his first fight and his first victory under his belt. It'd never been easier. His opponents were more concerned with attitude than winning. They stood toe to toe and slugged it out, even when they were conceding fifty pounds and a ten-inch reach advantage. They really didn't have any choice. The few who tried to keep away from him, to dance and jab their way to victory, were booed and jeered at by their own partisans. And the judges hadn't looked on their efforts any more kindly than the crowd.

The victories continued to come, one after another, for more than a year. And Moodrow had his sore right hand pumped by dozens of ranking officers, including an Irish inspector named Patrick Cohan with an unmarried daughter named Kathleen. Cohan, without ever saying it, became Stanley Moodrow's rabbi, bringing him to parties and functions, bragging about his exploits, encouraging his courtship of "my darlin' Kathleen."

"I would've preferred an Irishman," Patrick Cohan had explained when

Moodrow came to him for permission to ask Kathleen out, "but you're tough, smart and ambitious. Lord knows, there's no lack of tough, ambitious cops. It's the smart ones who're hard to find. So full speed ahead, boyo. Make her happy, if you can. Make her happy, but keep your hands to yourself. I want my daughter to come to the altar in a white gown, as pure as the day she made her first Holy Communion."

Moodrow didn't bother to look around when the door to his dressing room opened and Sergeant Peretti, Allen Epstein's assistant, announced, "Five minutes, Stanley. The light-heavies are outta the ring," but he felt his gut begin to knot up. It wasn't the importance of this particular tournament that bothered him. It was the caliber of his opponent.

Liam O'Grady was quick, smart, Irish and a lieutenant in the New York City Fire Department. He'd mastered a strategy available to few fighters, amateur or professional—the art of hammering his opponent while moving away. On the face of it, O'Grady's technique defied the laws of physics. A fighter had to be moving forward, to get his whole body into the punch, if he wanted to hit with power. But rules were made to be broken and Liam O'Grady had broken all of them (along with Stanley Moodrow's nose) a year before. O'Grady had danced around the ring like a giant Sugar Ray Robinson, while Moodrow, a clumsy Jake La Motta, lumbered after him, punching air.

There were differences, of course. Sugar Ray Robinson was a consummate professional. He could stay on his bicycle for fifteen rounds and still be throwing punches at the end. O'Grady, on the other hand, was only a gifted amateur. He could stick and move for three rounds, not fifteen. And *this* fight wasn't going three rounds. In deference to its importance, the bout, like every fight in this all-star tournament, had been scheduled for six. And the fighters were to wear eight-ounce gloves instead of the customary ten. Most important of all, the referees had been instructed not to stop a fight unless a fighter was out on his feet.

"You ready, Stanley?"

"Huh?"

Epstein frowned. "You're not focused, Stanley. You're not here."

"Then where am I, Sarge?" Moodrow began to put on his robe. He was smiling.

"You tell me?"

"What are they callin' this tournament? The First Annual Inter-Service Boxing Championships? The Golden Gloves and the Olympics all wrapped up in one?"

"So what, Stanley? This isn't the first time you've gone up against a fireman. You've gotta see it as just another fight. Stop putting pressure on yourself."

"Who's here tonight, Sarge? Who's out there screaming for blood?"

"This ain't helping you."

"The commissioner's sitting ten feet away from the ring. The chief of detectives is right next to him. There are city councilmen out there, the borough president, a deputy mayor. If I win, I'm a hero. If I lose, I'm a bum. My daddy always told me not to be a bum. He told me bums were the lowest form of life on the face of the earth."

Epstein draped a towel around his fighter's neck. "I could never tell you anything," he said. "You think you know it all."

"You could never tell me anything, because you don't *know* anything. Not about fighting. Let's go."

As they stepped into the narrow corridor connecting the boys' and girls' locker rooms with the gymnasium, the crowd in the tightly packed gym sent up a roar.

"O'Grady's in the ring," Epstein observed. "Now, it's your turn."

As if on cue, the crowd began a chant that was close to a moan. "Moooooooo-Drow, Moooooooo-Drow, Moooooooo-Drow."

"Your fans await you." Epstein's smile was closer to a grimace.

"You trying to say the vampires are hungry, Sarge? That's all that's happening. The vampires need to be fed. My blood or someone else's. It's all the same to them."

Epstein started to answer, but Moodrow turned away and marched into the gym. The room was packed, firemen on one side, cops on the other. Moodrow walked between them without turning his head, stepping up onto the ring apron and ducking between the ropes with practiced grace. Once inside, he raised his arms in premature triumph. The crowd went wild, stomping, whistling, cheering. He wondered if they even knew that Liam O'Grady had kicked his butt a year ago? Or cared, for that matter.

"Siddown, Stanley, lemme get the gloves on."

Moodrow dropped to the stool and extended his left hand. His head swiveled until he was staring directly across the ring at a smiling Liam O'Grady. Though he would have liked to return the smile, to meet arrogance with arrogance, he dropped his eyes to the canvas. If O'Grady wanted to think it was going to be easy, Moodrow had no objection.

"Whatta ya say, Stanley?" Ed Spinelli was a deputy supervisor in sanitation by day and a referee by night. He'd been chosen for his experience and his neutrality. "Lemme see the gloves."

Moodrow, without bothering to reply, held both gloves out for Spinelli's inspection. It was going to be a long night for the little referee, though he didn't know it. At a hundred and sixty pounds, Spinelli was too small to control a pair of determined heavyweights. He'd need the fighters' cooperation and he wasn't going to get it.

His gloves laced and inspected, Moodrow got up and began to move around the ring. O'Grady did the same. Both men were sweating profusely and neither wanted to cool off before the opening bell. Inevitably, they passed each other in the center of the squared circle.

"Do yourself a favor, flatfoot," O'Grady snarled. "Fall down early."

Moodrow let his eyes flick up to meet O'Grady's, then jerked them away. There were no scars over the fireman's eyes and his nose was as straight as a ruler. That was going to change. Liam O'Grady, the Fighting Fireman, might come out of this fight a winner, but he wasn't going to come out unmarked.

"Go back to your corners," Spinelli ordered. "They're gonna do the intros."

Deputy Mayor Gold was short and forty pounds overweight. Even with a cop and a fireman to hold the ropes apart, he had trouble getting into the ring. The crowd jeered, then broke into laughter. Moodrow heard none of it. He'd never been more focused in his life, never more determined. The Gold Shield was riding on the end of his right hand. Once he had it, he'd never again fight for someone else's amusement. He'd never hit or be hit, never taste the blood running from his nose or be sprayed as he drove his fist into a cut on his opponent's face. The glory he'd once reached for had died a second death at his mother's graveside, two years before. He'd gotten through his mother's death by deciding not to break down, by telling himself to "do what you have to do." He'd been living by that rule ever since.

"In the *red* corner, at two hundred and eight pounds, the *Fightin' Fireman*, 'Irish' Liam O'Grady." Deputy Mayor Gold, drenched with sweat, waited for the roar to die away before he continued. "And in the *blue* corner, at two hundred and forty-seven pounds, New York's *Fightin' Finest*, Stan 'The Man' Moodrow."

The referee motioned both fighters to the center of the ring and began to recite a set of instructions he'd already given in the dressing rooms. "All right, boys," he concluded, "touch gloves and let's have a clean fight."

It was supposed to be a gesture of sportsmanship, but that first contact, just the touch of leather on leather, coursed through Moodrow's body like a match tossed into a pool of gasoline. Now it was out in the open. It was war. You had to fight to survive.

When the bell rang, Moodrow moved to the center of the ring as if staking out a claim. O'Grady came out to meet him, then began to circle. Moodrow advanced at an angle, cutting the circle, and O'Grady reversed direction, then suddenly closed, throwing a quick combination before bouncing away. Moodrow took the punches, catching three out of four on his arms. The last one slammed into the narrow space between his left elbow and the top of his trunks.

Moodrow was aware of being hit, but he felt no pain. Tomorrow, he'd have trouble getting out of bed; tonight, he had a job to do. He continued to advance, forcing O'Grady back toward the ropes, throwing an occasional jab at his opponent's dancing head, punching air.

O'Grady gave ground willingly, just as he had in their first fight. Sooner or later his back would be against the ropes and both fighters knew it. Meanwhile, he continued to inflict damage, snapping jabs between Moodrow's gloves, following with short, vicious rights to the body, slipping Moodrow's clumsy attempts to counter.

It took Moodrow more than two minutes to force O'Grady into a corner, to render his opponent momentarily stationary. He absorbed a lot of punishment in the process, but found no reward at the end of the road. Before he could take advantage of his power, before he could throw a single punch, O'Grady ducked between his arms and grabbed Moodrow's huge chest. Now it was perfect. They'd come full circle, repeating every element of their first fight.

"New game," Moodrow whispered to O'Grady as Spinelli tried to pull the two fighters apart. He wrapped his left glove around the back of O'Grady's neck, pulling him forward and down, then jammed the point of his right elbow into the soft spot just behind O'Grady's collarbone. O'Grady tried to jerk away, but Moodrow, much the stronger, held him close.

"Hey, hey, hey," Spinelli shouted. "No holding, Moodrow. Don't grab him."

Moodrow let the ref tug on his arm for another few seconds before releasing his opponent. Grinning, he waited for O'Grady to move back to the center of the ring, then began to advance. For the first time, he allowed himself to look directly into O'Grady's eyes. He was hoping to find doubt, but he settled for anger. If O'Grady lost his cool and stood toe-to-toe, it would be a very short fight.

Moodrow moved a little faster this time, ignoring the jabs, not even trying to counter. O'Grady was staying closer, waiting for an opportunity to throw his best punch. He found it with fifteen seconds left in the round, a whistling right that slammed into Moodrow's forehead. Moodrow ignored the blow, didn't, in fact, even feel it. He pressed forward until O'Grady's back was against the ropes, then threw his own right. O'Grady's head moved slightly, avoiding Moodrow's fist, but not the forearm that followed. It smashed into the side of his skull, driving him sideways along the ropes.

Moodrow grabbed O'Grady behind the neck before he could escape and the fireman instinctively tried to pull away, lifting his body erect, opening his ribs to the right hand. The bell rang an instant before Moodrow could react to the opportunity, but that didn't stop him. He drove his fist into O'Grady's chest, then turned and walked back to his corner.

"You're cut, Stanley," Epstein said.

"Bad?" Moodrow suddenly became aware of the drops running along the outside of his right eye.

"Not yet." Epstein took the edges of the cut between his fingers, squeezing them tightly together. He held the cut closed until the bleeding stopped, then filled the gash with a thick coagulant. "You could use a real cut man for this one. If he keeps tagging you with the jab, it's gonna get messy."

"Don't worry about it, Sarge. They're not gonna stop this one for blood." He glanced across the ring, but O'Grady's handlers had him surrounded.

"Look here, Stanley." The referee's face swam into view. "I want you to stop the bullshit. Right now. Stop grabbin' him. Stop the elbows. I'll disqualify you."

"The crowd'll love that," Moodrow grunted. The truth was they'd probably tear Spinelli to pieces and Spinelli knew it. O'Grady was on his own.

The second round, in direct contrast to the first, was slow and dull. O'Grady got on his bicycle, staying far enough away from Moodrow to spin out before his back was against the ropes. The strategy was effective in that it prevented him from being trapped, but the distance was too great for any meaningful offense. O'Grady looked like a scared fighter and the few jabs he managed to land did nothing to change that impression. By the time the bell rang to end the round, the crowd, including a few of the firemen, was booing.

In the third round, O'Grady again reversed strategy, staying close to Moodrow, as he had in the first. Moodrow wasn't surprised. Irish fighters were expected to be especially courageous. O'Grady would have to return to the firehouse as soon as his injuries, should he suffer injuries, healed up. He couldn't very well go back to his buddies if he came out of this fight labeled a coward.

Moodrow led with a hard, straight right. It missed, but not by much. O'Grady didn't bother to counter. He came inside and banged his forehead into Moodrow's nose. Moodrow heard the cartilage in his nose snap, but he had no sense that it was his own flesh being torn. It was more like someone in another room had broken a pencil. O'Grady, aided by the referee, tried to pull back, but Moodrow held him long enough to put his glove on the fireman's cheek and rub the laces across his face.

O'Grady managed to jerk away and the referee, incensed, stepped between the two fighters before Moodrow could take up the pursuit. "I'm takin' a point," he shouted. "Y'understand? I'm takin' a point for that."

Spinelli signalled his decision by turning to each of the three judges and raising his index finger. The cops in the audience sent up a howl. They'd been fairly quiet before, not sure how to react to Moodrow's tactics. Now they were screaming for O'Grady's (and Spinelli's) blood.

The bell rang a few seconds later and this time O'Grady didn't wait to be hit. He bounced away like a puppet on the end of a string. Moodrow, standing in the center of the ring, turned to the crowd, spread his arms in a gesture of wonder, then minced back to his corner. The cops roared with laughter.

"How's the eye?"

"Forget the eye," Epstein nearly shouted. He pressed a hot-water bottle filled with shaved ice against his fighter's nose, trying to spread the swelling out over Moodrow's face. "Your nose is broken. I think it might be split."

"I know. I can taste the blood. It's kind of salty. Maybe we oughta save it and pour it over a hard-boiled egg."

"You're a funny guy, Stanley. But this ain't *The Milton Berle Show.*"

"The fight's over, Sarge," Moodrow replied calmly. "He's mine."

"This I already know."

O'Grady began the fourth round with a five-punch combination that stopped Moodrow in his tracks. Instinctively, Moodrow grabbed O'Grady and pulled him close. Spinelli, still furious, yanked at Moodrow's left arm, tugging it back far enough to allow O'Grady to drive his right fist into Moodrow's ribs.

Stunned at the turn of events, Spinelli let Moodrow's arm go and started to say something to O'Grady. He wasn't fast enough to get his message across. Moodrow grabbed O'Grady's face with his left hand and stuck the thumb of his glove into O'Grady's eye. Once again, O'Grady tried to pull away, but this time Moodrow's follow-up right caught the top of the fireman's head.

O'Grady responded by coming directly at Moodrow for the first time. And Moodrow, for the first time, began to give ground. He took a step backward, then another, then another, then set himself and put every ounce of his 247 pounds into a short left hook. O'Grady ran directly into the punch. It stopped him in his tracks, paralyzed him just long enough for the following right hand to catch him flush on the jaw. He trembled for a moment, like a sapling hit with a sledgehammer, then his body went limp and he dropped to the canvas. Moodrow, looking for any sign of consciousness, knew the fight was over when he distinctly heard the crunch of his opponent's skull smashing into the floor of the ring.

"Jesus, Stanley. Jesus Christ." Epstein ran to the center of the ring and tried to remove his fighter's mouthpiece.

Moodrow, his arms raised in triumph, ignored his trainer. He walked over to the ropes and saluted the assembled brass. The cheering continued for several minutes, then finally died away. Moodrow dropped his arms, weary for the first time. The pain was coming. He could feel it in his nose and ribs, only a dull ache now, but soon it would overwhelm him. Still, he wanted to drag it out as long as possible, to imprint his victory in the minds of every cop in the crowd.

"Go shake your opponent's hand, Stanley."

"What?" Moodrow looked down at his trainer as if surprised to find him there.

"Go shake his fucking hand. Tell him it was a great fight. Tell him anything, but don't leave him sitting there."

"You're right," Moodrow admitted. "I forgot."

O'Grady's handlers had him up and sitting on his stool when Moodrow approached. The fireman stared at the bloody apparition kneeling in front of him for a moment, then nodded his head. "You fought hard, Stanley," he said. "You deserve it. But I want a rematch. One more fight to settle the issue."

"Sorry, pal," Moodrow replied evenly, "but you're gonna have to learn to live with this one. I'm retired."

Three

JANUARY 3

PATRICK FRANCIS Matthew Cohan lingered in the bedroom of his ten-room Bayside home, despite the fact that most of his guests had already arrived. He knew his guests were out there, having met each of them at the door. He also knew about the gusty winds blowing through the borough of Queens. Those winds had greeted him each time he opened the door and now he was thoroughly absorbed in the task of patting rebellious strands of feathery white hair back into place.

Pat Cohan was always careful with his hair because he wore it long, despite the current fashion. There was no rebellion involved in the style he preferred. (Patrick Cohan was, after all, a full inspector in the NYPD, not some Greenwich Village beatnik.) It was just that a tall, broadly built, fifty-nine-year-old Irishman with a thick head of silvery hair couldn't, on pain of being declared a Protestant, wear that hair in a two-inch brush cut.

Pat Cohan thought of his hair as "the mane," called it that as he worked each strand into place. "Guess it's time to tame the mane." His daughter, Kathleen, liked to tease him about the amount of time he spent in front of the mirror. Pat didn't particularly like to be teased—he *only* took it from "my darlin' Kathleen"—but he also knew it was important that his hair always be neatly combed. Short hair, in 1958, was a badge of patriotism, the physical equivalent of a loyalty oath.

Satisfied that every hair was firmly in place, Pat Cohan drew himself up to his full height and measured the result of his efforts. His "mane" floated above a large skull, just as it was supposed to. It framed his broad brow, strong assertive jaw and blue, blue eyes. He liked to describe those eyes (to himself, at least) as the color of an Irish lake under a cloudless sky.

Of course, there were the negatives. (There were *bound* to be negatives when you were on the wrong side of fifty and tied to a desk.) His once-flat belly had gone the way of his colleagues' hair. And Pat Cohan had jowls, too, and the florid complexion and small broken veins of the habitual drinker. Not that he was a drunk, by any means. Alcohol was the curse of the Irish and every Irishman knew it. But the functions he was expected to attend as an NYPD inspector often required him to stand in a little circle of politicians with a drink in his hand. There were only forty-two inspectors in the 24,000-man NYPD and they spent as much time on the politics of the job as they did on policing the City of New York.

But not tonight. Tonight was special. This was a 'friends only' occasion and Pat Cohan's definition of the word 'friend' excluded all politicians. As far as Pat Cohan was concerned, politicians, with their addiction to public opinion, were only one step above the journalists who created that opinion.

"Not bad, Pat," he said to himself, pulling his vest down over his belly. He was wearing a black three-piece suit cut from the finest Irish broadcloth and tailored by a Lithuanian from the Yorkville section of Manhattan. The black suit was his trademark and, offset by a starched white shirt and a blue tie that matched his eyes, it made him instantly recognizable, even from a distance, whenever he was out of uniform.

Pat Cohan was just about to return to his guests when someone knocked softly on the closed bedroom door. The door opened before he had a chance to offer an invitation and Detective Lieutenant Salvatore Patero entered. Patero, Cohan noted, was wearing his customary white, two-button cardigan, a duplicate of the cardigans Bing Crosby wore on the golf course. Pat Cohan, who'd seen many similar sweaters on Salvatore Patero's back, felt that putting a guinea into the Crooner's cardigan was like putting the vestments of a Cardinal on a gibbering ape.

"Salvatore, my boy," Pat Cohan said quietly, "it's not polite to barge into another man's bedroom."

Patero's thick, dark eyebrows shot up in wonder. The gesture was habitual and every bit as conscious as Pat Cohan's hearty Irish handshake. "I knocked, didn't I? I mean, your wife's in the other room, Pat."

Cohan sighed and let the matter drop. The guineas were coming into the Department in larger and larger numbers. You had to make a place for them, but that didn't mean they were civilized. Civility would take another generation to master. At least.

"Let's hear the news, boyo. And would you try to make it *good* news. We're celebratin' my daughter's engagement tonight."

Everything about Salvatore Patero was sharp, from his chin to his chiseled Roman nose to his wiry hair. Even his slim, muscular body was all knees and elbows. Patero didn't particularly like cops. He didn't like *being* a cop, but "like" just wasn't part of the deal for kids from large families. Not when it came to choosing a profession. Patero had first gone out to work when he was eleven years old, carrying milk, eggs and butter from a horse-drawn cart to the doorsteps of Brooklyn housewives. He certainly liked being a cop better than *that*.

"I spoke to Accacio. I told him exactly what you said."

"Which was what, Sal?"

Patero held his temper. Maybe, one glorious day in the future, the pompous Irish assholes who ruled the Department would be driven out, but he'd be long retired before it happened. "I told him how unhappy the Department was about what happened at the whorehouse. I told him I didn't know if we *should* protect a guy who can't take care of his own business, who hires amateurs instead of professionals. I told him it's not nineteen twenty-five anymore. Civilians ain't supposed to get hurt, much less dead. You got a problem, put it in a Jersey swamp where it belongs."

"I'll bet he loved hearing *that*."

"He didn't react much. I mean he didn't seem frightened or anything. He told me the thing at the O'Neills' was an accident. He said if there was any heat coming down, he'd cut off the links between his people and the event."

"The lad is takin' steps to protect himself," Cohan interrupted. "How nice. Does he think we're worried about *him*?"

Patero threw his palms up in the air and shrugged his shoulders. "What could I say, Pat? It's the practical thing to do. I mean, I know you can handle your end, but there's pressure comin' down from the precinct."

"From exactly *who* in the precinct? I've already spoken to the captain and he assured me . . ."

"We're talkin' about a homicide, Pat, not about gambling and whores. It's not a thing a detective can ignore."

"Be serious, boyo. Dead Puerto Ricans are as expendable as you guineas were forty years ago. Tell our friend Accacio that he needn't fear the Seventh Precinct. He should be afraid of *me*."

"That's what I told him." Patero absorbed the remark about "you guineas." It was the price he had to pay and he knew it. "Look, Pat, I just wanna go on the record about this. We're not doing the right thing, here. I'm not saying we should go out and bust Steppy Accacio. But I *am* saying we should let the investigation take its course. It was a *homicide*."

"You finished, Sal?"

"Yeah."

"Good. Now, I want to speak to you about my prospective son-in-law."

"Stan 'The Man' Moodrow? The hero?" Patero laughed softly, covering his mouth with his hand.

"Shut up, Sal." Pat Cohan's voice demanded obedience. He waited until he got it, before continuing. "If you think what he did was nothing, boyo, you could always arrange to get in the ring with him. Maybe you could teach him a lesson."

Patero's face reddened. Like most cops, he didn't react well to having his courage challenged, but he couldn't very well punch the shit out of Pat Cohan, he being a lousy detective and Patrick Cohan a full inspector. Besides, Pat Cohan wasn't that far off the mark. Salvatore Patero would sooner have been assigned to the Bomb Squad than get in the ring with Stanley Moodrow.

"Don't take it the wrong way, Pat. I know Stanley's got the balls of an elephant. Besides, I like the kid."

"That's good to hear, boyo, because you'll be seein' a lot of him. Stanley's gettin' his gold shield tonight, though for the life of me, I can't see why he wants it." Pat Cohan had nothing but contempt for the "elite" Detective Division. They strutted through the precincts in their suits and overcoats like roosters in a barnyard, but they rarely had two dimes to rub together. You couldn't blame young cops for being drawn to the Gold Shield, but the truth was that there was no money to be made from assignments to the Missing Persons Bureau or the Photographic Unit or the Crime Laboratory. The only potential money maker in the Detective Division was the Narcotics Bureau. Fifteen years earlier, when Pat Cohan was a mere precinct captain, heroin had been a minor part of the crime pantheon. Now, it was the scourge of the city.

"What I want you to do, Sal," he continued, "is show him the ropes. I want you to take him around with you."

"Look, Pat, I don't give out assignments . . ."

"He'll be assigned to you. It's already taken care of."

Patero shook his head. "You're makin' a mistake here. You oughta put the kid in a decent squad and let him work his way up. The way you wanna do it, he's gonna be the most unpopular suit in the precinct."

"Stanley Moodrow's going to marry my daughter. I don't want him takin' her back to some Lower East Side tenement after the honeymoon." Pat Cohan's voice was devoid of any Irish charm. "Darlin' Kathleen" was his only child. His only *surviving* child. His son, Peter, had been lost in the waters off Omaha Beach. They hadn't even found his body.

"All right, Pat, I catch your drift. But I got my doubts that you'll get what you're after. The kid wants to be a *detective*. He wants to solve crimes, make arrests. It's only natural."

Pat Cohan thought it over for a minute. There was more than a little truth in Patero's argument. Stanley Moodrow *was* naive.

"Boyo," Cohan said, "you may be right, but the thing of it is that I've got a little problem. Stanley's tough as nails. He's also smart and ambitious, and I suppose that's all to the good. But he doesn't know anything about how the Department operates. I want him to find out *before* he marries my daughter."

Stanley Moodrow stood in the center of Pat Cohan's living room, his left arm draped about the shoulders of his fiancée, Kathleen, and recited the details of his recent victory to several newly arrived guests. It was the fifth re-telling of the evening, but there was no way he could get out of it. The guests were all cops and they all outranked him.

"Were you trying to get him to come after you? Was that a plan or a lucky break?" The cop standing in front of him (Moodrow couldn't remember his name or his rank) was middle-aged and stubby. As he spoke, he pulled on the thoroughly chewed end of a long cigar, sending clouds of smoke into the champion's face.

What Moodrow wanted, more than anything else, was to sit down. No, *lie* down. His upper body ached, every inch of it, from his neck to his waist. His right shoulder spit fire whenever he lifted it to shake another hand.

"I had to make him come to me," Moodrow said. "I knew I couldn't catch him."

What he knew was that he looked like one of the gargoyles on St. Patrick's Cathedral. X rays had shown that his nose wasn't as badly broken as he and Epstein had thought, but it was definitely broken. The doctor in the Bellevue Hospital emergency room had fitted his nose with a V-shaped metal plate, then covered the plate and half of Moodrow's face with white surgical tape.

But the doctor hadn't bothered to cover the eleven stitches he'd put in his patient's eyebrow. They stood out like insects, like ants, and drew even more attention to the swelling around Moodrow's eye. The bruise hadn't begun to darken yet. It was still red and puffy, but within a few days it would turn black, then green, then yellow. It wouldn't disappear for a week.

Moodrow's three inquisitors, the ritual of congratulations now complete, turned tail and headed for the bar. Moodrow watched them with contempt. How was it possible that what *he* did in the ring somehow made *them* better? It was funny how they were perfectly willing to share in the victory, but they couldn't feel any of the pain. They could raise their shoulders without a twinge and they did so eagerly, glasses of Irish whiskey clutched in their hands.

"How ya doin', Stanley?" Kathleen Cohan's arm encircled his waist and squeezed. The gesture was meant to be affectionate, but the sharp protest from his bruised ribs made it seem more like atrocious assault.

"Easy, Kate. My ribs are killing me. You got any aspirin?" He looked down at her upturned face and smiled. She was so perfectly, wonderfully Irish, with her pug nose and blue eyes and the spray of freckles high on each cheek. He could never quite accept the fact that she loved him. Especially since she hated violence. He'd managed to get the attention of half the Department with his fists, but what in the world had gotten *her* attention?

"Sure, I'll get you some," she said, but before she could move away, her father entered the room and approached the two of them.

"You okay, boyo?" he said to Moodrow.

"I'd like to make it a short night, if you don't mind, Pat. My face feels like a water balloon."

"I understand," he replied shortly. Moodrow's air of independence irritated Pat Cohan. It wasn't that Moodrow didn't want to show the proper attitude. He just didn't know how. "I'll make the announcements right away." Without waiting for a reply, he turned to his guests. "Your attention, ladies and gentlemen. Your attention, if you please. I've two important announcements to make." He paused while the assembled cops and cops' wives moved closer. "The first thing I have to say is that Patrolman Stanley Moodrow is a patrolman no more." He held up a thin leather billfold, hesitated for a moment, then let it drop open to reveal the coveted gold shield. "He is now to be called Detective, Third Grade, Stanley Moodrow." Cohan handed the billfold to Moodrow. "My heartiest congratulations." He grabbed Moodrow's sore right hand and gave it his Irish best. "If ever a man deserved his reward, it's you, boyo."

The guests, on cue, broke into light applause. Pat Cohan held up his hands, palms out, and the applause stopped. "I don't want to belittle Stanley's victory the other night, but . . ." He wrapped his arm around his daughter's waist and pulled her close. "But long after Stanley Moodrow's pugilistic skills have evaporated, long after his triumph is forgotten, he'll still be savoring the fruits of his second victory which I announce here tonight. Ladies and gentlemen, my good friends, and, you, too, Salvatore." He paused again, waiting for the laughter to fade. "As of this night, Detective Stanley Moodrow and my darlin' Kathleen, my one true treasure, are engaged to be married. May their union be long and healthy. And may they not wait too long to give me a grandson."

Pat Cohan raised his glass on high. Thirty other glasses rose to meet it. "Hurrah," Pat shouted. "Hurrah," they answered.

" 'Ah, my darlin' Kathleen,' " Moodrow imitated. " 'My one true treasure.' "

"Stop it, Stanley." Kathleen Cohan somehow managed to shake her head in disapproval and giggle at the same time. She loved her daddy with all her heart, but sometimes he *was* pompous. Kathleen was twenty-two years old, too old to be called 'my darlin' Kathleen,' but Daddy was Daddy and no one told Pat Cohan what to call his own daughter.

They were standing in a small closed porch. The front door was open behind them and they could hear the buzz of conversation from inside the house.

"And why would ya be so hard on me, girlo, when I'm only after larnin' the ways of the Department?"

"He doesn't talk like that." Now she was laughing out loud. "Stanley, you're terrible."

Kathleen Cohan, educated by the nuns and priests from kindergarten through college, had been a good girl all her life. Upon graduation from St. Mary's College, she'd chosen to teach at Sacred Heart Grammar School when she could have gotten a lot more money teaching public school. But she didn't want to get away from the faith any more than she wanted to get away from the father who needed her so much. Needed her because her mother had walked away from the family on the day the telegram had come, the one announcing the death of Rose Cohan's only son. Her only son and, for all the affection she'd ever shown her daughter, her only child. She'd walked away from the family and buried herself in the broad bosom of her faith.

Kathleen Cohan never spent much time worrying about her mother. She was a practical woman and there was too much to be done at home. The house had to be cared for and even if she didn't have to do it herself, she still had to supervise the colored girl who came in twice a week. And somebody had to balance Daddy's checkbook and pay the mortgage and get the plumber when the pipes leaked.

"Stanley?" she whispered.

"No."

"How do you know what I'm going to say?"

"I *don't* want to live here. I *don't* want to live with your father." He would have given her his most determined look, the one with the narrowed eyes and the pinched lips, but his face hurt too much. He had to settle for saying 'want to' instead of 'wanna.'

They'd been having the same argument for months, ever since her father made the offer. They'd probably be having it until the day he moved her into her own apartment. Not that he was complaining. What he liked best about Kathleen Cohan was her stubborn determination. Most of the time she dressed like a high-school girl. Right now, she was wearing a starched white blouse and a blue pleated skirt that covered her knees. Add that to the freckles and the long, honey-blonde hair and she *seemed* as insubstantial (and as sexy) as the fairy on a bottle of White Rock ginger ale. But underneath that schoolgirl uniform, she wasn't insubstantial at all. She was heavy-boned and solid and believed in herself as much as she believed in her God. Or her father.

Ignoring the sharp twinge in his shoulder, Moodrow put his arms around Kathleen and pulled her in close. He kissed her on the lips and felt her mouth open beneath his. He wanted to slide his hand down over her buttocks, but the door was open and there was always a chance one of the assembled cops would look up from his drink at the wrong time. Besides, she was undoubtedly wearing a girdle—she almost always wore a girdle under her dresses and skirts because it gave her that "smooth line." Girdles, in Moodrow's estimation, were the modern equivalent of the medieval chastity belt. You couldn't *seduce* a woman wearing a girdle. You couldn't *slide* a girdle over a woman's hips. It took so long to get it off, the act had to be deliberate, had to be premeditated. It couldn't just *happen*.

But maybe that was all to the good. More than a few of Moodrow's peers had gotten their girlfriends pregnant despite the conscientious use of Trojans. Almost all those peers had done the right thing, but he knew of one girl who'd gone uptown for an abortion and come back home on a slab. The suits had tracked down the doctor who'd implicated the boyfriend who was now doing eight to twelve in Sing-Sing. Moodrow, having listened carefully to Pat Cohan's warnings, would rather do the time than confess that he'd gotten the Inspector's daughter pregnant. Pat Cohan was president of the NYPD Holy Name Society. He was an officer in the Knights of Columbus and a patron of St. Patrick's Cathedral. He would neither be understanding nor forgiving.

Of course, that didn't mean there weren't times when they'd worked up enough heat to scorch the plastic cover on Inspector Pat Cohan's living-room couch. Times when darlin' Kathleen had pressed Moodrow's face into her breasts, not even bothering with the ritual "no," not protesting even when his lips and tongue ran over the smooth skin of her belly. Times when she'd opened her legs to allow his fingers to work their way under her slacks, her white cotton underpants.

"Doesn't this hurt?" Kathleen asked, pulling back.

Moodrow touched his fingers to his puffy lips. "It does, now that you mention it."

She reached out and took his left hand, bringing it to her cheek. "I have to go back inside."

"Why? Your father's in his glory. He wouldn't care if you stayed out here until tomorrow morning. He probably wouldn't even notice."

"Stanley, it's freezing. I don't have a coat on." She took a step back, but continued to hold onto his hand. "I won't see you for three days."

"Unless *you* visit *me*." Moodrow had three days' vacation coming to him and he intended to pass them going from his bed to a hot bath to the kitchen table. He was scheduled to report to the lieutenant at the 7th on Tuesday morning and he didn't want to walk into the squadroom a cripple.

"I can't, Stanley." She dropped his hand and looked down at her shoes. "Daddy . . ."

"I can understand 'old-fashioned.' Your father wants to protect you and I guess that's all to the good. But you're not sixteen years old. You're a college graduate, a working woman. And we're engaged, for Christ's sake."

"Don't use the Lord's name in vain."

Moodrow put his hands on Kathleen's waist—he wanted to put them on her shoulders, but he couldn't raise his hands that high—and looked directly into her eyes. "If you wanna wait until you're married to become a woman, that's okay with me. And I'm not talking about sex, either. But once the priest says 'I now pronounce you man and wife,' you've gotta stop being 'darlin' Kathleen' and start being Katie Moodrow. What scares me is that I don't think you have any idea who Katie Moodrow *is*. *I* can see the woman in you, but you can't. Or won't."

"You can be very hateful, Stanley."

"I don't wanna marry your daddy."

"He needs me, too."

"Katie, your mother spends half the day in church and the other half in her room with a rosary. It's sad, but it's not your fault. Just tell Pat that you're coming to see me and let that be the end of it. You're twenty-two years old and you're engaged to be married. That entitles you to come to my apartment when I'm too sore to get up and come to you."

She didn't want him to leave like that. Didn't want him to walk out carrying the same argument they'd been having for months. This *was* 1958. He was right about that. She should be able to do as she pleased, guided by her own conscience and *not* her father's.

"I'll try," she said. "I'm not promising, but I'll try."

"Good," Moodrow grunted, "because as soon as I get you inside, I'm gonna lock the door, rip off your clothes and force you to do ten or fifteen obscene acts I learned from all the prostitutes I was forced to arrest in the course of doing my duty."

"Stanley, you're impossible." She was grinning up at him, happy again. He had a way of making things better, of easing their arguments. As if *he* knew it would be all right, even if she didn't.

"Not impossible, Katie. Just very, very unlikely."

Four

JANUARY 4

JAKE LEIBOWITZ was sitting at the far end of his mother's kitchen table, the end closest to the living room. He had two reasons for doing this. First, it was as far as he could get from his mother, Sarah, who was cooking breakfast, and, second, he could see the open closet by the door leading out of the apartment. The closet held his "reward for a job well done." Jake *always* treated himself to a reward when a job came off successfully.

Of course, there were *some* people, like his mother, who thought it was stupid to spend two hundred on a reward when you only took in three hundred, but Jake had to disagree. He wasn't throwing his money away. Nor was he trying to play the big shot in front of his associates. He was conditioning himself for success.

Jake, as far as he could remember, had never liked to read. He tended to see letters upside down and words in reverse order. Not that he *couldn't* read. It was just that extracting the information locked up in those letters was closer to an all-out siege than a leisurely pastime. Still, there were lots of empty hours in prison, hours when time seemed to reach out to the edge of a very flat earth. Jake, like the majority of his prison peers, spent most of those hours lost in common, if complex, sexual daydreams. But he couldn't spend *all* the hours dreaming—there were just too many—so, somewhere in his fifth year of incarceration, he began to read *Life* magazine. He chose *Life* for two reasons. First, because it was on the warden's list of approved periodicals and, second, because it only came once a week. Jake needed a week to get through an issue. A week was an absolute necessity when you had to work on the words a letter at a time.

Jake was in his ninth year at Leavenworth when he came on the article in *Life* that changed *his* life. It was the missing link in Jake Leibowitz's formula for success. The article was on a Soviet psychology experiment which was called "conditioning." It was mostly about a man named Pavlov who did an experiment with his dog. He rang a bell each time he fed his dog and after a while the dog started drooling every time he heard a bell, even if there wasn't any food. At first, Jake thought this was pretty funny. He imagined Pavlov walking his dog down the street. Whenever the dog hears a fire bell or a church bell, it starts dribbling away. Like on some old broad's hightop shoes.

But the article stuck to Jake, despite its clownish aspects. The way he understood it, the commies were saying that you could make something happen by getting someone to *expect* it to happen. Maybe that was why he kept screwing up in life. He was always kicking himself when he made a bad move, always putting himself down. What he *should* be doing, he figured, is rewarding himself when he did something right. That way he'd get used to being successful. He'd get *conditioned*.

"Eat your eggs." Sarah Leibowitz banged the plate down so hard, the salami omelet bounced several inches into the air, then settled back on the plate with an audible plop.

"You still pissed off, ma?" Jake knew the answer to the question. He was sorry he'd asked it before the words were out of his mouth.

"He asks am I angry?" Sarah hugged her enormous belly with both arms and rocked from side to side.

"Don't do a speech, ma," Jake begged. "For cryin' out loud. Give it a rest."

"He asks am I angry," she repeated, ignoring him altogether. "Here is a boy goes out and buys *himself* a two-hundred-dollar overcoat when his mother is wearing a rag. A rag, mind you, that's not even *wool*. It's a cotton rag without a lining. Here is a boy who puts lambswool on his back . . ."

"*Cashmere*, ma. It's called cashmere."

"Lambswool on his back when his own mother is wearing a twenty-four dollars and ninety-five cents winter coat she got off the sales rack at Klein's. So why should I be angry that my son thinks he's gotta be Prince Jake, but it's okay his mother should freeze her *tuchis* off whenever she steps out of the house to go shopping for *his* dinner? Why, I'm asking?"

Jake wolfed the eggs down as fast as he could. He had work to do and he didn't want to distract himself by fighting with his mother. She never lost a fight, anyway, because she mostly ignored whatever he said.

"You're going where today?" Ma Leibowitz asked.

"*Mamaleh, mamaleh.*" Jake gave his mother a hug. She accepted his arms, but he knew what was coming next, so what he did was take three quick steps back after letting go. Ma Leibowitz's right hand just missed his face.

"Hugs are for cheapskates," she shouted. "Fur coats are for *mamalehs*."

Jake paused at the apartment door long enough to throw his new black overcoat a wistful glance, then took his navy peacoat off the hook and put it on. The peacoat was the cheapest coat in his closet, but it was warm and completely inconspicuous. There were thousands of them walking around the streets of New York. All on the backs of ordinary workingmen. Jake had nothing but contempt for wage slaves, but when he pulled the black watchcap down over his head and checked himself out in the mirror, he had to admit his mug would look perfectly normal behind the wheel of a truck.

The effect was exactly what he was looking for and he remembered to reward himself before he walked out the door. "You done all right, kid," he said, nodding the way his father would've nodded. If he'd had a father.

Jake felt good enough to take the four flights two stairs at a time, but when he opened the outer lobby door, the cold hit him like a hammer. It was twenty-four degrees in New York and the wind was blowing out of the northwest at twenty miles an hour.

"Damn!" Jake's eyes began to tear before the door closed behind him. He blinked rapidly for a moment, then opened them to find Abe Weinberg lounging against the side of the Packard as if he was basking in the July sun. Abe was wearing his favorite black leather jacket which he hadn't even bothered to zip up, because he wanted everyone to see the white T-shirt he was wearing underneath it. Abe, or so he'd told Jake, had seen *The Wild Ones* eighteen times.

"Whatta you, a fuckin' snowman?" Jake asked.

"You shouldn't talk that way in front of my new girlfriend," Abe said defensively. "It ain't right."

"Your new *what*?" Jake noticed the girl for the first time. She was also wearing a black leather jacket and black motorcycle boots. And she couldn't have been more than sixteen years old.

"This is Maria Roccantelli. She lives on MacDougal Street."

"Pleased to meetch'ya," Maria said, extending her hand.

"Likewise." Jake allowed his fingertips just to graze hers. He was familiar with the term jailbait and he was pretty sure it didn't apply to touching alone, but he wasn't taking any chances. "Don't you gotta be in school or some-thing?"

Maria giggled. "I just come by 'cause Abe said I should meet ya."

Jake looked at Abe, who was leaning against the car again. "Wake up, Abe. It ain't Rock-Around-the-Clock time. Say goodbye to ya girlfriend and let's get outta here."

"See ya later, alligator," Maria said jauntily.

"Take off," Abe hissed out of the side of his mouth.

The reason Jake held it in as long as he did—five endless minutes—was that it didn't matter much anyway. Maybe it made things harder, but it wasn't going to change the spots. He told himself that what's done is done, but what he said was, "How can you be so stupid as to bring your girlfriend along when we're goin' out on business?"

Abe, who was working on his pompadour with a long black comb, looked over in surprise. "We're only goin' out to check *locations*, right? It's not like we was doin' somethin' wrong."

"I don't give a shit. There's times when you're workin' and there's time when you're social. I been tryin' ta tell you that for the last six months. What I don't understand is how a guy who's been in the joint could be so goddamned casual. And that broad ain't *even* a broad. That broad is a *kid*. She can't be no more than sixteen and she looks like twelve. Here we are killin' ourselves to get in with the wops and you wanna pump some guinea's sixteen-year-old daughter. You gotta be stupid and I don't need stupid."

Abe Weinberg slouched down in the seat and drew his lips up into a sulky pout. It was the same pout Elvis had used in *Jailhouse Rock*, but it had no apparent effect on Jake Leibowitz.

"C'mon, Jake, smile. Ya gotta smile." Abe torched a Lucky Strike and blew a thin stream of smoke at the windshield. "Maria's *seventeen*, Jake. She graduates in *June*. Her parents *like* me."

"Do they know you're thirty years old? Do they know you're a *gangster*?"

Abe didn't answer and Jake didn't bother to pursue it, because it didn't matter anyway. Abe Weinberg was the kind of problem that could give Jake and all his efforts a bad name. It wasn't about putting on a show. It was about low profile. It was about doing what you had to do without the whole city knowing your business. Guys who got too much attention—who got their names and faces in the goddamned *newspapers*—ended up in a Jersey swamp. Which was exactly where they were going.

"You up for this?" Jake asked.

They were passing through the toll on the far end of the Lincoln Tunnel. Abe was practicing the art of curling one corner of his mouth into a sneer and the question caught him by surprise.

"Whatta ya mean?"

"I'm talkin' about what we're gonna do." Jake shook his head in disgust. If he didn't *know* Abe Weinberg was a Jew, he wouldn't believe it. "You're probably adopted, right? Tell me you're adopted. Your real parents were Okies who made a wrong turn and ended up in New York instead of California."

"C'mon, Jake. I just wasn't expectin' the question." Abe cracked the vent window and lit another cigarette. He liked the way he looked with a cigarette dangling from his lip, but the smoke was hurting his eyes. "The answer is, yeah, I'm ready. Like I already told ya when you first brought it up."

"You're ready to pull the trigger?"

"Yeah."

"You're sure you could do it?"

"If the money's right, I'll machine-gun Madison Square Garden on fight night. That answer your question?" This time he got himself so far down in the seat that his knees were up against the dash. "Didn't I do the fuckin' spic?"

"That was in a *panic*, Abe. That was *stupid*. I'm talkin' about doin' it cold."

Jake paused, waiting for a reply, but Abe stared out the window and began to hum the melody from Chuck Berry's tune, *Rock and Roll Music*.

"This is an honor the wops are givin' us here," Jake continued. "We do this right and we're on our way."

"Well, we're not doin' it today, right or wrong," Abe finally said. "All we're lookin' for is a place to dump a stiff that ain't even a stiff yet. So what I can't figure out is why you're makin' such a big deal outta nothin'."

This time it was Jake who didn't bother to answer. They were driving through a huge swamp west of Secaucus. It should have been beautiful, at least from inside the car. The cold winter winds had driven away most of the pollution and the sun was shining in the brown and gold tips of the cattails and reeds lining the roadway. It also shone brightly on mounds of garbage left by illegal dumpers, many of them commercial haulers.

Jake turned on an unmarked side road and began to criss-cross the swamp. He made lefts and rights at random, but he never got close to being lost. Abe, on the other hand, stared at the unfamiliar landscape as if he'd been transported to the moon on a Russian *sputnik*.

"You got a map, Jake?" he asked. "So we could find our way outta here." Though he didn't say it, the idea of being in the swamps late at night scared him a lot more than bumpin' off some guinea.

"In my head is where I got my map, Abe. I never get lost."

"The world's first *Jewish* Indian."

"Yeah," Jake laughed, "call me Tonto. Tonto Leibowitz."

A much-relieved Abe Weinberg joined in his pal's laughter. "Yeah, yeah. *Pathfinder* Leibowitz."

"Wait, this looks like a good spot." Jake stopped the car. "In fact, it looks perfect."

The road was so narrow, one car would have had to put two wheels on the shoulder to let another car pass. The reeds were higher than the car and the piles of garbage were higher than the reeds. A track leading into the swamp disappeared fifteen feet from the edge of the road.

"All right," Jake announced, "you wanna be an actor? You wanna be Marlon Brando? You wanna be Elvis Presley? Now's your big chance. We're gonna do this exactly like next week. I'm gonna be you and you're gonna be this guy who's gettin' what he's got comin' to him."

"Ya don't think we could reverse the parts, do ya? I kinda like bein' the hero."

"You tryin' ta tell me Elvis wouldn't end up in a swamp at the end of one of his movies? That's too bad, 'cause the way he sings, it'd be a *mitzvah*."

They were both laughing, now.

"Hey, remember Marlon Brando at the end of *Viva Zapata*?" Abe asked. "When they dump him in the street? The people couldn't even *recognize* him. That's how many times he got shot. If Marlon could do it, I could do it. An actor's gotta have range."

"Great." Jake opened the door and stepped out of the car. Abe followed a moment later. "I'm gonna talk it through while we're goin'. First, this is the gun we're gonna use." Jake held up a .22 caliber revolver. "We don't need no forty-five goin' off like a howitzer. From up close, a twenty-two is just as deadly and you're gonna be right on top of him. But remember, we wanna do this guy in the *swamp*. That means you can't shoot him before we get here unless you absolutely *gotta*. So, what you're gonna do is keep your finger *off* the trigger. Like this."

Jake held the .22 up again. He took his index finger off the trigger and laid it underneath the cylinder.

"What if he tries to run?"

"How's he gonna run when he's handcuffed inside a locked car? Ya getting me pissed off again, Abe."

"Ya can't learn if ya don't ask questions."

"Ya can't learn if ya don't ask questions," Jake mimicked. "What do I got here, a goddamned schoolteacher? What ya should be thinkin' is that ya can't learn if ya don't shut ya mouth and listen." He waited for the message to sink in before he continued. "When we get here, I jump out of the car first. I come around to your side and cover this guy in case he decides to run. *Then* you unlock the door and get him movin'. Now, we're both gonna go up the path here, but *you're* gonna be the one who's right behind him. *Don't* get too close. If ya get too close, he could turn and kick the rod outta ya hand. But, *also*, don't get too far away. If he jumps into them bushes, we'll never find him. Remember, it's gonna be dark. I don't wanna use a flashlight unless it's so black we're gonna fall over each other. What you gotta do is stay arm's length plus two steps away. Let's try it."

Jake walked over to Abe with his left arm outstretched. He stopped when his fingers were touching Abe's chest. "Now, take two steps back. Perfect. *Memorize* this distance. Ya don't let him get no closer and ya don't let him get no further away. Ya got that?"

"Yeah, but one thing. When we're marchin' him up the path, do I still keep my finger off the trigger?"

Jake looked up at the clean, blue sky. "How come it's always me, Lord?"

"What'd I say, now?"

"Abe, this is where we're gonna *do* it. Ya don't think he's gonna *know* that? Ya don't think he's gonna *know* this is his last chance? Once he gets outta the car, you gotta be ready. Don't be a *schmuck*."

"All right, all right. I get the point."

"Good, now let's walk in there and see what it looks like."

What it looked like was perfect. The narrow track wound among the cattails for a hundred yards, then ended abruptly in a small clearing. There was a pond on one side of the clearing (which would have been a great place to dump a stiff except that it was frozen like a rock) and a solid wall of reeds on the other. All you had to do was dump the body ten or fifteen yards off the clearing and by the time the rats got through with it, it'd be nothing but bones.

"Okay," Jake said, "we're here. Whatta ya do next?"

"I make him kneel with his head *away* from me so he can't see it comin'."

"Do it."

"C'mon, Jake. I'll ruin my pants."

"I'll buy you another pair."

Abe knelt down and stared into the reeds. "Is that all right? Do I pass, teacher?"

"I gotta give it to ya," Jake admitted, firing three shots into the back of his buddy's head. "You ain't as stupid as ya look."

Five

JANUARY 5

STANLEY MOODROW sat in the kitchen of his Avenue B apartment, thumbing his way through a copy of the *Daily News* while he waited for the coffee to boil. Moodrow had been reading the *Daily News* at the kitchen table for a long time. He couldn't remember exactly when he'd begun to take an interest in the news of the day, but he could clearly recall his father passing him the comic section at a time when he'd been too young to do more than look at the pictures. And he could remember his mother picking up the paper, too. *After* his father went off to work. That's when *she* got *her* breakfast.

The way Moodrow saw it, his family had gone through a lot of ups and downs when he was a kid, but there'd always been two fixed pillars in their lives. Heirlooms to be handed down from generation to generation. One was the *Daily News* and the other was a baseball team called the Brooklyn Dodgers. He was reading the *Daily News*, but the Dodgers were out of his life. Permanently and forever.

What did the sportswriters call Walter O'Malley? The most hated man in New York? And it was true—even Yankee fans hated O'Malley. For Dodger fans, the feeling was almost pathological. Moodrow could easily imagine putting a bullet into Walter O'Malley's fat carcass. All those years waiting for a World Series? His father hadn't lived to see it. His mother, either.

Moodrow got up to check the glass bulb on top of the percolator. The bubbling liquid wasn't really coffee yet, but it wasn't all that far away. He left it to boil and took a box of Cheerios out of the cupboard. Moodrow wasn't crazy about cereal, but the soreness in his ribs had eased considerably and he didn't want to upset the applecart by messing with pots and pans. He was scheduled to report for assignment in two days and he was determined to do nothing more than eat, read the papers and watch television in the meantime.

The doorbell rang before he could sit down. "Be there in a minute, Greta," he called, reaching for his robe. It was a little early for Greta Bloom, his mother's oldest old friend, to come up from the second floor, which she did whenever Moodrow was sick or hurt.

"I just wanna see you're okay. What's the harm?"

That was her answer whenever he tried to discourage her. Greta Bloom was a professional philanthropist. An *impoverished* philanthropist. Living on social security, the only thing she had to give was time. Greta went out to the *shul* on Clinton Street every day. She belonged to a dozen charitable "societies" and had more energy than Stanley Moodrow on fight night.

"Good morning, Stanley. I know it's early, but I wanted I should catch you before you went to work." Greta Bloom, in a worn yellow housedress, was barely five feet tall. She peered up at Moodrow through pale gray eyes. Her face was small and round with sharp, narrow features that complemented her nervous energy. Even the wrinkle-lines on her forehead danced in time to her enthusiasm.

"I'm not going to work today, Greta, so it doesn't matter."

"*Oy vey,* Stanley. You've been fighting again. I thought you gave that up. I thought you were a policeman."

"Sometimes a policeman has to fight, too. You want coffee?"

"I can't stay. The sisterhood meets at ten o'clock and I didn't even get into the shower yet. I was wondering could you do me a favor? Not for me, for a neighbor. Rosaura Pastoral who lives in 2D. You know her?"

"Maybe if I saw her, I . . ."

"It doesn't matter. So many people moving in, moving out . . . it's impossible to keep count."

"Unless you hang around the mailboxes and gossip all morning."

"Please, Stanley, I don't have time for your wiseguy remarks. I told you I'm in a hurry. Anyway, Rosaura has a boarder—*had* a boarder, I should say—named Luis Melenguez who got killed on Pitt Street the day after Christmas. With a gun, Stanley. Somebody shot him. It's been a week and nobody knows nothing. Rosaura went down to the precinct and the detectives wouldn't even talk about it. Told her to go home and mind her own business. Can you imagine?"

Moodrow *could* imagine. Cops know they have to take abuse from the victim's family. It's expected and you deal with it. But the *landlady*?

"You want me to teach them some manners?" he asked without so much as cracking a smile. "Slap 'em around a little bit?"

"Don't be ridiculous. And it's not *me.* It's not what *I* want. It's for your neighbor, for Rosaura Pastoral. She's a very nice woman."

"*What's* for Rosaura Pastoral. What do you want me to do?"

"Find out what's going on. You told me last time you were gonna be a big-shot detective. That's what I told Rosaura when I saw her last night. 'Stanley's gonna be a big-shot detective. He'll find out what's going on.' "

Moodrow knew better than to refuse Greta Bloom. A compromise was the most he could hope for. "I'll ask around, Greta. Find out who's handling the case and where it's going. But don't expect me to jump in and solve the crime. This isn't *Gunsmoke* and I'm not Matt Dillon."

"Stanley, don't have a heart attack. Nobody expects miracles. If *you* tell Rosaura that everything's kosher, I'm sure she'll be satisfied. Now, I gotta run, *bubbe*. And put some ice on your face. You look like Frankenstein."

He closed the door behind her, then headed back for the kitchen. The doorbell rang again before he got to his Cheerios. "What did you . . ." he asked as he swung the door open.

The sight of Kathleen Cohan in her new fox coat froze him in mid-sentence. It was funny how you could spend half the summer in a bathing suit, but you felt almost obscene in a striped bathrobe with your hairy calves sticking out.

"Jeeeeeesussss Christ."

"Don't take the Lord's name, Stanley. I'm hoping that Jesus isn't watching me, anyway."

"What are you doing here?"

"You invited me, remember? Anyway, I've come to observe your domestic habits." She pranced into the room and took off her coat. "I think it's important to really know a person *before* marriage. Especially if you're a Catholic and you have to stay married forever."

"Yeah? Great. Only don't put that coat down or the roaches'll kidnap it. My domestic habits ain't that good."

"Ugh. You have cockroaches? I *hate* them."

"*Everybody* in the city has roaches." He hung her coat in the hall closet.

"*I* live in the city and *I* don't have cockroaches." She snuck up behind him, put her arms around his waist and squeezed gently.

"Bayside, where you live, ain't the city." He paused for a second. "And that hug didn't hurt. I must be getting better."

"If Bayside isn't in the city, why do I pay city taxes?"

He turned and kissed her. "For kids who grew up in this neighborhood, *Bayside* is Never-Never Land. Peter *Pan* lives in Bayside."

"In that case," she giggled, "you can call me Tinkerbell."

He pulled her into his arms and kissed her. She responded eagerly, wrapping her arms as far around his back as they'd go. Moodrow, despite the fire pulling at his crotch, didn't quite know what to make of her sudden appearance. He'd been trying to get into bed with her for the better part of a year, but he'd always respected her whispered refusals. That was the way good girls were *supposed* to act. At least according to the prevailing mythology. Was it possible that an official engagement changed the rules? He let his fingers slide down her spine, expecting to find that latex chastity belt under her skirt, but what he felt was the firm globes of her buttocks.

"Kathleen . . ."

"I'm supposed to be with Joanna. At the movies." Joanna Buchanan was Kathleen's best friend.

"What?" Preoccupied as he was, Moodrow barely understood the words.

"Daddy thinks I'm with Joanna. I actually *was* with her. We had breakfast after church, but then I came to see you. Joanna went to the movies. With her boyfriend."

Moodrow didn't know what to say next, but he was smart enough to realize that she was running the show. And smart enough to let her, too.

"I thought I'd probably find you in bed," she declared. "I mean, if you're in too much pain to come out and see me, you should at least be flat on your back."

"Right now, you could definitely knock me over with a feather," Moodrow admitted. He waited for her to say something else, but she just stood there, grinning. Finally he asked her if she wanted a cup of coffee.

"Great."

"Sit on the couch and relax. I'll be back in a minute."

He was pouring the coffee when he figured it out. She'd come here to go to bed with him. Deliberately and consciously. Yet he *still* had to seduce her. The realization didn't come easily. The girls he'd known before he met Kathleen had mostly grown up on the Lower East Side. Some of them would do it and some wouldn't, but whichever way it went, they didn't need to play out this elaborate charade. Sex was a lot different in Bayside. In fact, as far as Stanley Moodrow was concerned, sexual politics out in the suburbs were more complicated than the politics at the U.N.

Moodrow congratulated himself on his insight ("pretty deep for a twenty-five-year-old kid," was what he told himself) and walked back into the living room prepared to do what he had to do. The only problem was that Kathleen wasn't there. He glanced over at the front door, half expecting to find it open, but it was closed and locked.

"Stanley?"

There were only two other rooms in the apartment and they were both bedrooms, so that was where she had to be. In a bedroom. If his career as a detective went anything like this, he'd be back to walking a beat in a month.

The bedroom was dark when he came in, but he could see well enough to know that she was in his bed. And that her clothing was draped over the back of a chair. He reached out to put the cup on the bureau and missed by a foot. The cup landed on the wood floor and splattered hot coffee over his right foot. He didn't notice it any more then he'd noticed the punch that'd broken his nose.

"I love you, Stanley," she whispered. "And I don't want to wait anymore.

Not another minute. Even if you *do* look like Frankenstein come back from the dead."

Moodrow touched a finger to the tape covering his nose. He thought about taking it off, then realized that what he was going to *have* to take off was his bathrobe. With Kathleen watching.

"I thought the *girl* was supposed to do the striptease," he said.

Kathleen giggled. "Take it off. Take it off."

"All right, I will."

Moodrow sat on the edge of the bed and slowly drew the covers back. Kathleen, surprised, started to cover her breasts with her hands, then fell back on the pillows. Her breath was shallow, her eyes half-closed. Moodrow laid the fingers of his right hand on her throat, then slid them gently down her throat, over her breasts and along her smooth, flat belly. When his fingers crossed the dark triangle of hair and dropped into the moist flesh below, she moaned softly and her legs came apart.

"Be gentle, Stanley," she whispered. "Don't hurt me."

But he knew he *was* going to hurt her. Of all the dirty tricks nature had laid on human beings, this was the dirtiest. There was no painless way, short of surgery, for a woman to lose her virginity. But that didn't mean there couldn't be pleasure, too. Moodrow had been thinking about it for a long time and he'd already decided what he was going to do. If she let him. If she didn't withdraw from what she had to see as a perversion.

He let his lips and tongue follow the line his finger had traced, though he took much longer, playing with her nipples and her belly and the soft hollow spot on the inside of her thigh. Her milky white skin reddened until it seemed like her whole body was blushing, but the deep, almost guttural sound coming from her throat indicated something other than embarrassment. At some point, she began to call his name. Repeating it until the single word became lost in a sound that was somewhere between a laugh and a scream.

Moodrow sat up on the bed and yanked off his bathrobe and his underwear. Kathleen, he knew, was as ready as a virgin, male or female, *could* be. Her eyes were joyous (if somewhat glazed) and her body was completely open to him. It was the perfect moment to enfold her in his arms, to gently lift her legs . . .

And that's exactly what he would have done. If he hadn't put the Trojan on backwards. If he hadn't ripped it and had to fumble in the nightstand for another one. By the time he managed to open the foil and get it on, the glaze in Kathleen's eyes had disappeared.

"I've never seen one of those before," she said.

"That makes *two* things you've never seen before."

She ignored the humor, reaching out to take his erection in her hand. He would have expected her to be reluctant, but she seemed more curious than naive. She drew him into her, opening for him, accepting his thrusts until he began to call her name, until he was lost in his own fire.

By the time Moodrow finally rolled over to one side of the narrow bed, they were both covered with sweat. He knew that he should take her in his arms, that she needed to be reassured, but somewhere along the line he must have smacked his nose, because it hurt like hell.

"Are you all right, Stanley?"

"My nose," he answered. "I think I broke my nose again."

He opened his eyes to find her propped up on one arm. Her breasts were inches from his face. Suddenly, the realization that he would marry this woman, that he'd spend his life with her, rushed over him. What he felt was grateful.

"I love you, Kathleen," he said, ignoring his nose.

"I love you too, Stanley." She leaned down to kiss him gently on the lips. "We're going to have a good life together. A great life."

Six

JANUARY 7

THE SERGEANT at the duty desk, Stefan Kirsch, grinned from ear to ear when Stanley Moodrow walked into the 7th Precinct.

"Jesus, Stanley," he said, "I thought you *won* the fight."

"That's just a rumor, Sarge. The *real* truth is that only the doctor won."

Moodrow felt awkward coming into the stationhouse in a suit and tie. He'd been proud enough when he'd examined himself in the privacy of his bedroom, but now he felt almost naked. He felt like a *civilian*.

"Well, congratulations, anyway. You deserve it."

"Thanks, Sarge."

There were several other uniforms in the outer lobby, all cops Moodrow had been working with for the past five years. They, too, greeted him like the celebrity he was supposed to be. One, James Curley, walked over and ran his fingers along Moodrow's lapel.

"Where'd ya get the rag, Stanley? Robert Hall?"

"Robert Hall? If you wanna say I'm cheap, why not try S. Klein's?"

"Alright, S. Klein's."

"Jimmy, the suit's *custom*-made." Moodrow wasn't lying, even if he'd left out the part about going down to Robert Hall and not finding a suit big enough to fit him. He didn't mention the part about the tailor, Larry Chin, working out of his apartment on Division Street, either. Or the one about the bolt of cloth being a factory second from a mill in South Carolina.

"I'm only kiddin' ya, Stanley." He took Moodrow's hand and shook it. "Congratulations on the Gold Shield. Lookin' at your face, I'd have to say you deserve it."

"That seems to be the general opinion."

The needling was just what Moodrow expected. After all, he (in *their* minds, at least) had been fighting for every cop in the Department and for the cops in the 7th in particular. That was why they'd come to watch two men beat the crap out of each other. Because they somehow shared in the victory.

"I'll see you later, Jimmy. I gotta report upstairs."

For Stanley Moodrow, walking up those stairs was a far greater reward than having the referee lift his arm. Uniformed cops almost never left the first floor of the 7th Precinct. The second story contained the captain's and the lieutenants' offices, as well as the detectives' squad room. Going up there was like being given a day pass to Mount Olympus.

Now, he'd be walking up these stairs every day. The squad room would be a second home, the other detectives a second family. Which is why he was hoping for a big hello from those detectives who happened to be at their desks. What he got, on the other hand, was ignored.

The 7th Precinct squad room (like every other detectives' squad room in New York City) was nothing more than a large room crowded with wooden desks. *Ancient* wooden desks. Desks blackened with decades of grime and covered with unfinished paperwork. The telephones were so old, the numbers had worn off the dials.

Moodrow picked his way between the desks. He knew a few of the detectives from one or another of his fights, but even the familiar faces kept their backs turned to him. Of course, there was always the possibility that this was the way they treated *all* newly appointed detectives, third grade. Maybe their studied indifference was a kind of initiation rite, like fraternity hazing.

Not that he had much time to think about it. He had to report to Detective Lieutenant Salvatore Patero, the precinct whip, for assignment to one or another of the many detectives' squads and Patero's office was just on the other side of the room. As he knocked on the door, Moodrow wondered just where he'd be assigned. He was hoping for homicide, but it was more likely he'd begin at the beginning, with vice or burglary.

"Come on in."

Patero's face was buried in the *Herald-Tribune* when Moodrow entered the small office. He took his time before looking up, but when he saw Moodrow, he managed a smile.

"Welcome to the detectives, Stanley."

"Thanks, Lou. Glad to be here."

"Siddown a minute. And don't call me 'Lou' or 'Lieutenant.' Sal'll be fine." Patero waited for Moodrow to seat himself before continuing. "You're gonna be working with me, Stanley. You're gonna be my personal assistant. At least temporarily."

Moodrow waited for Patero to say something else, to at least explain the nuts and bolts of personal assistantship, but Patero wasn't talking. He lit a cigarette, a Kent, and leaned back in his chair.

"Uh, Sarge," Moodrow finally said, "the thing is that I'm not sure that I'm qualified to be your assistant. I don't know anything about the paperwork or the procedure. I . . ."

"Can you drive a car?"

"Yeah. Of course. How can you be a cop if you can't drive?"

"For now, that's all you gotta know." Patero pushed back his chair and grinned. "What's the matter, Stanley? You don't look happy."

What Moodrow *felt* was cheated. He wasn't sure who'd done the cheating, but he knew that he hadn't fought his way to a Gold Shield in order to become Sal Patero's chauffeur. Or his secretary, either. Moodrow felt the anger begin to rise, but when he spoke, his voice was calm.

"I was hoping to, you know, just start in the regular way."

Patero leaned over the desk. "In that case, maybe you should've become a *detective* in the regular way. But you didn't, Stanley. You got here because you met the right people, not because of what you did on the street. Don't misunderstand me. I'm not puttin' you down. In the job, politics is what it's all about. Everybody knows that. But when your rabbi's an *inspector* and when you're engaged to your rabbi's *daughter*, there's no more regular to your career. You're gonna ride with *me* and neither of us has any say in the matter. If you got a problem with that, go to your future father-in-law. *Capish?*"

"I understand."

"I wanna get along with you, Stanley. Because, personally, I think you're a good guy. I doubt very much that Pat Cohan bothered to look at your service folder, but I went through every inch of it. I *liked* what I saw. And I'm also glad to hear that you want to go into one of the squads. Eventually, if I can swing it, you will. But right now your job is to learn how things work and my job is to teach you. Take the keys to my car and go make sure it isn't blocked in. You won't have a problem finding it. Being as I'm a big shot in the Seventh, I get a white Chevy instead of a black Chevy."

Patero's white '57 Chevrolet, though unmarked, was far from unrecognizable. Moodrow, sitting behind the wheel with the engine running, recalled a time when he'd been working traffic on the corner of Houston and Clinton. The kids were coming out of school and his job was to get them safely across

Houston Street's eight lanes of cars, trucks and buses. Patero had come cruising up Clinton in his white Chevy. A bunch of kids, *grammar* school kids, were following behind, yelling, "Here comes the lieutenant. Here comes the lieutenant."

Maybe, Moodrow figured, if he spent enough time with Patero, the kids would call out, "Here comes the lieutenant's *dog*."

Patero strolled out ten minutes later, still carrying the *Herald-Tribune*. He got in the car, instructed Moodrow to drive over to Madison and Montgomery Streets, then buried his face in the newspaper. Moodrow, not knowing what else to do, pulled the car away from the curb and began to work his way along the narrow Lower East Side streets. They were stopped at a light when Patero spoke up.

"Stanley," he said, "ya wanna hear somethin' funny?"

"Anything."

"Awright, you remember a kid named Bobby Gaydos?"

"The kid who killed his mother?"

"Right. Cut her throat with a Boy Scout knife last Thursday. Well, yesterday, four detectives take him over to the funeral home where she's laid out and he breaks down and cries for two hours. Boo-hoo-hoo. Whatta ya wanna bet some commie judge sends him to a nut house for treatment? Instead of the electric chair, where he belongs. I mean the kid made a goddamned *confession*."

"*Two* goddamned confessions." The truth, and Moodrow knew it, was that the kid had withdrawn his confessions and his grandmother was providing him with an alibi for the time of the murder. Moodrow also knew that interrogating officers routinely extracted confessions the way dentists extracted teeth. But he didn't say any of what he was thinking. Partly because his own thoughts ran counter to an official NYPD myth that blamed all crime on bleeding-heart judges and partly because *he* was a detective, third grade, and Sal Patero was a detective lieutenant. The difference between Patero's rank and his own was like the difference between champagne and vinegar.

When they arrived at the intersection of Madison and Montgomery, Patero ordered Moodrow to make a right and park.

"We're goin' in there," he announced, pointing to a candy store half way up the block. "When we get inside, I don't want you to say a word. Not a *fucking* word, *capish*?"

"Yeah, sure."

"You're here to learn. You don't have no *opinions* in this matter. But, maybe you could still help me out with somethin'. The guy I'm gonna be talkin' to— his name is Joey Fish—is givin' me trouble. I want you to stand there and stare at him. Don't say nothin', right? Just keep your eyes in his face. The way your mug looks, you could scare a gorilla."

Without waiting for an answer, Patero stepped out of the car and began to walk up the block. Moodrow, scrambling to follow, banged his ribs against the steering wheel (cars didn't fit him any better than off-the-rack suits) and let out an involuntary yelp.

"What'd ya say?" Patero stopped and turned to face his assistant.

"I hit my ribs. They're still pretty sore from the fight."

Patero's smile was friendly and open. "Jesus, Stanley, what you did to that fireman . . ." He shook his head. "Don't worry. You ain't gonna have to fight anyone today. The kind of problem we got with this jerk, we don't handle with our fists. You're kinda like a . . . What's the word? *Reinforcement*. That's right. You're a visual aid."

The candy store in question was as nondescript as any of the hundreds of others dotting the Lower East Side. Newspapers lay on a shelf near the cash register. A long counter, covered with formica and lined with revolving stools, ran all the way to the back wall. Racks of magazines, school supplies and greeting cards paralleled the counter. Moodrow had spent a good part of his childhood in stores exactly like this, graduating from penny candies to chocolate egg creams to banana splits as he moved through grammar school and junior high.

In the course of his candy store education, he'd also come to learn that many of these neighborhood establishments had back rooms that catered to the needs of adults. As he watched Patero cross the room without acknowledging the elderly man behind the counter, he had a pretty good idea of where they were going and what they were going to do. He was glad that he wasn't inside one of his old haunts, that he didn't, for instance, know either of the two customers sitting at the counter.

But Moodrow *did* know Joey Fish. Or, at least, he knew Joey Fish's kid, Alan, from high school.

"Jeez," Joey Fish said as Moodrow ducked through the doorway, "what happened to *him*?"

Moodrow responded with the blank stare requested by Sal Patero.

"I remember you." Fish shook his finger at Moodrow. "You're that kid who used to fight in the Gloves. The big one who went to school with Alan. Whatta ya, still fightin'?"

Moodrow continued to stare and Joey's face underwent a transformation as he put Moodrow's hostility together with his reputation. Joey Fish turned as white as the chalked odds scrawled on the blackboards covering the walls.

"Hey, Lieutenant," Fish said, turning to Patero, "whatta ya doin' here? You puttin' the muscle on me?"

"Cut the crap, Fish. You got what you owe me?"

"Lieutenant . . ."

"Just tell me. Yes or no. Without the bullshit."

Fish opened the desk drawer and withdrew an envelope. He passed it to Patero who weighed it in his palm.

"It's *all* here, right? Current and past due?"

"Every penny. And ya didn't need to bring in a palooka ta get it. I told ya I had a problem. Some of the boys was past-postin' at Hialeah and I got my balls caught in the squeeze. All I asked was a few weeks to recover."

"Don't bother me with ya problems, Fish. You got a business to run. Did ya call the phone company and tell 'em, 'I can't pay my bill because some hustlers past-posted in Florida'? What you shoulda done was collect from the bums that cheated you. Not hold out on me."

Fish glanced at Moodrow, then shrugged. "Some guys you gotta pay. Even if they're cheatin' ya. Even if ya *know* ya bein' cheated. Some guys ya gotta pay."

"Very sharp, Joey." Patero was already heading for the door. "Some guys ya *do* gotta pay. And *I'm* one of 'em."

They continued to make the rounds for the rest of the morning, neither of them speaking very much. Moodrow spent the time reflecting on the felonies he was committing, one after another. For Patero, on the other hand, the business they conducted was routine, a time-honored ritual that predated the existence of the modern NYPD by fifty years. Gambling and prostitution were tolerated in certain neighborhoods because the voters *wanted* gambling and prostitution. No matter how often or how loudly Cardinal Spellman condemned the sins of the flesh. Of course, the citizens weren't especially fond of the violence that flowed naturally from the existence of an institutionalized underworld. But wasn't that where the cops came in?

The unspoken policy was control and containment. And how could you complain if the cops in charge of implementing this policy, in return for breaking the oath they'd taken to support the Constitution of the United States and enforce the laws of New York State, felt they needed a bit of extra compensation?

"Stanley, you ready for lunch?"

"Whatever you want, Sal." It was the only thing he *could* say, under the circumstances. Besides, his stomach was rumbling like a Con Ed steampipe about to explode.

"See if ya could work your way over to Grand and Mott. The Castellemare Café."

Moodrow took a left on Delancey and began to fight his way through the traffic. Delancey Street was the connecting link between the Williamsburg Bridge on the east side and the Holland Tunnel. Jersey-bound trucks, loaded with Brooklyn freight and headed for points west, packed Delancey Street from early morning until after dark.

"Light up the bubble, Stanley. I'm in a hurry."

Moodrow put the red light on top of the Chevy and flicked the switch that set it spinning. The truckers, grudgingly, began to move out of the way. A cop directing traffic at Delancey and the Bowery stopped all north- and southbound traffic as he cleared a lane for the white Chevy. Moodrow recognized the patrolman. His name was Paul Scotrun and he'd made the mistake of spending most of a night tour in a bar on Second Avenue. The duty sergeant, by way of teaching him a lesson, had placed him in a position of high visibility. Now, his face red with cold, he managed a smile and a wistful salute as the Chevy passed.

Five minutes later they were seated at a small table in the Castellemare Café. The restaurant, in the heart of Little Italy, was decorated in the best tourist trap tradition. Gondolas made their way along the walls and the bar was dominated by a highly polished cappucino machine. All the waiters wore white aprons and the tables were covered with red-and-white checked tablecloths. The neighborhood had been solid Italian before the war. Now, the sons and daughters of the immigrants who'd founded Little Italy were leaving as fast as the moving industry could supply the trucks. On the other hand, the tourists, pie-fed Midwesterners mostly, couldn't seem to get enough *calamare fra diavolo*. They were thicker than ever.

"I gotta use the toilet, Stanley. Order me a Rheingold and get whatever you want for yourself."

Patero left without waiting for his assistant to answer. He made his way to the bathrooms in the rear, but instead of entering the door marked "KINGS," he knocked on an unmarked door, then quickly pushed it open.

"How come ya don't wait for someone to say, 'Come in'?" Joe Faci's tone was mild, his face expressionless.

"Because you already knew I was comin'. You knew I was here before I got to my table. Ain't that right?"

Faci shrugged. "It don't make a difference anyway." He opened a desk drawer and removed an envelope. "Mr. Accacio wants to know how things worked out. With the Puerto Rican."

"I'll bet he does." Patero put the envelope in the inner pocket of his jacket. Stanley, he reflected, wouldn't be seeing this one. "I'll bet it's real important to *Mister* Accacio. That's why I wanna deliver the message personally."

"I could take it to him. I got Mr. Accacio's complete confidence."

In Sal Patero's opinion, Joe Faci was an amazing guy. You couldn't make him mad—at least not so it showed—but it was fun trying. "Cut the crap, Joey. Stop makin' out like you got Lucky Luciano in the back room." He gestured to a door in the far wall. "Steppy's a neighborhood punk who's tryin' to make his way up. He ain't the fucking *capo di tutti capi* or whatever you're callin' the big boss these days. I got a message to deliver and I wanna deliver it personal."

Patero's message was simple enough: the situation had been contained, but *don't* let it happen again. *Don't* kill civilians. Except for the smell, nobody cares about dead gangsters in the trunks of cars. But if you start blowing away citizens, sooner or later you're gonna kill someone who matters.

The intercom on Faci's desk emitted a sharp buzz. "Send him in, Joey." The voice belonged to Steppy Accacio. "So I could hear his message personal."

Moodrow sat quietly at his table, sipping at a Schaefer. He was monumentally pissed off. Not that he was surprised by what Patero and he had been doing all morning. He wasn't even opposed to it. Not really. Cops referred to it as 'the pad' and it had been going on for a long time. Moodrow's Uncle Pavlov had explained it before Moodrow took the entrance exam.

"If you become a cop, Stanley, sooner or later people are gonna offer you money. What you gotta understand is that, as far as the Department is concerned, there's clean money and dirty money. The boss in the coffee shop won't let you pay for lunch? That's clean. That's *expected*. Likewise for the mechanic who tunes up your car for half-price. But don't take money from a burglar. Or a dope addict. Or, God forbid, a rapist. That's as dirty as it gets. You know about the pad?"

"No."

Uncle Pavlov had gone on to explain the setup. Every precinct had a bagman who collected from the bookies and the pimps. The captain took the biggest piece, then the lieutenants got theirs, then the sergeants, then a few detectives.

"Beat cops like me get nothing," he concluded.

"You're saying that the money just comes along like your paycheck?"

"See, that's the thing, Stanley. Is the pad clean or is it dirty? Not everybody participates. In fact, if the captain's clean, there ain't no pad. If the captain's clean, then it's every cop for himself. By the way, I'm sure you heard that gettin' transferred out to Staten Island is a horrible punishment for a cop. Ask yourself why that should be? A lotta cops *live* on Staten Island. There's no *violence* out there. You could do your tour without worrying that someone's gonna toss a brick off a roof. So I ask ya, Stanley, why is gettin' transferred out to the boondocks a punishment?"

"Because there's no money out there. No pad."

"Congratulations, my boy, you've just won a free trip to the real world."

What had stuck in Moodrow's mind was the part about "not everybody participates." He'd never given it much thought while he was fighting his way into the detectives, but he'd expected to have a choice, to think about it before it was shoved into his face. Sure, people wanted to make bets. They wanted to get laid, too. But when these same people got in over their heads, the bookies sent guys with baseball bats to do the collecting. And the pimps weren't any better. They controlled their stables with anything that came to hand. Fists, chairs, lit cigarettes, razors, knives. Anything.

Moodrow had seen it close up. It was always a beat cop who arrived first when the bookies got through collecting. A beat cop who picked up the pieces and loaded them into an ambulance. Besides, the story Moodrow kept hearing was that the bookies and pimps were employees. They worked for bosses who also distributed the heroin that'd hit the Lower East Side like a biblical plague.

What it needed was sorting out. No matter *what* the cops did, even if they never took a dime from *anybody*, the gambling and the whores would still be there. You couldn't stop it and the politicians would never legalize it. The cops were the regulators, the *only* regulators. It wasn't what they were set up to do, but if they didn't do it, the situation would be a lot worse.

"You in dreamland, Stanley?"

Sal Patero was smiling. He had no inkling of what was going on behind the swelling and the bruises on Moodrow's face. Fighters are trained not to show an opponent what they're feeling. A triumphant grin might inspire a beaten fighter to give it one more try. Showing fear or pain, on the other hand, encourages an even greater beating. If you were smart, you learned to show nothing. You learned, for instance, to hold yourself erect after a left hook just turned your liver to jelly.

"No, no. I'm here. I was just thinking."

"Have something to eat. It helps prevent that condition."

The waiter was already standing by the table. He took their order, veal for Patero and the shrimps in hot sauce for Moodrow, then disappeared into the kitchen.

"I was thinking about what we've been doing all morning," Moodrow said.

"I was afraid you were gonna say that."

"The thing of it is that if you'd given me a choice, I don't know what I would've done. Whether I would've gone into it or not. But now that I'm already in the soup, I wanna try to understand what I'm eatin'. So's I don't get indigestion."

"Keep goin', Stanley."

Patero was obviously irritated, but Moodrow wasn't really concerned about Patero. Pat Cohan had set this up and unless Pat Cohan decreed otherwise, they were stuck with each other.

"This is the pad we're doing, right?"

"Yeah."

"And you're the precinct bagman, right?"

"Don't make this into a cross-examination, Stanley. I don't feature being interrogated. Especially by you." Patero's ears were red, the veins along his temples swollen.

"How often do we have to do this?"

"Whenever I say so."

"C'mon, Sal. I got a right to know. Is this it? Eight hours a day, five days a week until I earn my pension?"

"You want out? There's ten thousand cops who'd give their right arms to be in your position. You want out, just say the word."

"That's not what you told me this morning. This morning you told me if I had a problem, I should take it to Pat Cohan."

"Fuck Pat Cohan."

"Ya know, Sal, you should try to put yourself in my position. Five years I'm a cop and the most I ever got out of it was a free hamburger. I'm a detective for five hours and I've committed five felonies. Five counts of bribery, if not outright extortion. Now don't get me wrong. I'm not blaming *you*. But I think I got a right to know what's going on. You haven't even told me what my piece is."

Patero stared into Moodrow's eyes for a moment. "You tryin' to tell me that Pat Cohan didn't spell this out for you? That's impossible."

Moodrow leaned over the table. "He didn't tell me shit."

Instinctively, Patero sat back in his chair. There was something unpredictable about Stanley Moodrow, something he didn't care for at all. "Pat Cohan is a prick."

"This I already know."

"He wants to see what you'll do. Before you marry his daughter. In a way, you can't blame him."

"But what does the pad have to do with it?"

"You grew up here, on the Lower East Side, right?"

"So?"

"Me, I grew up in Red Hook, near the docks. My father was a longshoreman. When I was ten years old, someone put a hook through his head. Left him in the hold of a banana boat. I never found out who did it. I never even found out why it was done. That's the way life was in those neighborhoods. Still is, for that matter. Anyway, right after I came into the job, I married a Jewish girl from Forest Hills, Andrea Stern. I loved the hell out of her, but our marriage didn't work out.

"Andrea grew up in one of those apartments on Queens Boulevard, the kind with the fountains in the lobby. That's what I liked about her. She was innocent, a child with a woman's body. In fact, I was so crazy about Andrea that I didn't give a lotta thought to what was gonna happen after we got married. Which I should've, because it turned out she couldn't take Red Hook. She tried like hell, but it was too much for her. Too rough in every way. Meanwhile, I'm makin' four thousand dollars a year and there's no way we can afford to go anywhere else. When Andrea offered to find a job, her parents went through the roof. They couldn't live with the disgrace of their daughter having to go out to work. They offered to *give* us money.

"I don't wanna make a long story outta this, but the moral is I should've thought things out *before* I got married. Only I was too much in love to think about anything but the wedding night. You? You're in the same boat. Or, at least, that's what Pat Cohan believes. You and Kathleen come from two different worlds. Her world is easy to get used to. Yours ain't.

"You know what a house costs today? Even a little house out in Flushing goes for nineteen thousand. Whatta you make, six thousand five hundred? You're on the pad for four bills a month. With that kind of money, plus what you're gonna get from the wedding, you could set yourself up with something nice. You could even afford to give your father-in-law the grandchildren he wants."

Moodrow took his time answering. He'd calmed considerably by this time. Mainly because most of what Patero was saying had already occurred to him. Most white people on the Lower East Side were either moving out or planning to move out. The Jews, the Italians, the Poles and Russians and Ukrainians—they were all heading for suburbia. "White flight" is what the newspapers called it. Moodrow wasn't sure whether they were fleeing the tenements and the poverty or the Puerto Ricans who were coming in by the thousands.

The Puerto Ricans didn't particularly bother Moodrow. He'd known any number of black and Puerto Rican fighters. Some of them were okay and some of them were assholes, just like his white neighbors. The problem was Kathleen. It was all right for a girl to work before she was married, but afterward she was supposed to stay home and take care of the house and kids. Kathleen might be willing to hold onto her job for a few years, but the Church (to say nothing of Pat Cohan) was opposed to any kind of birth control and Kathleen was as religious as they come. Once they were married, she'd want kids.

"Four hundred bucks a month, right?"

"Give or take a few. Plus it goes up if you get promoted or pass the sergeants' exam."

"What about being a detective? What about making arrests?"

Patero shook his head. "Ya still ain't figured it out, Stanley. I'm the precinct whip. My job is to supervise the detective squad, the *whole* squad, and I'm real good at it. The crap we're doin' now only happens the first few days of the month. The rest of the time, I do my work like any other cop. As for you, you don't have to worry about nothin'. You're gonna get your collars and you're gonna move up in the job. With Pat Cohan for a rabbi, it's guaranteed."

Seven

JANUARY 8

JAKE LEIBOWITZ, sitting in the back seat of his mother's Packard, was already bored with the New Jersey landscape. It was nothing but houses, dirt and trees. How could anybody live in a place like this? Why would they want to? That's what he'd ask Steppy Accacio if Joe Faci ever got around to introducing them.

Accacio had moved himself and his family out to Montclair more than two years ago.

"Wake up, Jake," he muttered to himself. "You're here on *business*. This ain't the guided tour."

"You say somethin', boss?" Izzy Stein asked, without turning his head. Izzy was as down to earth in his driving as he was in everything else, a fact Jake Leibowitz greatly appreciated.

"Nah, I'm just thinkin' out loud."

Jake liked sitting in the back seat. True, the move from riding shotgun to perched like a big shot, had been forced on him. Just like the wop who was riding shotgun in his place.

"I got a kid," Joe Faci had said. "He needs a job. Maybe you could take him with ya."

The 'maybe,' as Jake understood it, had meant 'do it or get the fuck out of here.' Well, what cannot be cured, must be endured, right? Life had a way of dumping on you and if you didn't learn to shovel in a hurry, you'd be buried up to your neck. The kid had turned out to be Santo Silesi, eighteen years old and just out of reform school. Santo seemed eager to please, but Jake understood that the kid's first loyalty would always be to the guineas. Jake Leibowitz was just a rest stop on the road to becoming a made man.

What it is, Jake decided, is that I'm never gonna turn my back on Santo Silesi. Because maybe Santo will become a made man by making Jake Leibowitz disappear. Like Jake Leibowitz made Abe Weinberg disappear. Which was most likely part of Joe Faci's plan for good old Jake, anyway. Faci hadn't exactly *ordered* Jake to eliminate his buddy, but he'd made his position perfectly clear. There was no way Steppy Accacio would continue to do business with a man who couldn't control his employees.

"So, do what ya think is right, Jake," Faci had said. "Then get back to me."

They were driving south along the Jersey coast on Route 9, making their way from town to town. Their target was a SpeediFreight tractor-trailer heading up from Virginia tobacco country to a warehouse near Matawan. The driver would be using the turnpike for most of his ride through New Jersey, but at some point he'd have to transfer to smaller, local roads. His final destination was twenty-five miles east of the turnpike.

There were any number of ways for the driver to go. (SpeediFreight encouraged its drivers to mix up their routes, especially when they carried cigarettes.) But in this particular case the driver would exit the turnpike near South Brunswick. He'd take Route 617 to a large truck stop outside of Old Bridge and go to lunch, making sure to leave the doors unlocked. When he came out, Jake would be waiting.

"This ain't the way I like to do things," Jake had informed Joe Faci. "I mean I don't have any *control*, here. Suppose I gotta get out in a hurry? One wrong turn and I'll be wanderin' through Jersey 'til the tires fall off. Or suppose the driver gives me trouble and I gotta do what I gotta do. Where do I dump the body? What do I do with the truck? No disrespect intended, Mr. Faci, but I wanna work as an *independent.*"

"Please, call me Joe." Faci, unperturbed, had sipped his espresso, then added more sugar to what was already a cup of black mud.

"Okay, Joe."

"I could understand ya reluctance, but I need ya ta do me this one favor. Because I'm in a bind. I got a regular crew for the job, but they had an unfortunate problem in Hell's Kitchen last week and they ain't available. So what I'm askin' ya to do is help me out this here one time. If it goes good, which I'm sure it will, I could set you up permanent. I could introduce ya to one of the dispatchers at SpeediFreight. After that, you're on your own."

Faci hadn't bothered to add "as long as we get our piece," but Jake had gotten the message. What Faci was doing by setting Jake up with the Speedi-Freight dispatcher was putting another layer between his boss and the operation. Jake could be trusted to do his time like a man if he got busted, but the dispatcher was probably some greedy citizen with a big family and a bigger mortgage. If the feds grabbed him, he'd roll over before they put on the cuffs.

"So tell me somethin', Santo," Jake asked, "where'd ya learn to handle a truck?" The plan was for the kid to drive the rig to a warehouse in Brooklyn where the cartons would be counted. Jake's cut was twenty cents per carton. The first thing he'd thought, when Faci had announced the price, was that he could get a dollar a carton if he sold them to someone else.

"Hey," Santo replied, "call me Sandy. I ain't in the 'Santo' generation." He turned to face Jake. "See, no mustache."

Jake unconsciously touched his own mustache. "You don't like mustaches? Well, a *blond* kid like you shouldn't grow a mustache, anyway. *Blonds* gotta have thick beards to make a mustache look good. It ain't for kids. Now why don't ya tell me where ya learned to drive a truck?"

Sandy Silesi turned away, concealing his face, but the tips of his ears, much to Jake's satisfaction, flamed red.

"My uncle had a trucking company. In the Bronx. I worked there in the summer. I used to move the trailers around the yard."

"Ya got a license ta drive a semi?"

"Nah."

"Then take it easy. *Real* easy."

"I'll try."

"Don't mouth off to me."

"I didn't mean nothin'."

"Because if ya mouth off to me, I'll pull ya baby ass outta this car and send ya back to Joe Faci in pieces."

The truck stop in Old Bridge turned out to be so big that Jake thought he'd turned into an army base. There must have been forty or fifty rigs parked in the truck lot and another fifty cars on the other side of the restaurant. Unfortunately, none of the tractor-trailers bore the name SpeediFreight, much less the number 114. Which is not to say that Jake was caught off guard. The drive up from Virginia took nine hours under perfect conditions. Which meant Jake had to be in Old Bridge nine hours after the rig was scheduled to leave Richmond. But suppose the driver ran into a bad accident? Or it was raining in Virginia? Or snowing in Pennsylvania?

"Me and Izzy are gonna go inside and get some lunch," Jake announced. "You wait in the car. If ya spot the rig, come and get us."

"Whatever you say."

Jake took his time getting out of the Packard, trying to decide if the kid was being sarcastic. He couldn't make up his mind, but then he figured it didn't matter, anyway. Maybe he *would* have to teach the kid a lesson. That didn't figure to be a problem. But this wasn't the time or the place to do it.

When they got inside, Jake asked the lady with the menus for a table close to the door. The lady dropped the menus on the first table she came to and walked away.

"I can see they like us already," Jake said.

"This kid is a piece of shit," Izzy replied. "Santo Silesi. He's gonna screw us first chance he gets."

"Jesus, Izzy, not again."

"It's *meshugah*, Jake. It's like carrying a snake in your pocket. Sooner or later, you gotta get bit, *nu*?"

"Don't talk that Jew talk, all right? This is 1958. Ya sound like a Lithuanian rabbi. Next thing I know you'll be growin' a beard."

"How I'm talkin' ain't the point."

Jake shook his head in disgust. "The point is that we *already* talked about this. Three *times*. Get it through ya head: we got *no* choice." Why was it that Jews never knew their place? Why couldn't they take no for an answer? It was a curse. The curse of the big mouth. "The point is that there's fifteen thousand cartons of cigarettes in that truck and we're gettin' fifteen cents a carton. That comes out to twenty-two fifty, our end. Ya wanna go back to gas stations and liquor stores? I could fix it."

"That ain't it, Jake. That ain't what I'm sayin'. I just don't wanna be a slave to some wop who can't write his own name."

"It ain't slavery. We give a piece to Steppy Accacio and he gives a piece to someone else and they give to someone else. I figure there's gotta be a big boss at the top, but I don't got the faintest idea who it is. Maybe it goes on forever. Maybe it goes in a circle. Whichever way, if ya don't give up that piece, ya can't operate. Ya might as well go out and get a job."

"C'mon, Jake, I ain't . . ."

They were interrupted by a tall, middle-aged waitress in a yellow uniform. The wad of gum she was chewing made a huge lump in her right cheek. It looked like she had a toothache. "What'll it be, folks?"

Santo Silesi appeared in the doorway behind the waitress. He nodded at

Jake, then spun on his heel and disappeared. "What it'll be," Jake said, "is some sandwiches to go."

"Take-out is at the counter."

"You couldn't get it for us?"

She walked off without bothering to answer. Jake grinned at Izzy, then stood up. "Must be an anti-Semite."

They found Santo in the parking lot. He nodded toward a SpeediFreight trailer parked off by itself in the back of the lot. "The driver's inside the restaurant."

"All right, you and Izzy go back to the car. And when we get movin', stay close. If I run into a problem with the driver, I want you right behind me."

He watched them walk away, then turned his attention to the SpeediFreight trailer. The way the driver had parked his rig, it could be seen from anywhere in the truck stop. If this was a set-up (and there was *always* that possibility— you couldn't ignore it), he, Jake, would be spotted before he got within fifty feet of the rig. And it might not be the cops, either. A company as big as SpeediFreight had to have its own security. For all Jake knew, the driver had been involved in a dozen heists.

The walk across the asphalt reminded Jake of the first time he'd walked across the yard at Leavenworth. He hadn't been able to shake the feeling that *everybody* was watching him. Just waiting for an opportunity to put a shiv in his back. Well, he'd survived that walk and he'd survive this one, too. He was sure of it, despite the fact that he was sweating, despite the fact that it was twenty-two degrees and windy. By the time he pulled himself into the passenger's side of the cab, he was breathing heavily, the icy air cutting into his chest like broken glass.

Jake took the .45 out of his waistband, laid it in his lap and immediately felt better. His little jaunt across the parking lot wasn't going to lead him back to prison. It was the road to Park Avenue. Once he got his hands on the Speedi-Freight dispatcher, he'd squeeze the bastard until his toes bled. SpeediFreight was one of the biggest outfits on the East Coast. They hauled everything— TV's, hi-fi's, clothing, furniture, appliances.

Six months of good luck. That's all he was going to need before he put a few goons (*Jewish* goons, naturally) between himself and the actual heist. Hijack-ings didn't really interest him, anyway. At best, they were no more than a means to an end. The end was the drug business, specifically heroin. Dope, horse, skag, doogie—no matter what they called the stuff, it came to the same thing. It came to profit margins that hadn't been seen in the criminal world since the end of Prohibition. Best of all, the industry was just getting off the ground. There was still room for an ambitious ex-con named Jake Leibowitz.

Jake didn't let himself become so lost in his plans for the future that he failed to keep an eye on the front door of the restaurant. He spotted the driver as soon as he stepped onto the asphalt. The man was tall, middle-aged and nearly bald.

Hatless despite the cold, he walked with his head down, flashing his shiny dome. He came directly to the truck, then hauled himself up and into the cab without looking at Jake.

"Ya know what this is all about, right?" Jake said.

"Yeah."

"I want ya to make ya way over to Route Nine, then head up toward the city. Any problems?"

"Naw." He pressed the starter button on the dash and the engine roared to life.

"What's ya name?" Jake asked as the rig began to move.

"Dayton. Dayton McNeese."

"You from down south, Dayton?"

"Mississippi."

"I guess that explains it."

"Explains it?"

"Explains why ya don't like hats."

Jake Leibowitz was so happy at the way things had turned out that he wasn't even bothered by the fact that he couldn't see the mustache he was attempting to trim.

"I'm movin' on dowwwwwwn the road," he sang in imitation of every colored inmate he'd run across in Leavenworth. "Movin', movin' movin on dowwwwwwn the road."

But the truth, as he saw it, was that he was moving *up* the road. And it wasn't a road, either, but a goddamned turnpike. They'd dropped off the SpeediFreight driver a mile from the Bayonne Bridge, then hotfooted it through Staten Island to a trucking warehouse in Brooklyn where the cartons had been unloaded and counted. The count had come out exactly as advertised, fifteen thousand cartons straight from the R. J. Reynolds factory. The payoff had been a little tricky, because Jake had told Izzy and the wop he was only getting fifteen cents a carton when he was actually getting twenty. But Joe Faci had been smart enough to hand over the money in the privacy of his office.

"Three grand," Joe Faci had said, "like I promised. And this here is the name and the phone number of the dispatcher at SpeediFreight who's been working with us. Call him and arrange a face to face. You should be aware that he sometimes needs a little encouragement."

Izzy's cut had been 30% of twenty-two fifty. Silesi had settled for 20%. Which had left Jake with a very satisfying eighteen seventy-five.

"As in one thousand eight hundred and seventy-five dollars and no fucking cents," Jake said, straightening his tie.

The first thing Jake had done was stop off in Mrs. Pearlstein's Ladies' Garments on Norfolk Street and pick up the largest rabbits' fur coat on the rack. Not that he was stupid enough to actually tell his mother it was rabbits' fur when he handed it over.

"It's raccoon, mama," he'd said. Then he'd broken into a sweat when she tried it on. If the goddamned thing hadn't buttoned over her fat gut, if she'd had to have her *raccoon* coat altered, if the equally fat woman who ran Mrs. Pearlstein's had laughed in Mama's face . . . But it hadn't happened. The coat had fit loosely enough and neither his mama nor her old-country girlfriends could tell the difference between mink and cat.

Jake hadn't forgotten about his *own* reward, either. He'd gone uptown, to Leighton's on Broadway, and bought himself a pearl-gray, double-breasted overcoat and a matching homburg. The homburg, with its softly rolled brim, made him look older, more mature. It made him look *established*. Which was the whole point, really.

"Ya beggin' days're over, Jakie-boy," he said as he dressed. "Time ta show the world where ya comin' from."

Fifteen minutes later, he was down on Pitt Street, stepping out of the Packard and walking up to a familiar door. He knocked softly and waited until it opened, until he was face to face with Al O'Neill.

"What could I do for ya, mister?" O'Neill asked.

"Ya don't remember me?" Jake took off his hat and leaned forward. "I'm insulted."

"Hey, mister, I see a lotta guys . . ." Then it hit him and he staggered back. "We're payin'," he said. "We're payin' *everything*. We're payin' on time."

"Relax, Al, I ain't here on business. I'm here on pleasure."

"Yeah?" O'Neill took another step back, then his face brightened. "Yeah?"

"Everybody gotta get laid, right? If it wasn't fa that, where would *you* be?"

O'Neill managed a laugh. "Can't argue about that one. Now, whatta ya intrested in? Ya got anything special in mind?"

"Young and willin', Al. That's all that matters."

Eight

JANUARY 9

STANLEY MOODROW, sitting at his kitchen table, a cup of coffee in one hand and the *Daily News* in the other, was more than annoyed. It wasn't the events of the last few days that had him going. He'd become reconciled to making the rounds with Salvatore Patero. Not that he actually *approved* (or even that he was committed to the money), but there was nothing he could do about it. Not in the short term, at least. The cards had been dealt and now he had to play them. It was like the sky falling on Chicken Little. The smart thing was examine the pieces, then do what you had to do.

He'd learned *that* lesson the hard way. He'd been fifteen when his father died quickly, twenty-three when his mother died slowly. Whatever he'd meant to say to his father or been afraid to say to his mother was going to go forever unsaid. For a few minutes, at his mother's wake, he'd thought he might die himself. Just stop where he was.

"If you can get through this, you can get through anything." That's what he told himself. And the truth was that compared to sitting on that folding chair by the coffin while friends and relatives murmured their condolences, his problems with Sal Patero and Pat Cohan were less than two piles of dogshit on the sidewalk. No, what bothered Stanley Moodrow as he dawdled over his breakfast was the weather.

It was cold and windy. Again. Looking out of his bedroom window as he'd dressed, Moodrow had followed the hunched backs of workingmen as they made their way to buses and subways. Checking the weather was a habit he'd picked up as a patrolman. It was funny, in a way. The newspapers wrote about cops all the time. Likewise the novelists. And while the reporters were mostly critical and the novelists full of bull, neither of them seemed to understand the physical aspects of the job.

On cold days, if you managed to keep moving, you'd stay warm from your neck to your ankles. Above and below, you froze no matter what you did. Your ears and feet would hurt for the first hour, then go numb and stay that way until you finished your tour. Which wasn't so bad until you came back to the station house and thawed out. On really cold days, the pins and needles would have more than one cop dancing in front of his locker.

The summer wasn't much better—you sweated all day and tended your rashes at night. By the time the dog days hit, your feet and armpits were permanently inflamed, the powder you put on in the morning was white greasy mud by noon, your balls were floating in a lake of sweat by ten o'clock. What got you through the discomfort was nothing more than dogged persistence. You learned to accept the discomfort like an ox accepting the yoke.

The telephone interrupted Moodrow's daydreams and he left the kitchen to pick it up. He was expecting to hear Sal Patero's voice, but found his fiancée on the line instead.

"Stanley," she said, almost whispering, "I only have a minute, but I have to talk to you."

"Are you at home?"

"No, I'm at Sacred Heart. I just went to confession."

"And?" The next part wasn't going to be any better than the weather and Moodrow knew it.

"What we did the other day, Stanley? It was beautiful, even if it was technically a sin."

"Did you tell that to Father Grogan?"

"It was Father Ryan. And no, I didn't. I told him that I knew I'd hurt Jesus and I was sorry for that. Which I am, Stanley. But the important thing is I had to promise not to do it again. You know that I *had* to."

Moodrow did know it. In order to make a true confession, in order to receive forgiveness, you had to do two things. You had to be truly repentant and you had to believe that you wouldn't go out and sin again. Moodrow had been all of fourteen when he'd realized that he *was* going to do certain things over and over again. No matter how many oaths he took in the confessional. He'd handled this insight by avoiding confession. Compounding the felony was what the lawyers called it.

"All right," he muttered. "I admit it. But you're also expected to avoid 'the near occasions of sin.' Does that mean we can't see each other until the wedding?"

"You don't have to be cruel, Stanley. You're a Catholic, too."

"I'm a *phony* Catholic, like ninety-nine percent of all the Catholics in the world." He hesitated a moment. "Look, I'm sorry, Kate. I don't want to attack your faith. The other day . . . well, if I gotta wait another six months, I'll wait. That's all there is to it."

"Actually, there's something else, Stanley. I probably shouldn't have gone to Father Ryan. I should have gone to Father Grogan, because he's a lot easier. Maybe I felt guilty. I don't know, but it's done now. Father Ryan wants me to tell my father. As part of the penance."

"*Jesus Christ.*"

"Don't take the Lord's name, Stanley."

As he made his way to the 7th Precinct, Moodrow was hoping against hope. He knew he was dealing with a fifty-fifty proposition at best. Maybe Kathleen wasn't a religious fanatic, but she did believe in sin and the ritual of forgiveness. Which always included a penance. Most penances consisted of saying a rosary or lighting a candle, but apparently Father Ryan had considered Kate's sin to be especially evil.

What Moodrow had managed to do, after much persuasion, was to make Kathleen agree to go back to Father Ryan and beg for mercy. At least that postponed the confrontation. Maybe, if he had a few days to think about it, he'd come up with a better plan. One thing for sure, he wasn't going to take a lot of shit from Pat Cohan. A rabbi was one thing—every up-and-comer in the Department had a rabbi—but Moodrow didn't figure he needed a master. He had no intention of playing the monster to Pat Cohan's Doctor Frankenstein.

He nodded to several uniformed cops inside the 7th Precinct's lobby, then quickly made his way to the detectives' squad room. Once again, the detectives working at their desks ignored him altogether. Moodrow had already stopped hoping that the cold shoulder was some kind of ritual. The truth was they resented the hell out of him.

Patero's door was open when Moodrow approached. There were two detectives sitting next to the Lieutenant's desk. Moodrow stopped for a moment, not quite knowing his place.

"Stanley, come in."

Patero was smiling, so, whatever was going on, it couldn't be all bad. Moodrow walked through the door and nodded to the suits. "Morning," he said.

"Stanley, this is Pete O'Brien." Patero jerked his chin at a tall, beefy cop. "And this here is Mack Mitkowski."

Mitkowski was small and wiry. His face was all flat planes except for a nose that seemed to jump out of his skull. He stared at Moodrow through dark blank eyes. "Whatta ya say, Stanley? How's it hangin'?"

Patero interrupted before Moodrow could reply. "We're gonna take a piece of slime off the streets today, Stanley. Ya know the guy they call the Playtex Burglar?"

"I know what he's done, but we've never actually been introduced."

The Playtex Burglar had been breaking into one or another of the small clothing stores clustered near Orchard and Delancey for the past six months. As far as Moodrow was concerned, he was strictly small-time, even if he was miraculously successful. What made him interesting to the cops (as well as a minor sensation in the newspapers) was the fact that in addition to a few decent suits and coats, he always grabbed several pieces of intimate lady's apparel. Lace bras, silk panties, a black shortie nightgown, a full-length slip. At first, the detectives who'd picked up the beef had assumed he was taking them home to his wife or his girlfriend. But as they'd gotten deeper into his m.o., they'd realized that he usually left a small pile of rejects in front of a full-length mirror.

"Well," Patero continued, "we got the little prick. Tell him, Mack."

"Piece of cake," Mack Mitkowski said. "He must've lost his regular fence, because last night he approached someone else for the first time. A new fence. This someone else (who I ain't gonna name) looks just like a rat, but he sings like a canary. He bought the whole load, then called me to come down and take a look at it. It matches with what went outta Kaufman's loft two days ago. The scum's name is Victor Zayas, a Puerto Rican. He lives on Avenue D, across from the projects. Works two blocks from here in the kitchen at Ratner's."

Patero shook his head. "Imagine. A spic who wears lace panties. Whatta ya think's gonna happen to him when he goes upstate? Think he'll be the belle of the ball?"

Moodrow started to laugh, then noticed that Mitkowski and his partner had maintained their neutral expressions.

"Mack and Pete are gonna toss the spic's apartment," Patero continued.

"We're gonna go over to Ratner's and bring him into the house. See if we can persuade him to own up to his foul deeds."

Questions began to form in Moodrow's mind, questions he was smart enough not to ask. First, he wanted to know if they had a warrant to search the apartment. If they didn't, they wouldn't be able to use what they found in court. And they probably *didn't* have a warrant, because if they did, they'd wait to see what they came up with before approaching Zayas. What Mitkowski was doing was protecting his informant. Or maybe the informant would never agree to testify in an open courtroom.

It amounted to the same thing. All they had was a name. That wasn't the same as proof or evidence or anything else that would stand up in court, even if they were *sure* Zayas was guilty. Of course, they could put Zayas under surveillance for the next month. They could try to catch him in the act. But it would take six experienced cops to maintain round-the-clock observation. Six cops times thirty days equals a hundred and eighty payroll days which equals eight or nine thousand dollars. Maybe the captain of the 111th out in Bayside would approve the expense. Bayside was a nice, safe, low-crime neighborhood. But the 7th saw crimes involving knives and guns every day, not to mention a flourishing heroin trade. Captain McElroy wasn't likely to invest that kind of money in the Playtex Burglar. The whole game hinged on getting Zayas to confess.

Moodrow stepped back to allow Mitkowski and O'Brien to get to the door. He sat down as soon as they were gone.

"Cheer up, Stanley," Patero said. "You're gonna get your picture in the papers today."

"What am I gonna do, kill somebody?"

"What you're gonna do," Patero said, "is bust the Playtex Burglar. I already called the reporters. They'll get the cameras down here whenever I give the word."

More questions to which Moodrow knew the answers. But this time he couldn't keep his mouth shut.

"How is it *my* bust? Mitkowski was the one who nailed him."

"It's your bust, because I say it's your bust." Patero's voice was sharper. He couldn't understand why Moodrow didn't just play the game. It was a gift, this arrest, and as far as Patero was concerned, Moodrow should be grateful.

"I hear what you're sayin', Sal, but what I'm seeing is that these guys hate my guts. I'm supposed to be out there developing my own pack of rats. A detective's only as good as his information. That's what everybody says."

"I thought we reached an understanding the other day." Patero lit a cigarette and sucked in a cloud of smoke. He held it for a second, then let it drift out through both nostrils. "I'm tryin' to cut down, but it only makes the ones I *do* smoke taste better." He took another drag before returning to Moodrow.

"First of all, it doesn't matter what Mitkowski and O'Brien think of you. They're nice guys and halfway decent detectives, but they're not going anywhere and they're not gonna complain. Second, them and everybody else in the squad would give their right arms to be where you are now. Third, what you're gonna learn, startin' today, is how to do something more important than beggin' some slimeball for a name. You're gonna become the Seventh's liaison with the DA's office. You're gonna be the one who makes sure that all the evidence and all the paperwork is in order before a case goes to trial. Take my word for it, Stanley. You won't believe what kind of assholes you're gonna be dealin' with. We had a detective, first grade, name of Galowitz who once sent a thirty-eight over to the lab without doing any paperwork at all. Just dropped it off on his way home. Naturally, it turns out the thirty-eight was used in a robbery in which a homicide occurred. Before we can arrest the scumbag who owns the gun, he shows up with a lawyer. The judge threw out the thirty-eight at a preliminary hearing and the perpetrator never went to trial. I've been asking the captain to give me a full-time assistant for the last two years. Just when I gave up hope, you dropped into my lap."

Victor Zayas didn't make any fuss when Sal Patero and Stanley Moodrow showed up in Ratner's kitchen. He didn't even glance at the badge Patero flashed.

"What do you want?"

"We want ya to come over to the precinct and model a pair of panties for us," Patero hissed. "Black silk panties. Trimmed with lace."

Zayas's face dropped through the floor. Scared shitless was the way Moodrow read it. When Patero put on the cuffs, Zayas began to tremble, a small, skinny kid made almost ghostly by his fear.

They marched him back to the 7th, letting the neighborhood get a good look at him. The idea, as Patero had explained it, was to break him down, then give him a way out. Most of the process would take place in a basement interrogation room, but it didn't hurt to begin at the beginning. Zayas was now in the hands of the police. They could hold him for seventy-two hours without charging him. More than enough time to do what had to be done. Moodrow didn't think the kid would last through the morning.

"All right, punk, welcome to your new home." Patero pushed open the door to a small room and shoved Zayas inside. The only piece of furniture in the room was an armless wooden chair. The chair was bolted to the floor. "If ya want room service, I'm afraid ya gotta yell. We ain't got around to installing telephones. Not that it matters. The filet mignon is shit here anyway." He shoved Zayas into the chair, then cuffed his wrists and ankles to the chair's legs. "Comfy?"

"What are you gonna do?" Zayas asked.

"We just wanna see what kind of panties you're wearing," Moodrow said. He noted Patero's approving grin, then loosened Zayas's belt and yanked his corduroys down. "Boxers." He shook his head in disgust.

"Why are you doing this?"

"You tell us," Patero said.

"I want a lawyer. I'm entitled to a lawyer."

"He talks pretty good for a spic. Don't he, Stanley?"

"My grandfather came here in nineteen oh-three. I know my rights. I want a lawyer."

"All right, already." Patero raised his hand defensively. "Don't get hot. We'll go out and find you a lawyer. You wait here."

Patero led Moodrow into a small anteroom. He closed the door, then turned out the overhead lights. Zayas was clearly visible through a glass panel, though what Zayas saw, when he looked at the glass, was himself, handcuffed to a chair.

"You're gonna be the *good* cop, Stanley," Patero said. "After Mitkowski and O'Brien get through with him. You know what to do?"

"I've seen it done, but I've never done it."

"Yeah, well, ordinarily I wouldn't expect ya to bring it off. I'd let ya watch a few more times, before ya tried it yourself. But this Zayas is a punk. We pulled his jacket this morning and he came up clean. Just wait until the boys soften him up, then go in and hold his hand." Patero took a sheet of paper out of his inside jacket pocket and tossed it over to Moodrow. "Here's a list of burglaries we'd like him to cop out on. Addresses and dates."

Moodrow scanned the list quickly. "These go back more than two years. I thought the Playtex Burglar's only been working for the last six months?"

"First rule of law enforcement, Stanley," Patero grinned. "The system runs on success. Ya gotta clear a certain percentage of the crimes committed in your command. It's a competition. One precinct against another. Second rule of law enforcement: everybody cheats. When I first got appointed to the detectives, I was stationed up in the Two twenty-second. In the east Bronx. The captain there had a motto: 'If it ain't dead, it ain't a felony.' We had the lowest felony rate in the city for six years running."

"Some of these burglaries were big," Moodrow insisted. "This one on Division Street netted thousands of dollars in furs. You put that on the kid, he's gonna go upstate for a long time."

Patero advanced until his face was six inches from Moodrow's chest. He looked ridiculous—like a chicken confronting a turkey—but he was much too angry to notice. "What're you supposed to be? Sir *fucking* Galahad? Why don't ya just give me your gold shield? Take it out right now and hand it over. I'll get the captain to put ya back directing traffic for kids comin' outta school. That way you'll sleep good at night."

The door opened before Moodrow could respond. O'Brien, carrying a paper bag, entered the room, followed by Mitkowski. If either of them noticed anything wrong, they didn't show it.

"Home run," O'Brien announced, emptying the bag onto a metal table. "Panties, slips, bras, nylons, garter belts. This one's my favorite." He held up a blue silk peignoir.

"He livin' with a broad?" Patero asked.

"Negative, Sal. No dresses, coats, shoes."

"Cosmetics?"

"A ton of it. Perfume, too."

Patero stepped away from Moodrow. He was smiling again. "Might as well get to it."

"I had a great idea on the way over," Mitkowski said. "Ain't that right, Pete."

"Great idea," O'Brien admitted.

Mitkowski took off his jacket, tie and shirt, then slipped into the peignoir. "Whatta ya think?" Mitkowski was small enough to button the peignoir, but his chest, covered with wiry black hair, somehow ruined the effect.

O'Brien took a scarred nightstick off the top of a filing cabinet and began to twirl it. In his expert hands, it spun like a yo-yo. "Just in case the punk ain't impressed with Mack's charms."

Patero flipped on the intercom as soon as O'Brien and Mitkowski were in the room with Zayas. "I'm gonna take off, now. I got some paperwork in my office needs takin' care of. You stay here. Do whatever you gotta do. One thing, though. You fuck it up, I'm takin' it back to Pat Cohan. I'm gonna tell him I can't work with you. I'm gonna say, 'You asked me to teach Stanley about the Department, but Stanley don't wanna learn. Whatta ya gonna do about it?' "

He left without waiting for an answer and Moodrow turned his attention to the interrogation room. The cops in the 7th called this room the Canary Cage, because so many suspects, caught within its walls, had been induced to sing whatever song the cops wanted to hear. Victor Zayas, however, was almost certainly a punk with no one larger than himself to give up. Which meant there was only one way out of the Canary Cage for the Playtex Burglar—his signature at the end of a confession.

Moodrow watched Mitkowski strut across the room, swinging his hips as he went. "And thith design," he said, "is *bound* to get hith attention. *All* hith attention." He sashayed over to Zayas and sat on the small man's lap. "Whatta think, Victor? Do I look the part? Or would ya like to show us how ya do it for ya boyfriend?"

"I want a lawyer," Zayas announced. "I know my rights."

O'Brien stepped forward, grabbed Zayas's nose between his thumb and forefinger, then twisted sharply. "I don't wanna hear that shit. Not from no faggot like you."

Zayas tried to pull away, but there was no place to go. The act was meant to remind him of his helplessness and O'Brien continued to drive the message home until Zayas cried out in pain. Then, seemingly satisfied, O'Brien strolled over to the far corner and picked a dusty telephone book off the floor.

"Did that bad, bad polithman hurt you, Vickie?" Mitkowski crooned.

"I want a lawyer." Zayas was near to tears. "I'm entitled to a lawyer."

"Oh Vickie, Vickie, Vickie." Mitkowski was having the time of his life.

When the boys in the squad room heard about this one, they'd buy his drinks for the next month. "Why are you rejecting me, Vickie? You know how thenthitive I am. Is it because I'm a fucking faggot? That doesn't make me a bad perthon. I could thuck every cock in Manhattan and still be a good perthon. I mean it's what's in your *heart* that counth. Ithn't it?"

This time Zayas kept his mouth shut. He sat in the chair, his eyes closed, clearly determined to ride out the storm. Of course, Zayas wasn't the first suspect ever to demand a lawyer. Suspects *were* entitled to speak with a lawyer before questioning, assuming they knew their rights and requested one.

Interrogating officers usually divided knowledgeable suspects into two categories: hardened ex-cons and well-informed citizens. Most of the ex-cons would take a beating and laugh in the cop's face. Having been through the game before, they knew that a beating only lasts for a few days, but prison goes on for years and years. Well-informed citizens, on the other hand, tended to see their right to a lawyer as an abstraction and the pain of a beating as very, very concrete.

"All right," Mitkowski said, getting up. "I know when I'm not wanted." He took off the peignoir, draped it over Zayas's shoulders, then buttoned it under his throat. "Here, it looks better on you, anyway. Pete, gimme the phone book."

O'Brien, standing behind Zayas, passed the phone book over to Mitkowski. "You gonna make a call, Mack?"

"Yeah, I'm gonna call Victor's conscience." He took the phone book and carefully dusted it off. "Wouldn't wanna get ya perm all dirty, would we, Victor?" He paused, but Zayas didn't answer. "What we're gonna do now is for your own good. Because what I noticed here is that ya got *very* bad posture and how could ya be a model if ya posture's bad? So what we're gonna do is put the phone book on the top of ya head. Your job is to keep it there, keep ya neck and head straight. Believe me, this is great trainin', Vickie. Course, ya *could* move and let the book fall down, but if ya do, I'm gonna take out my cock and make you suck it." Mitkowski's voice suddenly hardened. "You understand me, faggot? You understand what I'm tellin' ya? Don't try me, 'cause I never bluff."

"I want . . ."

Mitkowski slapped Zayas's face, a quick, sharp blow that would have knocked Zayas down if he hadn't been handcuffed to the chair.

"No more bullshit about a lawyer. Not one fuckin' word. Whatta ya think, we're playin' around here?"

"All right," Zayas muttered.

"That's better." Mitkowski laid the phone book on Zayas's head, balancing it carefully. "Very good, Vickie. See how ya holdin' ya shoulders? And how ya neck forms a straight line? Just hold it for another minute and I'll give you a nice reward."

The reward turned out to be O'Brien using the nightstick like an axe, bringing it in a long smooth arc, from behind his knees to straight over his head to the top of the Manhattan phone book. The crack was sharp enough to make Mitkowski wince. Zayas, on the other hand, did nothing for a moment. Then he screamed, a long howl so elemental it was neither male nor female. It filled the room, as solid as the walls and the floor, a single note, a song of sorrow as much as pain, freezing the two detectives until it finally died out. Until Zayas, head bent, tears streaming down his cheeks, began to sob uncontrollably.

"Look what ya did," Mitkowski said calmly. "Ya moved ya noggin and the phone book fell on the floor." He picked it up, then grabbed Zayas's face and lifted his head. "Now what I'm gonna do is put this phone book on ya head again. I know ya first instinct is gonna be to shake it off. Hey, it's only natural. But ya should think about *this*. If there ain't no phone book up there, then there ain't nothin' between ya faggoty skull and Pete's nightstick. See what I mean?"

Mitkowski didn't wait for an answer. He balanced the phone book on top of Zayas's trembling head, then stepped back and nodded to O'Brien who once again brought the club through its arc. This time Zayas didn't scream. He slumped forward, his eyes fluttering, nearly unconscious.

Zayas would have remained that way for a long time, preferring the blank dizziness to the reality awaiting him, but the sight of Stanley Moodrow crashing through the door overrode any common sense he might have had.

"What the fuck is goin' on here?" Moodrow demanded.

"Jeez." Even Mitkowski, who'd been expecting Moodrow's entrance, was impressed. Like most of the cops in the 7th Precinct, he'd witnessed the Liam O'Grady fight.

"I asked you a question," Moodrow repeated.

"Drop dead, Stanley," O'Brien said. "We're just doin' our jobs."

Moodrow strode across the floor and grabbed O'Brien's lapel, yanking him in close. "What you are is a fucking animal, Pete. And what I am is an animal *trainer*. I want you out of here. You and that asshole dwarf you call a partner."

"Take it easy. Take it easy." O'Brien instinctively pushed back Moodrow's chest. It was like pushing against a concrete pillar. "Jeez," he said, echoing his partner's sentiments.

"Look here, Stanley," Mitkowski muttered, "this asshole belongs to us. You try to play the big hero, we're gonna go to the lieutenant."

Moodrow released O'Brien and turned to Mitkowski. "Go anywhere you want, Mack. As long as it's out of here. And give me a key for those cuffs. Whatta ya think ya got here, public enemy number one?"

Mitkowski fished a key out of his pocket and threw it at Moodrow. "We'll be back," he announced.

"Don't slam the door on your way out."

Of course, they *did* slam the door. O'Brien slammed it as hard as he could and Moodrow had to wait for the crash to die down. When it was quiet in the room, he knelt beside Zayas and removed the handcuffs on the little man's wrists and ankles.

"That feel better, Victor?" Moodrow asked.

Zayas nodded. "Thank you," he whispered.

"What they did was wrong." Moodrow went back into the anteroom and picked up a small table and a chair. He carried them back into the interrogation room and set them in front of Zayas. "How do you take your coffee, Victor? Milk and sugar? Light and sweet?"

Zayas stared at Moodrow, uncomprehending.

"Your coffee, Victor. How do you like it?"

"Black."

"I'll be right back."

Moodrow reappeared a minute later with a steaming mug in his hands. He placed it in front of Zayas before sitting down. Carefully, almost reluctantly, he took out his ballpoint and his notebook. "You smoke, Victor?" he asked.

Stanley Moodrow sat at his kitchen table, an untouched bowl of Hormel chili (customized with strips of Kraft's Sliced American) in front of him. He was trying to read the *Daily News*, the same edition he'd been reading before Kathleen's call, but the stories seemed trivial, absurd. Albert Anastasia, the ultimate high-profile gangster, was in the headlines again. The reputed head of Murder, Inc., Anastasia had been gunned down in a barber's chair the previous October. Ever since, publicity-seeking DAs and congressional committees had been dragging in one mobster after another for what they called 'questioning.' Now it was Meyer Lansky's turn, Lansky and Sam Trafficante who were, according to the story, in Havana trying to buy the country of Cuba from its dictator, Fulgencio Batista.

Despite his best efforts, Moodrow kept asking himself the same question: what did Albert Anastasia and Meyer Lansky and the DA, Frank Hogan, have to do with what had happened in the Canary Cage? As Patero had predicted, the reporters had come to photograph Moodrow leading a handcuffed Playtex Burglar out of the 7th Precinct and into a waiting van. Would the story they printed have anything to do with what had gone on in that basement room? Would they, for instance, reflect Patero's anger? Because he, Moodrow, had never taken Patero's list out of his pocket. He'd simply written down whatever Zayas had said and had the kid sign on the bottom line.

Moodrow was honest enough to admit that he'd known about the game all along. His uncle had enlightened him before he'd entered the Academy. It was simple enough, really. The courts (the *lower* courts, at least) would admit any confession, no matter how it was obtained. The higher courts, assuming the convict had the money for an appeal, were as likely to reverse these convictions as not, but this meant less than nothing to the NYPD. As far as the cops were concerned, cases were cleared the minute a conviction was obtained, no matter what happened two years down the line. Of course, clearing cases wasn't the *only* way up for an ambitious precinct commander, but failing to clear as many cases as your competitors was a sure way down.

Maybe, Moodrow thought, it was like your first murder scene. You never forgot the first one—it dug under your skin like the teeth of a bloodsucking tick—but, after a while, you simply got used to the violence. After a while, you could stand there, inhaling the coppery stink of drying blood, and chomp on your doughnut like a real veteran.

The doorbell rang before Moodrow could drag himself back to the *Daily News.* He got up, hoping against hope that it was Kathleen come to tell him that Father Ryan could go to hell. But it wasn't Kathleen. It was his neighbor, Greta Bloom.

"Good evening, Stanley," she announced, marching past him into the apartment.

"Why don't you come in, Greta?"

"I'm already in, thank you." She turned back to the door. "Rosaura, please. Don't stay in the hallway. You'll get a draft."

The middle-aged woman who stepped into the apartment was so large that Moodrow couldn't believe that he hadn't noticed her in the hallway, had nearly shut the door in her face.

"Stanley," Greta said, "this is your neighbor, Rosaura Pastoral. Rosaura, this is our policeman, Stanley Moodrow."

Our policeman? Moodrow managed a nod despite his annoyance. He reminded himself that Greta had been his mother's best friend, had nursed her through her illness. If it wasn't for Greta Bloom, his mother would have spent the last six months of her life in a hospital.

"What could I do for you, Greta? Somebody lose a cat?"

"What you could do is ask us to sit down. And don't be a wiseguy, Stanley. I told you a million times about that."

"Greta, Mrs. Pastoral, please sit down."

Then he remembered. A homicide on Pitt Street. A stiff named . . . Melenguez, that was it. Luis Melenguez. He was supposed to ask around, find out what happened.

Greta perched herself on the edge of the couch. "*Nu,* you shouldn't bother with coffee and a *nosh.* It's late and we won't be staying long."

"Gee, Greta, I was just about to create my world-famous onion dip."

"Please, Stanley. This is serious business."

Moodrow sat down and looked the two women over. Rosaura Pastoral looked to be about five foot eight. She weighed maybe a hundred and eighty pounds. Greta Bloom, tiny, nervous, fluttering like a parakeet, had never weighed more than a hundred pounds in her life.

"What it is," Moodrow said, trying for a smile, "is I forgot all about it. I mean what you asked me the other day. Things got a little crazy in the precinct and I forgot to ask around."

"He forgets a *murder*? How is this possible?"

How could he explain it? All the times he'd responded to a crime scene to find a DOA lying in a pool of blood. It was always gruesome, no doubt about that, but it had long ago ceased to be exotic.

"What could I say? I'm sorry." What he wanted to do was get rid of them without listening to the harangue already showing in the expression on Greta's face. "I'll tell you what, Greta. As long as you brought Mrs. Pastoral with you, why don't you let *her* tell me why she feels something's wrong here. That way I'll know what to ask when I go into the precinct tomorrow."

Greta Bloom sniffed once. "That's smart, Stanley. But I'd be happy you shouldn't embarrass me again. If you're not interested in doing a favor, you should come right out and say so."

Moodrow turned to Rosaura Pastoral without answering. Now that she was sitting in front of him, he did recognize her. Maybe he'd seen her by the mailboxes or carrying a bag of groceries up the stairs. He couldn't really remember and that was too bad, because there was a time when he could name every family in the building.

"Maybe you better tell me about it," he said.

"*Señor* Moodrow," Rosaura Pastoral spoke for the first time. Her voice was deep and slightly hoarse. "This thing happens the day after Christmas. My boarder, Luis Melenguez, goes out for the evening and he don' come back. For five days I don' hear nothing. Then someone tell me he is killed in a house on Peet Street."

"Peet Street?"

"She means, Pitt Street," Greta interpreted.

"I'm sorry for my English is no too good. I try to learn, but it comes very slow."

"Don't worry about it," Moodrow said. "Just tell your story."

"When I'm hearing this about Luis, I go to the police station and talk to the officer at the desk. He is sending me to a man in a suit, Detective Maguire. Detective Maguire is telling me the investigation is . . . *progressing*. Tha' is the word he use. Progressing. Then I ask him why nobody come to see me. I am Luis's landlady. He live in my home. Why nobody come to as' me who is his friends? Who is his enemies? Ayyy, *Dios mio*, Detective Maguire get so angry. He say I don' know nothin' about it, so why don' I go home and mind my own business. I do like he say, but no is right thing. I don' think so."

Moodrow took a minute before he responded. He'd been in the final stages of training for his bout with Liam O'Grady on December 26 and knew less than nothing about the murder. But the fact that more than two weeks had gone by without an arrest meant that, statistically, at least, the murder was unlikely to be cleared.

"You say that *nobody* came to interview you. Nobody?"

"No, *Señor*. I never hear from nobody abou' this thing. Luis Melenguez is only in this country six months. He leaves his wife and his children in Puerto Rico to come here. Luis never hurt nobody in his life. In his country, he is a . . . I don' know the word for this."

"A peasant, Stanley," Greta said. "And believe me, from peasants I have experience."

The Department, Moodrow knew, cleared a high percentage of homicides, usually within the first forty-eight hours. And the *way* they cleared them was by investigating the people closest to the victim. Of course, there might be any number of reasons why Maguire hadn't followed standard operating procedure, not the least of which was the distinct possibility that Rosaura Pastoral was lying through her teeth. But even if Rosaura was telling the truth, even if Maguire had no good reason for sitting on his hands, there remained the question of what he, Stanley Moodrow, could do about it.

"You should understand something here," he said, more to Greta Bloom than Rosaura Pastoral. "I'm not the commissioner. There's not much I can do."

"Stanley, please, no one expects you should go out and make miracles. But also you should remember that Rosaura is your neighbor. She comes to you for help, because there's no other place for her to go. The *machers* at the police station don't have no use for a *pisher* like Rosaura Pastoral. Let me tell you a story so you should understand what I'm trying to say."

"Please," Moodrow groaned. Greta's stories had a way of extending themselves through several generations.

"Stanley, make me a promise you'll listen close and I swear I won't be too long."

"Keep it short and I'll repeat it word for word."

"Huh," she snorted, "always with the smart mouth. One day you'll get in trouble with a mouth like that."

"One day?"

"When I came to this country," she said, ignoring his response, "I was already thirty years old, a married woman with two children. This was in 1920. All my life before that I lived in a *shtetl* in Poland. A *shtetl* is a small village. For me, a *goy* was one of two things. A *goy* was a peasant with a club or a Cossack with a sword. Believe me, Stanley, I'm not exaggerating even a little bit. I saw plenty growing up—Jews beaten, robbed, killed. It was an expected thing. So, when I found out that my husband, who came here before me, was living in an apartment with a *goy* next door, I was so crazy I couldn't talk."

"There's a first time for everything."

"Little by little, I learned there were *goyim* in the world who didn't hurt Jews just because they were Jews. There were *goyim* who were neighbors, who helped you out when you were in trouble. This maybe sounds to you like nothing, but, for me, it was a revelation like even the prophets didn't know. It changed my life and all my thinking. Rosaura is like me when I first came to

America. She don't know a soul. She don't know how things work. But she's my neighbor and she's your neighbor, too. Just like her boarder, Luis Melenguez. From my thinking, when a neighbor asks for a favor, you do what you can. That's how we survived in 1920 and that's how we survive today."

"What's the favor, Greta? What exactly does she want me to do?"

"Stanley, don't be a *schmuck*. First you should find out what's going on. Then you'll think of something."

Nine

JANUARY 12

PAT COHAN was near to tearing his mane right off the top of his head. He just couldn't get it right. Just *couldn't*. Whenever he patted the last feathery wisp into place, whenever he was about to turn away from the mirror and face the plague that'd fallen on him over the last few days, another white knot popped out and fell over his eyes like the fine lace veil his wife put on every time she left the house.

What it made him feel was incompetent, disheveled, out of control. Which, in *his* mind, was the same as old. Which was the same as retired. Which was the same as *dead*. Which . . .

The point was that he could remember a time when he took problems in stride, when he actually looked forward to problems. Because if there was *anything* the Department appreciated, it was a cop who could make problems disappear. Especially the kind of problems that embarrassed the NYPD.

He looked at himself in the mirror, fingers automatically fluttering over his mane. His face was bright red, which meant his pressure was up again.

"Ya look like a boozer, Pat," he muttered to his reflection. "Ya look like a damned Irish drunk."

What he *felt* like doing was covering his head with vaseline like some punk rock-and-roll singer. Or just shaving the whole mess off. Wear it military-style and to hell with his image. But what he *did*, finally, was fish a can of Clairol hairspray out of a bureau drawer and coat his mane until it was stiff as a board. Which he didn't mind all that much. No, what *really* bothered him was the sweet perfumy smell. It would cling to him for the next hour, no matter what he did.

Sighing, he turned out the lights and headed downstairs to the den. Once there, once the door was closed and he felt safe, he intended to light the biggest cigar he could find and fill the small room with smoke. Unfortunately, in order to get to the den, he had to pass through the living room.

"What's that smell?"

Pat Cohan turned to confront his daughter. She was sitting in a leather wing chair. His *favorite* chair. And she was grinning like the Cheshire Cat.

"Isn't there something you should be doing, Kathleen? Maybe your mother needs help." Ordinarily, he enjoyed her teasing, actually encouraged it.

"Mother can pray the rosary without me, Daddy. But if you'd like to go up and ask her if she wants assistance . . ."

That was just what he needed. A visit to his wife's private hell, to windows and doors draped in black velvet, to an agonized, bloody Jesus hanging on the cross. The endless drone of his wife's prayers sounded more like the hum of a mindless insect than human speech. The dead mourning the dead.

"When Stanley shows up, I want to see him."

"Okay, Daddy. Sal's here, by the way."

"Patero?"

"Who else? I didn't want to disturb you, so I put him in the den."

Pat Cohan felt his face begin to redden. His fingers automatically drifted up to his hair, then dropped back to his side. He left his daughter and crossed the living room.

What he wanted to do was get it over with. He wanted to handle this problem the way he'd handled every other problem that stood between himself and the top of the heap. But this problem happened to be dope, and dope simply *refused* to be handled. It wasn't clean, like gambling or prostitution. Dope was an open sewer pouring disease onto the city streets. It infected everyone around it, the innocent as well as the guilty, with a mechanical indifference that was near to maniacal.

The only way to handle dope, he'd decided long ago, was to stay as far away from it as possible, to retire before he had to deal with it. That strategy had failed. It'd failed because the same people who controlled the gambling and the whores were moving into heroin. They had no choice in the matter. The potential profits were enormous. To surrender those profits to another gang would be the economic equivalent of cutting your own throat.

He opened the door to his den and stepped through it to find Sal Patero sitting behind his desk. His handcarved, mahogany desk with the eagle's claw feet.

"Get the fuck out of my chair."

"Good evening to you, too, Pat." Patero got up and moved around the desk. "Am I allowed to sit at all?"

"Cut the bull, Sal. I'm not in the mood for it."

"What's that smell? It smells like perfume. You wearin' some kinda sweet aftershave?"

Cohan felt his face redden. He closed his eyes and silently counted to ten.

"Take it easy, Pat. Ya gettin' ya pressure up. What's the matter with you, tonight?"

How could he answer *that* one? My hair won't stay put? I'm too old to handle the bullshit anymore? My only daughter's future husband is a fucking *fool*?

"All right, Sal, why don't we just get to it." He sat behind his desk, opened the center drawer and took out a long fat cigar. The cigar was a gift from the Chief of Detectives, a handrolled Cuban import. He unwrapped it quickly, snipped off the end and lit it up.

Patero leaned forward in his seat. "I spoke to Accacio again, like you said. To get a better picture of what he wants from us. Pat, he ain't askin' for protection. What he says he needs is information. Like where the narcs are operatin', their targets and like that. Accacio figures he can keep his boys out of trouble if he can see the trouble coming."

"I suppose he expects us to hand over all the paper in the Narcotics Squad?"

"No way, Pat. Accacio ain't stupid. He wants to operate along the East River, from Fourteenth Street down to the Brooklyn Bridge. All them projects? The ones already built and the ones goin' up? The Housing Authority is fillin' 'em with Puerto Rican welfare. Accacio figures it's like a captive market. Between the welfare and the low-cost apartments, they'll never move out. Every time one of them goes on dope, Accacio's got a customer for life."

Pat Cohan suddenly relaxed. He leaned back and tried, unsuccessfully, to run his fingers through his stiff white hair. "Sal, the public sees dope as worse than murder, worse than rape. We're under tremendous pressure to do something about it. Think for a minute. Drugs are federal. The FBI goes after drugs. The FDA goes after drugs. Suppose the feds *really* turn up the heat. Suppose they put a hundred agents in Manhattan. Suppose they analyze our paperwork and discover that arrests for heroin are virtually non-existent in a certain section of the Seventh Precinct. Suppose . . ."

"Accacio understands that, Pat. He told me he didn't care if we busted every junkie in his territory, because they come right back to the needle as soon as they get out of jail. He doesn't care if we bust a few of his street dealers, either. All he wants is enough advance warning to keep the people close to him out of it."

"That way he protects his dope, right? That way he makes sure we never seize enough to really hurt him."

"Pat, we could do this all night. My problem is I don't see an easy way out of it, short of committing suicide. We're in too deep. If Accacio drops a dime on us? I don't have to draw no pictures, do I?"

"Stop right there, Sal." Cohan set his elbows on the desk and leaned forward. "Are you tellin' me the little greaseball actually *threatened* us?"

Patero shook his head. "You know, it's funny, Pat. You didn't turn a hair at the idea of covering up a homicide. But now you've got your balls in an uproar because Accacio dared to challenge your authority. It sounds like you've got things all backwards."

Pat Cohan ignored the jibe. "What you said before? About Accacio dropping a dime on *us*? Well, Sal, *I've* never met the man, have I?"

It was Patero's turn to blush and Pat Cohan watched the process with satisfaction.

"We're the cops, Sal, remember? There's twenty-four thousand of us. Prostitution? Gambling? The last I heard, they were called vices. And we *own* the Vice Squad. What we could do, if we wanted to, is hit every one of Accacio's outlets on the same night. Teach the wop a lesson. If we wanted to."

"He could still give my name to Internal Affairs."

"Nobody cares about the pad, Sal. The pad is clean. Plus, the *one* thing we are in the Department is loyal. If Steppy Accacio breaks the faith, I'll see to it that he never operates in New York City, again. *Never.*"

"I appreciate that." Patero, much to his surprise, felt a wave of emotion roll over him. It took him a moment, but he finally recognized the emotion as pride, not gratitude. He was proud of an NYPD that protected its own, proud of a Pat Cohan who put loyalty before everything else, proud of himself for being part of the process. "I mean it, Pat. It makes a difference."

Pat Cohan cleared his throat and looked down at his hands. "Meanwhile, we haven't been threatened. All it is, when you think about it, is a simple request. So, let's consider it. How much are we talking about here?"

"Right now, we're gettin' a grand a month out of Accacio. Six hundred for you, four hundred for me. We help him out and he'll double that, for starters."

"Can we do it? Assuming we want to do it. The Narcotics Squad is pretty clean. If anyone's taking, they're keeping it to themselves."

"Pat, I'm a Boy Scout. I come prepared. Ya know Wolf? The Jew in Safes and Lofts? Well, he's in my pocket. Been there for more than a year, so I know he ain't gonna fold. What I wanna do is transfer him over to Narcotics. Nobody'll think twice, because I been under pressure to beef up Narcotics, anyway. Wolf'll be my ears inside the squad. Accacio says all he wants is information, so information is what we'll give him."

Pat Cohan relit his cigar. "The thing is we *can't* stop it. I mean the dope. Maybe if we'd started right after the war, when it was still small, we could've done something, but now it's out of control."

"For once, I gotta agree." Patero sat up in the chair and crossed his legs. "The only thing we can do is *regulate* it."

"Tell ya what, Sal. You go see Accacio tonight. Tell him we accept his offer, but it'll take some time to set things up. Which it will, of course. Just make sure you tell him we're expecting the first payment *now.* That'll give us a month to make up our minds."

They were silent for a moment, their silence constituting a kind of agreement. Pat Cohan, satisfied with his decision, let his thoughts wander lightly over his possessions—his home, his numerous bank accounts, his sad, sick wife, his only daughter. They finally came to rest on what had been bothering him all along. Stanley Moodrow.

"Let's talk about Stanley for a moment," he said.

Patero sighed, shrugging his shoulders. "I already clued you in, Pat. Stanley's not a bad kid, but these things we're doin' ain't right for him. And it ain't his fault. It's yours. You rushed him along too fast."

"But he hasn't actually *refused* to cooperate?"

"Do I have to go through it again? I gave Stanley a list of burglaries. I told him to include *all* of them in Zayas's confession. He didn't do it. Detectives, third grade, are not allowed to make their own decisions. It's that simple. Plus, even if he *did* go along on the collections, I could see he didn't like it. He *asked* to be put in one of the squads. Pat, I know you got a special interest here, but I ain't got the time to be your future son-in-law's psychiatrist. Either straighten him out or get Kathleen to find another boyfriend. Meanwhile, there's somethin' I ain't told ya, somethin' I didn't wanna talk about over the phone."

Pat Cohan sighed. "I can't wait to hear it."

"Ya remember the spic who got iced on Pitt Street? In the whorehouse?"

"I'm not senile. Yet."

"Well, Stanley asked me about him this afternoon."

Cohan's eyebrows shot up to his hairline. He rejected his first thought, that Stanley Moodrow was one of the headhunters from Internal Affairs, because it was too gruesome to contemplate.

"It ain't what ya thinkin'," Sal continued. "The spic, Melenguez, was a friend of one of Stanley's neighbors. All Stanley wants to know is how it happened and where the investigation's goin'. I told him I'd check on it and get back to him."

"This is what happens," Cohan grunted, "when you put a cop in his home precinct. Cases become personal. It destroys perspective."

"The *perspective* here is that we're not doin' shit to find the perpetrator. The *perspective* is that even if we don't know who the shooter is, we know who sent him. Now, whatta ya wanna tell Stanley?"

Pat Cohan took his time thinking it over. He re-lit his cigar, then blew on the ash until it glowed. "The first thing we better do is take it out of the precinct. Kick it up to the Organized Crime Task Force. They've already got a backload of mob killings that'll keep them busy for the next five years. I expect to see Stanley tonight. I'll tell him the spic was a pimp and we think his killing was mob-related, part of a turf war."

"Sounds okay." Patero glanced down at his watch. "Jeez, it's almost nine o'clock. I ain't laid eyes on my kids in two days. Lemme get the hell out of here. Maybe I'll be home before they go to bed."

Pat Cohan left his desk as soon as the door shut behind Sal Patero. He walked across the room, to a small table near the window, and sat down. A half-finished jigsaw puzzle lay on the table and he began to pick up individual pieces and fit them into an apple tree in the right hand corner of the puzzle. With his hands busy, his mind was free to consider his daughter's boyfriend.

That's the way he wanted to think of Stanley Moodrow—as a boyfriend, an unsuitable suitor, not as Kathleen's fiancé. Cohan had been aware of Mood-row's independent streak all along. Aware of it as a potential problem, especially if Stanley had a conscience to go along with it. Now the chickens were coming home to roost. Or, better still, the fox was in the chicken coop.

Like any good farmer, Cohan understood that the fox had to go. One way or the other. Unfortunately, the chicken, in this case, couldn't be replaced by a fertilized egg. He thought, briefly, about living alone in his fine big house. Alone except for his crazy wife. He was fifty-nine years old. Retirement was coming, whether he liked it or not. He'd been counting on Kathleen and the grandchildren she'd give him to make that retirement bearable. If he forced her to choose between himself and Stanley Moodrow, there was always the possibility she'd choose Moodrow. He, Pat Cohan, was far too close to the situation to make an accurate judgment.

What he needed to do, he decided, was to move slowly. Wait for Moodrow to fall on his face. The kid was headstrong, stubborn. Sooner or later, like any other beginner, he'd make a mistake. And when he did, Pat Cohan would be standing there, shotgun in hand, like any good farmer with a fox in the coop.

Ten minutes later, when Moodrow knocked on the door, Pat Cohan was ready.

"It's not locked," he called, moving back to his desk.

"Evening, Pat."

"Ah, Stanley. Yer lookin' good, son. Swelling's gone down. Bruises almost gone. Lookin' good, all right." He fumbled in his desk drawer. "Have a cigar?"

"No thanks, Pat. You know I don't smoke."

"Well, boyo, now that your fightin' days are in the past, it might be time to cultivate a few healthy vices."

"Maybe you're right, but I don't think I wanna begin at the top." He nodded toward the cigar. "One of these days, maybe I'll start with a cigarette and work my way up."

Pat Cohan chuckled appreciatively. He swiveled his chair away from the desk, opened a cabinet built into the bookcase behind him, and fetched a bottle of Bushmill's and two glasses. "Perhaps I might interest you in a different vice."

"Sure, Pat, that'd be great."

Cohan filled the two glasses halfway, then handed one to Moodrow. "Down the hatch, boyo."

Moodrow managed not to choke, despite the fire that raged in his throat. "Damn," he said, "I'm not used to this."

Pat Cohan allowed himself to chuckle sympathetically, then straightened in his chair. "I'm afraid we have something serious to discuss, Stanley. Something unpleasant."

"This I already figured out."

"Sal Patero's complaining. He says you're not cooperating. He *says* you don't care for what you're doing."

Moodrow sat back in his chair, looking for the right words, the words that would get his message across without offending Pat Cohan. He, too, had given the matter a lot of thought and he, too, was unsure of what Kathleen would do if forced to choose between her father and her lover.

"The *first* thing is that what Sal's got me doing came as a complete surprise. I know you're only trying to look out for me and Kathleen. I got no problem with that. But I gotta admit that I would've liked to work my way up. The other guys in the squad hate my guts and I always got along with everybody."

"Stanley, if ya want to get ahead, you can't worry about what some . . ."

"Let me finish, Pat. Before the lecture." The whiskey was rapidly going to Moodrow's head. Its main effect, at that moment, was fearlessness. "I went along with the collections, with the pad. I can live with that, because it's been goin' on for a long time. Also, the thing Sal's got me doing with the DA's office, the paperwork and that, is also acceptable. I'd rather be conducting investigations, but I understand that I'm doing something important. What bothers me is what he asked me to do with the kid, Zayas. I won't put these heavy beefs on some punk kid's head. It's not right."

Pat Cohan started to interrupt, but Moodrow waved him off, again. "Everything Zayas did, all those burglaries, don't add up to a thousand dollars. Zayas is nothing but an amateur who's small enough to get through a ventilation duct. I can't go along with making him into a major criminal."

"Is it my turn, now?" Cohan waited for Moodrow to nod, then continued. "It's a question of loyalty here, boyo. Not loyalty to me or to Sal Patero. We're talkin' about loyalty to the Department, to the tradition. The public doesn't give two figs for our problems. *All* the public wants is results. You really can't blame them. Between the papers and the TV, they're scared to death. I'm tellin' ya, Stanley, your average good citizen sees a mugger on every corner. They see rapists under their beds. Murderers in the closet."

Cohan took a minute to suck on his cigar. "There's no way to educate the public, boyo. There's no way to show them how things *really* work. Yet, we have to protect the Department from its enemies. Think about it, Stanley. Every time we turn around, we're being attacked by some nigger-loving politician out to pick up a few votes. We *have* to protect ourselves." Cohan sighed and leaned back in his chair. "I don't wanna turn this into a book, Stanley, because the answer is simple enough. We protect ourselves with statistics. As long as *our* bullshit statistics compare favorably with the bullshit statistics coming out of other cities, nobody can fault us. Now, it's true, boyo, some of the things we do to protect the Department aren't particularly pleasant. But those of us who've been in the game for a long time understand that our first loyalty is to the NYPD, not to some spic from the Lower East Side. And let me tell you one more thing, Stanley. A cop who fails to exhibit that loyalty, can't move up the ladder. I don't care if he's got the *mayor* for a rabbi."

"You have a point there, Pat, but I'm not gonna do it, anyway." Moodrow, to his surprise, answered without hesitation. "The bad guys are the bad guys. They have to pay for their crimes, even if it means doing what O'Brien and Mitkowski did to Zayas. But I'm not gonna frame some poor *schmuck*. If that means I never get above detective, third grade, then so be it."

Pat Cohan refilled his glass, then offered the bottle to Moodrow. "Have another, Stanley."

"No thanks, Pat. I'm still recovering from the first one."

"I know this is delicate, boyo." Cohan sipped at his drink, taking his time. "And the last thing I want to be is the interfering father-in-law. But, you know, Kathleen's my only child." He took another sip of the Bushmill's, swishing it over his tongue before swallowing. "The question I keep asking myself is whether Kathleen can *take* life on the Lower East Side. Everything looks so easy, when you're young, but . . ."

"I already got the lecture from Sal. Kathleen and I are gonna have to take our chances. Like every other couple startin' out. With both of us working, there's no reason why we have to live on the Lower East Side. That's even if you knock me off the pad, which I don't think you're gonna do."

"Damn it, I don't want my daughter working after she's married." Pat Cohan finally lost his temper. "I didn't want her to work *before* she got married."

"You trying to say she wouldn't listen to you?"

Cohan felt his face begin to redden. He couldn't believe this detective, third grade—who, by all rights, should still be walking a beat—had the gall to challenge him. Then he reminded himself that he'd already decided to dump Stanley Moodrow. "There's no sense in pursuing this, is there?"

"Pat, it's not like I'm talkin' about goin' to the press. Or Internal Affairs. I'm satisfied with what I'm doing. It's just that I'm not willing to send the Playtex Burglar upstate for the next five years to make New York's statistics better than Chicago's."

"Maybe you're right." Cohan let his fingers drift up to his stiff hair. "I'll calm Patero down. In fact, I'll *beat* Patero down, if I have to. You try to cooperate every way you can."

"No problem."

"Good, now there's one other thing. Sal told me you were asking after a stiff named Melenguez."

It was Moodrow's turn to blush. "This is embarrassing." He took a deep breath and launched into it. "I've got this neighbor. Greta Bloom. Used to be my mom's best friend. Greta's the kind of woman who sticks her nose any place it'll fit. I'm sure you know what I mean. Anyway, it turns out that Melenguez used to room with another neighbor, Rosaura Pastoral. Rosaura is also Greta's friend, so when Rosaura went to Greta, Greta came to me. She thinks I'm Dick Tracy or something. Anyway, I promised Greta I'd ask about Melenguez. It's one of those things you can't get out of. Like goin' to the dentist."

"Ya know, boyo, for a minute there, you had me worried. I was afraid you were *close* to this Melenguez. Now, as far as we can tell, Melenguez was a working pimp. From the way it went down, we're sure it was a contract killing. The case is in the process of being kicked out to boro-wide Homicide and Organized Crime. They'll share the information and work on it from different angles. It's funny, in a way. These little greasers come over here and start committing crimes before they put down their suitcases. Welfare isn't good enough for 'em. We do everything we can do to make their lives easy and this is how they reward us."

What Moodrow wanted was Kathleen Cohan back in his apartment on the Lower East Side. What he got was Kathleen Cohan so repentant that she was afraid to come within two feet of him. Kathleen had had her little talk with Father Ryan, a talk that turned out to be a lecture about the impossibility of forgiveness unless the penance was performed. And, of course, she would not be allowed to receive Communion until her sins were forgiven.

Moodrow, listening to Kathleen recite the details, felt his heart drop into his shoes. "Kate," he said when she was finished, "we've got enough troubles with your father. We don't need any more."

He went on to describe, in detail, the events leading up to his conversation with Pat Cohan. What he wanted, naturally, was for his fiancée to back him up a hundred percent. He wanted her to burn with indignation at the idea of forcing a man to confess to crimes he didn't commit. What he got was a puzzled, frowning Kathleen Cohan.

"This Zayas," she finally said, "is a homosexual and a thief. Did I get that right?"

"He steals women's clothes and dresses up in them. I guess that's a pretty big hint."

"Well, why do you care about him?"

If Kathleen's voice had been challenging or angry, Moodrow would have known how to respond. But Kathleen was clearly puzzled. She wanted an answer she could understand and Moodrow didn't have one. Or, at least, he didn't have one that would please her.

"Zayas was pitiful, Kate. Most likely, there are things happening to him right now that I can't even describe to you. They took him over to the Tombs and he can't make bail. I mean there's a fair chance that he won't even *survive.*"

"What I'm thinking," Kate interrupted, "is that some liberal judge is going to have the same attitude you do. I'm thinking he's going to give Zayas probation. Zayas is a *homosexual.* Do you want him out on the streets? Do you want him hanging around the schoolyards? Maybe homosexuality isn't a sin. Maybe it's a disease, like the psychiatrists say. But, even if it *is* a disease, it's a *contagious* disease. The only way I know to control a contagious disease is to isolate it until the doctors invent a cure."

Moodrow felt his mouth tighten down until it was a short straight line, almost a scar frozen on his face. "And what do you want me to do, Kate? You want me to be the judge and the jury? You want me to write my own laws? You want me to be God?"

Kathleen jerked backwards. The movement was involuntary and, for a few seconds, she was really frightened. She'd never gone to any of Moodrow's fights, never witnessed his potential for out-and-out ferocity.

"Stanley, please . . ."

"What?"

Suddenly, she reached out and pulled him toward her, burying her head in his chest. "I want you to get along with Daddy," she said, holding onto him as tightly as she could. "I'm begging you, Stanley. Daddy is all alone in the world except for me. It's been hard for him. When he lost Peter, when he lost his only son, he was devastated. In a way he's lost his wife, too. Maybe this is *worse* than losing her. What I'm saying is I need my father and he needs me. If I lost him, I think I'd die."

Ten

JANUARY 13

JAKE LEIBOWITZ was lost in dreams when the first blow struck the exposed flesh of his back. He was dreaming of prison, of cooking up and hiding a batch of prison hooch in his cell. Somehow, despite the sharp pain and the crack of the leather belt, he failed to wake up immediately. Only the character of his dream changed. It changed from the gleeful anticipation of alcohol intoxication, to a surprise visit by club-wielding prison guards. Still asleep, Jake did what any smart con would do under the same circumstances. He put his hands over the back of his head, curled himself into a ball and waited for the hacks to tire.

When he finally opened his eyes, only to discover his pillow instead of the concrete walls of a prison cell, Jake became slightly disoriented. Somebody was screaming at him, but he couldn't make out the words. Then, very slowly, inch by inch, it came to him. He wasn't in prison. He was home in his own bed. And the person beating him wasn't using a club. She was using a leather belt. And she wasn't screaming about prison contraband. She was screaming, "A *rabbit*? A *rabbit*? A *rabbit*?"

Timing the rhythm of his mother's assault carefully—the last thing he needed was to catch a shot in the face—Jake rolled away from the wall, grabbed his mother's arm as the next blow descended, and pulled her onto the bed.

"Jesus Christ, ma," he said, as he scrambled to his feet, "you shouldn't of . . ." He didn't finish the sentence, because he knew that he *did* deserve what he'd gotten.

"A rabbit for a *mamaleh*," she moaned. "A rabbit for a *mamaleh*."

"What did you do?" Jake gestured toward what remained of his mother's coat. She'd cut it into pieces and scattered it all over the floor. Which meant, Jake suddenly realized, that while he was sleeping, she'd been standing next to his bed with a pair of scissors. "*Mamaleh*, I'm sorry."

Jake's mother, still gasping for breath, slowly pulled herself upright. "You, you, you . . . you *goy*!" Fueled by this insult, she got to her feet and yanked the mattress off the bed. "Where is it?" she demanded. "Where is it?"

"Where's what?" Jake asked, though he knew *exactly* what she was looking for.

"Don't play the *shmegegge* with me. I'm looking for the money." She began to rip the drawers out of his dresser, scattering his carefully folded clothing among the bits and pieces of mutilated rabbit.

"Enough." Jake finally grabbed his mother, holding her arms tight against her sides. "There's no money here."

"Don't lie to me. A *goniff* doesn't put his money in the bank."

"The money's not here, *mamaleh*. Not that I have a whole lot, because I'm just gettin' started in business. But what I do have ain't here. Just try to calm down. I said I was sorry and I promise to make it up to you. I promise that tonight, when I come home, I'll have a *new* coat for you."

"You think I'd trust *you* to buy my coat? You think I'm a *schmuck*?"

"Okay, you're right. Tonight, I'll give you a hundred dollars to buy your own coat."

"*Five* hundred," she said calmly. "Not a penny less."

"I'm not made of money," Jake moaned. "For five hundred dollars, you could buy mink."

"Five hundred."

"Two."

"Two?"

"Two hundred."

"Four. I'll make do with four hundred."

"Two-fifty, *mamaleh*. And that's my last offer. If ya don't take it, I'm gonna move out and find a place of my own."

"You act like a big *macher*, but what you are is a cheapskate. A bum."

"I'm not changin' my mind." He felt her relax in his arms, heard her murmured assent, and let go.

"So, when do I get this money?"

"Tonight, when I come home."

"Tonight? It's already three o'clock in the afternoon. Tonight, for a big shot like you, means four o'clock in the morning."

"I'll leave it on the kitchen table."

"Okay, Jacob, I'm trusting you. But take one piece of advice from a poor old *mamaleh*. If you don't leave the money, don't go to sleep. Now, I'll make you a nice breakfast while you get dressed. And don't bother about the room. I'll clean it after you leave."

Jake got himself showered, shaved and dressed in record time. In a way, his mama had done him a favor. He was supposed to meet Izzy Stein at four o'clock. Not that Izzy wouldn't hang around if Jake showed up late, but Jake had made a very important decision about his own future and Izzy was a key part of that decision.

The rush didn't bother Jake, either. He and Izzy had business to take care of. Which meant he'd be wearing his working clothes. Somehow, a sweatshirt, khaki pants, work boots and an ancient peacoat didn't require a lot of care. His mother's salami omelet, on the other hand, went down very slowly. He couldn't understand why his mother insisted on adding a ton of garlic to everything she cooked. Not that he was foolish enough to ask her.

"Jake, you gotta get out of here," he muttered to himself, as he washed the omelet down with several mugs of bitter black coffee. It wasn't the first time he'd made the observation. He looked at his mama standing by the stove. She was nearly as tall as he was. And she outweighed him by fifty pounds.

"You said something?" she asked, dropping a spoonful of Crisco into the hot frying pan.

"We're a team, *mamaleh*. That's what I said."

"That's nice, Jakey. Such a sweet boy."

Ten minutes later, Jake was out in the street. He took a moment to note the overcast skies and the warmer temperature. It looked like rain, which was just fine with him. Rain would keep the honest citizens off the street, the ones who felt it was their *duty* to report a crime. The morons.

He walked the few blocks to Izzy Stein's hotel, the Paradise, and entered the lobby.

"You wanna go 'round the world with me, baby? Ten bucks. I do you good."

It was too early for the whores to be out on the street, but that didn't mean they weren't working. Jake ignored them, nodding to the desk clerk before climbing the stairs to the second floor. Izzy had had a number of rooms in the months since Jake had gotten out of prison, always on the second floor, rear. If worse came to worst, Izzy had explained, he could jump out the window without killing himself.

"Who is it?" The voice from inside 2C was sharp and suspicious.

"It's Jake." The door opened and Jake walked inside. "Who were you expecting?"

"Careless got me sent up the river. It ain't happening again."

Jake looked the small room over, shaking his head. A bed, a table, a chair, a tiny chest. "Damn, Izzy, you could do better than this. Ya movin' up in the world. It's time ya had a decent front. So's you could get respect."

Izzy sat on the edge of the bed. "Big places make me nervous. Too many rooms. Anybody could be hiding anywhere."

"Ya could still live in a hotel room," Jake insisted. "Ya could just make it a *better* hotel room."

"I hope ya didn't come down here to talk about my domicile. Because Sandy's gonna be here in half an hour."

"Sandy? Don't make friends with that wop, Izzy. I don't plan for him to be around too long. He's nothin' but a spy for Steppy Accacio."

"Ya know somethin', Jake, you got one big problem. Ya worry about the wrong things. Ya wanna find out how much I care about Sandy? Tell me to kill him. Then, you'll know. Now, what's up?"

Jake took a deep breath. "We're movin' faster than I expected. Maybe we got lucky or maybe we got so much talent we deserve it. Whichever way, if we don't look out, we're gonna get in over our heads. What we gotta do is organize."

"Ya don't hear me arguin'."

"Lemme explain, all right? Don't interrupt. Now, the way I see it is like this. First, we got the SpeediFreight thing goin' strong—next week, we're doin' another load of cigarettes and there's plenty more comin'. Plus, now Accacio's givin' us a piece of the dope. We're gettin' the retail for all the projects on Avenue D, from Fourteenth Street to Houston. There's ten thousand people livin' in those projects and we're gonna serve as many of them as we can. And that's the point, that bit about as many as we *can*. I don't know about you, but I got no desire to peddle dope on the street. If ya don't get busted, ya gotta worry that some junkie's gonna pipe ya for ya stash."

"Let him try it." Izzy lit a cigarette and tossed the match on the floor.

"Ya know what you need, Izzy? Ya need a woman. A Jewish man without a woman is helpless."

"C'mon," Izzy sighed. "Get to the point."

"The point is that we gotta find some help. We need a couple of young guys. Guys just startin' out. As long as they ain't wops. I don't care if they're fucking Chinamen, as long as they ain't wops."

"You got anyone in mind?"

Jake grinned. "That's where you come in, Izzy. You're gonna be my lieutenant and ya first job is to recruit us some employees. I'd do it myself, except that I don't know anybody. All them years in a federal joint in fucking Kansas? Talk about a wasted youth." He shook his head sadly. "See, what I'm hopin' is that in a few months, we won't personally touch nothin'. We organize. We collect. But we don't touch nothin'. Whatta ya say?"

Izzy took a moment to think it over. "I guess I could do it. You got any objection to the Irish?"

"Whatta you, an idiot? No Irishman's gonna work for a Jew. It's impossible."

"No Italians. No Irish. You want I should find some Apaches?"

"Look, Izzy." Jake took his time, reminding himself to be calm. "Try to remember what it was like to be a Jew inside the walls. How many cons could ya really trust? I know what I'm asking ain't easy, but it's gotta be done. Accacio thinks he can control us, because we're weak. Just a couple of kikes on a string. What we're gonna do is put together an organization that can stand by itself. That don't gotta go beggin' for crumbs. The dope business is the coming thing. It's gonna be bigger than Prohibition. Once I get my hands on a chunk of it, I don't have no intention of letting go."

Izzy managed a grin. "You shoulda been a lawyer."

"Then it's settled?"

"I'll get on it startin' tomorrow."

"Great, now I hope ya didn't tell Santo what we're doin' tonight."

"I didn't have to tell him. He already heard it from Joe Faci."

"Yeah? Well hearin' is one thing, but *seein'* is something else. He ain't comin' with us. I got a little surprise for young Santo."

Fifteen minutes later, young Santo knocked on Izzy's door. He came into the room with his habitual grin firmly in place.

"Whatta ya say, Iz? How's it hangin'?"

"Long and low, Sandy. How's by you?"

"Everything's everything. Whatta ya say, Jake? We workin' tonight?"

"*You* ain't." Jake was beginning to hate everything about Santo Silesi, especially his easy grin and his refusal to take offense, no matter how hard Jake pushed him.

"Whatta ya mean?"

"What I mean is I got a special job for ya. A job ya could be in charge of all by yourself. I'm sure ya relatives already told ya what we're gonna be doin' with the dope. Right?"

Silesi nodded. "They said somethin' about it."

"Yeah? Well here's what *I* got to say about it. I need someone to go in there regular. Somebody to take care of the customers. That's you, Santo. You're gonna have regular places to be and regular times to be there. According to ya relatives, we could dump between a hundred and two hundred bags a day. For starters. What you're gonna do is come to me every morning and every afternoon. I give you the dope and you give me the money. Any problems?"

"You want me to go in there alone, right? You're not worried that I'll get ripped off."

Jake laughed. "You tryin' to tell me ya scared of the Puerto Ricans? I thought you wops were supposed to be so tough?" He watched the blood rise into Santo Silesi's cheeks and ears. "Here's the thing, Santo. This is what I need ya to do. For now, anyway. You got a problem with it, you could always quit and go back to ya relatives."

"Why do you have such a hard-on for me, Jake?" Santo spoke quietly. "I've done whatever you asked me to do."

Jake walked across the room, stopping three feet away from the younger man. "People who work for me do what I say. And what I say is take a fuckin' hike. Ya don't like that? Well, there's nothin' between us, but air."

Santo Silesi broke for a moment. His friendly eyes turned to stone. The anger in them was cold and implacable, the icy glitter of sunlight reflecting off the face of a glacier. Jake grinned and braced himself. Twelve years in Leavenworth? A *Jew* in Leavenworth? If Santo Silesi came forward, Jake fully intended to kill him.

"Hey, guys," Izzy said. "This don't make no sense. It's stupid."

"Yeah, you're right," Silesi said, struggling to manage a smile. "I'll play it whatever way you want, Jake. As long as I get my piece."

"I don't welsh," Jake said. "So that ain't a problem for you. Now, take off. I'll see ya tomorrow morning."

Once Santo was out the door, Jake turned to Izzy. "Ya see that, Izzy? Ya see that?"

"I seen it," Izzy replied, calmly. "The wop's colder than he looks. So what?"

"One day, when Steppy Accacio don't need us anymore, this is the guy who's gonna try to kill us. *That's* 'so what.' " He paused to allow Izzy to reply, but Izzy kept his mouth shut. "Somethin' else I found out from Joe Faci last night. He says he's gonna feed us information on what the narcs are doin'. He says he's got a lieutenant from the Seventh in his pocket and this lieutenant's got connections higher up. If there's heat, we're gonna see it comin'."

"Ya wanna hear somethin' funny, Jake. It seems like this guy Faci's spendin' a lotta time lookin' out for us. I mean considering how you keep insistin' that he's gonna kill us."

Jake put his hands on Izzy's shoulders. "Listen, Izzy. We ain't family to Joe Faci. We ain't Sicilians or even Italians. We're *Jews*. When Steppy Accacio puts us on the line, he's only takin' a step back to protect himself. If protectin' himself means we gotta go, he'll put us down without thinkin' twice. Now, whatta ya say we get to work?"

Izzy shrugged into a black turtleneck sweater. He pulled a wool Eisenhower jacket over the sweater, then added a heavy watchcap and leather gloves.

"Is it cold out, Jake?"

Jake strolled over to the window. "For once, it ain't cold. But it's rainin'."

"Should we take an umbrella?"

"Sure, and don't forget to put on ya rubbers."

"Why, we gettin' laid?"

Jake put his arm around Izzy's shoulders. "Izzy, you're a riot. You oughta be on television."

They strolled out the door and down the stairs. The whores were still in the lobby. They'd probably stay there until their pimps forced them out into the rain. Several called out to Izzy and he acknowledged them with a nod and a tight smile.

"Hey, Izzy," Jake whispered, "maybe you're gonna need them rubbers after all."

They pushed through the doors and stepped out into a cold, steady rain. Jake turned up the collar of his peacoat. It was the only concession either of them made to the weather. The rain slowly worked through their jackets as they walked back to get the Packard. Jake knew that he should have driven the car over to Izzy's. He half expected Izzy to make some comment, but Izzy just kept walking. He didn't even hurry his pace when the car came into view.

Jake felt proud to have an associate like Izzy Stein. And happy to be rid of an asshole like Abe Weinberg. That was a lucky stroke, he realized as he started the car. If it wasn't for Joe Faci's demand, he, Jake, would still be dealing with that rock-and-roll moron.

"Here, take this." Jake handed a clean handkerchief to Izzy. "The defroster ain't workin' right. Ya gotta use the snot rag to clean the windows."

They drove over to a small playground on the north side of Houston Street between Avenue D and the river. There were no kids in the playground, only adults on business.

"You see our boy, Izzy?" Jake pointed at a tall man in a trench coat. "Name's Rocco Insalaco. Cute, huh? Like a rhyme."

Izzy peered through the small circle of clean glass. "You *sure* he don't have a partner watchin' out?"

"Faci says he works alone. He's connected, but his people don't approve of dope. Nobody's gonna come back on us for what we're doin'."

"I tell ya what I don't like, Jake. I don't like usin' this car. If some *schmuck* picks up the license plate, it'd come right back on us."

"Well, that's the fucking problem we were talkin' about. We need more guys. We need guys who can get into cars, guys who can do locks and safes. We gotta get organized, instead of takin' chances all the time. The way it is right now, we don't have no choices. Not that I'm expectin' problems. It's rainin' and the streets are empty. Besides which the people livin' here know the deal: you get in bed with the cops, you wake up in a swamp. Keep in mind that we ain't a couple of assholes workin' on our own no more. We're *connected.*"

One by one, the men in the playground, their business conducted, moved off to find a quiet place to enjoy their purchases. When the man in the trench coat was alone, Jake reached into the back seat of the Packard and grabbed two baseball bats. He handed both of them over to Izzy and grunted. "Ya know what to do." Without waiting for an answer, he climbed out of the Packard and walked into the playground.

Jake kept his right hand in his pocket. Gunshots weren't part of the plan, but if Rocco Insalaco picked up on what was about to happen and decided to run, Jake was determined to do what he'd come to do.

But Rocco Insalaco didn't run. He held his ground, eyeing Jake coldly. "Do I know you?" he asked when Jake was still ten feet away.

"That depends," Jake answered, pulling the .45 out of his pocket. "You know who *Malakh-hamoves* is?"

"Hey!" Rocco took a step back, then froze in his tracks. "I don't know nobody named Malik."

"I didn't think so. I didn't think a wop would be acquainted with the Angel of Death."

"Whatta ya want? Whatta ya want?"

Jake watched the man tremble, watched Izzy approach from behind, watched the bat as it whooshed through the air and slammed into the back of Rocco Insalaco's head.

"Ya must be losin' ya touch, Izzy. Either that or Rocco's got a skull like a nigger. Gimme a bat. We'll take turns."

They took their time about it. This was one body that wasn't going to end up in a swamp. Tomorrow morning, when the junkies heard about Rocco's fate, they'd have plenty of respect for the man who came to take his place. Santo Silesi wouldn't be operating on his own. He'd have the fate of Rocco Insalaco covering his back.

Eleven

JANUARY 15

STANLEY MOODROW sat at his kitchen table, a cup of coffee near his right hand and a bowl of untouched Cheerios in front of him. He'd already given up on the *Daily News*. In the first place, New York had been quiet on January 14th. There'd been no juicy murders, no subway wrecks, no crooked politicians to expose. The lead story concerned an unemployed chef who'd robbed a Queens bank with a non-existent bomb. The part about a "Queens bank" was the giveaway. The *Daily News*, not unlike New York City's politicians, rarely paid any attention to the outer boroughs.

In the second place, Moodrow couldn't stop thinking about his job and what it was doing to his plans for the future. He felt like Humpty Dumpty sitting on the wall. If he fell, if the hurricane pushing at his back shoved him over the edge, nobody would ever put his career back together again.

What made it funny was all the daydreams he'd had before he got his appointment to the detectives. He'd spent the six weeks before his bout with the "Fightin' Fireman" sitting in a training class at the Academy. Everyone else in the class had already been appointed, but the idea had been to give Moodrow regular hours while he prepared for the big fight. Moodrow found the classes easy, easy enough for him to dream about life as an NYPD detective. He'd imagined himself rising through the ranks, imagined his name and picture in the *Daily News*. . . .

Well, he'd gotten this name and his picture in the papers. The *Journal-American* had printed a photo of Moodrow leading the Playtex Burglar through the side door of the 7th Precinct. The contrast between the small, slender burglar and the giant cop hadn't been lost on the editor who'd written the caption. "Beauty and the Beast" was the way the paper had chosen to put it.

The notoriety hadn't given Moodrow any satisfaction, but that couldn't be said of the job he'd been doing for the last week. Sal Patero had been right about the cops in the 7th Precinct. They had an uncanny ability to mess up the paperwork. Maybe that was because the paperwork was irrelevant in all but a handful of cases.

Most of the felons on the Lower East Side couldn't afford a lawyer. They copped out to the charges, because demanding a trial inevitably resulted in a longer sentence, usually in one of the harsher prisons like Dannemora. But there *were* trials. There were hardened ex-cons who laughed at the third degree, who were smart enough to use their ill-gotten gains to keep an attorney on retainer. There were also first-time criminals—husbands who'd gone berserk on their wives, friends who'd cut each other to pieces in a bar—who simply had the money to hire a lawyer. In these cases, the paperwork had to be right and it almost never was.

Which is why, once they'd determined his competence, the DA's office had welcomed Stanley Moodrow like a conquering hero. Before he'd come upon the scene, they'd been cleaning up the mess by themselves. Now, they could put the burden on Moodrow. They could complain, order, cajole and, most importantly of all, blame someone else when cases fell apart due to sloppy policing.

Moodrow recalled a case that had had the prosecutors near to madness. Two patrolmen had arrested a man named Robert White for a double homicide. It should have been an open-and-shut deal, because even though the .25 caliber automatic they'd found on Mr. White hadn't exactly been smoking, ballistics had matched it to the slugs taken out of the victims' bodies. The only problem was that the gun couldn't be matched to the *perpetrator*. The special Property Clerk's Invoice used when firearms were confiscated was nowhere to be found.

The two patrolmen who'd made the arrest swore they'd done the paperwork. The detectives handling the follow-up thought otherwise.

"They oughta put them assholes in the Midtown Tunnel," one had insisted.

"Didn't *you* check the paperwork to make sure it was all there?"

"Hey, it wasn't my case. All I did was interview a few drunks who overheard White braggin' about the homicides."

Moodrow had chosen to believe the two patrolmen. Which meant the paperwork had to be somewhere in the precinct. The search had taken the better part of a day, but he'd finally run down the missing form in the file of a sixty-year-old pornography dealer named *Richard* White. The prosecutors had taken him to lunch. Better yet, they'd called Patero and thanked him for sending them Stanley Moodrow.

So, Moodrow supposed, he was a hero, now, instead of a stubborn, uncooperative bum. Now Patero, as Moodrow drove him back and forth from the 7th Precinct to NYPD headquarters on Centre Street, chatted easily. Now, there was no further mention of "first loyalties" or "acceptable statistics."

Moodrow had the distinct impression that he was being given a second chance, by Sal Patero if not Pat Cohan. Sooner or later, he was going to be invited to make another arrest, to pile on more charges. The only thing was that Stanley Moodrow wasn't sure he wanted a second chance. He'd taken a stand—at least, he *thought* he had—and stands were supposed to be final. Now, he wasn't sure what he'd do if faced with another Playtex Burglar. He even wasn't sure what he *should* do. That was why he'd invited his old trainer, Allen Epstein, to stop over for coffee. It was also why he answered the doorbell in his underwear.

"Oh, shit," he moaned, slamming the door on Greta Bloom, Rosaura Pastoral and a young woman he didn't recognize.

"I have to put something on, Greta," he shouted through the door. "I'll be back in a second." He ran into the bedroom, reached for a robe, then changed his mind.

"Lemme get this right," he muttered, tossing a clean white shirt and a pair of pants onto the bed. He threw on the shirt, buttoned it wrong, re-buttoned it, jumped into his trousers, fumbled in his drawer for a pair of socks without a hole in the toe, dug his slippers out from under the bed, ran a comb through his short hair. By the time he got back to the door, he was breathing hard.

"I'm sorry to keep you waiting," he explained. "I was expecting someone else."

"But I called last night," Greta said, pushing past him into the apartment. "Remember? You said you asked about Luis."

"Yeah, Greta, but you didn't say you were coming over at seven o'clock in the morning."

"So, when should I come? You work all day and at night you go out to Queens to see your girlfriend." She sat down on the couch. "You remember Rosaura, right? And this is Nenita Melenguez, Luis's wife. She came to New York to make arrangements."

"Mrs. Melenguez," Moodrow nodded. "Please, everybody sit down. Would anyone like coffee?"

"You are expecting the company," Rosaura Pastoral said, "so we should no be stayin' too long."

"Are you sure?" Moodrow was stalling for time. The slight figure perched on the edge of his couch looked like anything but a pimp's wife. She wore a beltless cotton dress that fell to her ankles and a cloth coat so thin it wouldn't keep her warm in Miami. Her eyes were riveted to the carpet, her head bent forward so that he couldn't see her features very well.

"So tell us what you found out," Greta said, smiling.

That was the problem. That was why he was stalling. How could he tell this woman that her dead husband was a pimp? Unless she already knew. Unless the dress and the coat were pure bullshit. Moodrow decided to find out.

"According to the lieutenant, Luis Melenguez was a pimp. A whoremaster. He was deliberately executed by person or persons unknown. The investigation's ongoing, but nobody expects a quick arrest. Right now, the case is in the process of being turned over to a squad that investigates organized crime."

He expected a reaction, but not the one he got. Nenita Melenguez, totally uncomprehending, looked up at Rosaura Pastoral and said something in Spanish. Moodrow understood the first words, *por favor*, but nothing else.

"She don' understand Eenglish," Rosaura explained. "I am suppos' to be translating, but I don know how I can say thees."

"She can't say it," Greta interrupted. "Stanley, you should please take a another look at this woman. Nenita is not the wife of a pimp. It's as plain as the nose on your face."

"My nose's been broken too many times to be plain."

"Stanley . . ."

"I'm not making this up, Greta. I went to the lieutenant, just like you asked, and I'm telling you what he told me. You wanna make up a story for Mrs. Melenguez, you go ahead and do it."

"No, I tell her wha' you say."

Rosaura Pastoral turned to Nenita Melenguez and quickly translated. The effect, though it didn't surprise Moodrow, wasn't the one he hoped to get. The woman raised her eyes to meet Rosaura's, then dropped them when Rosaura's message became clear. "No," she whispered. "Noooooo."

"Look what you've done," Greta said, taking Nenita's hand.

"What I did is what *you* asked me to do," Moodrow insisted.

Before Greta could respond, Nenita Melenguez began to speak. Her voice was soft and halting, the words spilling out in short, murmured phrases that Rosaura Pastoral easily translated.

"She say, 'I have know my husban' since he was a little boy. I know hees whole family. Luis marry me when I am fifteen. We have together three children. All hees life, Luis work in the sugar cane. He is wha' they call *palero*. Thees is a man who takes care of the *maclaines*. . . .' Wait, I don' know thees word *maclaines*."

Rosaura spoke quickly, then listened for a moment before nodding her head. "A *maclaine* is a ditch for bringin' water to the cane." She nodded to Nenita who continued. "She say, '*Palero* is a good job. *Paleros* sometime make fifteen dollars in a week. But tha' job goes away, because the *rematista*, the foreman, is bringin' a machine that digs the ditches faster than ten men. Luis goes back to cutting the cane, but the *rematista* brings other machines, like *arañas*, spiders, that load the cane onto the oxcarts. Then motors are put on the carts and all the *carreteros* who take care of the oxen are out of work. Luis's *papi*, who was a *carretero*, calls *la familia* together. He says someone mus' to go to *Nueva York*, to see if they can have a life in *El Norte*. Luis is chosen, because he is young and he is a hard worker, because he don' spend his nights in the *nickelodeons*. Luis is only here for six months. His letters tell me how hard it is for him. How he saves his money to buy tickets for *la familia.*' "

Nenita Melenguez fumbled in her tiny purse for a moment, then withdrew a worn photograph and handed it to Moodrow without looking up. Moodrow examined the picture carefully, noting the young-old man standing in front of a tin-roof shack, the narrow *Indio* eyes, the mahogany skin, the full lips and flat nose, the long oval face and sharp protruding chin.

"This is Luis Melenguez?" he asked.

"Tha' is heem," Rosaura answered.

Moodrow looked back at the photo. Melenguez was wearing a white *guayabera* shirt, baggy trousers and leather shoes without socks. His face was serious, composed. The posture of a man wearing his Sunday best.

"Look, I don't want to hurt anyone. But what can I do except report what I learned? I'm in an impossible position here."

Greta rose abruptly. "I think we better go," she said.

The two women followed her to the door, then Rosaura Pastoral turned to shake Moodrow's hand. "*Gracias, señor.* For takin' thees time for us."

Moodrow, properly chastised, at least in his own mind, opened the door for the three women. Greta, clearly unaware of his inner contrition, was the trailer.

"I'm only happy your mother didn't live to see this," she said, without looking at him.

It took all of Moodrow's self-control to close the door quietly. He went back into the kitchen, picked up his coffee then set it down again. The undeniable fact was that Greta Bloom had always been there for his mother. Nancy Moodrow had died of breast cancer, though Stanley could never figure out why it should have been called that because the cancer was everywhere in her body. It was in her lungs, her liver, her stomach, her very bones.

Death had been a long time coming. If it hadn't been for Greta, Moodrow would have had to put his mother in the hospital. And not in a private hospital, either. He would have had to put her in one of the city-run hellholes. No, there wasn't any doubt about it—Stanley Moodrow *owed* Greta Bloom. But did that mean he had to manufacture a story that fit her personal sense of justice?

What he'd do, he decided, was go down to her apartment and make it up to her. Maybe he'd bring her some *halavah*. There was a guy working out of a stall in the East Side Market who made his own. Greta's sweet tooth was legendary. . . .

The doorbell interrupted his thoughts. He answered it, half-expecting to discover Greta Bloom returning for a second assault, but found a smiling Allen Epstein, instead.

"Just like the old days. Right, Stanley? You ready for some road work?"

Moodrow managed a smile. "C'mon in, Sarge. You want coffee?"

"Sounds good to me."

Moodrow poured Epstein a mug of coffee, then topped off his own mug. Already depleted by Greta's visit, he launched into his story, detailing the events following his rise to the rank of detective, third grade.

"The thing of it is, Sarge," he concluded, "I don't want the money or the bullshit that goes with it. I just wish I could see a way to get out from under without screwing up the rest of my life."

Epstein took the time to put his thoughts together. He'd dealt with a lot of would-be fighters in his role as trainer-manager of the Manhattan South Boxing Club. Moodrow wasn't the only one who'd come to the ring full of ambition. But Epstein had never met a cop *or* a fighter as determined as Stanley Moodrow. It both surprised and saddened him to find his protégé floundering.

"Ya wanna hear something funny, Stanley?"

"Anything."

"Me, I don't take a dime. As a sergeant, I'm entitled to my piece of the pad, but I told the lieutenant to leave me out of it. He didn't like it, but there was nothing he could do. That's because I got my rank through civil service. Now, I'm not saying that I'm better than anyone else. It's just that I see a day coming when the pad is gonna explode in everyone's face. Sooner or later, some politician is gonna run through the department with a machine gun and I don't wanna get mowed down. It's happened so many times in the past that it's gotta happen again. It's *gotta*. Cops talk about 'clean money' and 'dirty money,' but the politicians only see cameras and votes."

"Sarge . . ."

"Wait a second. I'm not finished, yet. The way I see it, your problem isn't with Patero or with the pad, either. Your problem's with your girlfriend."

Moodrow snorted. "Ya wanna know something, Sarge, you're a better psychiatrist than you are a trainer. I could tell Pat Cohan to go fuck himself, but how do I explain it to Kate? How do I tell her that her father's a crook? Kate worships her old man."

"When are you getting married?"

"June fifteenth."

"You're gonna do it in a church, right? In a Catholic church?"

Moodrow smiled again. "Kate's religious. *Very* religious."

"So, once you're married, you're married forever, right?"

"What's the point?"

"The point is that you have to develop a strategy. And it has to be long-term. Right now, Cohan's holding an axe over your head. But after you're married, the axe is in *your* hands. Catholics marry for life. You wanna pick up stakes and move a thousand miles away, Kate's gonna figure it's her religious duty to go with you. It's just a matter of holding out. And *not* getting used to the money."

Moodrow shook his head in wonder. "You're a devious bastard, Sarge. But what about the Playtex Burglar? What do I do if they ask me to make another 'arrest'?"

"Look, Stanley, as slow as you were, you oughta be able to figure it out for yourself. Give ground. Take some punishment. Hold on when you're hurt. The closer you get to the wedding, the harder it's gonna be for Cohan to get between you and Kate. The thing is, Stanley, that I always figured you for a tough guy, but I only saw you in the ring. What you want here is a quick answer. It's only natural. But that isn't gonna happen. You gotta keep your guard up and go the distance."

"All right, Sarge, I get the picture. Maybe I should've studied for the sergeant's exam, instead of reaching out for the detectives. That's what I was doing before *you* came along."

Epstein looked at his watch. "I gotta get out of here, Stanley. It's almost eight o'clock. You goin' into the house?"

"Later. I'll be in later. I'm supposed to meet with an ADA at nine-thirty."

"Banker's hours. I guess being a big-shot detective isn't *all* bad."

Moodrow ignored the comment. "There's one other thing I wanted to ask you about, Sarge. You remember a guy named Luis Melenguez?"

"Can't say that I do."

"He got killed in a Pitt Street whorehouse the day after Christmas. A pimp."

"Oh yeah, I remember him. I responded to the scene. What makes you say he was a pimp?"

"That's what Pat Cohan told me. Melenguez was a friend of a friend. That kind of thing. I asked Patero about it, but it was Pat Cohan who told me it was a mob rubout."

"Pat Cohan told you bullshit. Melenguez was blown apart with a forty-five. I admit that the crime scene was pretty messed up by the time I got there—you can imagine what happens when a beat cop walks into a building with twenty half-naked women—but, from what I could make of it, Melenguez was standing in a doorway when he bought it. At the time, I figured he walked into the middle of a robbery. You know what I'm talking about, right? It was your basic wrong place/wrong time situation. We questioned the whores and the pimp who ran the place, but, naturally, nobody saw anything. The suits got there before we were finished and I turned it over to them. Standard procedure."

"Maybe that was the only chance the mob had to get him. Maybe they just saw an opportunity and took it."

"I can't buy that, Stanley. The guy was dressed poor. *Real* poor. He looked like he just came off the boat. Besides, nobody uses a forty-five to make a hit. Not if they know what they're doing. A forty-five sounds like a cannon when it goes off. Plus, when you're putting one behind the ear from six inches away, you don't need that much power. No, if Melenguez was a pimp, then I'm the Pope."

Moodrow sat back in his chair. "What I'm hearin' is that somebody's bullshitting me. And what I don't understand is why they're doin' it."

"Stanley, the job *runs* on bullshit. Get used to it. As for why? Well, you're a detective, right? You wanna find out the truth, go detect."

Twelve

JANUARY 16

FOR ANTONIO "Steppy" Accacio, this was the best time of the day. He was in the bathroom of his ten-room Montclair, New Jersey, home and his wife, Angela, was shaving his face. He would have preferred to have his own barber, his *personal* barber, do the shaving, but the ungrateful bastard simply refused to make the trip from Mulberry Street to Montclair despite everything he, Steppy Accacio, had done for the man.

But that was the way it was in life. You had to accept the bad with the good. Sure, you found some piece-of-shit swamp guinea and lent him the money to start his own business. Sure, you *expected* a little gratitude, something over and above the 20% interest you were charging. That didn't mean you'd get it.

"Hey, no laugh. You laugh, I cut."

Steppy opened his eyes to look at his wife. She was leaning over him, patiently scraping away at his heavy beard. As usual, his eyes dropped to her breasts. Angie was ten years younger than he was and her jugs were still firm. He wanted to touch her, to feel her dark nipples pushing against the palm of his hand. But the last time he'd tried that move, she'd sliced him so bad, he ended up with four stitches in his right earlobe.

"Almos' finish," Angela said.

"Looks like I survived again. Right, Angie?"

"No talk."

She wiped his face with the hot towel she'd used to soak his beard, then slapped on the aftershave. Steppy inhaled the fragrance of Roma Brava. It was sweeter than Aqua-Velva. More in keeping with the old country, which was where it came from. Which was where his *wife* came from. Steppy had no particular love for Italy. He'd never been there and had no desire to go, but these little touches impressed the 'mustache Petes' who still clung to the reins of power. Who needed to be impressed as much as they needed the millions of dollars pouring into the pockets of their six-hundred-dollar suits.

Steppy got off the chair and shrugged into the silk dressing gown his wife held out to him.

"We're havin' company," he announced. "Three, four guys. Make sure you got enough coffee and pastries." He threw her a hard look. Like most Sicilian women, she had a sharp tongue. He'd been trying to break her of the habit, but had yet to come up with a method that didn't require breaking her body as well.

"You tell me this lassa night. Why you gotta repeat? I'm no *stupido*."

What you are, Steppy thought, is halfway to being a fuckin' nigger. It was funny how her cousins' descriptions had left that little fact out. *Olive* was how they'd described her complexion. Well, there were two kinds of olives, green and black, and Angela was a lot closer to the black kind. Not that she *really* looked like one of *them*. Not that she had a flat nose and big lips. Not that anyone would actually *say* anything about her complexion. But, still, the cousins *should* have told him.

He watched her butt twitch as she walked through their bedroom, then turned to admire his own complexion in the mirror. The simple fact that *his* parents were *not* from Sicily stared back at him. Blond hair, blue eyes, milky skin that burned in the sun. One thing for sure, *his* ancestors hailed from the highlands of Tuscany, not the mountains of Sicily, a fact which (at least according to the prevailing mythology) meant he couldn't rise much beyond his present station.

"Let 'em keep their secret fuckin' society," Steppy muttered, patting his blond hair into place. "I know where I'm goin', even if *they* don't."

He left the bathroom, crossing his bedroom and going downstairs to the den. The journey didn't take very long. How could it? The small frame house wasn't exactly a mansion in Upper Saddle River. On the other hand, it was a long way from the roach-infested tenements of lower Manhattan.

The deep chimes of the doorbell interrupted his reverie and he quickly took a seat in the leather chair behind his desk. He loved making his workers come all the way to New Jersey for business meetings. He loved it as much as they obviously hated it.

"Ya company's here," Angie yelled from the living room.

"Send 'em in," Steppy called back, his face reddening with anger. The bitch was supposed to usher his guests into his presence, not scream like a vendor in the Fulton Fish Market.

"Steppy," Joe Faci said, walking into the room, "sorry we're late. The snow held us up. How are ya doin' this morning?"

"That depends, Joe." Steppy rose to offer his hand to Joe and his companion, Santo Silesi. "It depends on what you're gonna tell me. Siddown."

Before they could begin talking, Angie Accacio appeared, pushing an oak serving cart. A small pot of steaming coffee, a creamer and sugar bowl, three small cups and saucers, and a plate of small pastries were carefully arranged on its polished surface.

"Would yiz serve, Angie?" Steppy kept his voice even, despite the fact that it wasn't a request. He waited patiently as she filled the cups and handed them, first to the guests and then to him. Until she walked out, closing the door behind her.

"All right, enough with the bullshit," he snapped. "The Hebe'll be here in a few minutes. Let's get to it. How'd ya make out, Sandy?"

"What they did to Rocco? I didn't see any of it. The Jew wouldn't let me near it."

"This I already know. Joe told me."

"Then you also know that he's got me standing around in project playgrounds with fifty bags of heroin."

Steppy Accacio smiled indulgently. Santo Silesi was his oldest sister's firstborn, a Tuscan on both sides. That was one thing the Sicilians had right. That bit about the family. It wasn't a foolproof protection against treachery, but it was as close as you could get.

"Just be a little patient, Sandy," Accacio said. "I'll pull ya outta there as soon as possible. Meanwhile, ya should watch everything goin' on with the Jew. Where he lives. Where he goes. Who he hangs out with. When the time comes, I wanna be able to find him."

Silesi raised his hands, palm up. "Whatever it takes, right? That's the only way to look at it. By the way, sales were better than we expected. I moved three hundred bags yesterday."

"The take's better," Joe Faci interrupted, "but that might not be so good for us. The Hebe wants to buy in quantity. He claims he's got the bucks to go for half an ounce. He'll package himself."

Accacio bit into a cannoli. The crust was flaky, the filling moist and sweet. "I don't mind so much that the Hebe's ambitious. I mean where's he gonna go? He can't do nothin' without we say so first. *My* problem is that I had a bitch of time gettin' hold of the territory we got. Which, you mighta noticed, ain't all that big. What I figured on doin' was maximizing the profit. If I sell to the Jew wholesale, I'm gonna have to expand and I ain't too sure I can get permission. Not right away."

"Why don't we just shoot the mother-fucker," Santo blurted out. "I mean every time I turn around the sheeny's makin' me eat shit." He didn't bother to add the simple fact that he was *afraid* of Jake Leibowitz.

"Yeah," Steppy said, "I heard about that. What you gotta do, Sandy, is keep ya self-control. Like I said, I'm gonna pull you outta there soon. And when I do, I'm gonna make the Hebe report directly to you. I'm gonna put you in charge."

"He ain't gonna like *that*," Joe Faci said.

"*That's* the idea."

All three were laughing when the doorbell sounded. They were still wiping the smirks off their faces when Angie led Jake Leibowitz into the room.

"Jake," Steppy Accacio said, rising to offer his hand, "we meet at last."

Stanley Moodrow spent most of the day thinking about what he was going to do. Thinking about whether he should do *anything*. Greta was *already* pissed off, whereas Sal Patero had stopped being pissed off. Pushing his nose into Patero's business wouldn't necessarily make Greta happy, but it was guaranteed to make Sal unhappy. It would be the same as calling Patero (and Pat Cohan) a liar. Of course, there was always the chance that Patero *was* a liar. Moodrow wasn't sure he wanted to know that, either.

But there was also the chance that Patero was right, that Allen Epstein was simply mistaken. Maybe the sergeant was confusing Melenguez with someone else. Maybe, despite all appearances, Melenguez's death *had* been a mob hit. Maybe the detectives had concluded that Melenguez was a pimp on the basis of information from their informants.

In the end, there were too many 'maybes' for a man as inherently curious as Stanley Moodrow. What he did was go down to the files and pull the paperwork. He didn't expect anyone to notice and nobody did. Paperwork was Moodrow's job.

He went through the file systematically, beginning with the patrolman's report and proceeding to Epstein's observations, the preliminary reports of the two detectives and the forensic unit's description of the crime scene. Melenguez had been gunned down from inside an office on the first floor, rear, of 800 Pitt Street with a .45 caliber pistol. There was no doubt about it. Melenguez had been hit four times and all four slugs had been recovered, two from the hallway behind the victim and two from the victim's body.

Moodrow turned to the Medical Examiner's report. The M.E.'s description was gruesome enough—the first shot, the one that'd killed him, had blown away half his face; the next three had turned his abdominal cavity into tomato soup—but there was nothing in it to contradict the detectives' preliminary assessments.

The witness interviews came next. There were fourteen interviews with women and one with a man, a further indication, assuming 800 Pitt Street wasn't a nunnery, that Melenguez had been gunned down inside a whorehouse. Moodrow scanned the interviews as quickly as possible, noting the name of the only man.

Finishing, Moodrow realized that Epstein had been right about one thing: none of the witnesses, even though all had been isolated during the questioning, had been willing to admit they'd eyeballed the shooting. Which raised several questions. Melenguez had been standing in the doorway. The perpetrator had been standing inside the office. Epstein was of the opinion that

Melenguez had wandered into a robbery in progress. But wasn't it also possible that Melenguez had *been* the robber? According to the preliminary reports, no weapons of any kind had been found at the scene. If Melenguez had been armed, someone had taken the time to remove the weapon. Or maybe one of the whores had scooped it up with the intention of selling it on the street.

Moodrow turned to the follow-ups, the DD5's. The two detectives handling the case, John Samuelson and Paul Maguire, had interviewed Melenguez's employer, a trucker named Levy, as well as several co-workers. The portrait that emerged was of a hard-working, ambitious immigrant. Melenguez had been in New York for slightly less than six months. He'd shown up for work every day. He had no friends outside of his fellow workers and spent his nights listening to the radio and writing letters home.

Moodrow recalled the picture Nenita Melenguez had shown him. He tried to imagine the tiny man with the jug ears packing a rod, pulling it on the pimp who ran the whorehouse. He couldn't even come close.

The obvious next step was to speak to the suits who'd handled the case before it was farmed out of the precinct. As it happened, Moodrow knew Paul Maguire fairly well. Maguire had still been in uniform when Moodrow came onto the job and for a short time before Maguire's appointment to the detectives, the two of them had walked overlapping beats.

That was on the plus side. There was a minus side as well. Moodrow knew he could return the file with no one the wiser. He could still put it back and forget the whole thing. But once he started talking to other cops, he had no way to predict who might whisper what message into Sal Patero's ear. Paul Maguire had always been friendly, but how was Moodrow to know where Maguire's loyalties lay? Ordinarily, jobs were given out to any detective foolish enough to be loitering in the squad room when a call came into the precinct. On the other hand, Patero might have personally assigned the case to Maguire because he knew Maguire could be trusted to do what he was told.

Moodrow went back to the filing cabinets and replaced the paperwork, then strolled over to the squad room and poured himself a cup of coffee. Samuelson and Maguire had back-to-back desks in a far corner of the room. Moodrow looked over, hoping they were out in the field, but found both men pounding away on their respective Underwoods. He recalled what Epstein had told him about going the distance, using time to his own advantage.

What I oughta do, he thought, is forget about this bullshit. What I oughta do is stay close to Kate and brown-nose her old man until after the wedding. What I oughta do is find an apartment in Flushing and move out of the Lower East Side. What I oughta do . . .

Sound advice, he couldn't deny it, but his long legs kept moving across the squad room. Kept moving until he was standing next to Paul Maguire's desk.

"How ya doin', fellas?"

Maguire and Samuelson looked up in surprise. Just as if they hadn't seen him coming.

"What's goin' on, Stanley?" Maguire said.

"You know the Melenguez case?" Moodrow paused, but neither man spoke. "Well, I was looking over the paperwork."

"Somethin' missing?" Samuelson asked. "Not that it matters, because the case is goin' away from us. In fact, it's already gone."

"No, that's not it. Nothing's missing." Now that he was in the middle of it, Moodrow couldn't decide what he wanted to ask. The two detectives weren't any help. They continued to stare at him with blank expressions. "All right, there's a couple of things bothering me. If Melenguez was shot from inside the office, either the pimp or someone the pimp knows had to be the shooter. How else would the perpetrator get in there? Sal thinks Melenguez was hit by a professional. But that doesn't make sense, either. Why would anybody want to rub out Luis Melenguez?"

"Wait a second, Stanley," Maguire interrupted. "Are you saying the lieutenant's not happy with the work we did?"

"Just the opposite. Sal's already signed off on the case. What I'm doing here is personal. Rosaura Pastoral, Melenguez's landlady, happens to live in my building. She asked me to check it out."

As far as Moodrow could tell, his explanation had exactly no effect on the two detectives. Their faces remained blank. They didn't even look at each other.

"Everything's in the file," Samuelson finally said. "Whatever we found out, that's where it is. We got nothing to add."

Moodrow remembered to thank the men before walking away. He felt like an idiot, but the feeling didn't make him unhappy. No more bullshit, he told himself. No more Sherlock Holmes. Mind your own goddamned business before you do something to put your ass in a permanent sling.

He went back to his own desk and began to review a case the ADAs had sent over in the morning. There were two statements missing, one from the complainant and one from the accused. The defendant's lawyer was demanding both and the prosecutor intended to drop the indictment if they couldn't be located.

Two hours later, the missing statements found and already on their way to the DA's office, Moodrow signed out and began to walk through the remains of the morning's snowstorm to his apartment a few blocks away. He was due out in Bayside at eight-thirty and his thoughts were on Kate and what she might have told her father. The last time they'd spoken, he'd begged her to defy the priest. Kate, after much argument, had agreed to think about it. What bothered her was the distinct possibility that Father Ryan might decide that, despite the theoretical sanctity of the confessional, it was his Christian duty to have a little talk with Pat Cohan. It had happened too many times in the past to be entirely discounted.

"Stanley."

"Huh?" Moodrow turned to the man who'd fallen into step beside him. It was Paul Maguire.

"Just keep walkin', Stanley. I wanna have a little talk with you."

"Whatever ya say, Paul."

"The thing of it is, Stanley, that this conversation never happened. Understand? *Never*."

"Sure."

"Because if it gets back to Sal Patero, I'll be walkin' a beat in Far Rockaway. It gets real cold out there near the ocean. The wind never stops blowin'."

"Paul, I get the message."

"Okay, what you said about Melenguez? You're right. There was no hit and Melenguez was in the building to get laid. One of the whores told me she'd just finished takin' care of him."

"I didn't see that in the interviews."

"Maybe somebody took it out. Maybe your buddy, Sal Patero, took it out. I'm not here to solve this crime. All I wanna do is whisper a few words in your ear. Then, it's up to you. You hearing me?"

"Loud and clear."

"O'Neill runs the house. Him and his wife. I'd bet my gold shield that both of them were in the office when the shooting went down. Someone put a heavy beating on the pair of 'em and it sure as shit wasn't Melenguez."

"The beating wasn't in the files, either. What you're sayin' is that somebody's covering up a homicide. A fucking *homicide*."

"Stanley, I'm here to give you a piece of advice. If you're smart, you'll keep your nose out of it. This goes a lot further than Sal Patero. But, if you're stupid, here's what you should do. O'Neill and his old lady are still running the show on Pitt Street. Squeeze 'em. Squeeze 'em like tubes of fucking toothpaste. I got a hundred bucks here that says the same guys who pounded on O'Neill and his old lady shot Melenguez. I got another hundred that says O'Neill knows the shooter."

Stanley Moodrow knew he'd stepped in it when the door of Kate's home opened to reveal her mother, Rose. Decked out in widow's weeds, the small slight woman took a backward step and raised her fist to her mouth. A rosary, its onyx beads as black as her dress, dangled from bony fingers.

"Mr. Cohan wants to see you," she hissed.

"Where is he?"

She continued to back away until her heels were against the first riser of the staircase. Then she turned and fled.

Moodrow stood in the open doorway for a moment. A mixture of emotions coursed through him—dread, rage, fear. He didn't want to sort them out; he wanted to flee from the situation, just as Rose Cohan had fled. It's bad, he thought. It's so bad it can only get worse.

He recalled a day, early in his fighting career, when he'd been asked to spar with a hotshot middleweight named Virgil Thomas. Already over a hundred and seventy-five pounds and cocky as hell, he'd jumped at the chance. Thirty seconds later, as the slap of leather against flesh echoed through the small gym, he'd known he was in deep trouble. He also knew there was no remedy except to go through with it and that was what he'd done. Now, he was going to have to go through with it again.

Moodrow crossed the living room and opened the door to Pat Cohan's den without knocking. He'd been hoping against hope to find Kate inside, but Cohan was alone.

"You don't knock?" Cohan asked.

"Where's Kate?"

"What's the hurry, Casanova? You so horny you can't spend a few minutes talking to me?" Cohan lit the stub of a cigar and sucked it into life. He was fully dressed, his jacket and vest buttoned, his hair sweeping out and back like the lion's mane he imagined it to be.

"Where's Kate?" Moodrow stepped forward. There was a chair between him and Pat Cohan's desk. He swept it away with a casual wave of his right hand. "Where's Kate?"

"I thought it best she not be here for this."

Moodrow watched Cohan shrink back in his chair. The Inspector was staring, not into his eyes, but at the still-red scar on his brow. Moodrow, like all fighters, drew energy from his opponent's fear.

"Why's that?"

"Look here, boyo . . ."

"I'm not your fucking 'boyo,' Pat. I'm twenty-five years old. And Kate's not your 'darlin' Kathleen,' either. She's a twenty-two-year-old woman. You can't keep her in diapers forever."

"I didn't call you in here to fight with you, Stanley."

"This I already figured."

Pat Cohan's face contorted with anger. "Listen, you little prick, I made you and I can break you."

"That works both ways, Pat. The way I see it, we're in this together. Till death or the Department do us part."

Cohan managed a thin smile. He sucked on his unlit cigar. "That's not entirely true, Stanley, but I'm not here to threaten you. If you remember, I only asked one thing of you when you requested permission to see Kathleen. I asked you to keep her pure until after the wedding."

Moodrow finally sat down. He shook his head in disgust. "Why don't you cut the bullshit. Stop living in Never-Never Land. She's a woman, that's all. And this ain't the fucking junior prom. Nobody cares unless the woman gets pregnant. And the people I grew up with don't even care about *that*. As long as you do the right thing."

"She committed a *sin*, Stanley. And *you* should have known better. *You* should have stopped her. Kate is innocent. She's inexperienced, naive."

Moodrow thought back to that morning when she'd shown up on his doorstep. Innocent? Naive? What she *really* was was stupid for going to the wrong priest. What she *really* was was weak for not telling him to stick his penance in his breviary.

"All right, Pat. Let's say it was a sin. Let's even say that I took advantage of a naive young girl. So what? It's over now and there's nothing you can do to fix it. Kate and I are engaged. That means whatever advantage I took, I'm gonna be makin' it up to her for the next forty or fifty years. Ya know, when I went to Catholic school, the nuns taught me that my sins were between me and God. So what are you doing here? You so high up in the job, you think you're God?"

Pat Cohan put the stub of his cigar in the ashtray. He ran his fingers through his silvery hair and leaned forward. "What I want, Stanley, is for you to go away. Take it from a man trapped in a miserable marriage, you and Kate aren't right for each other. You're not even close. So why don't you tell me what *you* want?"

"What I want is Kate. And if you say she doesn't want me, if you put that lie in her mouth, I'll drive my fist through the back of your head."

"I believe you would, Stanley. But I'm not here to lie to you. I haven't sent Kathleen to a convent. She'll be home tomorrow. In the meantime, why don't you think about what I've said? Do you want Homicide? Narcotics? Safes and Lofts? How about a jump in rank? Detective, second grade, with a guarantee of first grade in a year."

Moodrow felt his anger begin to evaporate as the central truth of Pat Cohan's message sunk in. This man, Kate's father, had decided to prevent the marriage. It was just that simple.

"Why are you doing this, Pat? And don't tell me it's because we went to bed together. You don't give two shits about the Church. You're the biggest god-damned thief in the Department."

"I'll ignore that last comment, boyo." Cohan opened the center desk drawer and took out a fresh cigar. He studied it for a moment, then turned to Moodrow. "As for my reasons, I don't know where to begin. I thought you were a tough guy, but I was wrong. You're only tough in the ring. Mentally, you're not prepared to do what's necessary to guarantee Kate and her children the kind of life I want them to have. I wouldn't say it's your fault, exactly. No, I'd have to say the error was mine. But that doesn't change anything, does it?"

"Keep going."

"You're impulsive and headstrong. Maybe that's what comes from being victorious. You fought your way into the detectives, just like you fought your way into your engagement. But you never stopped to consider the conse-quences. You're like a traveler who desperately wants to arrive at a certain destination without any clear understanding of what he'll do after he gets there. Patero's afraid of you. He thinks you're unpredictable. Of course, Patero's right in the middle of it, so perhaps he has a right . . ."

"Bullshit." Moodrow stood up. "All those rounds? All that training? I knew what I wanted. I wanted to be a detective. *You* made me into the precinct bagman. As for Kate, you think I'm using her the way I used the ring, but that's not true. I love Kate and I want her to be my wife. Now, here's something you might wanna think about: if you fight me and I win, I'm gonna take Kate and migrate to California, like everybody else in the country. Kate's a religious girl, Pat. She takes all that bullshit about 'love, honor and obey' very seriously. If I tell her we're going, she'll pack her bags and get on the plane."

"You're quick with the threats, Stanley."

"What have I got to lose?"

"Everything, boyo. *Everything*."

"Ya know what I think, *boyo*? I think your promises are bullshit. Once you've got Kate under control, you'll fuck me any way you can. That's your rep, Pat. That's what they say about you. Inspector Cohan *never* forgets. Never forgives, either. I got nothing to lose."

Moodrow backed toward the door. He expected Cohan to make some sort of protest, but Cohan merely lit his cigar and leaned back in the chair.

"Something else you might wanna think about, Pat." Moodrow opened the door without turning away. "Luis Melenguez. You lied to me about Luis Melenguez. It wasn't a little white lie, either. It was a big *black* lie. Go confess to Father Ryan. Maybe he'll order you to tell me the truth."

Thirteen

JANUARY 17

STANLEY MOODROW, sitting down to breakfast, knew he had to make a decision about Luis Melenguez. He'd been angry the night before, angry enough to threaten his benefactor, Pat Cohan. He'd also been shrewd enough to recognize (and enjoy) the fear his threat inspired. But that didn't mean he would or should follow through. Sure, he wanted Kate Cohan. That was obvious. But he couldn't see how investigating the murder of Luis Melenguez would result in the two of them walking down the aisle. In fact, no matter how Moodrow examined the situation, it seemed that tracking down Melenguez's killer would have the opposite effect. Especially if Pat Cohan was trying to cover it up.

What he needed to do was think it out. The only problem was that he couldn't manage to concentrate on anything more complex than the *Daily News*. His eyes scanned the paper while his brain spun like a raindrop in a tornado.

A Brooklyn judge named Leibowitz had ordered a special grand jury to investigate the practice of giving high school diplomas to kids who couldn't read above the fifth-grade level. This was the same judge who'd charged the grand jury to investigate "the tide of terror and lawlessness" in Brooklyn schools, then later approved the grand jury's recommendation that cops be stationed in every high school.

Moodrow started to lay the paper down when another headline caught his eye. *Housing Board Bias Probe Is Voted by Wagner Group.* The charge, "racial and religious discrimination" in the projects, was nothing new. When the first of the projects had gone up before WWII, they'd been used to service individual neighborhoods. On the Lower East Side, for instance, the Italians had gotten the Governor Smith Houses while the Jews had gotten the Jacob Riis Houses. The policy had seemed reasonable at the time, an attempt to keep neighborhoods and traditions intact. The only problem was that five hundred thousand impoverished Puerto Ricans had migrated to New York in the ten years following the war. More than a million blacks had come as well, fleeing southern poverty and Jim Crow legislation. The city had responded by constructing tens of thousands of low-income apartments, but no matter how fast projects went up, there were far more applicants than apartments. Waiting lists were created, lists based on ethnic, racial and neighborhood considerations. Now, the chickens were coming home to roost.

Moodrow discarded the *Daily News* and went to refill his coffee cup. It was funny, in a way. New York City, at least according to the newspapers and television, was a filthy, dangerous place. The schools, for instance, were so violent that Judge Leibowitz wanted cops stationed in every high school in Brooklyn. So why did Melenguez and half a million of his countrymen leave their homes to come here? And why did they stay? The Republicans blamed it on easy access to the welfare system, but there hadn't been any welfare at the turn of the century when the Jews and the Italians arrived. Nor when the Irish and the Germans had come before them.

The answer, when Moodrow hit on it, was obvious enough. They were coming to occupy the same tenements that *he* intended to flee. If the Lower East Side was so horrible that a girl like Kathleen Cohan couldn't be expected to live there, Luis Melenguez didn't stay because he loved the Big Apple. He stayed because what he'd left behind was worse. Which was exactly why Moodrow's own parents had come and stayed.

"Fuck them," Moodrow said aloud. *Fuck who?* he thought.

Another idea popped into his mind before he could even consider the question: Luis Melenguez has a *right* to revenge. Because that's what the cops really did. Ordinary citizens weren't allowed to get even. If they tried it, they were subject to arrest. Punishment? Retribution? Justice? There was only one safe way for Joe Citizen to go and that was to the cops, the courts and the prisons.

But I could *still* make it right, he thought. If I go to Pat and apologize, if I promise to love, honor and obey. . . .

Stanley Moodrow giggled, the sound spilling from his lips unbidden. The truth was that Pat Cohan was determined to break him. *If* he got the chance. The situation was funny, because he and Cohan were going to have to do a little dance while they slugged it out. They were going to dance a minuet around "darlin' Kathleen," neither sure of her reaction when she found out what was really happening.

And Kathleen Cohan wasn't the only issue. Moodrow's career, his very job was at stake. Detectives, third grade, didn't challenge inspectors. Pat Cohan had a reputation as a man who always got even, no matter how long it took. Moodrow had threatened to break the Inspector's bones. He'd questioned Pat Cohan's physical courage, the ultimate slight to every cop's self-image. Inspector Pat Cohan wouldn't react to the insult by meeting Stanley Moodrow in some back alley. He'd either wait for Stanley Moodrow to make a mistake, to drop his guard, or he'd try to set him up.

"He thinks he's got all the ammunition," Moodrow said aloud. And that was obvious, too. Cohan's arrangement with Patero was basically unprovable. Especially considering that he, Moodrow, had a personal interest. Any charge he leveled at Cohan would be extremely suspect. Cohan, on the other hand, could use Patero (and God only knew who else) as an instrument of revenge.

What you are, Stanley, he thought, is a schmuck. You're supposed to lead with your left, not with your chin.

He should never have challenged Cohan directly. He should have retreated, begged for mercy, promised to reform. He should have played for time while he gathered ammunition of his own.

And that was assuming there was anything out there to gather. Because it was just possible that Pat Cohan *hadn't* been lying about Luis Melenguez. In fact, it was more than possible that Cohan was simply repeating what Sal Patero had told him. Cohan's office was down on Centre Street, not in the 7th Precinct, and Cohan's job was purely administrative. He played no direct part in the investigation of criminal complaints.

Still without any clear line of action, Moodrow went to the phone, called the 7th Precinct, and told the duty sergeant that he wouldn't be coming to work.

"A personal matter," he explained before hanging up. One good thing about his job as Patero's assistant: no cop below the rank of captain had the guts to challenge him.

He went back to his bedroom and looked out the window. It was eight-thirty and the streets were alive with workers trudging through the remains of yesterday's snowstorm. Moodrow noted the coats buttoned to the throat, the caps pulled down low to cover the ears. Well, he could deal with the cold. He laid out a set of long johns and two pair of heavy wool socks, then began to dress.

The doorbell rang while he was buttoning his shirt. For a fleeting moment, he managed to conjure up a picture of Kate Cohan standing on the other side. Then he returned to reality.

"Hello, Greta," he said, as he swung the door inward.

"Stanley, how are you this morning?"

"I've been better. C'mon in." The truth was that he had no way to keep her out and he knew it. "You want coffee?"

"Please."

He poured out the coffee, then waited for her to speak first. He didn't have to wait long.

"So what did you find out?"

"About what?" If he couldn't actually discourage her, he could at least break her chops.

"About Luis Melenguez, of course. His wife went home yesterday."

"I'm sorry about the other day, Greta. I didn't want to hurt Mrs. Melenguez, but I was only repeating what I was told."

"I understand. And I'm also apologizing if I said anything nasty. So, *nu*, what did you find?"

"Look, Greta, you've got to try to understand that I'm just starting out in the detectives. I got no connections for information. I got no informants out on the street, either. I'm not gonna argue that Melenguez was a pimp. I know he wasn't. For whatever reason—and I don't *know* the reason—the lieutenant decided to lie to me. The only thing is that I'm not sure what I can do about it. If anything."

"Please, Stanley, you shouldn't get so discouraged. Let me tell you a story."

"You always do."

Greta was the only person Moodrow knew who spoke in parables. And it was impossible to discourage her. She was incredibly strong-willed, as were most of the women his mother knew. Maybe the simple fact of their gender made them even stronger. They couldn't get their way by ranting and raving the way men did when they were angry. The women persisted, no matter what obstacles were thrown in their way.

"Do you know how your grandmother died, Stanley?"

Moodrow felt the hairs on the back of his neck begin to rise. "I know she died twenty years before I was born. My mother never talked about it."

"Your grandmother's name was Trina. She came here from Poland when your mother was only a few months old. Came with her brother and his wife. She had no husband, because he'd been taken into the Polish army right after Trina became pregnant and from there nobody knows what happened to him. The army told the family he was dead, but in those days men who went into the Polish army seldom returned anyway. I don't want to make such a long story that you miss your lunch, but . . ."

"Just say what you have to say, Greta." Moodrow had spent a good part of his life avoiding Greta's stories, but this time he was all ears.

"After she got settled, Trina went to work like everybody else. She got a job as a helper in the Triangle Shirtwaist Factory across the street from Washington Square. When I tell you this job was hell, you should believe me. The girls were paid according to how much they did and Trina had to bring work home to make four dollars a week. The factory was, you should pardon the expression, a shithole. Fabric piled everywhere. Lint and dust so thick you couldn't see from one wall to the other. The owner paid off the fire inspectors so that when there came a fire in 1911, the workers couldn't get out. The emergency exits were chained because the boss didn't want the girls to sneak off. Why the boss should worry that girls would sneak off I can't understand, since they were getting paid according to how much work they did and not by the hour, but that's the way it was. The fire only lasted eighteen minutes, but a hundred and forty-six workers died, most of them young Jewish and Italian girls. The flames were so hot the workers jumped out the windows to escape. Your grandmother was one of the women who jumped."

"What happened to the owner?"

"Nothing happened except he lost his factory. You can't look at these things like it was today, Stanley. The bosses were kings in 1911. They paid off the police and the firemen and the politicians. When the workers tried to organize, the strikebreakers attacked the picket lines and the police sat on their horses and laughed. Or they joined in with their billy clubs. And this is the point I'm making here. Your mother was only fifteen when the union put her to work as an organizer. She was so young and pretty, the bosses didn't suspect her. But on the picket lines she was a demon. What I'm telling you now, I saw with my own eyes. So many times she had her head cracked I couldn't even count them. And she gave as good as she got. One time I remember like it was yesterday. The cops were driving their horses into the picket line, hammering the workers with their clubs. Your mother pushed a hatpin into the horse's *tuchis*. I'm telling you, Stanley—right in there. The horse jumped up and the cop fell off. He fell into a circle of strikers. That day we got even a little."

"I don't know anything about this."

"That's the point. Your mother was not a young girl when you were born. She was almost thirty and she figured she'd done her duty. The garment workers were mostly organized by then, anyway. What was the point of looking for trouble? She decided to stay home with you while you were young. Then came the war and everybody went off to fight Hitler."

Moodrow refilled Greta's cup without asking. He put a few jelly doughnuts on a plate and set them out on the table.

"My mother must have been pretty disappointed when I became a cop," he said.

"If she was, she didn't say anything to me about it. I think by that time she was just happy you weren't going to be a boxer. She was afraid you were some kind of a savage. Also, times had changed. When there came a strike, the cops protected the workers instead of attacking them. And remember, your father's brother was a policeman and your mother knew he wasn't a bad man."

"Greta, I know I asked you this before, but what do you expect me to do here? About Melenguez. I . . ."

Greta Bloom, straightening up in her chair, seemed to transform herself. The kindly neighbor disappeared and her eyes grew hard. "Nothing happens without risk. When your grandmother died, your mother could have said, 'See, this is what happens. This is the way it is. What can I do about it?' Instead, she fought back. That thing with the horse? It didn't just happen. She brought the hatpin with her, because she knew the cops would use their horses and there was no other way to bring the horses down. Now, I have to go. I got the laundry and my shopping to do. Plus, I also have a Hadassah meeting at the *shul*. I tell you, Stanley, I'm busier now in my old age than when the children were young."

"Wait a minute, Greta. This time I have a question for *you*. Did you tell these stories to your own children? I mean your kids went to City College. They're professionals. Now they live out on Long Island somewhere."

Greta Bloom sighed. "I told them, but they don't wanna know from the old days. What's the use of complaining? Every time I turn around, somebody's kids are moving out. But you, Stanley, you're different. You're a fighter like they never were. You could understand what I'm trying to say. Luis Melenguez's killer should not go unpunished."

Fourteen

GRETA BLOOM departed, carrying her little circle of energy with her. Moodrow finished dressing in the island of calm she left behind, then he, too, left. It was cold outside, as expected, and Moodrow felt the urge to break into a trot, to begin his roadwork as he had so many times before. It had been much simpler when he was still fighting. An opponent stood in front of you, gloves up, and you either beat him or you didn't. The whole thing was over in a few minutes. It was over and the result became part of your record forever.

Now, he could see any number of ways to win and lose at the same time. For instance, to put Inspector Cohan where he belonged while losing Inspector Cohan's daughter. Or to marry Kate and find her dragging a lifetime load of resentment into their marriage. What was clearly lost was the fantasy that'd carried him through all the hours in the gym. The June-moon-spoon fantasy that had the two of them, Stanley Moodrow and Kate Cohan, living happily ever after.

He walked down First Avenue, past Houston, to Stanton Street, then turned left for a block, then right on Orchard. In the summer, the shopkeepers along Orchard Street stood outside, hawking their wares to passersby. Now, the doors and windows were shut tight against the cold, but, still, an occasional shopkeeper stood by the glass with his back to an empty store. One and all, they knocked on the window and waved to the former cop who'd protected their merchandise, to the local boy who ran through the streets in search of glory.

Moodrow waved in return, but kept on walking. He was a block from Pitt Street before he admitted where he was going. Begin at the scene of the crime. That's what the instructor at the Academy had told the new recruits. In this case, of course, the crime scene wasn't exactly fresh, but, according to Maguire, there were witnesses who hadn't come forward with the truth, who could make sense of Pat Cohan's bullshit.

He went over it in his mind as he walked toward the doorway of 800 Pitt Street. The pimp's name was Al O'Neill. His wife's name was Betty. The prostitute who'd serviced Melenguez was named Mariana. He had no last name for her and no intention of questioning her, either. At least not right away. He had to assume that Patero and Cohan were covering for somebody. If he left O'Neill alone for any length of time, O'Neill would call that someone and that someone would call Patero. The last thing Moodrow needed was Patero showing up before the interrogation was completed.

Moodrow rapped sharply on the door, then stepped in front of the peephole, which looked newly installed. After a moment, a man's voice called out: "Whatta ya want?"

Moodrow held up his shield. "Police," he announced.

"Whatta ya want?"

"Open the door."

"You got a warrant?"

Moodrow answered by driving the heel of his right shoe into the peephole. The door held, but the muffled cry of pain from inside the building was so pleasing that Moodrow decided to give it another try. The door opened before he could deliver.

"Ya cut me." The man holding his eye was fat and middle-aged. A thick bandage covered his forehead and his mouth was grotesquely swollen.

"Try being more hospitable. Then you won't draw these hostile reactions." Moodrow stepped inside.

"I can't give no more. Ya hittin' me up every other day." The fat man stood his ground, arms folded across his chest.

"I don't know what you're talking about, Al. I'm here to investigate a homicide. You remember Luis Melenguez? Got blown away on December 26. One day after Christmas."

O'Neill, shocked, took a careful look at the huge cop standing in front of him. He, himself, was a large man, heavily muscled beneath the fat that coated his body, but his head barely came up to the detective's shoulder.

"The cops already checked that out," he said. "It's been taken care of. You should call your boss before . . ."

"I wanna go back in the office where it happened."

"Look . . ."

"Just fucking do it, Al."

O'Neill shrugged and led Moodrow past the staircase and down a hallway to the back of the building. The office, Moodrow noted, was a long way from the stairs. Melenguez didn't just happen to wander back here. Something must have drawn him down the corridor. Something loud and violent.

"Okay if I make sure my wife is dressed?" O'Neill asked.

Moodrow answered by drawing his .38 and holding it down by his side. "Don't say a word, Al. Not a word. And you better hope there's no surprise behind that door. Because if there is, I'm gonna shoot you first."

"Are you crazy?"

"Open the door."

Betty O'Neill was seated behind the desk when the door swung open. She looked up in surprise, muttering something inaudible.

"Her jaw's wired," O'Neill explained. "She had an accident."

"What about her hair? That an accident, too?" Betty O'Neill's skull was shaved in three places.

"Yeah. She had stitches."

"Where'd the accident happen?" Moodrow shoved the .38 back in its holster.

"On Houston Street. She got hit by a car."

"That right, Betty? You get hit by a car?"

"Yeah," Betty mumbled. "I got run over."

"You make a report?"

"Huh?"

"An accident report. Did you make an accident report?"

No answer. Moodrow let the silence stand while he checked the room. He went through the desk, finding a .22 caliber revolver which he pocketed, then walked over to a door at the back of the room and opened it to reveal a tiny bathroom. There was a window set high up on the wall, too narrow and too far up for an adult to crawl through.

"All right, here's what we're gonna do," Moodrow announced. "Betty, you're gonna go in the toilet while I question your husband. When I'm finished with him, I'm gonna bring you out and ask you the same questions. What I'm sayin' here is that I wouldn't like it if you gave different answers. Let's go."

Betty O'Neill's face reddened. She tried to protest, but her words were a hopeless jumble. Not that it mattered, because Moodrow wasn't interested anyway. He took Betty's arm and hauled her to her feet.

"Well, well, well. Take a look at this." He ran a finger along the dark scars on the veins of her left forearm. "Ya know somethin', I bet if I looked real hard I could find where you hid your dope. And if I did, I bet I could get you thrown in the Tombs for a few days. And if that happens, you'd have to kick the habit cold turkey. You probably wouldn't like that, would you?" The look in her eyes, a mixture of absolute terror and fierce hatred, gave him all the answer he needed. He stroked her face and smiled. "But don't worry. What I'm doing here is investigating a homicide. You help me out and I'm willing to overlook your nasty habit. You fucking lie to me, on the other hand, and you'll be puking your guts out before the sun goes down. And you might wanna keep in mind that sunset comes early this time of year."

Betty O'Neill walked into the small bathroom and closed the door. Moodrow motioned Al O'Neill into the chair behind the desk and turned on a small radio, setting the volume loud enough to guarantee that Betty wouldn't overhear the conversation. Then he sat on the edge of the desk, two feet from Al O'Neill, and grinned.

"You did it, Al. You killed Melenguez."

"You're crazy."

"Melenguez was shot from inside this room. This room just happens to be your office. I know Melenguez came here to get laid, because I know the name of the girl who took care of him. *You* killed him. You or your junkie wife. What I wanna know is why."

Moodrow was sure that Al O'Neill hadn't killed Luis Melenguez. He was *almost* sure that the killer and the man who'd smacked Betty O'Neill around were one and the same. His problem was that he couldn't come back to 800 Pitt Street. The minute he left, O'Neill would call his contact who'd call his contact who'd call his contact. Eventually, it would get back to Patero and Cohan. That would be the end of that.

"I didn't kill him. I wasn't even here. I was checking one of the girls. Ya know what I'm sayin', right? She didn't wanna service her john. Didn't wanna do what he asked her."

"And the little lady? Where was she?"

"Betty was visiting her mother."

"Wrong, Al. According to the first cops on the scene, the little woman was in the building." Without shifting his weight, Moodrow slapped Al O'Neill across the face. It wasn't much of a blow, by Moodrow's standards, but it came so fast that O'Neill, unprepared, flew out of the chair.

"The thing about it is," Moodrow said calmly, "that I know you keep your money and your records in this office. Which means that nobody gets in here without your permission. You were here, Al. In the room. Now, I can accept that maybe it wasn't a murder. Maybe he surprised you and you shot him because you thought he was a thief. I could buy that. But what I can't buy is that you weren't here. And I'll thank you for not insulting my intelligence by insisting on that particular piece of bullshit."

O'Neill dragged himself off the floor, then pulled the chair upright. "I didn't do it. I didn't kill Melenguez. How could I mistake that little spic for a thief? He looked like he was right off the fuckin' boat."

"You saying your old lady killed him?"

"No, I ain't sayin' that."

"Lemme see if I got this straight. You were in the room, you and Betty, but neither one of you killed Luis Melenguez. Does that mean someone else was here, too?"

O'Neill slumped in the chair. "Figure it out for yourself," he muttered.

Moodrow held out his hand, palm forward, then slowly curled his fingers, one at a time. His hands, small for so large a man, were still huge by ordinary standards. The knuckles had been so flattened by years of workouts with a sixty-pound bag that his fist looked like a block of wood.

"I'm not leaving here without answers, Al. It's that simple."

"So what're you gonna do? Kick my ass? Throw me in jail? If I talk to you, I'm dead. Simple as that, cop. I'm dead."

"You might wanna consider something, Al." Moodrow, knowing that if he was in O'Neill's position he wouldn't talk either, was thinking as fast as he could. Which translated as saying the first thing that came into his head. "New York is a death penalty state. Now, I got a good idea who's covering for you down at the precinct, but this case isn't in the precinct anymore. The Hispanic Improvement Society is pushing the mayor and the mayor's pushing the commissioner. That means the case has got to get cleared. Somebody's goin' down, Al, and I don't see any reason why it can't be you."

"It wasn't me."

"You're not thinking logically, Al. You were here. In this fucking room. You think I can't prove it? Look, I'd like to nail the bastard who pulled the trigger. I'm a cop, a hunter. I don't like settling for a rabbit when I'm after a bear. But if I *gotta* settle, I gotta settle. I'm not in a position where I can go back without a trophy." Moodrow paused long enough to grab O'Neill's face and raise it up until their eyes met. "You know what's gonna happen if I walk upstairs and start leaning on the whores? I'll tell ya, buddy. What's gonna happen is two or three of 'em are gonna say they saw you come out of that office right after the shots were fired. That gives you opportunity. The same two or three, plus two or three more, are gonna say they heard your wife screaming just before the shots were fired. If you and Betty were the only people in the room, then you were the one kicking her ass. Now here's what the prosecutor's gonna say. He'll say that Melenguez, on his way out, heard the screams and came riding to the rescue. He came through that door and you, in a blind rage, shot him down. Which gives you a motive. Motive and opportunity. When the jury sees the medical reports on your wife, they won't be asking what happened to the gun."

"Whatever you're gonna do, it's better than dyin'. I talk to you, I won't live a week."

Moodrow let his left fist fly. "You *don't* talk to me, you might not live through the day." He peered down at O'Neill, wondering if he'd actually knocked the man out. He'd never knocked a man out with a jab. But no, O'Neill wasn't unconscious, he was just smart enough to stay on the floor.

"Hey, Al, I'm sorry," Moodrow continued. "I don't actually wanna hurt you, but I need to make you understand that I'm serious here. I need to make you understand that after I establish motive and opportunity, I'm gonna drag your ass uptown and persuade you to confess to this awful crime. Now, you shouldn't take this to mean that I can't appreciate your point of view. I can see you're in a tough spot and maybe it's better you should risk gettin' electrocuted five years from now than risk gettin' blown away next week. But I got my own priorities."

Moodrow reached down, grabbed O'Neill by the shirt, hauled his 225 pounds upright and slammed him into the chair. He was about to resume his interrogation when he heard a voice in the hallway.

"Al, where the hell are you? What're you doin'?"

Moodrow, caught by surprise, looked around for a place to hide, then thought better of it. The panic in Al O'Neill's face gave him a better idea.

"C'mon in," Moodrow said. "I'm in the office."

The man who walked into the room was young and blond. He hesitated when he saw Moodrow, but only for a second. "Hey, what's doin'?" he said.

"Nothin' much," Moodrow answered. "How's by you?"

The man turned to O'Neill without answering. "I got a delivery for you, Al," he said. "Collect." He dropped a small paper bag on the desk and stepped back while a sweating Al O'Neill counted out two hundred dollars, then handed it over.

"All right?" O'Neill asked without looking up.

"Fine, Al. Just fine." The man started to turn away, then checked himself. "I think you cut yourself, Al. Up there next to your eye. Better put some iodine on that. You don't wanna get infected. Also, your front door's open. That's why I came in. I figured something might be wrong."

"Nothing's wrong," Moodrow said, standing up and turning toward the much smaller man. "We're just havin' a conversation. A private conversation, if you take my meaning. You could shut the door on your way out."

"I'll do that."

Moodrow watched the man retreat, heard the front door slam, then turned back to Al O'Neill. "What's in the bag, Al? You gettin' a condom delivery?"

O'Neill groaned, but made no effort to prevent Moodrow from emptying the contents of the paper bag on the desk.

"This looks like dope to me." Moodrow pointed at the forty small glassine envelopes. "It looks like a *lot* of dope. The little lady can't be using all this horse. You gotta be supplying it to the girls. At a profit, of course."

O'Neill, to Moodrow's surprise, burst into tears. "He made you for a cop," the fat man blubbered. "I know he made you."

"You worried about a small-time pusher? A big man like you?"

"He's connected. If he talks, I'm dead. And he's gonna talk."

O'Neill was close to caving in, to spilling his guts. Moodrow could feel it. The fat man was like a little kid standing by the edge of a swimming pool. He was afraid of the water, but once he got wet, he'd stay in there all afternoon. The temptation was to push him over the edge, but Moodrow instinctively knew that wouldn't work. He knew that this particular child had to be convinced that jumping was in his own best interest.

"Tell me what you wanna do, Al," Moodrow finally said.

"What?"

"Look, whoever that kid was, he's already seen you, right? We can't take that back. Plus, a murder was committed in this room. We can't take that back, either. So, you take it from here. You tell me what you wanna do."

"I wanna get my ass outta here in a hurry," O'Neill said without hesitation. "I got money put away in the bank. I wanna take it and run."

"Good. I'm glad you said that, because it means you know that going to jail won't protect you. Whoever's after you can reach right into the Tombs and pluck you out. Am I right?"

"Keep goin'."

"Okay, you told me what *you* want. Being that fair is fair, I'm gonna tell you what *I* want. I want you to tell me what happened here on December 26. All of it. I wanna know who was here and why they were here. I wanna know who they worked for and if any cops were involved. Once you make me believe that you're telling the truth, you get to write everything down in your own hand-writing and sign it. Then your wife does the same thing and we stroll over to the drug store on Delancey Street so we can have your signatures notarized. After we're all finished, I'll let you run as far and as fast as you can. And I won't ask where you're going. How's that sound?"

O'Neill stared up at Moodrow, his look a mixture of confusion and hope. "I don't know what to do," he admitted. "All I know is that I'm screwed."

"Why don't you start with the night of December twenty-sixth. Somebody came into this office and assaulted your wife. Why? Were they here to rob you? Was it another pimp? Tell me what happened, Al. These people are gonna to kill you if they get the chance. You don't owe them anything."

"There were three of them," Al O'Neill finally began, "and they were here because I was late with my payments."

Fifteen

JANUARY 18

STEPPY ACCACIO was in a towering rage. In the first place, it was only eleven o'clock in the morning, *way* too early to be dealing with major problems. In the second place, his bitch of a Sicilian wife was nowhere to be found.

"Where ya hidin', Angie?" he shouted. "Ya humpin' the paperboy? Ya humpin' the goddamn Fuller Brush man? Who ya humpin', Angie?"

Accacio roared through the house, screaming his wife's name at the top of his lungs. He knew he was wasting time, wasting *valuable* time, but he couldn't help himself. When his temper went off, it went off. There was nothing he could do except ride it out.

Still, he'd feel better when he found his lazy wife and gave her a few good reasons to answer him the first time he called her name. When he let the pressure roaring in his temples out through his fists.

He was down in the basement, still shouting, when he heard his Cadillac (his brand-*new* Cadillac) pull into the garage. There she was, out shopping when he wanted her. Playing around in the department stores. Buying some kind of bullshit they didn't need and never would need.

"Welcome home, bitch," he hissed as she came into the kitchen with a bag of groceries in her arms.

"I got fresh rolls," Angie said, holding the paper bag between them. "And some fruits. For you breakfast."

Steppy Accacio slapped the groceries out of her hand. The truth was that he didn't care *what* was in the bag. He didn't give two shits if it was filled with hundred-dollar bills. The bitch was gonna get what she deserved. Even if she didn't deserve it. He slapped her in the face, then slapped her again.

"I want you here when I want you here," he shouted. "I don't want you somewheres else."

She made no move to defend herself, her arms limp at her sides, head lowered. For some reason, this made Steppy Accacio even angrier. It made him want to *really* work her over, to bust her ribs, crack her nose, split her lips. He could almost taste the blood.

But there was no time for it. Joe Faci and Santo Silesi were on their way over. If he did the job on Angie, she'd require some kind of medical attention and that would only complicate what was already getting out of hand.

He reached out and pulled her coat off, then grabbed her blouse and yanked it so hard the buttons flew across the kitchen.

"Get out of those clothes," he ordered. "You could sit up in your bedroom for the rest of the day. I don't wanna see ya dressed. Maybe you won't go nowheres if ya tits're hangin' out."

Angie, already tugging at the hooks on her bra, started to walk past him, but he pushed her back against the kitchen table. "Do it here. I wanna make sure ya don't defy me. Bein' as ya not a person I could trust."

Steppy grinned, enjoying her obvious humiliation. She was probably blushing, he decided, even if you couldn't see it through that dark Sicilian skin. Angie was a devout Catholic, and despite all the bullshit about Sicilians being so lusty, sex with her was an obligation, like going to church on Christmas and Easter. Ordinarily, he much preferred the kinds of games he played with the whores under his control, but this was different. This was an opportunity. He felt the blood pounding in his temples start to pound in his crotch.

"Nice tits, Angie. I admit it. Ya got a nice set of bazoomas."

And it was the truth, too. Maybe, someday, their kids (if they ever managed to *have* kids) would drag those grapefruits down to her waist. But for now they rode high, pointing right at his lips. He reached out and took her nipples between his fingers and twisted until he was sure it hurt. She didn't cry out, of course. She *never* cried out.

"Keep goin', Angie. I'm gonna give ya what ya deserve."

He watched her step out of her shoes. Watched her wriggle out of her skirt, then slide her panties down over her hips.

"Open ya legs. Open 'em wide. That's a good girl. That's a very good girl. See how nice I am when ya give me what I want? Now, turn around, Angie. Show me that sweet brown ass."

He stepped forward, pushing his crotch into her buttocks, then slammed her down against the tabletop.

"Reach behind ya, Angie," he hissed. "Reach behind and take it out for me. I'm feelin' lazy at the moment."

Thirty minutes later, when Joe Faci and Santo Silesi finally arrived, Steppy Accacio's mood had gone from bad to good to bad again. The way Accacio saw it, the small, fragile niche he'd managed to carve for himself on New York's Lower East Side, his stepping stone to bigger and better things, was being threatened by forces he'd thought were under control. True, he didn't have all the facts yet. Maybe, just maybe, his young nephew had misjudged the situation. Maybe Sandy had simply panicked. But one thing for sure, the bosses who'd given him permission to occupy his little niche would yank that permission the minute they felt he couldn't control his territory. There was no shortage of aspiring businessmen looking for the same chance he'd been given.

Accacio didn't bother showing Faci and his nephew into the den. With Angie naked in their bedroom, there was little chance of being overheard. He didn't bother with espresso and pastries, either. What Accacio felt as he led the two men into the living room was cold hard fear. It was like being nineteen years old and back in the army again, back in that minefield in France. The lieutenant had led them into that field as if they were taking a stroll through Central Park. It wasn't until the first mine exploded, showering the platoon with bloody chunks of PFC Trevor Jones, that the dumb bastard figured it out. The following hour had been the longest in Steppy Accacio's life. He still dreamed about it.

"Awright, Sandy," Accacio said, his voice surprisingly quiet, even to himself, "let's hear it."

"There's not much to tell. I'm supposed to go into O'Neill's twice a week to drop off forty bags of dope. If he needs anything extra, he sends one of the whores out to pick it up. Yesterday, I'm making my regular delivery and I find the front door wide open. I knock and call out, but O'Neill doesn't answer, which is very unusual because he mostly stays by that door. Now I don't like the situation, but I still wanna deliver the dope because I'm finished for the morning and if O'Neill doesn't take it, I'm gonna have to hold onto the forty bags all day. So, I'm walking back to the office, still calling O'Neill's name, when someone says, 'C'mon in.' Me, I think it's O'Neill, but when I go inside, I find this cop sitting on O'Neill's desk. My first instinct is to get the hell out of there, but I manage to hold together and make the delivery. I figured the cop would be more suspicious if I ran."

"But you didn't actually *hear* what they were talkin' about," Accacio said. "For all ya know, they coulda been talkin' about the weather. I mean it coulda been the cop was tryin' to shake the pimp down. Happens all the time."

"I thought about that and I guess it's possible. But what keeps bothering me is the look on O'Neill's face when I walked into the office. I thought the pimp was gonna have a heart attack. I'm telling you, Steppy, his face was dead white, like he was looking into his own coffin. Then the cop tells me that him and O'Neill are having a *private* conversation."

"Did O'Neill say anything? Anything at all."

"Not a word. But his hands were shaking so bad, he could hardly count out the two hundred."

"If the situation was so fucking serious, how come you waited this long to tell me?" Accacio's voice rose as he asked the question. He could feel his anger returning.

"The kid didn't do nothin' wrong," Joe Faci interrupted. "Him and the hebes had to go to Jersey in the afternoon. Then he had to go back in the projects at night. He called me as soon as he was finished, but you was already outta touch by then."

"Yeah," Sandy said quickly. "The thing was I didn't wanna tell Jake before I spoke to you. The job we had to do in Jersey with SpeediFreight? If I didn't show up for that, Jake would've *known* something was wrong. He's not a dope, Steppy. He's smart, like all the Jews. What I did was go through the day like nothing happened. Then, after I got finished in the projects, I found Joe and told him exactly what I'm telling you."

Steppy Accacio leaned back in his chair and rubbed his eyes. His nephew's story was based on nothing more than instinct. Instinct, Steppy knew, was important. You couldn't really make your way in this business without it, but you could also let it get away from you. Facts were a lot better, but sometimes facts were hard to come by. You might spend weeks digging out the facts and, meanwhile, your whole life was going down the drain.

"Could you describe this cop? Would you know him again if you saw him?"

"That's easy," Santo Silesi replied. "He was a fucking giant. Six-five, at least, and built like a refrigerator. Plus, he had a scar in his eyebrow. The scar was still red, so he must've gotten it recently. I could make out the stitch marks."

"I seen this cop before," Joe Faci said quietly.

"You know him?" Accacio asked. "You know who the fuck he is?"

"I didn't say that, Steppy. I didn't say I actually *knew* him. I only said I *seen* him."

"You wanna tell me *where* you seen him? Or do you wanna make it a goddamned mystery."

"The last time Patero came in for his piece, the big cop was with him. The reason I remember it so clear is because the cop still had the stitches in his eye."

"Holy shit," Accacio shouted, jumping out of the chair. "Holy shit. Holy shit. Did Patero bring him into the office?"

"Nope. Left him outside at a table. They had lunch after you and Patero finished ya business."

Accacio sat back down. "Maybe it's not so bad. Maybe O'Neill got behind on his payments to Patero, like he did with us. Maybe the cop was there to teach him a lesson. Jesus, if the sheeny didn't shoot that spic, we wouldn't be worried about this bullshit. Sandy, you didn't say nothin' to the Jew, right?"

"Right."

"Okay, we gotta move fast. And it ain't the cops I'm mostly worried about. We're just startin' out, just gettin' established. If we look like a bunch of fuck-ups, Tommy Rosario's gonna cut us out like he was pullin' a used rubber off his dick. Sandy, you go back to Leibowitz and tell him Joe Faci wants to see him. Joe, you tell Leibowitz that O'Neill and his old lady gotta go. What I'm thinkin' here is that even if this bullshit with the cop ain't directed at us, O'Neill's junkie wife is a liability. They *seen* the spic go down. It's like a sword hangin' over my head and I want it outta there. You tell the sheeny to do it quiet, Joe. Like he done his buddy. I want them two pimps should disappear like they never been born. Meanwhile, I'm gonna personally call Lieutenant Patero. I'm gonna tell him that if he can't control what goes down in his own precinct, he can take his protection and shove it up his fuckin' ass."

Pat Cohan was so pissed off he couldn't believe it. He hadn't felt this way in years, not in *years*. What he wanted to do was fire his long-unfired .38 into Stanley Moodrow's chest. Except that Stanley Moodrow wasn't there and Sal Patero was. Sal Patero was sitting in a chair with his legs crossed like nothing was happening.

"You know what's buggin' you, Pat?" Patero said. "What's buggin' you is that you totally fucked up when you picked this kid out to marry your daughter. You misjudged his character and you put him in a position he couldn't handle. Now you got your family mixed up in it and you don't know what to do."

"Listen, you little wop," Cohan screeched, "don't tell me what I shouldn't have done. You're the one who put me onto Steppy Accacio. I was clean before that. You hear me? *Clean.*"

"You never been clean a day in your life. And what you're doin' right now leads me to believe it's time you got out of the game. You're not being objective. You oughta be thinking about what you're *gonna* do. Instead, all you can think about is what you've already done."

"What I wanna do is *kill* the bastard." Cohan, once he'd gotten it out, began to calm down. Patero was right, of course. The important thing was to stop Moodrow before he did any damage.

"You wanna go out and kill a cop, Pat? Is that what you wanna do?"

Cohan sat in a chair behind his carved mahogany desk. He lit the stub of a Cuban cigar and blew out a cloud of gray smoke. "I'm not sayin' we should actually kill him."

"Why don't we talk about the future? Let's talk about what we *are* gonna do."

"I suppose you've got that all figured out."

"I haven't been wasting my time thinkin' about the past."

"Look, you guinea bastard, keep the sarcasm to yourself. I don't need that crap."

Patero laughed. "Hey, Pat," he said quietly, "you and me are sleepin' in the same bed. If I get fucked, you get fucked. Why don't you try to clear the potatoes out of your stupid Irish brain? Just long enough so you could hear what I'm gonna say. The first thing is we gotta separate young Stanley from the Seventh Precinct. I'm not talkin' about a suspension. Just a two-week vacation, followed by a transfer to the Hundred and First in Far Rockaway. That's step number one. Step number two is I make it clear to the squad that Stanley Moodrow is not to have access to the paperwork in the Melenguez case. Under pain of following young Stanley out to the boonies. Maybe we could also spread the rumor that Stanley is talkin' to the press, that he's tearin' down the blue wall. I'm not sure the boys'll buy it, but it can't hurt us."

"Wait a second, Sal. How do you know he hasn't already seen the file?"

"Seeing the file is one thing. Copying it is something else. Now, step number three is we prepare a case against Stanley for corruption. Or dereliction of duty. Or disobedience. Or spitting on the sidewalk. Something to use if he doesn't take the hint. Because the thing about it is we can't call him off. Any cop has the right to investigate any crime when he's off-duty. It's a tradition and we can't mess with it. Now . . ."

The doorbell rang, interrupting Patero's lecture. Pat Cohan knew who it was. He also knew that he should stay in his den, that there was nothing to be gained from a confrontation with Stanley Moodrow. But he got up anyway, got up and walked out of the den to find his darlin' Kathleen in Stanley Moodrow's arms.

"Lord Jesus," he muttered. "What have I done to myself?"

The young couple gave him plenty of time to think about it. Reacting like any pair of lovers after a separation, they continued to hold each other, continued to press their lips together.

"Stanley," Pat Cohan said when he could stand it no longer. "Stanley."

Kate jumped back, her hands unconsciously smoothing her skirt. "Daddy," she said, "I didn't know you were there."

"It's all right, darlin', I was young once, too. Stanley, boyo, do you think I could have a moment? Just a moment, then I'll leave you two lovebirds alone."

"Sure, Pat. Whatever you want."

Pat Cohan felt his ears begin to redden. There hadn't been a *hint* of fear in Moodrow's voice. It was as if he was totally unaware of what happened to cops who made enemies of NYPD inspectors. Unaware or unconcerned.

"Hey, Stanley," Patero said as Moodrow came into the den. "What's goin' on?"

"Nothing much, Sal. How's by you?"

"Enough of the bullshit," Cohan said, trying to keep his voice down. "Just what in hell do you think you're doing?"

"I'm visiting my fiancée."

Cohan's mouth opened, but no words came out. Stanley Moodrow was staring directly into his eyes.

"Relax, Stanley," Patero said. "You know what Pat's talkin' about. He's talkin' about your visit to the Pitt Street pimp. Can I assume you weren't there to sample the merchandise?"

"What I do on my own time is my own business. The job doesn't own me twenty-four hours a day. Maybe you wanna tell me why you bullshitted me about Luis Melenguez."

"If you had a problem with what I told you," Pat Cohan shouted, "you should've come to *me*."

"Sal," Moodrow said, ignoring Cohan altogether, "We're talking about a *homicide*. You're a cop. How can you bury a homicide?"

"What makes you think I'm burying *anything*?"

Moodrow hesitated, then smiled. "Melenguez was my neighbor. I saw his wife the other day. She came from Puerto Rico to pick up her husband's effects. We talked for a long time. A *long* time. What you told me about Melenguez being a pimp was pure bullshit. He was just an ordinary citizen who happened to be in the wrong place at the wrong time. Think of it like this, Sal—if you're not guilty, then you got nothin' to worry about."

"You," Pat Cohan said, "you have plenty to worry about. I'm going to bury you so deep, they won't be able to find you with a steamshovel."

"You already gave that speech," Moodrow growled, turning back to the inspector. "Two days ago. Wanna hear something funny? I believe you a hundred percent. Which means I don't have a hell of a lot to lose."

"All right, enough small talk." Patero got up and approached Moodrow. "Here's what's gonna happen, Stanley," he said, poking his index finger into Moodrow's chest. "You're on vacation, starting right now. You got a problem, take it to the P.B.A. Plus, I don't wanna see you in the Seventh. Maybe I can't lock the door, but I got a lotta friends in that building. You come in there, someone's gonna be watchin' you every minute. Besides which the Melenguez paperwork's already gone over to Organized Crime. Where *everybody's* my friend."

Patero continued to jab Moodrow's chest as he spoke, his thin smile gradually widening into a grin. "You figure out what I'm sayin' yet, Stanley?"

"I know what you're trying to do, Sal," Moodrow answered. "You want me to hit you. You want me to hit a superior officer in front of an officer who's even superior to him. But I gotta tell you something you haven't figured out yet." He grabbed Patero's wrist and held it motionless. "If it comes down to a street-fight, you're gonna get your ass kicked. Now, if you don't mind, I think I'll go join my fiancée."

Pat Cohan waited until the door closed behind Moodrow before he spoke. He was much calmer now. "Know what I'm gonna do, Sal? I'm gonna transfer the bastard out, just like you said. Then I'm gonna wait. A year. Two years. Until he thinks I've forgotten. When the right time comes, I'm gonna set him up. I'm gonna put him in prison, then I'm gonna visit him and tell him what I did. Because nobody . . ."

"Look, Pat, you're . . ."

"Don't interrupt me, Sal. I want you to get to Faci tonight. I want you to tell him the shooters have to go. I don't care if he ships them across the ocean to spaghetti heaven or buries them in a swamp. They gotta vanish."

"I'm not gonna say any such thing, Pat. It's much too early to panic. How do you know what Stanley's gonna find out? Besides, Faci and his boss aren't stupid. If we let them know what's happening, they'll handle things on their own."

"Give me a number, Sal."

"What?"

"Give me a phone number. Faci's. Accacio's. I don't care which one. Give me the number and I'll take care of it myself."

Stanley Moodrow couldn't stop thinking about how easy it would be. He and Kate were sitting together on the living room couch watching television. Pat Cohan was upstairs, presumably asleep. The image on the screen was revolving wildly, but neither he nor Kate showed any inclination to adjust it. They'd just come out of a long embrace, an embrace that had begun with Kate's lips drawn tightly together, then quickly escalated to all-out passion. Kate had pulled away first, as expected, but she continued to breathe heavily as she straightened her skirt.

What Moodrow figured he could do, assuming he wanted to, was draw Kate Cohan into his bed. Despite Father Ryan's penance, despite all the good-girl myths, despite her fear of her father, Kate's body would get the better of her. He could seduce her and get her pregnant and that would be all she wrote.

"Maybe we ought to talk about something else," Kate said.

"I don't recall us talking at all."

She took his hand and squeezed it. "Stanley, what were you and Daddy fighting about? I heard him shouting."

What could he say? Your father's pissed off because I'm trying to prove he covered up a murder?

"I think his hair got messed up."

"Don't be evasive, Stanley. What were you fighting about?"

"I know you love your father, Kate, but you have to admit he has his faults." He waited for her to nod in agreement. "And one of his faults is he thinks of you as a medal he's giving out. If I want the medal, I have to earn it. Which basically means obeying *him*, even if what he wants has nothing to do with your welfare."

"Daddy's just being protective. The way fathers are supposed to."

"But where does that leave *me*? I'm not a dog on the end of his leash. I have to live my own life. And after we get married, your life and mine are gonna be one and the same. The point I'm making is that sooner or later your old man has to let go."

What he wanted to do was bury his lips in her throat, to run the tips of his fingers over her body, to join their flesh until neither of them could tell where one body left off and the other began. But he didn't do any of that. It was the wrong time and the wrong place and he knew it.

"I suppose he does," Kate said, "but I think it'll come naturally. After we're married. Daddy respects marriage."

"Yeah, well, I hope so. But there's something else we have to get straight and that's where we're gonna live." The issue had been bothering him ever since he'd realized they were going to have to survive on his salary. If they saved their pennies, they might someday be able to afford a home of their own, but that was going to be in the future. *Way* in the future. "Because the thing of it is that I've already got a two-bedroom rent-controlled apartment right now. For which I'm paying eighty dollars a month."

"But the neighborhood, Stanley. It's falling apart."

"Look, I know the Lower East Side isn't much. It never was. But half a million people live there and they mostly get along. What I want you to do is come to see me tomorrow. It's Sunday so you oughta be able to get away. Let me take you around, show you what the neighborhood's really like. If you still think you can't live there, we'll find some other place. But at least come and take a look."

Sixteen

JANUARY 19

THE THING about Jake Leibowitz, Jake Leibowitz thought, is he never kids himself. He faces up to the crap reality throws at him is what he does. He *deals* with the bullshit.

When Santo Silesi brought him the word that O'Neill and his bitch had to go, Jake'd seen it as a routine piece of business, as the price you pay for your mistakes. That *routine* had changed dramatically when he, Izzy and young Santo found 800 Pitt Street deserted. Jake had figured it out right away. The O'Neills were a link between Steppy Accacio and the electric chair: O'Neill to Jake to Faci to Accacio. That's how it went. Take the O'Neills out and the chain breaks.

But with O'Neill and his old lady most likely talking to the cops, the only sensible thing for Steppy Accacio to do was move up to the *next* link. Which happened to be Jake Leibowitz. Jake and his buddy, Izzy Stein.

Well, Jake Leibowitz wasn't going to run. Not from Accacio and not from the cops. And he wasn't going to panic, either. He'd waited too long to get his piece of the action. What he'd do is watch his back at all times. Watch his back and wait for Santo Silesi to make a move.

"Yoo-hoo, Jakey, are you decent?"

Jake, staring at his reflection in the mirror, rolled his eyes. "Yeah, ma, c'mon in."

Sarah Leibowitz pranced into the room, her rotund body encased in the rattiest fur coat Jake had ever seen. "You like?" she asked, spinning around to give him the big view.

"Great, ma. What kind of fur is it?"

She threw him her darkest look. "A hundred percent fox. If you knew from fur, you wouldn't ask."

"That's what I was gonna say. Only I didn't wanna look bad in case it was mink."

Ma Leibowitz sniffed. "So why are you dressed so fancy-pancy? You getting married?"

"I gotta go out, ma."

He looked back at the mirror, at his beautiful gray suit. The suit he'd almost *fought* the salesman at Leighton's to get. "Continental," the salesman had insisted. "Continental is the fashion now." Then he'd brought out a three-button jacket and a pair of trousers with a little buckle in the back. "I'd rather wear a fucking dress," Jake had said. "What I want is double-breasted and no bullshit about it." The suit he ended up buying was a compromise because even though it *was* double-breasted, it only had one button. Way at the bottom.

"This is crap," he'd told the salesman, but then he'd tried on the jacket, looked in the mirror and known right away. The damn thing draped his chest like a Roman toga. He looked like he'd just stepped off the cover of *Esquire*. "Do the cuffs. I'll pick out some shirts while I'm waitin'."

Now, he *never* wanted to take the suit off. Even though his business this morning was routine. He was supposed to meet Santo Silesi in the projects on Houston Street and hand over the day's supply of heroin. Dope was a seven-day-a-week business. Miss a day, even a Sunday, and your customers went somewhere else. Later, after Santo had his pockets full, Jake and Izzy were going to meet down at Katz's Delicatessen for some breakfast and a strategy session. The strategy wasn't hard to figure: locate O'Neill before it's too late. Find him or get ready to fight. Jake wanted to know if Izzy had come to the same conclusion. Especially about the fighting part of it.

Jake took his .45 from under the pillow and shoved it into his belt.

"What's with the gun?" Sarah Leibowitz asked.

"You want fox, mind your own business."

"For me he has no respect," Sarah moaned. "For me . . ."

"Cut the crap, ma. I ain't got the patience for it."

"Huh," she sniffed. "You could at least straighten your tie."

He *did* straighten his tie. Then he left the bedroom. "I'll be back when I'm back," he said, shrugging into his black overcoat. "Don't wait up."

It was cold outside, cold and windy, as usual. Jake held his hat with one hand as he walked along Avenue D. It was like being in Kansas, in *Leavenworth*, Kansas, where the wind came across the prairie like a bullwhip in the hand of a sadistic hack. The only good thing about this winter of 1958 was that Santo Silesi had to spend hours every day standing in it.

"I'll bet the little prick has a face the color of Santa Claus's costume," Jake said to himself as he hurried along. "I'll bet his face is so raw he screams when he shaves."

When he finally located Silesi in a park near the river, Jake's first thought was, "Good, he's got customers." But as he moved a little closer, Jake realized that something was very wrong. Silesi was surrounded by five Puerto Rican kids wearing identical baseball jackets. Jake could see young Santo's head swiveling as he tried to watch everyone at the same time. What it was, what it *had* to be, was a rip-off. Pure and simple.

Jake pulled the .45 and laid it alongside his coat. Santo and the five kids were standing just off the path and Jake waited until he was abreast of the group, then turned, stepped forward and smashed the .45 into the nearest kid's head. The kid dropped without so much as a groan.

"Who's talkin' here?" Jake asked, looking from one kid to another. "Who's the big shot?" He paused, allowing the barrel of the Colt to swing in a slow half-circle. "What's the matter? Nobody got nothin' to say? You a bunch of *patos*? You a bunch of faggots?"

Their eyes were riveted to the .45. They couldn't even *think* of anything else.

"Somebody better wake the fuck up," Jake said. "Because I ain't gonna *slap* the next one." He drew the hammer back.

"I am the president," a tall, slim kid announced.

"That's funny," Jake said, pointing the .45 at the center of the kid's chest, "you don't look a bit like Dwight David Eisenhower. Not with all that greasy hair. Ike's bald."

"I am president of the Tenth Street Dragons."

"Dragons? More like the Tenth Street *Cucarachas*."

"You have the gun, *señor*."

"Here, Santo, take this." Jake passed the .45 to Silesi, then took off his overcoat, folded it carefully and laid it on a bench. His hat followed, then his jacket. "Okay, *El Presidente*, let's see what you got."

Jake could see the kid was scared. He was scared, but he couldn't chicken out. Not with that macho attitude every Puerto Rican was supposed to have. He *had* to fight.

"Ya know somethin', kid? I was havin' a *very* bad day. But since I met *you*, it's picked up considerable."

The kid threw a slow clumsy left. Jake took it on the forehead, a nothing punch that made no impression whatsoever, then slammed his right hand into the kid's face. He felt the kid's nose flatten under his knuckles, watched him fall.

"What's the matter, *El Presidente*, you don't wanna get up?" The kid *didn't* want to get up. That was obvious. He was sitting on the frozen ground, holding one hand to his face, trying to shake off the dizzyness.

"C'mon, don't be a pussy." Jake drove the toe of his fifty-dollar Bostonians into the kid's ribs. That got him going. The kid rolled away, trying to get to his feet, but Jake moved with him, waiting for an opening. When he saw it, he kicked the kid again, this time right in the balls.

"Guess the party's over," Jake said. "*El Presidente* musta ate somethin' that didn't agree with him. He's pukin' all over his sneakers. What I gotta say to the rest of you punks is that ya boss is lucky. He's lucky he ain't fuckin' dead. Which is exactly what *you're* gonna be if ya try this bullshit again. Look at yourselves. Wearin' them stupid jackets and them sneakers in the middle of winter. Why don't ya get a goddamned suit? A decent pair of shoes?" He paused for an answer, but nobody said a word. "Awright, pick up ya buddies and get your asses outta here. And don't come back. Next spic that fucks with me is goin' for a swim in the river."

Jake took the .45 from Santo, then waited in his shirtsleeves until the kids disappeared into the projects. What he was *showing* them was that he didn't feel the cold, but what he was *doing* was freezing his ass off. The minute they were gone, he put on his jacket, overcoat and hat. Then he started walking.

"Let's move up to Sixth Street. In case somebody's momma decides to call the cops."

They walked over to Avenue D, then turned north. "What were ya doin', Santo?" Jake asked. "Were you just gonna let 'em rob ya?"

"They weren't thieves," Silesi replied evenly. "The Dragons aren't a fighting gang."

"Then what the fuck did they want?"

"They wanted me to stop bringing heroin into the neighborhood. They said it was destroying the community."

"No shit?" Jake shook his head in wonder. "Puerto Rican social workers. Who woulda believed it."

"What could I say, Jake? It surprised me, too."

"Did they happen to mention what they were gonna do? In case you decided not to take their advice."

"You showed up before they got to that part."

"Well, you could forget about them. They ain't comin' back. There's somethin' else I wanna talk about anyway. Ya told me your uncle had a police lieutenant in his pocket. Remember?"

"I remember."

"So what I wanna know is how come we gotta worry about the cops? Because Joe Faci told me it was fixed. I mean was he bullshitting me or what? It seems to me if ya *really* got a lieutenant in ya pocket, you could find out where the cops hid the pimp and his old lady."

"That's not my end of it, Jake. All I know is some cop's making a fuss and Steppy's dealing with it."

They were interrupted by what Jake, thinking about it later, called a miracle. A woman, dressed in a dark cloth coat and a woolen scarf, stepped out of a doorway and approached them. Her hands were shaking, her nose running freely.

"Sandy," she said, "ya gotta help me out."

Jake recognized Betty O'Neill immediately. Which is not to say that *she* recognized *him*. She wasn't even looking at *him*. The bitch only had eyes for her pusher.

"I'm sick," she said. "I gotta have a fix. I *gotta*."

"I just dropped off forty bags the other day," Silesi said calmly. "You must have some kind of habit, Betty. Maybe it's time for you to kick."

"It ain't that," Betty said. "Al dumped it in the toilet. He said that dope is what got us into the mess we're in. I asked him, 'What mess?' but all he can say is we gotta run. I don't know what's the matter with him, Sandy. He's turned into some kind of a pansy."

"Was he talkin' to the cops, Betty?" Jake asked. Now she was looking at him, trying to place him. He smiled innocently. "I mean I'm only askin' because there's rumors goin' around and what with you and Al takin' off, people are startin' to get worried."

"A cop *did* come to the house, but Al didn't tell him nothin'. I swear it."

"Then why did he run away?"

"Because he's a damned coward, that's why." She paused long enough to run the sleeve of her coat across her mouth and nose. "Al figured that when Santo seen him and the cop together, he'd jump to conclusions."

"Betty," Jake said, "do you know who I am?"

"You're Santo's boss."

"That's right." He took a small paper bag out of his overcoat pocket and let her take a look at what was inside. "You know what that is, don't ya?"

"Dope." Her hand floated up for a moment, then dropped to her side. "I got money. I'll take it all."

Jake shook his head. He counted out ten caps, then handed the rest to Silesi. "Go take care of business, Santo. You got customers need servicin'." He waited until he and Betty were alone before speaking again. "What would ya give for this, Betty?" he asked. "What would ya give?"

Betty managed a crooked smile. "I'd give ya whatever ya wanted." She put her hand beneath her coat and let it slide down her belly.

"What I want is your husband. And I ain't no fag, either. I just gotta make sure he's all right, that he ain't talkin' to the wrong people."

"That chicken ain't talkin' to nobody. He don't hardly answer the door."

"I got an idea, Betty. Why don't you and me go some place private? That way you could take care of what you gotta take care of. When you're all better we could talk about this . . . this problem."

"Where are we goin'?"

"To paradise. The Paradise Hotel. A friend of mine has a room there."

The news, as far as Jake was concerned, was all good. Al O'Neill wasn't being protected by the cops. He had to be holed up somewhere on his own, because if the cops were involved, Betty wouldn't be roaming the streets looking for dope. She'd be climbing the walls in some locked room.

Jake led the way down Avenue D and across Houston Street. He didn't bother watching Betty O'Neill. (He could hear her sniveling as she trotted alongside him like a stray dog sniffing at a roast beef sandwich.) Instead, he thought about what was wrong here. If Al O'Neill was talking, the first thing the cops would've done is drag his sorry ass into the precinct to look at the mug books. Jake was in those books. Izzy and Abe, too. So, how come . . .

Maybe O'Neill hadn't talked to anyone. Maybe it was all Santo Silesi's imagination. Maybe Silesi was only trying to make himself more important to Joe Faci and Steppy Accacio. Maybe Accacio himself was nothing more than a chickenshit sissy who panicked every time he heard a noise in the house. Maybe, maybe, maybe.

But none of that mattered and Jake knew it. Because what he *should've* done was take care of Al and Betty when Abe plugged the spic. What he should have done was eliminate the witnesses on the spot. He'd made a mistake, just like Abe Weinberg had made a mistake, and now he had to pay for it. Or Betty O'Neill had to pay for it. That was closer to the truth. Betty and her old man had to pay the price. Permanently.

Jake wasn't surprised to find the lobby of the Paradise Hotel deserted. The assorted whores and hustlers who lived in the Paradise weren't exactly early risers. Plus it was Sunday, and the desk clerk wouldn't come on duty until noon. Jake led Betty up the stairs to Izzy's room on the second floor.

"Good morning, Izzy," Jake said when the door opened. "I brought a guest."

Betty O'Neill may not have recognized Jake Leibowitz, but she knew Izzy Stein well enough. "Oh, Lord," she muttered. "Lord, Lord, Lord."

"Don't be shy, Betty," Jake said, pushing her into the room. "Izzy won't hurt ya. As long as ya tell the truth."

"Where'd ya find her?" Izzy asked. "She fall down outta the sky?"

"Next thing to it. She come lookin' for dope." Jake took out three bags of heroin. "Here ya go, Betty. Have a party."

"It ain't enough," she said. "I gotta have more than that."

"Do this much first," Jake said. "I don't need ya so stoned ya can't get off the floor."

Betty took the heroin, then stripped off her coat and rolled up the sleeves of her blouse. She fumbled in her purse for a moment, then found a cracked leather billfold and dumped its contents on the table: a crusted eyedropper, the tip of a reusable needle, a bent, blackened tablespoon, a wad of cotton, a narrow strip of paper torn from a dollar bill. Despite her trembling hands, she fitted her works together in record time, wrapping the strip of paper around the open end of the eyedropper, then forcing the needle over it.

"I need water," she said.

Izzy retrieved a glass of water from the table next to his bed. It'd been sitting there for two days.

"Thanks." Betty tested the works by filling and emptying the eyedropper and needle several times. When she was satisfied, she squirted water into the tablespoon, added the heroin, then lit a match and heated the mixture until it came to a boil. Finally, she dumped a small piece of cotton into the spoon and set it down to cool.

"Better not leave that too long," Jake said. "The roaches'll drink it."

"Ha, ha." Betty fumbled with her sleeve again, trying to roll it up past her bicep. "Goddamn winter. It gets in your way." She pulled her blouse off, stripping down to a lace brassiere, then wrapped a cloth belt around her upper arm and pulled it tight with her teeth. The veins at her elbow and along her bicep were black with scar tissue, but she patiently worked her finger along the dark lines until she was satisfied, then picked up the dropper and jammed the needle into her flesh. Almost miraculously, a crimson drop blossomed in the clear liquid. With a sigh, she let the belt drop out of her mouth and squeezed the bulb.

Her hands stopped trembling and her nose stopped running within seconds. Her whole body straightened as the knotted muscles in her back began to smooth out.

"That better?" Jake asked.

"Listen," Betty said, ignoring the question, "ya gotta understand that I didn't say nothin' to that cop. I don't know what's happening to Al. Maybe he's gettin' soft in his old age. But I didn't have nothin' to do with nothin' as far as the cop is concerned."

"I believe ya," Jake said. "That's how come I know ya wouldn't mind helpin' us out here. I mean you was there and I wasn't." He waited for Betty to nod before continuing. "What'd the cop want?"

"He was askin' about the john who got killed right after Christmas."

"And what'd ya tell him?"

"I didn't tell him nothin'."

"What'd *Al* tell him?"

"See, that's the thing. The cop locked me in the toilet so's I couldn't hear what was goin' on."

"You were in there all the time?"

"No, he took me out later and locked Al up. Then he asked me a whole lotta questions about that night the john got shot. But I didn't say nothin' except I wasn't there. I told him I got run over by a car and I was sleepin' upstairs at the time."

"If you were in the toilet, how do ya know Santo was there when Al was talkin' to the cop? Santo didn't say nothin' about seein' *you*."

"Al told me."

"What else did he tell ya? What'd he tell the *cops*?"

"That's what I'm tryin' to say. I don't know. All Al said is Santo seen us so we gotta run. I told him we can explain it. I mean what're we supposed to do? Ya can't stop the cops from comin' around, can ya?"

"Maybe Al has a guilty conscience."

Betty didn't answer and Jake let it go. He looked over at Izzy and smiled. "Gimme ten caps, Iz. I got a feelin' Betty's gonna need it."

Izzy crossed to the far corner and yanked up one of the floorboards. He pulled out a mason jar filled with small bags and counted out ten of them.

"See, Betty?" Jake said. "I could keep ya high forever. I mean if you was *my* woman, that's what I'd do."

Betty attempted a coquettish smile. She squared her narrow shoulders and pushed her chest out. "I don't know what's happened with Al. He ain't the man I married, that's for sure. I mean he ain't come near me in years. If I want some, I gotta go to one of the girls. Ain't that unbelievable?"

Jake took the heroin from Izzy and tossed five bags on the table next to Betty's eyedropper. Betty started to go for it, but Jake caught her arm. "It ain't time yet. First I gotta get some answers." He flipped her onto the bed. "I'm not gonna blame you for what ya husband said to the cops. But I don't want no more bullshit. Ya either come clean or what I'm gonna do'll make what Izzy done to ya seem like a honeymoon hump."

Betty's head swiveled back and forth, from the heroin to Jake's face. "You ain't gonna kill me, are ya? For what Al said?"

"As a matter of fact, I got a proposition for ya. In Providence, Rhode Island. See, ya can't stay around here 'cause the cops'll find ya. But I got a small establishment in Providence that's runnin' all fucked up. The woman there can't keep the whores in line. I figured maybe you could take it over. Get it back to makin' a decent profit. All I need to know is what Al told the cops and where he's hidin' out."

Betty leaned back, letting her head fall against the pillows. "Ya know I used to be pretty good. When I was in the trade."

"Cut the crap. I been patient long enough."

She sat back up and straightened the straps of her bra. "He told the cop that Santo and the guys that beat us up both work for Steppy Accacio. The cop made Al write it out and sign a paper. Then he let us go."

"He didn't take ya down to look at no mug shots?" Jake felt himself getting excited. Maybe this wasn't as bad as he'd thought. An idea began to form in his mind. The cop had eyeballed Santo Silesi, but he didn't know who Jake was or what he looked like. If the cop went after Santo and Accacio, if he took them out of the picture, there'd be a big hole in the Lower East Side heroin business. A hole for Jake to fill if could find himself another dope connection. What Jake didn't know is why the cop had released Al and Betty. It didn't make a lot of sense, but if Al was holed up by himself, it also didn't matter.

Betty shook her head. "I got the feeling he was in a hurry. Maybe that's why he didn't work me over."

"Where's ya husband now?"

"He went out to Jersey. To visit his mother. That's how come I got out. I ain't good enough for his mother."

"I mean where's he stayin'? In the city."

"We got a room in Hell's Kitchen. That's where Al grew up. We had the room for years. Use it once in a while to get away from the business."

"Could we go there *now*? Could we go over and wait for Al?"

"Just lemme do up them caps first. Then, whatever ya want. I mean Al gotta pay the price, right? If he didn't wanna pay, he shouldn't've done what he done."

"That's the right way to look at it, Betty. The dope is yours. Take ya time. Enjoy."

Jake nodded to Izzy and both men crossed the room. They waited patiently until Betty pressed the bulb of the eyedropper, until she rocked back in the chair, her eyes fluttering. "Bring the saps and a knife, Izzy," Jake whispered. "We wanna do this quiet."

Seventeen

STANLEY MOODROW, unwashed and unshaven, was spooning Maxwell House coffee into his percolator when he suddenly realized that he was having the time of his life. Sure, he was in a battle (a war, really) and there was always the possibility of losing, but it wasn't the kind of useless combat that fed the dreams of bloodthirsty spectators. He wasn't likely to come out of it with a cracked nose or a split eyebrow, either. No, what he was doing, he told himself, was hunting for truly dangerous game. Like that Englishman who went from one Indian village to another, shooting man-eating tigers from the back of an elephant.

He dumped the percolator on a burner and went into the bathroom to shave. The water was barely warm, which wasn't so great because Kate Cohan had telephoned the night before and told him that she'd decided to give the Lower East Side a chance.

"Show me around," she'd said. "And I promise to keep an open mind."

Moodrow wondered if her open mind extended to an occasional lack of hot water. Not having a ready answer, he worked up a lather and quickly brushed it across his face. He grabbed his razor, examined it closely, then decided to change the blade. Usually, he managed to squeeze three or four shaves out of a Gilette, but the last couple were only bearable when he had plenty of hot water. When the water was this cold, he either changed the blade or his face ended up the color of a ripe strawberry.

He stared at himself in the mirror for a moment before he began to scrape at his beard. Mornings were special times for him. Ever since his mother died and he'd awakened to find himself alone, he'd used the early hours to analyze his problems. At first, he'd concerned himself with other fighters, their strengths and weaknesses. Then he'd turned his attention to the job and his personal ambitions. Now, he found himself preoccupied with the details of the hunt. Much to his surprise, they threatened to overwhelm all other considerations, even his impending marriage.

After leaving the house on Pitt Street, he'd done what any good detective had to do. He'd canvassed the immediate neighborhood, knocking on doors, hoping that someone had seen or heard something on the night Luis Melenguez had been murdered. What he wanted was a witness, but he wasn't surprised to come up empty. Not only had the murder taken place more than two weeks before, the Lower East Side wasn't the kind of neighborhood where good citizens eagerly came forth to share information with the police. As far as most residents of the Lower East Side were concerned, the cops were as dangerous as the criminals.

The whole thing would have been a lot easier if he could have dragged the O'Neills into the 7th and had them look at mug shots until they put names and faces on the men who'd come visiting the day after Christmas. That wasn't going to happen, of course, but he, Moodrow, had gotten a good look at the drug dealer called Santo, and Santo, according to Al and Betty O'Neill, worked for Steppy Accacio, the man who'd sent the shooters. Which meant that Stanley Moodrow could look at mug shots, too. Or he could if the 7th wasn't off-limits.

Moodrow wondered what would happen if he just walked in there, pulled the mug books and started turning the pages. He couldn't imagine Patero trying to stop him from doing what his badge entitled him to do. No, Patero would simply get on the phone and make Santo vanish. Much better to let Patero and Pat Cohan think they were in control of the situation.

What he needed was a photograph to show around. Maybe he didn't have a stable of informants like most of the veterans, but he'd grown up on the Lower East Side. He knew a lot of people, people on both sides of the law and people who straddled the fence. If he had something to show, he'd find Santo easily enough.

The doorbell rang. He answered the door, finding Allen Epstein, as expected, and Paul Maguire.

"Hey, Paul, whatta ya say? C'mon in. You, too, Sarge." Moodrow led the two cops into the kitchen and poured out the ritual mugs of coffee.

"I hope you don't mind that I brought Paul with me," Epstein said. "Paul's an old friend of mine. You could trust him a hundred percent."

"That mean you wanna go on the record, Paul?" Moodrow asked. He couldn't shake the simple fact that Maguire had walked away from a homicide. Sure, Patero had *ordered* him to walk away, but if that was a good excuse, what would Maguire do if Patero ordered him to get Stanley Moodrow?

"Look, I'm willing to help you out," Maguire replied evenly. "As long as I don't have to put my head on the chopping block. You hear what I'm sayin', Stanley? I got three kids and a heavy mortgage."

What Moodrow wanted to say was, "Luis Melenguez had a wife and kids, too," but he held his tongue. Antagonizing Maguire wouldn't get him any closer to the man who'd killed Melenguez. Still, he couldn't help but wonder how many other cops hid behind their families and their mortgages when a superior officer snapped his fingers.

"Why don't you start by telling me what happened with Patero? Did he just *order* you to stop investigating? Did he give you an excuse?"

"The first thing you gotta understand is that my partner, Samuelson, is in Patero's pocket. He wants to make detective, first grade, and Patero's his rabbi. As for Melenguez, we did all the usual things. Interviewed everyone in the house, recovered the slugs, diagrammed the crime scene, took blood samples, dusted for prints. We knew that O'Neill was bullshitting us, but him and his old lady were busted up pretty bad, so we let 'em go off to the hospital. What I figured to do was come back and squeeze 'em, but then Patero says to lay off. He says the investigation's going over to Organized Crime, that certain people (which he naturally can't name) are registered informants in a city-wide probe and we don't wanna blow their cover. I figured he was full of shit, but I kept my mouth shut. I'm not sayin' it didn't bother me, because it did. That's why I'm here . . ."

"Wait a minute, Paul," Moodrow interrupted. "You said you dusted for prints?"

"Yeah."

"You come up with anything?"

"The problem is that we came up with too much. According to the lab boys, we got eight identifiable unknowns. You get one print, you can try to match it up. It takes about a week, but it *can* be done. You get *eight* prints, you gotta have a suspect before it does you any good."

"I get the message."

"What about you, Stanley?" Epstein said. "What have you been doing?"

Moodrow took a moment to think about it, then detailed most of his visit to the O'Neills, leaving out any mention of notarized statements. Up to this point, he'd trusted Epstein completely. But Epstein had kids and a mortgage, too. "What I need is a photo," he concluded. "Something to show around the neighborhood. The story is that Santo and the men who killed Melenguez all work for Steppy Accacio. If I can run down Santo, I can use him to find the shooters."

"You're most likely right, Stanley," Epstein said, "but what're you gonna do when you find them? With the O'Neills on the run, you haven't got any witnesses."

"Maybe I'll find the gun they used. Maybe I'll encourage them to confess to their evil deeds. Maybe I'll take their statements and hand them over to the newspapers."

"You can't do that," Maguire said. "You can't go to the papers."

"Why not?"

"Try to understand," Epstein said. "There's a lot of good cops out there, cops who *hate* guys like Patero. Believe me, Stanley. You haven't been around long enough to know. Those good cops'll help you when they can. But not if you're gonna take it outside the Department."

"That means they'll help me as long as there's no risk to their precious reputations."

"Yeah," Maguire shouted. "As long as they don't get hurt. What do you think, everyone's got your balls? Lemme tell ya something, Stanley, your chances of getting out of this are about a hundred to one. If you go public, if you crack the blue wall, you won't have a friend in the job. Nobody. That'd reduce your chances to a *million* to one. You gotta find another way."

Moodrow sipped at his coffee. He needed friends, that was obvious enough, friends with access to the pool of information available to every detective. If he lost his temper, he'd have to dial the operator for information.

"You're right," Moodrow said. "And I know it. I just got pissed for a minute. But it couldn't hurt if Patero and Cohan . . ."

"*Pat* Cohan?" Maguire shouted.

"That's right. *Inspector* Pat Cohan. Like I was saying, it couldn't hurt if Patero and Cohan *believe* I'll go to the papers. Think about it. As long as Patero and Cohan are willing to protect the shooters, nothing's gonna happen. What I have to do is convince the bastards that an aggressive prosecution is in their own best interest. Patero and Cohan may be accessories after the fact, but they didn't pull the trigger. They weren't in that office when Melenguez showed up. The way I see it, my job is to put a killer in the electric chair, not reform the New York Police Department. But that doesn't mean I can't bluff."

As he spoke, Moodrow began to ask himself questions. *Would* he be satisfied to get the killers of Luis Melenguez? Or did Patero and Cohan have to pay as well? How would he accumulate enough real evidence to convict the shooters? Forced confessions were fine for criminals like the Playtex Burglar, but judges were quick to toss them out in trials involving the death penalty. Defendants in capital cases always had lawyers who always appealed their convictions.

"What I need right now is a photograph of Santo. A photo and a last name. Which means I have to gain access to the mug books."

"You *know* he's got a record?" Maguire asked. "Suppose he's not in there."

"He's there, Paul. I could smell it on him. But even if I'm wrong, I could always go with my memory and . . . but don't worry about it. He's there."

What Moodrow was about to say, what he held back, was that he could always go with his memory and a police artist. It was the word 'police' that brought him up short. There were any number of artists living on the Lower East Side. They came because the neighborhood bordered fashionable Greenwich Village and because the rents were cheap. There was no reason why

Moodrow couldn't go to one of them. No reason why he couldn't keep his business to himself.

"The books can't leave the precinct," Maguire said. "You'd catch a suspension for even tryin' it."

"What about Inzerillo?" Epstein asked. "He still the desk officer on the late tour?"

"Yeah, last I heard."

"I think what he oughta do is get Stanley inside late at night, when it's quiet. We could stash him in the basement, bring him the books one at a time. Inzerillo's a decent guy. I think he'll go along."

"I got a better idea. I wanna send him over to the Thirteenth on Twenty-first Street. I got some friends over there. Detectives. I could just take him over, show him the books."

Epstein shifted in his chair. He picked up his mug, found it empty and handed it to Moodrow for a refill. "It's too risky. Half the cops in the city know Stanley's face. It might get back to Patero. We have to get him in without being seen. The duty sergeant's the ranking officer on the late tour. If we can get Inzerillo to cooperate—and I'm *sure* he'll cooperate—we can bring Stanley through the side door. It's not that big a deal, really."

"No," Maguire admitted, "it's not such a big deal. I've done it myself. Sometimes with a reluctant witness, you have to guarantee they won't get recognized. How long will it take you to set it up with Inzerillo?"

"A few days. At most."

It was only eleven-thirty and Moodrow's patience had already worn down to nothing. What he wanted to do was get to work. He could smell his quarry, like a hungry wolf crossing the track of a lame deer. The whole thing was going to be easy. He was sure of it. Find Santo and use him to find Luis Melenguez's killers. What could be simpler?

But there was no way he could avoid spending the afternoon (and the evening, too, in all probability) with Kate. After all, she was coming at *his* request.

It wasn't, he told himself, that he didn't love and want her. It wasn't that at all. But love wasn't something you felt every minute of the day. Sometimes you were preoccupied. Sometimes you had important things to do. Sometimes you had *better* things to do.

Moodrow looked around his apartment, trying to imagine Kate Cohan living there. He saw a living room, two bedrooms and an eat-in kitchen. Nine hundred square feet, all furnished in solid maple. Maple was better than pine, but it was still a long way from the oak and mahogany Kate Cohan was used to. Plus, the living room carpet was threadbare. And the walls needed painting. And the windows stuck in their frames. And whenever he tried to do something about the cockroaches, they retreated to the Sawitzkys' apartment, only to be chased back. Mrs. Sawitzky was a demon with the Flit.

What was the point? The Lower East Side of Manhattan was never going to be suburbia. No matter how many coats of paint Moodrow threw up on its walls. No matter how many gallons of insecticide he poured beneath the sink or behind the icebox. Kate would just have to live with it, because he wasn't about to move. He wasn't about to spend the rest of his life chasing her middle-class dreams. The price was too high. Just ask Pat Cohan.

He tried to picture Kate's face, the spray of freckles across the bridge of her nose, the firm jaw and bright blue eyes. But the image that kept forcing itself into his mind was of his mother armed with a hatpin, of mounted cops urging their horses into a crowd of striking workers. He could hear the accents: Italian, Yiddish, Russian, Polish. He could hear the horse scream as the hatpin slammed home. He could hear the terrified shout of the cop as he came off the horse.

The phone rang and Moodrow, still preoccupied, was halfway to the door by the time he realized it wasn't the doorbell. He walked back into the kitchen and picked up the receiver.

"Hello?"

"Stanley, it's me."

"Kate?" Moodrow looked up at the clock. It was almost noon. "Where are you?"

"I'm home."

"Home?"

"In Bayside. Daddy and I had a terrible fight. I can't come over. Daddy's *forbidden* me to come over."

What it is, Moodrow thought, is that if you're not an adult at age twenty-two, you never will be.

"Why don't you tell your *daddy* to go fuck himself."

"Stanley, don't use that language."

"Because your *daddy's* a crook."

"What?" Her voice rose an octave. "How can you say that?"

"That's why you're living in that house in Bayside. Because your *daddy's* been taking bribes for the last thirty-five years."

"That's a horrible thing to say. Daddy would never . . ."

"You're gonna find out about it sooner or later, Kate. Pat Cohan is as crooked as they come and what he's trying to do is have me follow in his crooked footsteps."

"Why are you telling me this? What do you want me to do?"

Moodrow took a moment to think about it. "What I want you to do is go into the bedroom, undress, and step in front of the mirror. Take a good look at yourself. What you're gonna see is the body of a woman, not a child. And what you have to do is let your mind catch up to your body. The shit's gonna hit the fan, Kate. It's gonna hit real soon and your father's got his face right in front of the blades."

It was Kate's turn to think about it. When she spoke again, she was in control, her voice almost cold. "Are you telling me that you, Stanley, *you* are going to do something to get my father in trouble?" She hesitated again. "That you're going to put my father in *jail*?"

"I'm a detective, Kate, and I'm investigating a murder. Your father didn't commit the murder, but he's trying to cover it up. He's impeding the investigation."

"Can you prove this?"

"Not in a courtroom. Not yet."

"I didn't think so."

"Look, Kate, I didn't set out to *get* your father. Things just happen. They happen and then you have to make decision. A decision about yourself. Remember Father Ryan's penance? I'm sure it came as something of a surprise, but once he gave it out, you had to do what your conscience told you was right. Personally, I don't think there's anything wrong with making love. In fact, I think there's something wrong with *not* making love. But fornication is nothing compared to murder. Nothing. Go talk to your father. Tell him everything I've told you. See what he says."

There was nothing more to be said, but Moodrow couldn't bring himself to hang up the phone. "Listen, Kate," he continued after a moment, "I know how much this is hurting you. I know how much you love your father. But there's no escape, now, for either one of us. What you have to do is look at it straight up and make a decision. There's lots more I could tell you. About me and Sal Patero collecting payoffs from every pimp and bookie in the Seventh Precinct. About me not wanting to be anything more than an ordinary detective. About a neighbor of mine named Luis Melenguez who's being shipped back to Puerto Rico in a box. You go talk to your father. Then, if you're still interested, I'll go through it blow by blow."

As he hung up the phone, Moodrow was only vaguely aware of what Kate's loss (assuming he did lose her) would mean to him. He saw it as an obligation, a debt to be paid sometime in the future. Would it be crushing? He didn't know. All he knew was that it wasn't crushing at the moment. At the moment, what he wanted to do was get to work.

He walked into the bedroom, found his jacket, shrugged into it, then went back to the living room for his overcoat. As he opened the door and stepped into the hallway, he felt absolutely certain that whatever happened, even if Kate walked away, even if they took his badge and gun, he could deal with it. Maybe he was the proverbial fool, rushing in where angels feared to tread, but if that was the case, he'd rather be a fool than an angel, anyway.

It was cold outside, bitterly cold, but the small shops along Orchard Street were doing a brisk business. Feltly Hats, Sidney Undergarments, Blue Chip Handkerchiefs, Jack Zabusky's Housewares. Many of the shops were down in basements, others up a half-flight. Merchandise was piled outside in cardboard boxes and housewives struggled to control their bored children as they pawed through the goods. One shop, the one Moodrow was looking for, bore the legend Seidenfeld Shoes in red letters. Below, in deference to a new breed of customer, a hand-painted addition announced *Zapatos*.

The interior of Seidenfeld's was so crowded with piled shoeboxes that Moodrow could barely move through the aisles. The younger students at St. Bridget's were going to make their First Holy Communion on the following Sunday, and the girls needed white patent-leather shoes to go with their frilly white dresses.

"Hey, Moe, where ya hidin'?"

A completely bald head emerged from behind the cash register. "Ah, Stanley, so how's by you? I heard you became a big-shot detective. Congratulations."

"Thanks, Moe. I'm looking for Marty."

"My son, the beatnik?"

Moodrow grinned. He and Marty Seidenfeld had met in grammar school, attending the same classes with the same teachers through junior high. Then Marty had gone off to the High School of Music and Art while Moodrow remained on the Lower East Side. On Sundays, to make a little extra money, Marty often worked the shoppers, doing charcoal sketches (caricatures when he could get away with it) for a dollar apiece.

"I need him to do me a favor, Moe. Is he around?"

"He's in the basement. Most likely smoking marijuana."

"Are you kidding?"

"Do I look like Milton Berle? You can see the customers for yourself. An hour ago, the beatnik went to bring up fresh stock. Wait, he'll come back walking like a drunk."

"Maybe you should call him up. If he's doing what you say, I don't wanna see it."

"You shouldn't take offense, Stanley, but I can't leave now. I'm the only one here. If I leave, the merchandise will follow me out of the store. Besides, a night in jail would do him some good. Maybe they'll give him a haircut."

Moodrow walked out of the shop and down a flight of steps into a cold, musty basement.

"Hey, Marty, you down here?" Much to Moodrow's relief, there was *no* smell of marijuana in the basement.

"Over here."

Moodrow made his way to the back of the room where he found Marty Seidenfeld squatting in a tiny cleared space. Surrounded by shoeboxes, Seidenfeld was mixing oil paints on a small palette. The colors, applied directly from small tubes, must have been brilliant, but in the dim light cast by a single bulb they seemed as dull as a newspaper photograph to Moodrow.

"Stanley Moodrow," Marty called. "Like, what's happening, man? What brings the po-lease to Seidenfeld's glorious emporium?"

"How can you paint in this light, Marty? How can you even *see* in this light?"

"I paint in the dark to paint the darkness," Seidenfield replied. He shook out his shoulder-length black hair, ran his fingers through a beard that would have been the envy of an Hasidic rabbi.

"I need a favor, Marty. Not a battle. For old time's sake."

The beat generation's presence on the Lower East Side had been the subject of endless newspaper and magazine articles. Most condemned the movement for its open advocacy of free love and its covert advocacy of experimentation with drugs. A few journalists tried to be understanding, but the beats themselves couldn't have cared less. They turned up their collective noses at all authority. Especially cops.

"Check it out, baby, the man comes in the name of the past. He invokes the glory years of St. Stephen's."

"C'mon, Marty, don't bust my chops. I need you to do a sketch."

"Of what?"

"Of someone I saw a few days ago."

"Like, you got a photograph I can use for a model?"

"If I had a picture, what would I need you for?"

"An attitude. The man comes with a chip on his shoulder."

"We're talking about murder here. You understand, Marty? We're talking about a poor slob who just happened to be in the wrong place at the wrong time."

"Oh, man, you're breakin' my heart."

Marty Seidenfeld's dark eyes bore into Moodrow's without flinching. Moodrow had expected some kind of recognition. The two of them had spent nine years in the same school and even if they'd never been especially close, they'd played the same games on the same teams in the same schoolyards. It should have counted for something.

"It might have been you or anyone you know. The victim's name was Luis Melenguez. He was gunned down for no reason at all. He wasn't a criminal. He wasn't robbed. He was killed because he was in the wrong place at the wrong time."

"Man, you already *made* that point."

"It means nothing to you?"

"*Nada*, as they say in *el barrio*."

"Well, maybe you should do it for old time's sake. Because we've known each other for so many years. Or maybe you should look on it as a favor, a check you can cash some time in the future. Or maybe you should do it because, if you don't, I'm gonna shove them tubes of paint up your ass."

"I must admit that last reason is cool, Stanley. In fact, it's colder than this goddamned basement. But I can think of an even better reason. One that guarantees the full employment of my considerable talents."

"Say it, Marty."

"Like, if I do your sketch, you're gonna come up with twenty beans. You're gonna do it because you sincerely believe an artist should be paid for his work."

"Twenty bucks?" Moodrow could see the new tires his car needed flying out the window.

"That's right, Stanley. And if I didn't know ya from the old days, I wouldn't do it at all."

Eighteen

PAT COHAN, perched on the plastic slipcover of his living-room sofa, enclosed his "darlin' Kathleen's" hands in his own. He hung his head, refusing to meet his daughter's eyes, and took a deep breath.

"Kate," he whispered, "I don't know what to say."

"My whole life's falling apart, Daddy. You have to say *something*."

"I'm not surprised, of course. Not surprised at all."

"You were expecting this?"

Pat Cohan sighed. He ran his fingers through his mane and looked at his daughter for the first time. "There's one thing I want you to keep in mind, Kate. Stanley Moodrow, whatever his faults, loves you with all his heart. If he didn't love you, he wouldn't take the trouble to lie to you the way he did. The truth, girl, the *truth* is that Stanley's not long for the Department. He's been takin' with both hands from his first day on the job."

"I can't believe it, Daddy. Not Stanley."

"Ah, yes. 'Not Stanley.' That was my first thought when Internal Affairs came to see me last week. But I'm an old cop. I've been around too long to let my emotions get in the way of the facts. They've got him dead to rights and he knows it. Stanley went into Sal's office yesterday afternoon. He blamed me for his problems and he made all kinds of threats. This is his way of following through."

Kate Cohan pulled away from her father. She got to her feet and walked behind the couch.

"If he did it, he did it for me," she said. "Because I didn't want to live on the Lower East Side. Because I wanted things he couldn't afford."

"It's not true, Kate. Stanley began taking the day he put on a uniform. Years before he even met you. Just little things, in the beginning. A few dollars to let the truckers park on the sidewalks. Or to let the liquor stores open up on Sundays. After a while, it got worse. That's what happens when a cop surrenders to greed. There's plenty of gambling in the Seventh Precinct. Bookmakers and numbers runners both. Some of these gamblers have to work the street and Stanley made sure they paid for the privilege. There's prostitution as well. Along Third Avenue where they tore down the El. Stanley . . ."

"He says you're trying to cover up a murder, Daddy. You and Sal. There's no truth to that? None at all?"

Pat Cohan buried his face in his hands. When he finally raised his head and turned to his daughter, there were tears running along the broken veins on his cheeks. "As God is my witness, Kate. As God is my witness."

"Daddy . . ."

"It's so hard." Pat dried his tears on a freshly pressed white handkerchief. "I've given my whole life to the New York Police Department. My whole *life*."

"I'm sorry, Daddy. I know you couldn't do something like that."

"The other day, Kate, when you told me about . . . that thing between you and Stanley . . ." He looked up into his daughter's eyes. "I used it to drive a wedge between the two of you, because I couldn't bring myself to say that your fiancé was a crook. I couldn't say it out loud. I was wrong, of course. I should have been honest with you."

Kate sat down next to her father. "Is Stanley going to be arrested? Is he going to jail?"

"I'm not about to let that happen. I may be the next thing to an old horse put out to pasture, but I still have *some* influence." Pat Cohan's voice was very gentle. Gentle and kind. "Stanley's badge and gun will be taken away, of course. He'll be suspended and a departmental hearing scheduled. If he has enough common sense to resign before the hearing, that'll be the end of it."

"He's not going to resign, Daddy. Stanley's a fighter and you know it."

Pat Cohan looked away from his daughter. "I'm hoping he won't be foolish, Kate. I'm hoping he'll read the writing on the wall. If he doesn't, if the evidence is put into the official record . . ."

What Jake Leibowitz understood was that all his plans for the future were coming apart. Despite the fact that he'd left the pimp and his wife in a pool of blood. Despite the fact that he'd buried Abe Weinberg. Despite everything he'd done to further and protect the interests of Steppy Accacio and Joe Faci, the dagos wanted him to take a long vacation on the West Coast. Just give it all up. The dope, the hijackings, everything.

"Whatta ya think, Izzy?" Jake asked. "Whatta ya think we should do?"

"I don't know what we *should* do, but I got a good idea of what we're *not* gonna do. And that's run off to Los Angeles. How could I go to Los Angeles? They stole the Brooklyn Dodgers, for Christ's sake."

Jake managed a smile. "Ya wanna go down in a blaze of glory? It ain't gonna be like John Wayne, Izzy. Where he rides into town and kills all the bad guys? The wops probly got twenty shooters they could send after us. We might get a couple of 'em, but sooner or later . . ." He put his index finger against the side of his head. " 'Pow! Right in the kisser!' "

Izzy lit a Pall Mall and blew a stream of smoke across the room. "I got an idea, Jake. Ya think ya could listen without gettin' all crazy?"

"Whatta ya talkin' about?" Jake pushed his chair far enough back to guarantee he wouldn't get ashes on his suit.

"I'm talkin' about how you don't like it when someone else gets an idea."

"Look, Izzy . . ."

" 'Cause this is important. You're talkin' about the two of us, me and you, like we was married. The wops say we gotta get outta town? I got relatives in Chicago. There's no reason I couldn't go out there. Alone."

"Whatta ya sayin?"

"I'm sayin' this bullshit about you're the boss has gotta go. If I'm gonna take any chances for you, I want a fair split. Like fifty-fifty, for instance. See, what I got in mind could pull us outta this hole. The only thing is that it's a long shot. A *real* long shot. I ain't playin' those kinda cards unless I'm a full partner."

"Can I hear what you got in mind before I make a decision? If it ain't too much trouble?"

"Actually, I gotta start with a question."

"That figures."

"How long do we have?"

"Before what?"

"Before we lose the dope in the projects."

"We got until we run outta product. Two days, maybe three."

"Awright, here's step number one. I want ya to look for Steppy Accacio. If ya can't find him, then find Joe Faci. Whichever one, I want ya to get down on ya knees and kiss his ass until ya nose is so brown people take ya for Jackie Robinson. Then I want ya to start beggin' for time. Tell him he don't have to panic. Tell him the O'Neills are dead and there ain't no other witnesses. Tell him we already bought our tickets to L.A. and we're ready to leave any time things get too hot. Tell him he's payin' off a lieutenant in the precinct, so he'll get plenty of warning before the shit hits the fan. Tell him anything, but get us a couple of weeks."

"A couple of weeks to do what?"

"A couple of weeks to find another connection. See, the way I figure it, Accacio took our territory from somebody else. That's how come we had to do the job on Rocco Insalaco. Whoever controlled the projects before we showed up can't be too happy. Maybe he's got a lotta product and no way to dump it. Maybe we could explain that his best move is to sell his product to *us*. Maybe he's got enough juice to keep Accacio off our backs."

"That's a lotta 'maybes.' "

"That's where the two weeks comes in. It looks like things are goin' bad, we could always run. If it looks like things are cool with the cops, we could stay with Accacio. If we find ourselves a connection with some muscle, we could become independent. There's all kinds of possibilities, but none of 'em work out unless we can buy us some time."

"Ya know, it's funny, Iz. I mean what ya talkin' about. Because I been doin' some checkin' on my own. Accacio ain't such a big shot. In fact, except for the olive oil and the spaghetti, there ain't too much difference between him and us. Wanna hear somethin' funny? Steppy Accacio ain't even a Sicilian. It might be the people over him wouldn't see too much difference between a mountain guinea and a Jew."

Steppy Accacio sipped at his espresso and nodded thoughtfully. He was practicing what he called "my great stone face" and doing a splendid job of it. His goal was to scare Jake Leibowitz without actually making any threats. Like a judge making a defendant piss his pants just by clearing his throat.

"It's good to see you again, Jake," Joe Faci said. "Have ya been thinkin' about what I mentioned?"

"I already bought train tickets," Jake responded, holding them out. "Only I didn't put no date on 'em. That's what I come to talk about. See, I don't have no objection to leavin' New York if that's what I gotta do. The whole thing's my fault anyway. If I hadn't of taken that asshole over to the pimp's, none of this woulda happened. But what I'm thinkin' is, maybe we're jumpin' the gun a little bit. I mean how's it gonna come back on us? There ain't no witnesses left. And even if the cops do have somethin' goin' down, ya connections'll let ya know in plenty of time."

"Los Angeles ain't a death sentence," Joe Faci interrupted. "It's like a precaution. Go out there for a few months. Catch yaself a nice tan. If everything's copacetic, you could come back and do what ya gotta do."

"I hear what ya sayin', Joe. And I'm only askin' ya to think about it before ya make a final decision. Ya know I done a lotta time and I ain't no spring chicken. Now that I finally got a piece of the action, it's a bitch for me to walk away unless I know I gotta. I mean you guys've been great to me and Izzy. Ya gave us a chance. Ya . . . ."

"Awright, Jake, we catch ya drift." Joe Faci spoke without looking at his boss. "But we think it'd be better if ya took a little vacation. There's a lotta cops in New York. Just because we know a couple who do business don't guarantee our safety. It don't even guarantee the cops doin' the business won't come around with handcuffs and a warrant. Ya can't trust the cops. They only think about themselves."

"How 'bout this, Joe? It's gonna take me a couple of days to get rid of the dope I got on hand. Maybe ya could just *think* about it? Make a final decision when the dope's gone."

"We already thought . . ."

"Hold up a second, Joe." Steppy Accacio finally spoke. "The truth is that I feel bad for ya, Jake. Except for that one mistake, ya been doin' a great job for us. SpeediFreight? The projects? Everything goes like clockwork. So what I'm sayin' is, it ain't right that you should have to run all the way to a place like Los Angeles. A place that stole the Brooklyn Dodgers. Also, it could be that I'm actin' too much like a little old lady. People think ya panickin', they get ideas. Ain't that right, Joe?"

"They don't reward ya for lookin' weak," Joe Faci responded.

"That's right." Steppy Accacio leaned over to fill Jake's cup. "What I think we oughta do here is play it from day to day. I'm impressed that ya bought them tickets and I believe ya when ya say ya ready to use 'em. What is it from the Lower East Side to Penn Station? Ten minutes by cab? All I'm askin' from you is that ya should stay in touch."

"No problem, Steppy. I ain't the wanderin' type."

"Also, I'm gonna pull Sandy outta the projects. My sister's goin' crazy about the kid bein' out on the street. She thinks he oughta be an executive. That ain't a problem, is it?"

"Hey, family's family, right? I got a *mother* drives me crazy."

"So it's settled. We take it as it comes."

Jake stood up and offered his hand. "All I could say is thanks for givin' me another chance. Ya won't be sorry."

Joe Faci waited until the door closed behind Jake Leibowitz's back, then turned to his boss. "Whatta ya wanna do, Steppy?"

"What I wanna do, Joe, is kill 'em both. Soon."

Sal Patero, more than annoyed to be summoned out to Bayside on a Sunday night, watched Pat Cohan's tirade without changing expression. If the situation wasn't so potentially devastating, he would, he decided, personally nominate Stanley Moodrow for Cop of the Year.

"My family," Pat Cohan nearly shouted. "He attacked my family. It's getting to the point where nothing's sacred. *Nothing.*"

"You already said that. Ten fucking times. Enough already."

"And I suppose you think attacking a man through his innocent family is just ordinary business?"

"For Christ's sake, Pat, Kate's his fiancée. There's no way you were gonna get through this thing without her finding out. Be realistic."

"That's easy for you to say. Your family isn't involved."

Patero chose to ignore the comment. What he was trying to do was bring a little sanity into the conversation. He'd made a decision and he wanted to put it on the table and go home.

"The way I look at this, Pat, what we should've done was let Samuelson and Maguire do their jobs. Which is what I told ya from the beginning. If we'd kept our hands off, most likely Don Steppy would've taken care of it by himself."

"It's easy to say that now, Sal. But how were we supposed to know that Luis Melenguez was Stanley's neighbor? Do *you* have spics for neighbors?"

"Look, it doesn't really matter what you say. The thing of it is that I've had enough. I'm jumpin' ship. You wanna get Stanley, you gotta do it yourself."

"You're as dirty as I am. Dirtier, from a legal point of view."

"You can't threaten me, Pat. Ya can't threaten me because I don't care. But I got a real good piece of advice for you. This homicide isn't in the precinct anymore. You had it sent out to Organized Crime. Well, if you got friends on Organized Crime, grab that phone and tell 'em to find the man who killed Luis Melenguez. Find him before Stanley does."

"And why should I take advice from you, a man who's taken bribes from dozens of assorted bookmakers and pimps?"

"Wanna hear something funny, Pat? I think that without knowin' what I was doin', I somehow walked into a loony bin on December twenty-sixth. Just an accident, right? Could've happened to anybody. Meanwhile, I been wanderin' through the place ever since. Covering up a homicide? You *gotta* be crazy. Which is what I was and what I'm not gonna be anymore. Take my advice, Pat. Find the killer yourself and lock him up in a cage. That's your only hope."

"Well, boyo, thanks for the advice. Now, being as you're no longer involved, I can't see as I have any more need of your company this evening. *Adios*, as they say in the projects."

Pat Cohan, calm for the first time in many hours, waited for the front door of his Bayside home to close, then picked up the phone and quickly dialed out. He listened for a moment, the fingers of his free hand absently running through his silky white hair, then said, "Get me Joe Faci. Tell him, Patrick's on the phone."

Nineteen

JANUARY 20

"STANLEY, I'M heating up my world-famous cheese blintzes. You're maybe interested in one or two?" Greta Bloom set a mug of coffee in front of her guest, then turned back to the stove.

"I'd be *more* interested in ten or twelve," Moodrow said, pouring cream into his mug. "How come you're not making me use that white powder in my coffee?"

Greta shook her head. "From kosher you'll never learn. I'm making blintzes. That's dairy. With dairy you can have cream. So, how many blintzes should I put up?"

"A dozen'll do."

"Just like your father. Max wasn't as big as you, but no one could fill *him* up, either." She turned back to the stove, then began to giggle. "I just remembered a story about your mother and father. You wanna hear?"

"As long as you don't forget the food."

Greta pushed a cookie sheet dotted with cheese blintzes into the oven and closed the door. "Your mother was a very pretty girl. Even with a ring on her finger, men didn't leave her alone. As it happened, we were working in a loft on Grand Street, sewing lace onto satin wedding gowns. This was considered skilled work by the bosses and the pay was good for that time. Anyway, there was a foreman in the loft named Kawitzski. A *brute*, Stanley, and always making remarks to the girls about coming into the storeroom. He went crazy for your mother. Every *minute* he was standing by her machine."

"Wait a second. My mother was married at this time? Or single?"

"Married. And practically a newlywed. You can believe me when I say Nancy Moodrow had no use for Kawitzski. But what could she do except laugh it off? It was common for men in the garment business to makes passes at the girls. Bosses? Foremen? They strutted like Cossacks in a peasant's cottage. A few of the girls went along, too. It means a lot to get the better jobs when you're doing piecework. But that's neither here nor there. One day this Kawitzski touched your mother in a way he shouldn't have. It was not a thing you could throw off with a laugh. When your mother left work, she was so mad that she told your father what happened the minute he got home."

"Pop always had a temper. What'd he do, kill the guy?"

"Killing is what he *wanted* to do, but like I already said, this Kawitzski was a brute. He saw your father coming and hid behind a door. When your father walked past, Kawitzki jumped out and hit him a *tremendous* punch. Down goes your father and Kawitzki starts to jump on top, but Nancy has a little trick of her own. Five rolls of pennies in a tiny purse. She hit Kawitzki such a blow I don't think he woke up to this *day*. Then we all ran out before the cops came. Your father was so mad he didn't talk to your mother for a week. Everybody was laughing at him for hiding behind a woman's skirts."

Moodrow blew on the steaming coffee, then sipped carefully. "I never got to know my father. He was always out working and he died before I was old enough to really talk to him. It was different with my mother. Especially after my father passed. I was serious about my boxing at that time, so I didn't go out much. Between school and training, I had no time for a social life." He hesitated for a moment, took the mug in his hands, then set it down. "I think what I'm trying to say is that I miss her. Things fall away and you can't get them back. It makes you crazy if you think about it too much."

"I miss her, too, Stanley." Greta took the blintzes out of the oven and set them on top of the stove. "To tell you the truth, the way I feel this morning, pretty soon I'll miss myself." She crossed to the refrigerator, took out a bowl of sour cream and put it on the table. "*Nu*, so tell me. With the case, what's happening?"

"I kind of messed it up." Moodrow dug out the sketch of Santo Silesi and laid it on the table. "This guy's first name is Santo. He's a small-time heroin dealer. The men who killed Luis Melenguez work for Santo's boss. What I'm trying to do is locate Santo so I can ask him a few questions, but I think I'm going about it the wrong way."

"You're going about it how?"

"The story I got from O'Neill . . ."

"O'Neill?"

"O'Neill ran the house of prostitution where Luis was murdered. The killers were there to teach O'Neill a lesson and Luis Melenguez walked into the middle of it. O'Neill gave me a statement, but you can forget about him testifying in court. He's running for his life."

"You're a cop, Stanley. You could protect him."

"I could if there weren't other cops protecting his killers. You think those blintzes are ready?"

Greta forked several blintzes onto a plate and passed them over. "Stanley, would the cops doing this protecting be somehow related to your father-in-law?"

"I'm not married, Greta. I'm engaged."

"Don't be technical. Answer the question, please, or tell me I should mind my own business."

"*Yes*, my father-in-law *is* protecting the killers. And you *should* mind your own business." Moodrow cut a blintz in two, covered the half on his fork with sour cream and popped it into his mouth. "I spent most of yesterday knocking on doors in the projects where I think Santo works. I didn't run into anyone I know and I didn't get anywhere, either. I'm gonna go about it a little different today. I'm gonna visit some of the guys I grew up with and some of the guys I met when I was boxing. Even if nobody recognizes the picture, I'll still be ahead of the game, because at least I can be sure I'm not being lied to."

"To me it sounds good." Greta said, shoveling blintzes onto Stanley Moodrow's plate. "And I hope things work out with Kate. It's not your fault her father's a crook."

The phone rang before Moodrow closed the door behind him. What he wanted to do was let it ring, to grab his gun, badge and coat, then get on the street where he could work. Unfortunately, the caller, almost as if he could read Moodrow's mind, refused to hang up.

"Yeah?"

"Stanley, it's Allen Epstein. I been phoning every ten minutes. Where you been?"

"I been having breakfast with my girlfriend."

"Is Kate there?"

"Just kiddin', Sarge. What's up?"

"The pimp and his wife are dead. The cops in the Tenth found them last night. The way I hear it, the apartment was a slaughterhouse. There was blood in every room, even the toilet."

"Sounds like somebody put up a fight."

"Yeah, but not the pimp. He was sitting on the couch when the killer sliced his throat. It must have been his old lady. *She* was stabbed twenty-seven times."

"Any chance the killer was injured? Any chance some of that blood was his?"

"It's too early to know. With that many samples, the lab'll need at least three days to separate them out. Anyway, I got something better than blood. There was a witness."

"You're bullshitting."

"Oh, so I got your attention, eh?"

"Don't play with me, Sarge."

"Awright, I don't have a name or an apartment number. I don't even know if it was a man or a woman. What I do know is the witness lives in the building. Apparently, the killers made a lotta noise and the witness opened the door as they were leaving."

"Ya know somethin', Sarge," Moodrow said after a moment, "this doesn't have to work in our favor. If Patero and Cohan find out there's a witness, they're gonna pass the information on to Accacio. Any idea who caught the squeal?"

"Not yet, but soon."

"So we don't know if the witness is being protected or not."

"Protection can work both ways, too. Whatta you lookin' for, a guarantee?"

"No guarantee, Sarge. But I'm not gonna sit on my ass, either. I'm heading out to work."

"Can't wait to get busy, right?"

"Right."

"It's kinda funny you haven't asked me about getting a look at the mug shots."

Moodrow hesitated for a moment, then laughed. "You should've been a cop, Sarge. You got natural suspicion."

"Forget the bullshit, Stanley. What's goin' on?"

"I already have what I need. I went to an artist I know and had him make a sketch. It's not a photo, but it'll do for a start."

"I take it you don't trust me, Stanley. Being as you didn't mention this before."

Moodrow took his time answering. When he finally spoke, his voice was cold. "Up until right now, I didn't trust anybody. Not you. Not *anybody*. But if you were in bed with Patero and Cohan, you never would've told me about this witness. Or about the O'Neills, either. I'm sorry if I hurt your feelings, but I know what I have to do and I'm gonna do it the way I see it."

It was Epstein's turn to think it over. He waited a long time, until Moodrow was ready to hang up, before he finally spoke. "I guess I can't blame you. The way you went from walking a beat to the bullshit you're in now would shake anybody up. Most likely it would've worked out better if you'd spent the first five years of your career learning the politics of the job instead of waltzing around a boxing ring. But what's done is done. You still wanna get inside the precinct?"

"It depends on whether I have any luck on the street. What I'd like to do, assuming I can't find Santo by myself, is give *you* the sketch and let *you* go through the books. It can't hurt if Patero and Cohan think I'm sitting on my hands. If they think I'm scared shitless."

"All right, Stanley. But one piece of advice before you hit the bricks. You're gonna need friends if you expect to get through this in one piece. And I'm in a much better position to know who to trust. I've been living with the bullshit for a long time. If I tell you somebody's okay, they're okay."

"Yeah? You sayin' you wanna come out in the open on this? You wanna put your name right next to mine on Inspector Pat Cohan's shit list?"

"If you're asking me to step into your shoes, the answer is 'go fuck yourself.' What you have to realize is that you *can't* do it yourself. Once you get that tiny little thought firmly planted in your tiny little brain, you'll stop taking so many punches."

Moodrow, stepping out onto the street, looked up at an overcast sky and shook his head. After weeks of freezing days and below-freezing nights, it was finally warming up. That was the good news. The bad news was that it'd be raining by noon. And it'd probably keep raining until strong Canadian winds pushed the soup back toward Virginia where it belonged.

It was eight o'clock in the morning and Moodrow was headed for Berrigan's, an amateur boxing gym on Allen Street that had to work around school schedules in order to train its aspiring champions. The gym was run by Father Samuel Berrigan, a no-nonsense Catholic priest who used early-morning workouts as a way to separate the serious from the merely foolish. He lectured his boys constantly, insisting that the most important factor in a fighter's career was simple desire. Stanley Moodrow had been his favorite example.

"He's slow. He's ugly. He fights with his face. Stanley has no right to win, but he wins anyway. That's because he *wants* to win. He *desires* victory."

By the time Moodrow ran into a fighter with equal desire and far more talent, he'd moved through several trainers, leaving Father Sam far behind.

The gym was open and functioning when Moodrow walked through the door. There were fighters on both speed bags, sharp middleweights competing with each other to make the bag dance. Moodrow watched them for a minute, then drifted over to a boxing ring in the center of the gym. The two kids sparring inside couldn't have weighed more than a hundred and ten pounds, but they were giving it all they had. The shorter of the two, stocky and short-armed, was bobbing and weaving frantically. The other kid was firing one jab after another, following each jab with a crisp left hook or a straight right hand. The only problem was that the short kid didn't know how to close the space between himself and his opponent, while the taller kid didn't have the timing to hit a moving target.

"I do believe those boys're doin' the lindy hop. There's no way you could call it *boxing*." Father Sam was short and bow-legged. He'd been a fighter before he'd turned to the priesthood and his rapport with the tough, street-wise boys of the Lower East Side was legendary. His gym was open to everyone and many a Jewish father had dragged his troubled son through Father Sam's door.

"I can remember when you trained 'em to be a lot meaner," Moodrow said, turning away from the ring.

"You can't teach mean, Stanley. Can't teach brave, either. I saw your last fight."

"Against the fireman?"

"Yeah. Pure desire. It made me proud. What're you doin' here. You slummin'?"

"I'm lookin' for somebody."

"One of my boys?"

"No." Moodrow fished Santo's sketch out of his jacket pocket and passed it to the priest. "This guy's dealing dope somewhere in the neighborhood, probably out of the projects by Avenue D."

"What'd he do, kill somebody?"

"Dope dealing's not enough?"

"It's enough, Stanley. It's enough to mess up more than one of my boys. Only I didn't think you cops *gave* a damn. Being as they're dealin' it right out in the open."

"Look, Father, I can't speak for the entire Department. No more than you can speak for Cus D'Amato." Cus D'Amato, Floyd Patterson's manager, refused to let the champion fight serious contenders, preferring rank amateurs and club fighters. The sportswriters never lost an opportunity to rake him over the coals. "But you've known me for a long time, so you can believe me when I tell you that the people I'm after need to be taken off the street. Permanently."

The priest took Moodrow's arm and pulled him to one side of the gym. "Now, Stanley, I know you're talkin' justice here, but it seems more like a *favor* to me. Of course, people in the community *should* be doin' favors for each other. It's the neighborly thing, right? Now, I've got this Jewish boy. Joseph is his name. Joseph Green. The boy got himself in a little trouble. Drinkin' is what it was. He got so drunk, he smacked a cop."

"The cop was in uniform?"

" 'Fraid so." The priest shrugged. "Joey's not a bad kid. Stupid, yes, but not really bad."

"Is he charged with assaulting a police officer?"

"Yeah, that's it. They're gonna give the boy hard time if he goes to court and loses. The boy doesn't deserve hard time just for smackin' somebody. I don't care if it was a cop. People down here smack each other all the time."

"Was the cop hurt bad?"

"Now, that's the thing. Joey knocked the cop down and he hit his head on the sidewalk. I understand there were some stitches involved."

"What's the kid's name again?"

"Joe Green."

"Okay, Father. I'll ask around, find out what's happening. Maybe I know the cop."

"Go see the boy, Stanley. Talk to him. He's not a bad kid. Just stupid, like I said."

"I'll do what I can, but don't expect miracles. If he's got a record, he's goin' away." Moodrow held up Santo Silesi's picture. "You know this guy or not?"

"Well," the priest scratched his head, then smiled, "I don't believe he shows up for the six-thirty Mass at St. Ann's."

"This is serious, Father. If you don't wanna bother, don't waste my time."

"Patience, Stanley. Isn't that what I taught you? Slow fighters have to be patient. Now, it happens there's a boy changing up in the locker room named Henry Sanchez. He lives in those projects. If you think you can refrain from callin' him 'Chico,' we could ask him to look at your picture."

"I'll do my best."

They walked through the gym, Father Sam leading the way, to a small locker room at the far end of the building. Henry Sanchez was pulling on his shoes when they entered the room. He looked up, glanced at Moodrow, then turned to his trainer.

"Wha's up, Father."

"Give me the picture," the priest said, pulling it out of Moodrow's hand. "You recognize this man, Henry?"

Sanchez took his time studying the sketch, then handed it back to his trainer. "Why you wanna know?"

"It has nothing to do with me," Father Sam said. "This here's Stanley Moodrow. He used to fight for me. Now, he's a police officer. Stanley's looking for the man in that picture. Says that man's dealing dope in the projects."

"Tha's funny," Sanchez said, staring straight up at Moodrow, "I been thinkin' the cops don' arres' no dealers. The headknockers only arres' the junkies."

"Now, that's your *whole* problem, Sanchez. *That's* why you can't learn to hook off the jab. You think you know all there is to know. *I'm* tellin' you that Stanley's on the up and up."

"I still wanna know is he gon' to arres' this man?"

"Look, Henry," Moodrow interrupted, "There was a killing on Pitt Street the day after Christmas. The victim's name was Luis Melenguez. The man in the sketch, his first name is Santo, knows who the killers are. If I find Santo, I'll find the killers. Simple as that."

Sanchez took a minute to think it over. "Tha's the name," he finally said. "Santo. Every day he's bringin' dope to the projects. I seen him down by tha' little park on Houston Street. Near the river."

"Any special time?"

"Mos'ly I seen him when I'm comin' back from school. But, like, he ain' punchin' no clock."

"He come alone?"

"*Si.* Only I ain' watchin' thees *maricon* every minute."

"All right, thanks Henry. I appreciate the information."

Moodrow headed for the door, Father Sam trailing behind. "Slow down, Stanley," the priest demanded. "You were never in a hurry when you were trainin' for *me*."

"Sorry. I can't think about anything but what I have to do."

"You were like that as a fighter, too. That's why you won. Lord knows, you didn't have any talent."

Moodrow turned to face the smaller man. "Is there a point here, Father?"

"Now, don't go workin' yourself up. Just think about how easy it was for you to waltz in here and find out what you needed to know. This gym could be a real nice connection for a cop like yourself. A cop with *desire*."

"Enough with the lecture. Whatta you want?"

The priest managed a beatific grin. "What I'm gettin' at is how I could use some help. Somebody with desire to show these boys the fundamentals. Every time I turn around, they're out there smokin' marijuana cigarettes. Or some gangster is tryin' to make 'em turn pro before their ready. Could be if you start comin' down regular, you'd be doin' yourself a favor."

Twenty

IT *SOUNDS* great, Izzy Stein thought. The dope business *seems* like the greatest thing since chopped liver. But what it really is, is standing out in the rain. It's looking over your shoulder for the narcs and the thieves. It's sick, sniveling junkies begging for an extra bag. Or for credit. Or for *anything* to relieve the endless misery of their endlessly miserable fucking lives.

"Oh, man, you gotta take this watch. It's a gold Lady Hamilton, man. With *diamonds*. It's gotta be worth ten bags. I got it *uptown*."

"It ain't worth shit to me, pal. My girlfriend's already got a watch."

"Please, man. I'm *sick*."

"Whatta ya want me to do about it? Do I look like a fuckin' doctor? Go out an sell the watch to the guy you stole it from. Me, I'm only interested in cash."

"But *everybody* takes merchandise. *Everybody*."

"Yeah? Well, maybe you should go find *everybody*."

"I would, man. I ain't bullshittin'. But like it's *late* and I don't know if anybody else's around. If you could do me this favor—just this one time—I'll never bring you nothin' but cash."

And that was another thing. *That* was the worst thing. You couldn't discourage a sick junkie. No matter what. You could punch 'em, kick 'em, stab 'em. It didn't matter. They popped up like balloons, wiped the snot off their lips and continued to beg. *Please, please, please. Gimme, gimme, gimme.* It was disgusting.

"Lemme see the fuckin' thing." It was a Lady Hamilton, all right. But that could mean *anything*. The watch might be gold or it might have been dipped in yellow paint. The little stones on the face might be diamonds or they might be paste. How was *he* supposed to know?

What Izzy *did* know was that he was standing in the rain, in the projects, with ten junkies waiting their turn, and he wasn't going to get warm and dry until he took care of everybody. On the other hand, if he accepted the watch and it turned out to be a piece of shit, Jake would most likely go through the roof. Well, maybe Jake could give it to his mother.

"Three bags. Take it or leave it."

"Oh, man, three bags won't even get me straight. Like, I gotta go through the whole *night*. Plus I got a job lined up. I got a fucking *warehouse*. In Greenpoint. Just gimme ten bags and I'll make it up to ya tomorrow mornin'. I swear it on my mother."

"You could swear it on ya fuckin' needle tracks and it still wouldn't mean shit to *me*. Take the three bags or go find somebody else. And don't interrupt me, 'cause I'm runnin' outta patience."

"Five, please. Five bags. The watch's worth at least a hundred bucks. Five bags is only twenty-five dollars. Ya gotta help me out here."

What Izzy was tempted to do was pull his .38 and relieve this miserable junkie of his miserable sickness forever. But what he did was count out the five bags, take the watch and motion the next junkie forward, the one pulling a wire cart stuffed with rags.

"I got a radio," the junkie said as he approached Jake. "A fucking *Motorola*, man. Like it's worth a hundred bucks. At least."

It took Izzy an hour to finish up. An hour standing in the rain with the prospect of another session with a dozen sick junkies still ahead of him. Well, at least Houston Street was the last stop. Then he could walk back to the Paradise and catch a hot bath and a couple of shots of bourbon. Maybe he could even figure a way out of this bullshit. Maybe he could talk Jake into taking a turn standing in the projects. Being as they were fifty-fifty partners.

Izzy, despite his years on the street and his prison experience, was so wrapped up in his own misfortunes that he failed to notice the elderly man in the black trenchcoat until the man spoke. By then, it was too late to run.

"Police. Stop right there. You're under arrest."

Izzy's mouth said, "What?" But the gun in the cop's hand left no doubt as to his intentions.

"Get up against the car. Spread your legs."

The hands crawling over Izzy's body were experienced. Experienced and confident. They relieved him of his .38 and his dope, then slapped on the cuffs. All in less than thirty seconds.

"I want a lawyer," Izzy said. "I wanna make a phone call."

"Don't worry, boyo," Pat Cohan replied. "You're going to get everything you deserve. Now, why don't you hop in the back seat like a good little criminal? Then we can drive on down to the stationhouse and give you that phone call."

There was nothing to be done about it. At least, not right away. The cop had searched him without a warrant and maybe a good lawyer would find a way to prove it to a judge. But that was in the future. The first step was to establish himself in the Tombs. Which was where they'd eventually take him. The second step was to find a lawyer. The third step was to make bail. The fourth step was to find a way to pay the . . .

The Ford screeched to a halt on 11th Street, between Avenues A & B. Izzy looked up, expecting to see the 7th Precinct, but they were parked next to an alley.

"Well, boyo, bein' as I've an appointment elsewhere, I think I'll be off. But have no fear, the officer in front will see you safely to your destination."

Only "the officer in front" wasn't an officer. The "officer in front" was Santo Silesi. And he was holding a small automatic. And he was smiling.

The door opened, then closed, then opened again before Izzy could pull his thoughts together.

"Hi, Izzy," Joe Faci said, squeezing into the back seat.

"What's the game?" Izzy finally said.

"No game. Just that I gotta thank you for giving my friend this opportunity to make his bones. I'm sure Santo, when he remembers his manners, will thank you, too."

Izzy took a moment to think it over, then smiled and spit directly into Joe Faci's face. Despite the handcuffs. Despite Santo Silesi's automatic which began to bark, to spit fire, to project small chunks of lead into Izzy's chest.

"Jesus, Santo, what you done is stupid," Joe Faci said. "This is no place to be shootin' nobody."

Izzy heard that, though he missed Santo's reply. He couldn't move and, for a few seconds, he couldn't remember why. It was very strange. His eyes were closed and somebody was kicking him. They were forcing him onto the floor of the car, covering him with an overcoat. He felt shoes on his back, then remembered what had happened. Oh shit, he thought, I've been shot. Oh shit, I'm bleeding. Oh shit, I'm dead.

What saved Moodrow's butt, in the end, was simple habit, a series of reflexes built up over years of practice. But what got him into trouble was simple inexperience. Moodrow spent eight hours sitting in his car on the south side of Houston Street. It was his first stakeout and, all things being equal, he would have had a veteran detective sitting next to him. He would have had a guide to warn him against falling into a mental state that was closer to sleepwalking than alert and ready.

Eight hours in the rain, Moodrow supposed, thinking about it later, is enough to blur anyone's concentration. Eight hours peering through the drops at a tiny park jammed between twelve-story brick buildings. What it did was get your mind to drifting, to thinking about what you'd spent the last couple of days trying *not* to think about. Which was Kate Cohan.

There was a basic unfairness in his relationship with Kate that went beyond the sins of her father. The simple fact was that if he wanted to marry her, to spend his life in her company, he was going to have to leave his world and enter hers. The reverse, he'd come to think, could never happen. In fact, whenever he tried to imagine Kate in her fox coat strolling down Avenue C, he was tempted to laugh out loud.

And the change would involve much more than packing a suitcase and moving the twenty miles from the Lower East Side to suburban Bayside. He'd have to leave his attitudes behind, have to build up an entirely different way of addressing the world. And their children would never understand. No more than Kate understood. Bayside, as far as Moodrow could make out, didn't have a history at all. It was a place to go after you made it. After you escaped.

What it is, Moodrow thought, is that the suburbs mean the same thing to the second generation that the Statue of Liberty meant to the first. And maybe that's what Kate Cohan means to *me*. Maybe all I want to do is get away from the junkies and the projects and the rotting tenements. Maybe I'm watching all the kids I grew up with stuff their crap into moving vans and I think I'm being left behind.

He closed his eyes for a moment, concentrating until Kate's image, nearly solid, floated behind his eyes. For some reason, she was smiling that same quick smile that flashed across her face whenever he said something wicked. The spray of freckles running across the bridge of her nose was especially vivid, a burnt-orange contrast to her innocent blue eyes.

Innocence. That was another thing. The women who'd come in and out of his life before he'd met Kate had been any number of things, but never innocent. They'd all seen too much, grown up too fast. Some would stand beside you in a bar fight. Others would sell you out in a hot flash. Yet, for all their variety, they never represented anything more than aspects of a world he already knew. A world that, waiting in the rain, wishing he smoked cigarettes so he'd have some way of passing the time, didn't seem all that bad to him. There was something about sitting in Greta's apartment and hearing the living history of the neighborhood (*his* neighborhood) that yanked at him like a magnet grabbing a paperclip.

He spent a moment trying to put a name to that attraction. Pride? No, it wasn't pride. He was aware of the flaws, of the poverty and the violence, the alkies sleeping in doorways on the Bowery, the junkies looking for something to steal, the prostitutes (most often junkies themselves) parading up and down 3rd Avenue. Maybe there wasn't a name for what he was feeling. Maybe he was just looking for something to hang onto. Maybe, maybe, maybe.

It was nearly eight o'clock when he gave it up. The junkies had come and gone, apparently unsatisfied. Which, Moodrow supposed, was better than having a dealer other than Santo show up to service them. Tomorrow was another, hopefully dry, day.

There was no place to park in front of his building, a fact which came as no great surprise to Stanley Moodrow. The space he eventually found, nearly three blocks away, was par for the course. He pulled the key, turned up the collar of his overcoat and stepped out of the Ford. The streets were deserted and he let his thoughts drift from Santo to Kate to a mystery witness somewhere up in Hell's Kitchen. Epstein had urged him to be patient. Father Sam, too. Still, he'd begun the day with every expectation of finding the killers of Luis Melenguez.

What I am, he thought, is a rookie. An amateur. What I should be . . .

He didn't notice the man behind him until the bat was actually in motion. Even then, he had no more than a split second to react. Not enough time to think, much less plan a response. He did what any experienced fighter would do, what every trainer from Sam Berrigan to Allen Epstein had taught him to do—he pulled his shoulder up to protect the side of his face. The bat struck the point of his shoulder, then clipped the top of his head.

Damn, he thought, I'm bleeding. I don't want to bleed anymore. I'm through with that.

He was facing his attacker, now, though he couldn't remember turning around. He watched the bat drift away, then begin its arc. Once again, he reacted instinctively. Instead of pulling his head away, he stepped forward and the bat curled over his shoulder, thumping harmlessly against his back. Moodrow grabbed his assailant's throat with one hand, then began to drive his fist into the man's face. He didn't stop until bat and man were lying motionless on the sidewalk.

The first thing Moodrow thought was that the man was dead and he, Moodrow, was going to spend all night in the precinct filing reports and being interviewed. Dropping to one knee, he turned the man over and began to search for a pulse. He was still searching when the man began to moan and tried to sit up.

"Stay on the ground," Moodrow growled. "Don't move your hands. I'm gonna frisk you and if your hands move while I'm doin' it, I'm gonna slow 'em down by smashing your face into the sidewalk."

The search turned up nothing, neither weapon nor identification. Moodrow put his hand up to the right side of his scalp. The blood was still flowing, a thin trickle that mixed easily with the rain soaking his shirt collar.

"You better have a good story," Moodrow said. He rolled the man onto his stomach and cuffed him tightly. Very tightly.

"You're gonna cut off my circulation. I'll lose my hands."

"Guess that means you won't be swinging any more baseball bats. You got a name?"

Nothing. Moodrow's attacker spit up a wad of blood-soaked phlegm, then turned his eyes to the ground.

"C'mon, pal, you ain't gettin' out of this without some answers. Gimme a name. Yours or somebody else's."

"Joe Jones," the man said without looking up.

Moodrow spun Joe Jones around and drove his right fist in the left side of Joe Jones's lower back. He was rewarded with a scream.

"Ever piss blood, Joe? Lemme tell ya, the first time it happens, it really shakes you up. And it can do a lot of long-term damage." Moodrow smashed his fist into Joe Jones's ribs. "When you crack a rib, on the other hand, all the damage is done on impact. If, God forbid, the rib breaks up, you gotta worry about splinters cutting into the lung. *That* can make the lung collapse, which, believe me, leads to all kinds of complications. Are you listening?"

Moodrow's breathless soliliquy was interrupted by the sound of a car horn. He turned, reaching for his gun with one hand while he held onto Mister Jones with the other.

"Take it easy, Stanley. It's me, Samuelson. What's going on here?"

It took Moodrow a moment to realize that "Samuelson" was Detective Paul Samuelson. He was accompanied by a second detective, a man unknown to Moodrow.

"What're you doing here?"

"We're working, whatta ya think? Comin' back from a homicide on 14th Street. Figured to make a stop on First Avenue for coffee when we heard this guy scream. What's goin' on here? You're bleedin'."

"Well, that's what happens when you get hit on the head with a Louisville

Slugger. You bleed." He put his hand up to his scalp. The bleeding had slowed considerably. Slowed, but not stopped.

"You're gonna have to get that sewn up. Why don't you give me the basics? I'll take the bastard over to the house and book him. Tomorrow morning, you can drop by the Seventh and do the paperwork."

"The basics are this asshole attacked me from behind and I punched his face in. Meanwhile, he's not carrying i.d. What I'd like you to do is take a hike while I ask him a few questions about his secret identity."

"I'm afraid we can't do that." Samuelson's companion stepped forward. "We can't allow you to abuse a prisoner."

"Stanley," Samuelson said, "this is Detective Lieutenant Rosten."

Moodrow managed a smile. "You slumming, Lieutenant?"

"Patero's transferring out to Forensics at the end of the month. What I'm doing is getting my feet wet."

"You'll get your head wet, too, standing out in the rain."

"It doesn't bother me. In fact, it reminds me of the old days. When I used to walk a beat. Samuelson's right, by the way. You'd do yourself a favor by getting that wound sewn up. We can handle the details."

Moodrow knew he could insist on coming into the precinct to make sure the details jibed with his own version of what happened, but he didn't see what good it would do him. The idea that Samuelson, accompanied by Sal Patero's replacement, just happened to be driving down the street was too stupid to contemplate. Most likely, his assailant (along with Detective Lieutenant Rosten) had been sent by Pat Cohan. Most likely, his assailant was a cop. Most likely, if he went down to the 7th Precinct, he was the one who'd be arrested. For the first time, Moodrow had the sense that he'd bitten off more than he could chew.

"I think you're right about the cut," he said. "It's still bleeding. Why don't we get in a car and write up a preliminary report. You got complaint forms in there, right?"

"Yeah, sure." There wasn't anything else Samuelson could say. Every detective carried a variety of forms. It went with the territory.

"Great, because the thing of it is, I want a copy. A signed copy. Everything I say, plus everything *you* saw. And don't forget to put the bat in there. I haven't touched it, so any fingerprints have to belong to this slimeball. The blood, on the other hand, which you're gonna have tested, belongs to me alone."

"Is that necessary?" Rosten asked. "It sounds like you don't trust us."

"Well, let me put it this way. If you refuse, I'm taking this asshole to the Thirteenth Precinct and book him there. It's closer than the Seventh and being as I'm not in the greatest shape, it doesn't make a lotta sense for me to walk all the way down to Clinton Street. You try to stop me and I'll put your face through the windshield."

"You're crazy."

"Thank you." Crazy was the ultimate street compliment.

"I won't forget this."
"That's just what I was hoping. That you won't forget *anything*."

Jake Leibowitz was just a little pissed off. Maybe it wasn't necessary and maybe they hadn't talked about it, but the least Izzy could have done was call to wish him luck. After all, their future hinged on what he, Jake, was going to do tonight. It hadn't taken long to find out who Steppy Accacio's rival was. The gangster (a wop, naturally) who'd controlled the dope in the projects before Accacio took over was named Dominick Favara. In a way, he and Steppy could have been brothers. Despite the fact that Favara was as dark as Accacio was fair. They were both young and ambitious, both trying to work their way up, both trying to impress the mobsters who ran New York City.

Well, Izzy or no Izzy, Jake was determined to pull it off, to make the switch from Accacio to Favara before Accacio knew what was happening. He was wearing his absolute best, his black cashmere coat over his double-breasted gray suit. Even his mustache was perfect. He'd allowed Mama Leibowitz to trim it, despite the anxiety he felt whenever she had a sharp object in her hands.

"All right, Jake," he said aloud, "this is it. Ya fuck this one up, ya gonna have to leave town tomorrow."

He pushed open the door of the Ragusa Social Club and walked inside.

"Yeah?"

The man who stepped in front of Jake was as wide as he was tall. One of those monsters, Jake thought, who spend their days collecting for the bookmakers and the shylocks.

"I'm here to see Dominick Favara. He's expectin' me."

"Ya got a name?"

"Jake Leibowitz."

"Leee-bowww-wwwitz?"

"Listen, tubby, if you don't turn ya fat ass around and go tell ya fuckin' boss I'm here to see him, I'm takin' a powder. That's after I kick ya face in."

"Could I help somebody?"

Jake answered without looking away from the man in front of him. "I'm lookin' for Dominick Favara."

"That's me."

"I'm Jake Leibowitz. We got an appointment."

"I been expectin' ya. Come in the back."

"You oughta put a chain on ya dog," Jake said. "He ain't trained yet."

"Don't let Carmine bother ya. That's just his way."

"Yeah," Carmine said, "that's just my way. No offense."

"None taken. And please forgive me for threatenin' to kick ya face in."

Jake crossed the room, shook hands with Dominick Favara, then stepped through the doorway into Favara's small office.

"Pull up a seat, Jake. Take a load off ya mind."

Jake removed his hat, then carefully arranged his cashmere overcoat before sitting down. "Hey, Dominick," he said, "I'm sorry I lost my temper. What happened was I started off the day on the wrong side of the bed. I ate my mother's cookin'."

Favara chuckled appreciatively. "I heard you was a tough guy, Jake. In fact, I been hearin' a lot about you lately. Ya did some time, didn't ya?"

"Some? Try forever and a day." Jake quickly outlined his problems with the army.

"Tough break. I mean ya had a perfectly good plan, but nobody could read the future. Sometimes it don't turn out like you expect."

"Yeah, but *sometimes* ya get a chance to make it right before the sky falls on ya head. I'm hopin' that now is one of them times. Ya know what I'm doin' in the projects?"

"I heard all about it."

Jake, noting the sudden gleam in Favara's eye, was careful to keep his own expression neutral. *Now*, they understood each other. "What it is is I ain't happy with my current supplier. He thinks I'm an employee, but what I wanna be is an independent contractor. I mean, I been givin' it a lotta thought and what I come up with is this. If I got plenty of cash, if I don't need credit, why can't I deal with more than one supplier? Competition. Ain't that what America's all about? Ain't it competition that makes people work harder?"

"I think I get the point."

"If ya do, then ya one up on Steppy Accacio. Steppy don't want me buyin' from anybody but him. That way he can make the price as high as he wants."

"Can ya blame him?"

"Can ya blame me for not goin' along? I didn't do all those years in the joint so's I could end up bein' a flunky."

Favara stood up and walked over to the window. "So that's what ya want from me? To buy dope? Ya don't want nothin' else? You ain't, for instance, askin' me to watch ya back when Steppy comes lookin' for ya?"

"Ya gotta protect your interests, right?"

"That guy you did in the projects? With baseball bats? Ya know he worked for me?"

"Not at the time."

Favara walked back over to his desk and sat on the edge. "What I hear is that you're crazy, Jake. What I hear is that you been killin' people right and left. Like that spic in the whorehouse."

"It was a mistake. Jesus Christ, does the whole world know about it?"

"You went in there for Steppy is what ya did. To do the job on the pimp and his old lady. They used to be my customers. Before Steppy took over the projects. O'Neill talks too much. Just like the rest of the micks."

"Yeah? Well, he won't be talkin' no more. I ain't pretendin' to be no saint,

Dominick. But I only made one mistake and there ain't no witnesses left. I did what I had to do. I'm *still* doin' what I have to do."

"I ain't sayin' ya not, Jake. What I am sayin' is if ya wanna buy dope from me, I'll be glad to sell it to ya. But only for cash. As for the rest of it, I ain't interested in coverin' ya butt, because ya too fuckin' hot. If ya happen to survive, which ain't too likely, we could maybe do business long-term. But first ya gotta survive."

Jake took a minute to think it over. Access to a dependable supply of dope would give him an income, but it wouldn't protect him. He had to have help.

"On the other hand," Favara said casually, "it happens I know some right guys who ain't got work at the moment. If ya don't mind dealin' with Puerto Ricans, I could talk to 'em. Tell 'em you got a proposition to make."

"Shit, Dominick." Jake smiled for the first time. "I'm a Jew, ain't I? I gotta take my friends where I can find 'em."

Twenty-one

JANUARY 21

MOODROW WAS still in bed, still asleep, when the phone began to ring. He glanced at his Big Ben, saw it was after eight o'clock and jerked himself upright. The intense jab of pain that shot through his skull reminded him why he hadn't set the clock. Then the phone rang again and he realized that it didn't take movement to set his head to throbbing. Sound would do, as well.

Let it ring, he thought. Just let it go away. Just let the whole goddamned morning disappear.

But whoever it was apparently knew Moodrow was home, because they wouldn't hang up. Not after five rings, not after ten, not after fifteen. Moodrow got out of bed and crossed the room, desperately wishing for a cup of coffee.

"Yeah?"

"Stanley? It's me, Epstein."

"Jesus, Sarge, you could've picked a better time."

"Why? What's wrong?"

"I got attacked is what's wrong. I got smacked on the head with a baseball bat. Louisville Slugger, Gil Hodges model, to be exact." He went on to give the details, including the sudden appearance of Samuelson and Detective

Lieutenant Rosten. "I'm looking at the complaint right now," he concluded. "They both signed it."

"This Rosten is a lieutenant?"

"That's what Samuelson said. I didn't ask for i.d."

"The rule is one detective lieutenant to a precinct. Something must be happening with Patero."

"You haven't heard any rumors?"

"I didn't go into the house yesterday. That's what I'm calling to tell you. I've got the name of the witness, the one in the O'Neill killings. Pearse O'Malley. Another Irishman."

Moodrow didn't know how to respond to the last part. Hell's Kitchen had been Irish for a long time. The Lower East Side, too, back when it was called the Fourth Ward. In fact, the whole damn city had been Irish once. Finally, he decided to ignore the comment altogether.

"This O'Malley, he talkin'?"

"I don't know, Stanley. I know he's being protected, but my man inside the Tenth warned me to stay away from the two suits who caught the squeal. Names are Gordon and Russo."

"Where they keeping the witness? West Street?"

"He's in his apartment, with a cop sitting out in the hall. A uniform."

"You got an address and and an apartment number?"

"Yeah, 2211 Tenth Avenue. Top floor, 6B."

Moodrow sighed. "I guess I gotta go up there. Try to bluff my way past the uniform."

"You do that, you're gonna tip your hand to Patero and Cohan. That what you want?"

"Somebody's gotta warn the guy, Sarge. That cop sitting in the hallway isn't protecting Pearse O'Malley. He's keeping him prisoner."

"You don't know that."

"Yeah? Well, I'm not gonna take the chance. Besides which O'Malley might be able to identify the men who killed the O'Neills. I'm not saying I know the O'Neills' killer and the Melenguez killer are the same person. But I *am* saying if I get my hands on either one, I'll find the other."

"I can't argue with that. Anything else I can do for you?"

"Yeah, Maguire said the lab boys lifted some prints at the Melenguez scene. You think you can get me a copy of those prints?"

"Why, you got a suspect?"

"I just wanna be ready when the time comes. Those prints are the only physical link we have and I got a funny feeling they're gonna disappear. That's if they haven't disappeared already. It shouldn't be a problem, because there's gotta be several copies in the files. Forensics always makes up a bunch in case they're needed in other precincts. Just pull one and send it out to me."

"Those prints could belong to anyone. I'm not saying I mind snatching them for you, but don't get your hopes up. It's most likely a wild goose chase. Mob killers don't leave fingerprints."

"These guys didn't go to the O'Neills' with any intention of killing. They were there to teach a lesson to a couple of pimps who couldn't complain to the cops. Plus, they had to figure Patero would cover for them if anything went wrong. Get the prints, Sarge. It couldn't hurt."

Pat Cohan took the envelope in his hand, thanked the officer who'd delivered it, then closed the front door of his Bayside home. Don't smirk, he told himself. In fact, don't even smile. Model yourself on Little Jack Burns. No one's seen him smile in years.

Little Jack operated Burns Funeral Parlor on Utopia Parkway. His gravely sympathetic expression never changed, not even when he added up the tab and took your check. Not even when he *deposited* your check. The rumor was that his wife had left him because she didn't like sleeping with a corpse. Little Jack put that same expression on the face of every stiff he touched. What Mrs. Burns didn't know (and didn't *want* to know) was who was imitating who.

So that was it. Jack Burns all the way. In recognition of Kate's loss. Which, Pat Cohan supposed, must seem just like a real death.

"Daddy? Breakfast's ready."

"Be right there." He took a second to examine his reflection in a mirror hanging over the mantle. His hands fluttered up to his hair, but there was nothing for them to do. His mane was perfect.

He came into the kitchen to find his wife sitting at the table. Rose was praying over her food, as usual. Or, at least, he *guessed* she was praying. He couldn't understand a word of it. Her mumbling sounded more like a continuous low belch than human speech.

"Morning, Kate," he said.

"Is something wrong, Daddy?"

"Why do you ask?"

"I don't know." Kate shook her head and laughed. "You sounded like you were going to a funeral."

"A funeral? Well, I suppose it's not so far off."

Kate put down the pot she was scouring and shut off the water in the sink. "What's wrong, daddy?"

He took a deep breath before speaking. "Stanley's going to be arrested, Kate. You don't know how sorry I am to have to tell you, but it's better you hear it from me. I've got a copy of the warrant in my hand." He passed it over and waited until she was looking at it before continuing. "It happened last night. Stanley assaulted another police officer."

"But, why?"

"The officer was on surveillance. He was following Stanley when it happened. I can only assume that Stanley lost his temper. The nets are closing,

Kate, and he knows it. Maybe the pressure was too much and he reverted to
what he spent so many years training to do. It doesn't matter. The officer was
badly beaten. He's in the hospital and he'll stay there for a week."

Pat Cohan watched his daughter cry for a moment, then reached out and took
her in his arms. Her sobs, he noted, blended nicely with his wife's mumbling.
They gave some variety to the general drone.

"My darlin' Kathleen," he whispered, "my darlin', darlin' Kathleen. Life
doesn't always work out the way you expect it to. Sometimes there's an awful
lot of pain. What you've got to be is strong, girl. Strong enough to face the
losses. Now, there's something I think you should do. I think you should call
Stanley."

"I can't, Daddy. I can't do that."

"He's going to need a lawyer, Kate. The sooner, the better. Somebody has to
warn him and I think it should be you."

"Please, Daddy. You do it. I can't."

"He needs to know that *you* know."

Kate shook her head. "You're talking like it's all over, but I still love him. It
doesn't just disappear."

"All the more reason. If there's any hope for the future, you've got to be
honest with him."

Pat Cohan could read his daughter's indecision, see her mind jumping back
and forth. Yes or no? Yes or no? Like pulling the petals off a daisy. In the end,
he knew, she'd decide to obey her father. Yes, she'd decide to obey, and that
decision, once made, would cut Stanley Moodrow out of her life forever. It was
her father she'd be choosing, whether she knew it or not. Her father over her
lover. Not that he, Pat Cohan, enjoyed seeing his darlin' Kathleen in such
obvious pain. He was doing it because it was necessary. Because if he let
Stanley Moodrow, a rookie, triumph over Inspector Pat Cohan, he might as
well hike on down to Jack Burns's place and pick out a coffin.

"All right, Daddy, I'll do it. But I want you to listen to what he says. If he has
a defense, I want you to hear it."

"Fine, Kate. I'll pick up in my office."

He was tempted to run for the phone, like a kid for a cookie, but he held
himself in check. What he had to do was savor the moment. That was his first
obligation. Stroll through the parlor, light a fat Cuban cigar, blow a thick white
smoke-ring at the ceiling. Sure, he was getting old. Sure, he was rushing
headlong toward retirement and a rocking chair. But, still . . .

When he finally picked up the phone, it was already ringing.

"Hello."

"Stanley, it's Kate."

"How ya doin', Kate?" Moodrow's voice, much to Pat Cohan's disgust, was
soft and gentle. "I've been thinking about you. Wondering when you'd call."

"Don't, Stanley. Please don't make it any harder. I'm calling to say you're about to be arrested for assaulting a police officer. I'm warning you, so that you can get a lawyer."

" 'Get a lawyer?' " Moodrow began to laugh. "That's gotta be your father talking. *Gotta* be."

"You think it's funny. I've *seen* the warrant."

"That sounds like your father, too. Tell me something, Kate, did he bring it home or did he have it delivered? Maybe he *suggested* that you call me?"

"You're laughing at *me*, aren't you?" Kate was close to an explosion. It was obvious to both listeners.

"Look, Kate, I've got a terrific headache. I looked in my medicine chest and all I can find are Carter's Little Liver Pills. What I was trying to do, before you called, was figure out how they got there. It's a mystery, see. Like how I can be arrested for getting smacked on the head with a baseball bat. What I'm laughing at is the way things work out."

"Are you saying you're innocent?"

"What I'm saying is that your father's guilty. He's guilty and he's gonna pay."

"Stanley, the arrest warrant's for *you*, not Daddy."

"What happened to 'innocent until proven guilty'?" He waited for Kate to respond, but she kept silent. "The thing is that you've already made a choice. Whether you know it or not."

"But I still love you. I do."

"Love isn't enough. It just isn't."

"So, that's it? There's nothing more to be said?"

"That's it for now. Later on, maybe . . ."

"Goodbye, Stanley. And good luck. You're going to need it."

Pat Cohan, puffing at his cigar, imagined his daughter sitting by the phone in the kitchen. He could almost see her shoulders heaving as she sobbed into her cupped hands. He should, he knew, go out to comfort her. He should take her in his arms, hold her gently until her tears dried, tell her that he'd do everything possible for poor, misguided Stanley Moodrow. But there was one more thing to be accomplished before he saw to his daughter's needs. He picked up the receiver and quickly dialed Stanley Moodrow's number.

"Yeah?"

"Stanley, boyo, how's it going? How's your headache?"

"Gettin' better, Pat. I found some Bufferin over the sink. How's things by you?"

"Couldn't be finer."

"Glad to hear it. By the way, did Samuelson tell you that I have a signed copy of the complaint? He tell you there's a baseball bat with *my* blood on it? He tell you the suspect wasn't wearing gloves, so if the bat's wiped clean of prints, someone's got a lot of explaining to do? He . . ."

"Don't waste your breath, Stanley. I'm not a fool. I know the arrest won't stick. But it *will* take your gun and badge away. It *will* tie you up for the next couple of months. It *will* give me time to think of something else. How does corruption sound?"

"It sounds like you've gone off the deep end. It sounds like you're ready for a straitjacket. It sounds like you're willing to sacrifice your daughter to get to me."

"Ah, Kate. Well, boyo, I've made a few mistakes in my life and matching you up with Kate was the worst of 'em. Not that mistakes can't be corrected. Not that I won't have grandchildren to comfort me in my old age."

"Tell me something, Pat. What're you gonna do when she figures it out?"

"That's never going to happen, boyo. You and Kate are finished."

"Don't count your chickens, Pat. It only leads to disappointment. By the way, you got your people waiting outside to arrest me?"

"Actually, I do. And as soon as I make a phone call, they'll be on their way up. See you in jail, boyo."

Moodrow, working quickly, gathered up the statements given by Al and Betty O'Neill, the complaint form signed by Rosten and Samuelson, and his personal notebooks. What he had to do was get them safe. If the arresting officers decided to search his apartment (which they would) and found the papers (which they also would), he'd have about the same chance of survival as a mouse in a lion's cage.

He left his apartment, walked down two flights and knocked on Greta Bloom's door.

"Stanley, come in, please."

"I haven't got time, Greta. What I've got is a problem and being as you're the one who got it started, I figure you won't mind helping me out."

Greta stepped back and folded her arms across her chest. Her head barely came up to Moodrow's lower ribs. "Maybe you could stop with the remarks and tell me what you want?"

"I'm about to be arrested. What I need you to do is hold onto these papers and find me a lawyer in case I have to make bail."

The look in Greta Bloom's face went too far back for Stanley Moodrow to read. It went all the way back to a small village in northeastern Poland.

"The bastards," she whispered.

"Say that again."

"It doesn't matter. Quick, come in. I'll hide you."

"Just the papers, Greta. I'm too big to hide."

"You can't let them take you."

"Hey, this is 1958. It's not like the old days." Moodrow could read Greta's disbelief in the way she held her head off to one side, in the thin line of her tightly pressed lips. "Look, I could run away, find someplace to hide, but if I do that, I'm finished. I won't be able to go out on the street. I won't be able to *investigate*. But if I let myself get arrested, I'll most likely be released without posting bail. Which means that as long as I don't break any laws, they have to leave me alone."

"Don't believe it, Stanley. Once they put you in a cage, they can do anything." She reached out and touched the wound on the side of his head. "You've got stitches. Tell me what happened."

"That's what I'm being arrested for."

"Somebody breaks your head and *you* get arrested?"

"The other somebody, who got hurt much worse than me, is also a cop. And *he's* singing a different song. Those papers you're holding? They're gonna get me out of this."

"Tell me, Stanley. Your father-in-law is involved here?"

"Jesus, you're a nosy old woman."

"Jesus don't have nothing to do with it. Better you should call on Moses or Abraham. Anyway, please answer the question."

"My father-in-law, Pat Cohan, is what they call a *full* inspector. Do you understand? There are twenty-four thousand cops and forty-two full inspectors in the Department. That's one for every . . ."

"Five hundred seventy-one regular cops." She sniffed loudly. "Don't give a look, Stanley. I worked twenty years in retail. And we didn't have no adding machines like today."

"Did I open my mouth?"

"You were thinking. I could hear you."

"I gotta go, Greta. I wanna be upstairs when they come for me. If I'm not, they're liable to wreck my apartment when they search it."

"First say what you were gonna say."

Moodrow sighed. "The point I was gonna make is that I don't know who I'm fighting. It's a problem for me. A big problem. For instance, the Patrolman's Benevolent Association will supply me with a free lawyer. Only I don't know if I can trust them. I don't know if I can trust anyone. Except you, of course."

"Of course."

"So what I want you to do is, first of all, keep these papers safe. Second, stay by the phone for a few hours. If I need a lawyer or they start talking bail, I'll call you. Third, leave the hatpins in the hats."

Twenty-two

ON THE way back to his own apartment, Moodrow fought the urge to peer down each hallway, to crane his neck at every turn of the stairwell. He knew, from long experience, that fear can be crippling, that a scared fighter usually leaves his fight in the dressing room. Besides, the fear, if he should allow himself to feel it, would be out of all proportion to the threat. How had Greta put it? "When they get you in a cage, they can do anything." Moodrow wasn't worried about physical abuse. It'd take a squad to put the cuffs on him. As for being killed, the rule of thumb in the NYPD was that cop killers weren't taken alive. Not unless they surrendered on the steps of St. Patrick's Cathedral with the Cardinal in attendance. And even if they did survive the actual arrest, the only thing gained was a free trip to Sing-Sing and a late-night appointment with the electric chair. If there'd been an unsolved cop killing in Stanley Moodrow's lifetime, he didn't know about it.

Still, for all his bravado, Moodrow took a quick look down an empty hallway before opening his door, stepping inside and locking it behind him. He went directly to his bedroom, took the better of his two suits out of the closet and laid it on his bed. A clean white shirt and a brand-new tie followed. He began to dress, then noticed his mud-stained shoes. If you're gonna do it, he told himself, then do it right.

Ten minutes later, he was pulling on his newly polished brogans and straightening his tie. He took a moment to admire his reflection in the mirror, then strolled into the kitchen, poured himself a cup of coffee and picked up the *Daily News*. He could feel his mind racing, the way it often did before a bout. It was exciting, all right, but not the kind of excitement that helped fighters to survive. He tried to concentrate on the paper, but except for a couple of headlines, *U.N. Girl Is Stabbed by Teener in Park* and *City Aide Advises PR's to Learn English First*, he didn't understand a word he read.

He was wondering who was going to come for him. It wouldn't be Pat Cohan. He was out in Bayside and he'd said the arresting officers would be on their way up as soon as he made a phone call. Samuelson would be there, of course, looking to get his hands on the complaint he'd signed the night before. That would get *him* off the hook. Detective Lieutenant Rosten, too. If they recovered the complaint, they might even be able to make a case against him.

Patero was the question mark. Precinct detective squads were invariably commanded by a single lieutenant. His functions were almost entirely administrative as he attempted to deal with Department politics as well as precinct crime. So what was Rosten doing in the 7th? And why was he riding with a detective, second grade? Samuelson had said that he and Rosten were coming from the scene of a homicide. *That* was a straight-out lie. The only legitimate reason for Rosten's presence in the precinct would be as head of a special task force investigating a single crime or a single category of crime. He would never, for political as well as practical reasons, involve himself in day-to-day precinct business.

A knock on the door interrupted Moodrow's thoughts. He pushed himself away from the table, took a moment to straighten his tie, then strolled through the kitchen and the living room.

"Who is it," he called. "Is that Mayor Wagner? Cardinal Spellman? President Eisenhower?"

He opened the door without waiting for an answer, expecting to find a dozen uniforms massed in the hallway to protect Samuelson and Rosten. What he found, much to his surprise, was Sal Patero, a briefcase tucked under his arm, standing by himself.

"Morning, Stanley," Patero said. "You mind if I come inside?"

"That depends, Sal. Whatta ya want here?"

"I wanna talk, Stanley. If you can spare the time. If you can't, I'll take off."

Moodrow, thoroughly confused, looked over Patero's head at a still-empty hallway. Where were the arresting officers? Did Patero think he could make the bust by himself? He'd have to be insane.

"You wanna come in, then come in. But I'm telling you, Sal, I'm not in the mood for bullshit."

"When you hear what I have to say, you're not gonna think it's bullshit."

Patero walked into the apartment, found an overstuffed chair in the living room and took a seat. Moodrow, after locking the door carefully, slipped on the safety chain and followed.

"I didn't expect to see you, Sal. Being as you're not the precinct whip anymore."

"Who told you that?"

"I made an arrest last night. Maybe you heard about it. Funny thing was two cops showed up just as I was about to interrogate my prisoner. One of them was a detective lieutenant named Rosten. I figure he was doing your job."

Patero sighed. "You wouldn't consider giving me a cup of coffee, would you? Being as I'm a guest in your house."

"A guest or a prisoner," Moodrow said evenly. "I can't make up my mind which category you fall into."

"Very funny. Considering that *you're* the one who's gonna be arrested. That's what I came here for. To warn you. The guy who attacked you last night was a cop. His name's Michael Reina. They dragged him all the way from the One-Eleven in Bayside to do the job."

"Bayside, huh? Pat Cohan's hometown. So how come they want to arrest *me*? Being as even *you* know that I was the victim? And if there's already a warrant, how come nobody's showed up to bring me in? Or maybe that's *your* job?"

"That's a lotta questions, Stanley. A cup of coffee would go a long way toward keeping me alert enough to answer."

"All right, Sal. A cup of coffee it is. How do ya take it?"

"Light, two sugars."

Moodrow walked back into the kitchen. He took his time with the coffee, stalling, really, while he tried to grasp the significance of Sal Patero's warning. Had Patero really had a change of heart? Had his conscience finally got to him? Or was this just another chunk of Pat Cohan humor? Another twist of the knife.

And even if Patero *had* come to his senses, what did that mean to Stanley Moodrow? The warrant was still out there. Pat Cohan was still out there. Melenguez's killer was still out there.

"You said two sugars, Sal?"

"Yeah."

Moodrow took the mug and carried it back into the living room. He half-expected to find Patero crouching in the middle of the room, .38 in hand, but Patero hadn't moved. If he was acting, Moodrow decided, he was doing a hell of a job of it.

"Thanks, Stanley."

"You're welcome, Sal." Moodrow sat on the couch and crossed his legs. "You think maybe you could answer a few of those questions I asked? Now that you have your coffee?"

Patero leaned forward in his chair. "You have a lot of support in the Seventh," he began. "I mean a *lot* of support. That's why nobody's come down with the warrant. Rosten can't put a squad together. Ordinary beat cops are telling him to go fuck himself."

"Why doesn't he come down and do it himself?"

"*That* question doesn't need an answer. Michael Reina was beaten to a pulp. And he was the one with the baseball bat."

Moodrow managed a smile. "Well, I thought I'd ask you the easy questions first. From now on they get harder. I want you to tell me what you're doing here. I wanna know what's happening in the house."

"Look, Stanley, I never wanted to go along with Pat on the Melenguez thing. I got sucked into it. I'm not making myself into some kind of a hero, but most of what happened after the killing came from outside the precinct. That's because Pat Cohan was pulling the strings. The decision to transfer the case out to Organized Crime, for instance. I had no control over that."

"But you *did* control Samuelson and Maguire. The way I hear it, you're Samuelson's rabbi. The two of them, they didn't interview Melenguez's land-lady. Which, considering they didn't have a suspect, they *should've* done the first day. You pulled them off *before* the case was transferred out. You, Sal. You."

"I knuckled under, Stanley. I'm not saying I didn't. But it's done now, and I can't take it back. I have to go on from here and do what I think is right."

"That mean you're willing to give a statement?"

"A statement?"

"Yeah. Put it all down on paper. Get it off your chest?"

"What'll you do with it? If I give you what you want?"

"Well, I don't figure the *Times* would be interested, Sal. That's because it's not 'fit to print.' But the *Daily News* might run with it. That's my favorite paper, anyway."

"You can't do that, Stanley. You can't go outside the job. You *know* that."

"All right, all right, I was only kidding. I won't take it to the papers. I'll take it to Internal Affairs. How'd that be?"

Patero took a long pull on his coffee. "Forget Internal Affairs. The Inspector running I.A.D. has been buddies with Pat Cohan for thirty years. They were in the same class at the Academy."

"Lemme see if I've got this right, Sal? What you're saying is I can't go outside the Department and I can't go inside the Department. Tell me something, my supporters down at the precinct, what exactly do they want me to do?"

"They want you to get Melenguez's killer."

Moodrow slammed his fist into the arm of the couch. "Do I look like some kind of human sacrifice?"

"What're you talking about?"

"I'm talking about the fact that I'm tired of bleeding for other people. I had one too many fights and I don't wanna get hurt anymore. I'm talking about *you* giving me a statement that I can use to protect myself."

"Look, Stanley, I brought you the entire Melenguez file. I had it copied before Rosten took over. They're transferring me to the Crime Scene Unit. If I can, I'll copy their files, too. But that's as far as I'm willing to go."

"It's not right, Sal. And you know it." Moodrow waited for Patero to respond, but Patero just shook his head. "Well, what can I say? If that's the way it's gotta be, I'll just have to live with it." Moodrow let his shoulders drop to their normal set. He took a deep breath and shrugged his shoulders. "Being as the Department is the Department, I guess I oughta be thankful that I'm getting any help at all. Tell me something, Sal, you recognize this guy?"

Moodrow took the sketch of Santo Silesi from an end table drawer and passed it to Sal Patero. Patero looked at it for a moment, tapping the edge of the paper with his forefinger. "I'm not a hundred percent sure, but I think I've seen him with Joe Faci. I don't know his name, though."

"Who's Joe Faci?"

"Faci works for Steppy Accacio."

"This Accacio, he's Mafia, right?"

"No." Patero laughed softly. "He's not even Sicilian. Look, Steppy Accacio is a small-time punk who's trying to work his way into the big time. He's ambitious, Stanley. Like you *used* to be. There's a dozen Steppy Accacios on the Lower East Side. They come here like actors go to Hollywood. Looking for the big break."

"Then why deal with him? Why deal with a punk?"

"We take money from street pimps, don't we? I'm telling you that Steppy Accacio is only two steps removed from the street."

"Did he pull the trigger, Sal? Did Accacio kill Melenguez?"

Patero looked directly into Stanley Moodrow's eyes. "I don't know who killed Luis Melenguez. Accacio told me he wasn't there. He claimed it was an accident and that he and his boys would take care of the shooter. 'It won't happen again.' That's what he said. 'Just help me out this one time.' "

"You think he was telling the truth?"

"Yeah, I believe him. I know that he was trying to expand and the rumor is that he hired outside talent."

"How far outside? Boston? Chicago? Los Angeles?"

"More like Avenue B. I think they're still working for him." Patero looked at his watch and began to rise. "Stanley, I gotta go."

"Wait a minute, Sal, there's something else. Look, sooner or later Rosten's gonna come for me. How am I supposed to operate with a warrant hanging over my head? Maybe I should go down to the house and surrender."

"Don't do it. Don't give up your badge and your gun. Without a badge, you got no right to stop people on the street, no right to question suspects, no right to make an arrest."

"But if I make bail, I can move around freely until the trial and we both know it's never gonna come to a trial. If I don't surrender, I'm gonna spend all my time looking over my shoulder."

"So what? When they come, they come. It's not gonna be any worse if you wait until they find you. Same warrant. Same charges. The main thing is to hang onto your badge and gun as long as possible. If I was in your position, that's what I'd do."

Moodrow offered his hand. "Maybe you got a point. I gotta think about it." He took Patero's hand in his. "It's good you came here today. I mean it, Sal. It's good. Unfortunately, it doesn't get you off the hook."

He yanked Patero's right hand forward and down, simultaneously driving a left hook into the right side of the lieutenant's face. The force of the blow drove Patero over the back of the couch and onto the floor. Moodrow, worried about the Smith & Wesson nestled in Patero's shoulder rig, circled quickly. He needn't have bothered. Sal Patero was lying motionless on the rug.

"Never drop your right hand, Sal. Not when you got a glass jaw. It just gets you in trouble." He scooped Patero off the rug, tucked him under his arm, trotted off to the kitchen and sat the lieutenant in a chair. "Here you go, Sal. Your home away from home."

If Moodrow had had four sets of cuffs, he could have done the job right, but he had only two, his and Sal Patero's. Still, he managed to secure Patero firmly, wrists to the right rear leg of the chair, ankles to the left front. When he was finished, he left the kitchen, and rummaged in the hall closet until he found his old nightstick and a copy of the Manhattan yellow pages.

"Ya know, Sal," he called as he walked back to the kitchen, "I wish I had a girlfriend living here. Because, the way it is, I haven't got a nightgown for you to wear. But we can always pretend, right?"

"What, Stanley, what . . . ?" Patero was starting to come around. He was lost in confusion for a moment, staring blankly up at Stanley Moodrow. Then he realized that his hands and feet were cuffed and he began to panic. "For Christ's sake. For God-almighty-sake. Jesus Christ."

"This isn't gonna be difficult, Sal. Being as you've been through this drill once or twice, I won't have to soften you up. What I want is a signed statement. In your handwriting. I want everything. Names, dates, places."

"You're crazy."

Moodrow smiled. "Not crazy, Sal, just greedy. I want Melenguez's killer and I *don't* wanna be crucified in the process. I don't wanna end up being some kind of noble sacrifice. Does that sound unreasonable? Your statement, along with everything else I've managed to accumulate, is gonna keep me off that cross. And I think I should warn you about something else. I found out more than you think I did. Much more. If you lie to me, I'm gonna know it. Lemme tell ya, Sal, lying is not your best option. Now, you wanna start talking? You could begin with your first contact with Accacio after Melenguez was killed."

"This is bullshit. You think a forced confession is gonna stand up in court?"

"If the confession's bullshit, you shouldn't mind giving it to me. C'mon, Sal, make up your mind. How do you wanna play it?"

"Fuck you, Moodrow. Go fuck yourself."

Moodrow giggled. The sound startled him and he quickly brought his hand up to his mouth. "Excuse me, Sal, for being so rude. Now, here's what's gonna happen. I'm gonna put this phone book on top of your head and you're gonna keep very, very still. That's so it stays balanced. Then, I'm gonna take my nightstick and smash it down on top of the phone book. One thing I gotta warn you about, if you move your head and the book falls off, I'm gonna crack your fucking skull open. You gettin' my drift, Sal?"

"You'll pay for this. I mean it."

"Do you *really* mean it. Would you swear on your integrity as a police officer?"

"Fuck you."

"Now you're repeating yourself."

Moodrow laid the phone book on Patero's head, holding it there with his left hand. He raised the nightstick over his head. "Say 'cheese,' Sal."

"Don't hit me. Don't. Don't." Patero was close to tears. "I'll do what you want."

Moodrow slapped his nightstick into the phone book. He didn't use much force, but the sharp crack was impressive, nonetheless. Patero screamed first, then began to sob.

"That was for old times' sake. Now, we can get to work."

Twenty-three

"TWO-GUN JAKE," Jake Leibowitz said to himself. "Fastest Jew in the Wild Wild East." He admired himself in the mirror for a moment, adjusting the two .45's. One, his own, rested in a custom-made shoulder rig. The other, formerly the property of Abraham Weinberg, was snugged into the waistband of his trousers.

What a fool he'd been to hold onto Abe's automatic. It was a *murder* weapon, for Christ's sake. What a double fool he'd been for believing Joe Faci when Faci insisted the matter had been taken care of. Well, it didn't make any difference now. Because he'd decided not to run. Because the wops had killed Izzy. Because he'd had enough bullshit to last for a lifetime. A *short* lifetime.

Who are they gonna send? he thought. It won't be Steppy or Faci or Santo, because he'd kill any one of those bastards the minute he laid eyes on him. No, they'd have to find a stranger, one of those faceless guineas who hung around the social clubs looking to get discovered. If Accacio was *really* connected, of course, he'd bring in a pro from out of town, but Jake had long ago stopped believing that Steppy Accacio was anything more than an ambitious neighborhood punk.

Jake thought of all the crow he'd eaten trying to get in with Dominick Favara. What a waste of time *that* had been. Favara wouldn't save him. Not with Izzy gone. Why should he? Favara could wait for the garbage to sort itself out, then make his move. One thing for sure, there wasn't going to be any dealing in the projects on Avenue D while Jake Leibowitz was alive. Not by Accacio, not by Favara, not by nobody.

"I hate this shit. I hate it."

God, how he missed Izzy. God, how he hated being completely alone. It was like being locked up in isolation with the hacks on the way to administer a midnight beating. You could play the wall, take out one or two with your fists, but sooner or later you'd be overwhelmed and the beating would be all the worse because you had the balls to fight back.

"Maybe I oughta take a trip," he said. "Maybe I oughta take a trip out to New Jersey, stop in and see old Steppy."

"Jake? Who ya talkin' to?"

Mama Leibowitz came through the door like she owned the place. Which, Jake supposed, she did.

"This is my *bedroom*, ma," Jake said. "You could at least ask if I'm decent."

"As if you got something I ain't already seen. What's with all the guns? You think maybe you're Jesse James?"

Jake sighed. "We got trouble, ma. And we gotta be careful. Don't open the door to anyone ya don't know, even if it's the cops. Let 'em kick the door in, but don't open it voluntarily. And don't stand in front of the door when you're askin' who it is, either."

"*Pogrom*," Ma Leibowitz whispered. "*Pogrom*," she repeated.

"Yeah, ma, only this time they're doin' it with *Italian* Cossacks." Jake had heard all the stories about the old country, about living on the Polish-Russian border, about soldiers who killed Jews because the soldiers were drunk and didn't have anything better to do. Or because it was Christmas and driving a sword through a Jewish body seemed like a good way to celebrate the birth of Jesus.

"Wait here a minute, Jakey. There's something I gotta show you."

Damn, Jake thought, for a fat woman, she can sure move fast. He watched his mother fly out the door, then reappear a moment later with the largest revolver Jake had ever seen. The barrel was at least eight inches long.

"Where the fuck you get *that*?"

"Your grandfather bought it when he first came over. That was 1891. He gave it to his son, your father, when your father went into business for himself. 'This,' he said, 'is what makes America great. In Poland, only the *goyim* have guns.' "

Jake shook his head in wonder. "Lemme see it, ma." He took the revolver and hefted it in his palm. The damn thing felt like it weighed ten pounds. And it was so dirty, it was more likely to kill the person holding it than anyone else. He cracked the cylinder open and yanked out the swollen cartridges.

"Jeez," he said, "forty-five caliber. Did Poppa use this on jobs?"

"You think he pointed with his finger? Bang, bang, bang?"

"Take it easy, ma. I ain't bustin' balls . . ."

"Stop with the language, already."

"Sorry. What I'm gonna do is clean this sucker up good and load it with new ammo. If you gotta shoot it, hold it with both hands, because it's gonna kick back hard. In fact, don't shoot at all if ya don't absolutely *have* to. Better you should just whack 'em with it. A good crack with this gun'd most likely kill a moose."

Ma Leibowitz sat on the edge of the bed. "Do you think we should maybe leave town?"

"They killed Izzy, ma." Jake noted his mother's sharp reaction. "And they killed Abe Weinberg, too. Me, I don't feel like runnin'."

"Ha, just like your father. So tell me, what am I supposed to do in my old age? Maybe I could shrivel up like a dried bug. From starvation, already."

"I got a few grand stashed away. That oughta hold ya for a year or so."

"Jakey, listen to your *mamaleh*. It's better we should leave the Lower East Side. We could maybe go out to Williamsburg."

"Jesus, ma, Williamsburg's only a mile away. It's right over the goddamned bridge."

"But it's not *here*. That's the difference."

Jake smiled. He couldn't help it. "You're nuts, ma."

"All right, then. Brighton Beach. We could move to Brighton Beach. That's practically a foreign country."

"It's still *Brooklyn*. Sooner or later, they'd find me, the cops or the guineas. What am I supposed to do, spend my whole life tryin' to watch my back? I'd rather go out in a blaze of glory. Like Poppa did."

Stanley Moodrow pulled back the curtain and stared down at the street below. It was pea soup out there again. A blend of morning fog and fine rain obscured a winter sun that wouldn't get high enough to shine between the tenements, anyway. He dropped the curtain and plucked a black trenchcoat from the hall closet. As he pulled open the front door, he took a moment to admire himself in the mirror.

"Ya know something, Stanley," he said, "you're in danger of looking like a goddamned detective. Your whole body's shoutin' *Cop, Cop, Cop*."

It was funny. One of the prime benefits of the Gold Shield was not having to wear an NYPD uniform, not having to carry all that crap around your waist. What did everyone, patrolman and detective alike, call detectives? Suits? So why did the "suits" end up looking so much alike they might as well be wearing uniforms?

Moodrow was carrying a small bag when he left, enough underwear and socks for a few days, plus his shaving kit and toothbrush. He stopped down at Greta's to hand over Sal Patero's signed statement. Patero, uninjured, had been gone for almost an hour. Moodrow wasn't worried about what the lieutenant might or might not do. Most likely, the worry was coming from the opposite direction.

"Another Christmas present, Greta," he said as she opened the door.

"Hanukah *gelt*, more likely," Greta answered, taking the folded looseleaf sheets.

"I'm gonna be gone a couple of days. Something came up and I decided not to surrender. If you need to get in touch with me, I'll probably be sleeping at Berrigan's Gym. It's in the phone book. If not, I'll give you a call as soon as I can."

Greta nodded thoughtfully. "You're sure you don't want to stay with me?"

"No, they'll be watching the building."

"Well, good luck, Stanley. And be careful."

"Caution. That's my middle name." Moodrow started to turn away, then thought better of it. "Greta, if something should happen to me . . ."

"Don't talk like that, *kayn aynhoreh*."

"It isn't the evil eye that worries me, Greta. It's the evil forty-five. Anyway, if something happens to me, something permanent, I want you to take those papers and burn them. Understand?"

"No, I don't."

"They're insurance papers. *Life* insurance papers. No life, no insurance." Greta sniffed loudly. "From revenge, you don't wanna know, right?"

"What's the point of revenge if you're not around to enjoy it? Those papers are like a virus. You put them out in the world, you don't know who's gonna get hurt."

Moodrow was tempted to sneak out through the basement, but decided against it. What was the point? He wasn't particularly afraid of an arrest and he didn't intend to crawl through the Lower East Side. In fact, what he intended to do was pay a visit to Pearse O'Malley, who was being guarded by a cop. If the cop had been warned to look out for a certain detective, third grade, named Stanley Moodrow, he wouldn't make it through the morning.

Still, he found himself looking in both directions as he stepped onto the sidewalk. He didn't see any cops, but a brand-new Cadillac parked across the street caught his attention. The man sitting behind the wheel certainly appeared to be on a stakeout, even if the Cadillac was a bit conspicuous.

Moodrow's first impulse was to cross the street and confront whoever it was, but before he could move, the man rolled down the window and waved to him.

"Hey, Stanley," he yelled. "C'mere."

C'mere? Moodrow stood on the sidewalk and stared across at the Cadillac. The car was parked in shadow and he couldn't make out the features of the man sitting behind the wheel. As he watched, the Cadillac pulled out into the center of the one-way street, then backed up until it was right in front of him.

"Don't be a hard-head, Stanley. I just wanna talk to ya."

"Carmine?"

"Ya remember me. I'm flattered."

Carmine Stettecase was a notorious bully who'd gone through St. Stephen's two years ahead of Stanley Moodrow. They'd had any number of battles until, somewhere toward the end of grammar school, Carmine had decided to leave his younger schoolmate alone. Predictably, Carmine had left school in ninth grade to go into business with his Uncle Stefano, a small-time bookie. Five years later, when Uncle Stefano dropped dead in a bar on Grand Street, Carmine had recruited his old buddy, Dominick Favara, another of Moodrow's contemporaries, to help him out with the business. Over time, as they'd moved into prostitution, loan-sharking and heroin, Favara had become the boss and Carmine the worker.

Moodrow knew all about Stettecase and Favara. Their progress had been a common topic of conversation among St. Stephen's alumni. He recalled standing in the rain one day, in his uniform, when Dominick had come sailing down the street in a new Chevy. Favara had gone out of his way to run through a puddle, sending a wave of muddy water splattering against Moodrow's black rubber raincoat.

"What's up, Carmine," Moodrow said casually. "You decided to confess to your crimes?"

"Yeah, ha-ha, that's a good one. Hop in, Dominick wants to talk to ya."

Moodrow felt his heart begin to pound in his chest. For a moment, he was too excited to answer. This was the way it had to be. You pounded the streets, screamed in people's faces, ate slammed doors, walked until your feet fell off. You kept doing it until something gave. It wasn't about clues and brain power. It was about persistence. Persistence and, as Sam Berrigan had insisted, desire.

"What's he want?" Moodrow asked. There was nothing to be gained by showing his excitement to Carmine Stettecase. "And why doesn't he come to *me*? I'm not too crazy about taking orders from punks like Dominick Favara."

"He *can't* come to you. Whatta ya, crazy? I'm takin' a big chance myself, so if ya don't mind, let's get outta here before someone sees me talkin' to a cop."

Moodrow strolled around to the passenger's side and got in alongside Stettecase. "This better be good, Carmine. If it isn't, I'm gonna haunt your ass for the next twenty years."

"Jeez, Stanley, you ain't changed at all. I mean I woulda hoped ya matured a little, but ya still a hard-head. Only *you* could think I'd do this and not be playin' square."

Moodrow expected a quick ride over to Little Italy, but Stettecase steered the car onto the East River Drive and headed downtown.

"Where we heading?" Moodrow asked, as they entered the Brooklyn-Battery Tunnel. "I oughta warn you, if you're kidnapping me, I'm not worth shit."

"That's good, Stanley." Carmine turned his moon face away from the line of traffic. "It's good to see you're loosenin' up, because this here is your lucky day. I wish I could tell ya the thing Dominick's gonna tell ya, but, hey, loose lips sink ships, right?"

"How about telling me the price I have to pay. Or are you and Dominick giving out charity in your old age?"

That was the whole thing, of course—the price. Moodrow had no doubt that Dominick Favara knew the identity of Melenguez's killer. Or that Favara would use that information to bury Accacio. It made perfect sense. They were both from the neighborhood, both young and ambitious, both trying to find a niche in the ever-expanding heroin trade. Moodrow wondered, for a moment, if Accacio was from the neighborhood. He hadn't gone to school at St. Stephen's, but that meant less than nothing. There were a dozen Catholic schools in lower Manhattan.

"You didn't answer my question, Carmine. Where we going?"

"There's a lunchwagon on Bond and President Streets. Dominick's waitin' for us there."

The hand-painted sign read *Louie's Luncheonette*. Stuck between two small warehouses, it was little more than a shack with a kitchen, the kind of a place that opened at four in the morning and closed as soon as the local workers went home in the afternoon. It sold soup and sandwiches, coffee and soda, cigars and cigarettes. The french fries would be so greasy you could wring them out like wet laundry.

"Hey, Stanley," a voice called from the back, "over here."

"He's in the booth," Carmine said, as if Moodrow had suddenly gone blind.

"I could figure that out," Moodrow said. He strode to the back of the lunchwagon, ignored Favara's outstretched hand and sat down hard on the bench. "What's up, Dominick?"

Favara frowned, letting his hand drop into his lap. "I don't see why ya takin' that attitude," he said. "Bein' as we was always friends at St. Stephen's."

"We were never friends," Moodrow said quietly. "You were the class bully. You bullied anybody weaker than yourself. Correction, anybody you *thought* was weaker. I was the kid who kicked your ass."

"He ain't bullshittin'," Carmine said. "Ya remember in seventh grade, Dominick? What we decided after gettin' into about ten fights with this kid?"

"*Leave Stanley alone*," the two men said in unison, then broke out laughing.

Moodrow felt his face redden. He wanted to reach across the table and smack Favara's face, but he held himself in check. "Enjoy your joke, Dominick," he said, "but not for too long. You got five minutes to get this over with."

"Whatta ya gonna do?" Carmine asked. "Walk home?"

"What I'm gonna do is take the keys out of your pocket, Carmine, and drive back to the Lower East Side. That's after I smack the shit out of you."

"Listen, you prick . . ."

Dominick Favara put a restraining hand on Carmine's shoulder. "Ya gotta forgive Carmine," Favara said. "He ain't used to havin' people call his bluff."

Moodrow grinned. "I forgive you, Carmine. But you'll still have to stay after school and wash the blackboards. Now, what's the story, Dominick? You gonna tell me who killed Judge Crater?"

"Would ya believe Harry Truman?"

"I'll arrange a press conference for high noon."

"See, Carmine?" Favara slapped his partner's back. "I told ya he'd loosen up."

Moodrow leaned his elbows on the table and rested his chin on his closed fists. The truth was that Dominick Favara and Carmine Stettecase could have busted his chops for a week and he still wouldn't walk away. He felt almost feverish, the flush of excitement something like the few seconds between knowing your opponent's helplessness and finishing him off. Now the tension would would go on for days while he gathered enough evidence to make an arrest. Until he slapped the cuffs on a killer for the first time. What Moodrow suddenly realized, his eyes boring into Dominick Favara's as if they could push their way into Favara's brain and pluck out the information, was that he loved his job. And that he wanted to continue doing it until he was too old to tie his shoes.

"Jeez, I hate fighters," Favara said. "They don't blink. You can never beat 'em when it comes to hard looks."

"C'mon, Dominick," Moodrow whispered. "Let's do business."

Favara leaned over the table, putting his face within inches of Moodrow's. "Here's what I heard, Stanley. I heard you're lookin' for the people who blasted that spic on Pitt Street. I can tell ya who was there and why they were there. I can tell ya, for instance, that the whole thing happened because some asshole panicked. I can tell ya that same asshole is now dead. Also one of his partners. I can tell ya . . ."

"Get to the point," Moodrow said. "What do you want from *me*?"

"Nothing. Right *now*. But maybe, somewhere in the future, I'll ask for a favor. Nothing big, Stanley. I ain't gonna ask ya to fix the grand jury. Sometimes I get a phone number and I need an address. For you, it's nothin'. For me, it's a royal pain in the ass. Plus . . ."

"So you can find the deadbeats, right?" Moodrow interrupted. "That's why you'd want an address."

"Yeah. Like that."

"And then you can send Carmine with a baseball bat to make the collections."

"Hey, Stanley . . ."

"Forget it, Dominick. Wipe that crap out of your mind. It ain't gonna happen." Moodrow pulled his head back, freeing his hands. "I'm gonna tell you what I told your partner. If you brought me here to jerk my chain, I'm gonna make your life miserable for the rest of my career. You're gonna be my personal project. Days off? Vacations? Some guys take up fishing to pass the lonely hours. *I'm* gonna take up Dominick Favara."

"You expect me to give it up for nothin'? I tell ya, Stanley, I'm startin' to lose my temper."

"Go ahead, Dominick. Go ahead and lose it. See what happens." Moodrow leaned back and smiled. "The way I see it, Dominick, is that you and Carmine are a couple of ambitious punks. You're both trying to move up in the world and if you can do it by putting me onto Steppy Accacio, so much the better. Look at it this way, Dominick, you tell me who killed Luis Melenguez, you're payin' yourself."

"If you got all the answers, whatta ya doin' here?"

"I'm waiting for you to cut the bullshit and say what you have to say."

Favara looked over at his partner for a moment, then turned back to Moodrow. "That part of the Lower East Side, Pitt Street and along the river, is being run by Steppy Accacio, who you already know about. Nobody operates east of Avenue B without payin' Steppy off. The pimp got behind on his payments. He was makin' noises like he didn't see why he should have to pay at all. Accacio can't ignore this. He's *gotta* do somethin', because if he don't, *nobody's* gonna pay. You gettin' the picture?"

"Keep goin', Dominick. And don't forget the punch line."

Favara grinned. "I won't forget, Stanley, but I gotta save it for the end. Like any good comedian. Now, what Steppy does is hire three outside guys, three Jews, to break the pimp's face. It's supposed to be a lesson for everyone, a real simple deal. Only this little spic walks into the middle of it and one of the Jews plugs him. The shooter, by the way, ain't been seen since right after it happened. The word on the street is that he was punished by his partners for makin' everybody's life miserable.

"That was *supposed* to be all she wrote. It was supposed to be the whole story. Only last night, one of the Jews comes to me and says he ain't happy with Steppy. He's lookin' to be on his own. Then, today, I hear from a guy who's very close to Steppy, a mug who *also* wants out. He tells me the Jew's partner got into a car with the wrong people. Now he's sleepin' in the trunk. Steppy's runnin' scared, Stanley, because the cops are puttin' the heat on him. Which is very interestin', seein' as it was the cops who were supposed to fix it."

"What about O'Neill and his wife? You know about them?"

"They seen what happened, Stanley. They had to go."

"Who killed them?"

"The Jews. The ones who killed the spic. At least, that's what I *heard*. I don't want ya to think I was there."

"Anything else?"

"Just the punch line, Stanley. One little, two little, three little Jewboys, right? Number one, the shooter, was named Abe Weinberg. Number two, who's sleepin' in a trunk, was named Izzy Stein. Number three, who's still walkin' around, is named Jake Leibowitz. If ya wanna play Dick Tracy and solve this crime, ya better move fast, Stanley, 'cause Mister Leibowitz ain't gonna be around much longer. Steppy's cuttin' his losses."

Twenty-four

IT WAS raining hard by the time Carmine Stettecase dropped Moodrow off by his car on the Lower East Side. The battered Ford looked like a poor relation next to Carmine's blue Cadillac, and Carmine didn't waste any time making the obvious comparison.

"That ya car, Stanley?" he asked. "That what ya drivin'? Christ, you'd be smarter takin' the subway."

Moodrow turned up the collar of his trenchcoat and tugged on the brim of his hat. "Maybe you should stick around, Carmine. In case I need a push. My Ford doesn't like to start in the rain."

"That's a joke, right? Me pushin' that piece of shit with my Fleetwood?" Carmine shut down the windshield wipers and a curtain of rain swept across the glass. "Lemme ask ya somethin', Stanley. And don't get all hot, 'cause I ain't bustin' balls. I really wanna know. I wanna know how ya could live like this when ya could do so much better? Why do ya give a shit about Jake Leibowitz? Or that spic, Melenguez? Dominick and me, we're goin' up in the world. We ain't stupid, like that mountain guinea, Accacio. We ain't gonna leave bodies on the street. You could play along with us or not play along with us. Nothin's gonna change. No matter *what* ya do, the neighborhood's gonna stay the same sewer it always was."

Moodrow opened the door without replying. He stepped out into the rain, Carmine's voice following him all the way. "Ya wanna be a hero, Stanley? That what it is? Protectin' the weak and the poor? You're a dope, Stanley. You was always a dope."

But Moodrow was past replying. His mind, having already shifted gears, was busy sifting information, casting about for a course of action. Moodrow had been surprised to hear that Leibowitz was a neighborhood kid, but then Favara had filled in the details and it had all made sense. Leibowitz had spent twelve years in a federal prison. He'd left the Lower East Side just about the time Moodrow had become aware of the streets and the animals who inhabited them. Jake was back, now. And Stanley Moodrow was all grown up. Stanley Moodrow had become the cop who was going to put Jake Leibowitz in the electric chair.

The Ford refused to start. As predicted. The engine turned over, but except for an occasional backfire through the carburetor, never came close to actually starting. Which meant his basic strategy, to cruise the Lower East Side until he found Allen Epstein, was out the window.

What he had to do was get into the precinct. He needed Jake Leibowitz's photograph and fingerprints. There was a witness up in Hell's Kitchen, a witness whose identification could be used to produce arrest and search warrants. Once the process got started, once a judge put his name to the paperwork, Pat Cohan would have to back off and let the system operate. Maybe after Jake Leibowitz figured it out, he'd trade Steppy Accacio for a life sentence. Maybe Accacio, just as guilty of murder as Jake Leibowitz in the eyes of the law, would turn on Patrick Cohan and Sal Patero.

And maybe if he, Moodrow, didn't find Allen Epstein and gain access to the information he needed, Jake Leibowitz, Steppy Accacio, Pat Cohan and Sal Patero would have the pleasure of toasting Stanley Moodrow's mug shot.

Moodrow got out of the car and began to walk south, toward Delancey Street and the Williamsburg Bridge. There was an alley beneath the bridge, just off Willet Street. It ran between two small businesses: MYRON KOSHER: LIVE POULTRY PICK YOUR OWN and B&B PLUMBING: SECOND-HAND AND NEW. Officer Joseph Gerber would be sleeping inside that alleyway. He'd be sitting on the passenger's side of his squad car, his head slumped against the window, a pint of PM whiskey tucked under the seat. The booze wasn't there to get him stoned. It was there to keep him functioning through roll call.

Every precinct had a Joseph Gerber (or two or three or four), a dedicated lush with a few years to go before earning a right to the magic pension. They were tolerated, as long as they stayed out of trouble. Gerber was a master of the coop. His main goal in life was to mind his own business, to avoid anything remotely related to the concept of work. He pursued this end, especially on rainy days, by hitting the bottle until he was too stewed to answer the radio.

It took Moodrow fifteen minutes to walk down to the bridge. He stopped once, to pick up several containers of hot coffee, but saw no one he knew. The rain fell steadily, puddling up in the gutters. It carried all the garbage left behind by thoughtful residents since the last rain—cigar butts, candy wrappers, orange rinds, sheets of newspaper.

Moodrow kept his eyes on the sidewalk, stepping around, over and through the muddy water as he made his way along empty sidewalks. He took out his gold shield when he entered the Willet Street alley, then quickly walked the fifty feet to Gerber's old green and black.

"Joe. Hey, Joe." Moodrow tapped gently on the window, hoping to wake Gerber without scaring him to death. The tapping had no effect, it being entirely overpowered by Gerber's own snoring.

"Hey, Joe!" Moodrow shouted. "Get the fuck up!"

Gerber woke in a panic, his hand dropping to the Smith & Wesson in its holster. Moodrow pressed his badge against the window and Gerber's panic turned to mere confusion.

"What the, what the, what the . . ."

"Unlock the door, Joe. I gotta talk to you."

"Stanley? That you, boy?"

Gerber unlocked the door and slid across the front seat. Moodrow got in next to him, then rolled down the window as he caught a whiff of Gerber's breath.

"I need a favor, Joe. I want you to get the sergeant over here."

"How do I do that?" Gerber asked.

"With the radio. How the fuck else?"

"It ain't workin'." He turned up the volume and the two cops listened to the radio pop and crackle for a few seconds.

"Have some coffee, Joe. Take a good slug, then start the car and drive it fifty feet to the end of the alley. The radio'll work just fine."

Ignoring Moodrow's coffee, Gerber retrieved the bottle of PM and took a quick sip. "The sergeant don't like me, Stanley. I don't wanna see the sergeant. Why don't ya go down to the house and get the duty officer to hail him?"

"I'll take care of the sergeant. You just get him on the horn."

Gerber took a much longer pull then sighed. "All right, Stanley. But if I get in trouble, I ain't gonna forget." He grinned. "Not before I finish the bottle, anyway. You want a shot?"

Jake Leibowitz, cruising past Steppy Accacio's two-story frame house, had murder on his mind. Murder and revenge, the noble motives. Not that he had any illusions. Not that he had any hope of getting out of this in one piece. Even if he managed to blast Accacio (and his partner, Joe Faci, and his nephew, Santo Silesi), he'd still have to deal with the guineas who'd set Accacio up in the first place. Not to mention the rest of Accacio's little mob.

No, his chances of survival were about the same as those of a lobster on display in a seafood restaurant. Unless, of course, he got out. Unless he ran.

Right now, he *couldn't* run. It wasn't in him to lose everything while Accacio came up smelling like a rose. Besides, where could he go? Boston? Chicago? Los Angeles? The wops were everywhere. Sooner or later they'd catch up to him and that would be all she wrote. He did have one idea, though. It had come to him as he sat in traffic outside the Lincoln Tunnel. Maybe there was one place a Jew could go where he wouldn't be outgunned. Maybe he could even take his mother with him. Maybe he could go to Israel and help kill Arabs when the next war came.

But running, if it came to that, was way in the future. The present was how to get inside Accacio's house without being spotted. How even to get *close*, considering it was winter and there were no leaves on the trees and bushes to give him cover. Montclair, New Jersey, wasn't the Lower East Side. This was the kind of neighborhood where citizens reported prowlers and the bulls actually came out to check.

The rain would help, the rain and the fog. They'd help even more if he waited till dark. But he wasn't going to do that because there wasn't any place to wait. And besides, people were already looking for him, maybe *lots* of people.

Jake parked the car half a block away from Accacio's and opened the door. "Time to go to work, Jakey," he said aloud. "None down and three to go."

His black cashmere overcoat was soaked before he took a dozen steps. Not that it mattered, because soon he wouldn't need an overcoat. There was only two places in Jake Leibowitz's future, Israel or hell. As far as he knew, there wasn't any cold weather in either one of 'em. Still, as soon as he got within sight of Accacio's house, he stepped beneath a huge pine tree and tried to brush the water off. When he looked up, he saw a woman standing on the front porch. She opened the mailbox, pulled out a few letters, then saw him standing there.

"Shit," Jake said, "I ain't even gonna get *one* of the bastards." His hand was already sliding toward the butt of Abe Weinberg's .45, when the woman put a finger to her lips.

"Shhhhh," she said, beckoning him with a finger.

Jake peered through the mist, trying to make out the woman's features. "Goddamned eyes," he muttered.

Now the woman was using her whole hand to beckon him forward. And she was looking over her shoulder, signaling to someone in the house. Or making sure there was nobody watching her.

Jake was tempted to run for it. Jump in the Packard and get his ass back to the Lower East Side before he got it shot off. But then the woman did something completely amazing. She stepped off the porch and walked straight at him. That was when he recognized her, though he couldn't remember her name. She was Steppy Accacio's wife.

"Shhhhh," she whispered. "You no make-a no noise."

Jake tried to meet her eyes, but she wasn't looking up. She was looking down at the .45 he held in his right hand.

"Are ya crazy?" Jake asked. "Comin' out here like this. Whatta ya want?"

"Uppa-stairs," she answered. "Antonio. Uppa-stairs. He sleeps."

"Who the fuck is Antonio?"

"Steppy, Steppy. Uppa-stairs." She closed her eyes and rested her head on her shoulder for a moment. "Sleepa. He sleepa." Then she grabbed the lapel of Jake's cashmere overcoat and half-dragged him across the lawn and into the house.

"There." She pointed to the staircase before walking into the kitchen and closing the door behind her.

Jake didn't waste any time. What was the point? He was *inside* the house which is exactly where he wanted to be. If Steppy Accacio had been waiting for him, he'd be dead already.

His grip tightened on the butt of Abe's .45 as he quietly made his way up the stairs. Five closed doors, two on either side and one at the end of the hallway, led to the various bedrooms and to the toilet. Jake didn't have to guess which one belonged to Steppy Accacio. Accacio's loud snoring left no doubt. Jake, his shoes squishing with each step, walked down to the second door on the left. He put his ear to the wooden panel and listened for a moment. Somebody was sleeping in there, all right. Or some*thing*. Jake wasn't absolutely sure it was a human being. It sounded more like a bear.

Jake looked down at Abe Weinberg's .45. What had Abe called it? Little Richard? Yeah, Little Richard. Abe was dead. The wops had made *him* kill Abe. Izzy was dead, too. Lying in some Jersey swamp. And what had they done, Izzy and Abe, except follow orders? Maybe they *had* made that one mistake, but they'd done a damn good job of the rest of it. So why didn't any of that matter?

"Because we're Jews," Jake muttered, pushing the door open. "And nobody gives a shit about us."

Steppy Accacio was sprawled on the bed. His red silk pajamas contrasted sharply with the starched white sheets. A black mask covered his eyes, making him look like a chubby Lone Ranger.

The mask, Jake decided, had to go. He wanted Steppy Accacio to see what was coming and who it was coming from. He walked over to the bed and slapped Accacio's face with all his strength.

"Ahhhhhh." Accacio's head came off the pillow in a hurry. He ripped at the mask, cursing at the top of his lungs, then froze when he saw Jake Leibowitz and the .45 he held in his hand.

"Whatta ya say, Steppy? Surprised to see me?"

"Don't do it, Jake. Don't shoot me."

"Is that what Izzy said?"

"Izzy? I don't know any Izzy. Whatta ya . . ."

Jake smashed his fist into Accacio's face. It felt so good, he did it again. Then he stepped back to watch the blood flow from Accacio's broken nose down over his mouth and chin.

"It ain't right, what you done, Steppy. I mean after we took care of the pimp and his old lady, that should'a been the end of it. What'd ya think, the bulls'd take me and I'd turn canary? Ya promised us a little time and then ya went out and killed Izzy. It ain't right."

"Ya should've gone to Los Angeles," Accacio mumbled. He licked at the blood on his lips, then shuddered.

"Why didn't *you* go to Los Angeles? Why couldn't ya leave me and Izzy to deal with the cops? See this gun? It's got a name. Little Richard. That's what Abe Weinberg called it. Now Abe's dead. And for what? For killin' a spic?"

"You *kept* the gun?" Accacio's amazement overrode his fear. "You kept a murder weapon?"

"Why shouldn't I keep it? Didn't Joe Faci tell me everything was fixed up? Huh? Didn't he?"

"We thought it was handled, Jake. I swear."

"Thought? Ya pretend ya such a big shot. 'Don't worry about nothin', Jake. We got it covered.' Next thing I know the cops are sniffin' around and I gotta go to Los Angeles. Well, I ain't ya fuckin' dog, Steppy. I ain't *nobody's* dog."

"Look, Jake, I got money . . ."

"Here? Ya got it right here in the house?"

"No."

Jake pulled the trigger without thinking. The slug caught Steppy Accacio in the right shoulder, spinning him into the headboard. It glanced off bone and tore down the soft tissue in his arm, ripping arteries and veins before exiting just behind the elbow. The blood spread across the sheets, soaking them before either man could speak.

"Ya killed me," Steppy Accacio finally said, trying to lift his shredded arm. "Look what ya done. Ya killed me. I got killed by a Jew."

Twenty-five

IT WAS eight o'clock when Moodrow finally decided to give it up. What was the sense of pretending to be patient? Who did he expect to fool? He was the only one there and he definitely wasn't fooling himself. If he had a rope, he'd be skipping it. If he had a heavy bag, he'd be hitting it. The truth was that he'd never been this jumpy in his life. Not even before his first fight, when Uncle Pavlov had to hold him on the stool while the introductions were being made.

Despite his earlier decision to stay away, Moodrow was back inside his own apartment. He was waiting for Allen Epstein to arrive with the package on Jake Leibowitz and his impatience was only partially due to the desire for combat and the fear of arrest. He wanted Jake Leibowitz, no question about it. From that narrow point of view, he'd be a lot better off going to Pearse O'Malley with Leibowitz's photo in hand. But that didn't mean he could ignore the fact that O'Malley was in danger. If Sal Patero had been telling the truth (and Moodrow had no doubt that he was), there were at least four bodies tied to the shooting of Luis Melenguez. One more wouldn't matter. Not to the killers.

Moodrow finally decided to wait until eight-thirty. If Epstein didn't show by eight-thirty, he'd go up to Hell's Kitchen and warn O'Malley, even if that meant losing him as a witness. This decision firmly made, Moodrow pulled a chair up to the window and sat down to watch for Epstein's patrol car. It was a Tuesday evening and despite the dry streets and warm temperatures, the block was nearly empty. The few pedestrians strode purposefully, heads down, arms pumping. The press liked to call New York "The City That Never Sleeps," but that description didn't really apply to working-class neighborhoods where the kids had to be fed, the garbage put out, the dog walked . . . all before *The Perry Como Show*. Or *Gunsmoke*. Or *The $64,000 Question*.

Still, there'd be action on Third Avenue. The hookers would be coming out now that the shops and businesses had closed for the night. Customers were already drifting south from their uptown hotels. The flesh trade worked all night, every night.

The bars were open, too. There was one on every corner and two in the middle of the block. Some catered primarily to the Puerto Ricans, some to the Poles, some to the Italians, some even to the beatniks. There were no Jewish bars, as far as Moodrow knew. Jews, if they drank, had to migrate across cultural borderlines.

At eight-fifteen, Moodrow saw a squad car turn onto the block and his heart jumped in his chest. He had the entire Melenguez file in his possession, complete with the prints lifted at the scene. All courtesy of a repentant Sal Patero. It wouldn't take more than twenty minutes to match them with Leibowitz's prints. Assuming there was a match to be made. If not, he'd still have a photo. And not a mug shot smuggled out of the precinct, either. Leibowitz had been in an army prison, a *federal* prison. The photo would come from J. Edgar Hoover's boys and Moodrow could take it wherever he liked.

The cruiser drove past Moodrow's window, hesitated at the corner, then jumped the light and disappeared. Moodrow's rising excitement disappeared with it. Then the phone rang and Moodrow found himself cursing Ma Bell. It had to be Allen Epstein and it had to be bad news. Maybe the FBI was stalling. Or, worse yet, maybe they'd refused Epstein's request altogether. There was no way to predict what the feds would do in a given situation. And no way to apply pressure, either, because FBI agents answered only to J. Edgar Hoover and Hoover answered only to God. (Or to Satan, depending on whose opinion was asked.)

Moodrow, as he picked up the phone and muttered a greeting, was totally unprepared to discover Kate Cohan on the line. He was even more unprepared for the sorrow in her voice. What he heard was near to grief. He'd been telling himself any number of things about Kate. Telling himself that, for instance, Luis Melenguez's right to justice overrode Kate's pain. Or that there was nothing he could do about it, anyway. Or that Pat Cohan, at least for the time being, was holding all the cards, but he, Stan 'The Man' Moodrow, would someday make it up to her.

Maybe all of that was true, but now he could actually feel Kate's intense confusion as she bounced from her father to her lover like a medicine ball tossed between two heavyweights. He could feel it and he wasn't sure the injustice done to her didn't equal the injustice done to Luis Melenguez.

"Crime would be a lot easier," he said, "if innocent people didn't get hurt. It'd be a lot easier if it was just one crook killing another crook. If there were no families, no innocent bystanders, no . . ."

"Stanley, what are you talking about?"

"I'm talking about you, Kate. Your father wants to put me in jail, but the funny thing is that I'm not worried about myself. Maybe I should be, but I'm not. I'm worried about *you.*"

"I'm all right, Stanley. It was really bad for a while, but I'm better now. I want to hear your side of it. That's what I called for. I realize you don't have to tell me anything, but I need to hear it."

She didn't sound all right. She sounded like she was about to burst into tears and Moodrow didn't have the faintest idea what to do about it.

"Is your father there? Is he listening? Like the last time you called?"

"Daddy went out. I'm alone." She hesitated for a moment. "How did you know Daddy was listening?"

"He called me. Right after you hung up. He called to rub it in."

"Have you been arrested, Stanley?" Kate abruptly changed the subject. "Are you out on bail?"

"No, I'm still walking the streets. A couple of detectives and half a dozen patrolmen came down this afternoon, but I wasn't here. They questioned all my neighbors."

Actually, Greta Bloom had given him hell for coming back, but he really hadn't had any choice. Father Sam had refused to give him anything more than a place to sleep. The priest had drawn the line at having Allen Epstein (or *any* cop except Moodrow, for that matter) come into his gym on business.

"I can't do it, Stanley," he'd explained. "I got kids here who've been in trouble a time or two. If I go takin' sides in a cop war, it could be the winner'll come out with a grudge against Sam Berrigan. Too much of my funding comes from the Police Athletic League for me to take that risk. You wanna stay here, fine. But no calls and no visitors. My boys come first."

"Stanley," Kate said, "are you there?"

"Yeah, I'm here." Moodrow took a deep breath. "You want to know the whole story? That's what you said?"

"I want to hear your side of it. I'm not saying . . ."

"Wait a minute, Kate. There's someone at the door."

"Don't answer it."

"I'd better. It sounds like the son-of-a-bitch is gonna break it down." Moodrow covered the receiver with his hand. He knew who it was. Allen Epstein had knocked three times, then stopped, then knocked again. "Wait a minute, Sarge. I'm on the phone."

"Stanley? Stanley?" Kate was near to panic. Her voice quivered like a plucked guitar string.

"I gotta go, Kate," Moodrow whispered into the phone.

"Are you being arrested?"

"No, it's something else. We're almost to the end, now. In a few days, you should know everything." But would she? Even as he spoke, Moodrow had the sinking feeling that Kate would never really know why her world had suddenly collapsed.

"Be careful, Stanley. Take care of yourself. I . . . Oh, damn, I don't know what to say. I can't stand this."

She hung up before Moodrow could reply, leaving him with a surge of emotion, a mixture of guilt and rage that threatened to overwhelm him. What he wanted was the simplicity of a movie western, but all he could see were victims, some dead and some living. Would arresting Jake Leibowitz or Steppy Accacio or Pat Cohan ease Nenita Melenguez's suffering? Would cop justice, courtesy of Stanley Moodrow, feed her children?

Moodrow walked over to the front door and pulled it open. "Give me some good news, Sarge," he said. "I could use it."

Epstein stood in the doorway for a moment. "What's the matter with you?"

"I just spoke to Kate. I feel like I'm killing her." Moodrow stepped back. "Get inside. Let's at least close the door."

"What could I say? If there were no victims, we'd be out of business." Epstein walked into the apartment and waited for Moodrow to close the door. "I got everything you wanted, Stanley. Or Maguire got it. His brother's an agent, so it didn't turn out to be a big problem."

Moodrow sighed. "All right, let's go into the bedroom. I don't wanna show a light. And thanks for the sympathy."

The bell rang before they could move.

"Who is it?"

"Police, open up."

"Give me your hands, Stanley," Epstein said matter-of-factly. "I been thinking about this for the last four hours." He snatched a pair of handcuffs off his belt, slapped them on Moodrow's wrists, then smiled. "Wouldn't it be funny if me and Pat Cohan have been working together all this time?"

Moodrow grinned. "I think I'm starting to feel a lot better," he said.

"That not an appropriate response, Stanley. Maybe you should see a head-shrinker."

Epstein lifted Moodrow's .38, then opened the door. The two detectives in the hallway performed a double-take that would have made the Three Stooges proud.

"What the fuck is this?"

The one who spoke, the oldest, was short and fat. His three chins wobbled obscenely as he jerked his head from the stitches in Moodrow's head to the stripes on Epstein's sleeve. The second detective was taller and smarter. *He* kept his eyes on the Smith & Wesson in Epstein's hand.

"What's with the gun, Sarge?" he asked. "And what're you doing here?"

Epstein grinned. "My name is Allen Epstein. *Sergeant* Allen Epstein. This is my precinct, the Seventh. And *my* bust. Who are you?"

"I'm Donnelly," the short one said. "And this is Wittstein. We're from Midtown North. We got a warrant for a cop named Moodrow. I take it this is him."

"What about it?" Epstein asked.

The two detectives looked at each other. The obvious (though unasked) question was how do you arrest someone who's already under arrest? Especially when you, yourself, have been caught in the wrong place at the wrong time.

"And why is it," Epstein continued, "that two suits from Midtown North come all the way down to the Seventh to make an arrest for a routine assault that didn't occur in their precinct? How is it that you even *know* there's a warrant out for Detective Stanley Moodrow? Who sent you down here? Who put the warrant in your hand?"

"Wait a second, Sarge," Wittstein said. The tips of his ears glowed red. "You got no right to question us."

"Wrong," Epstein said. "I outrank the both of you. Unless one of you passed the sergeant's exam. The fact that you're wearing a cheap suit and a spotted tie doesn't mean squat. I outrank every detective in the job."

"That's just technical," Wittstein hissed.

"Technical? I could order you off the scene, but I'm not gonna do that. In fact, even though it's my bust and two dicks from Midtown North are trying to take it away from me, I'm gonna let you accompany me down to the house so I can book this vicious criminal. While we're there, maybe I can get you an appointment to see the captain. He's a busy man, the captain, but I think he'll wanna know what two precinct detectives from Midtown North are doing on the Lower East Side. I think the captain'll give us a little personal time."

"We have a right to make an arrest anywhere in the city." Wittstein was livid. "Who the fuck are you to tell us where to operate?"

"Because it never happens innocently," Epstein ignored the challenge. "*Never.* You're down here because someone sent you. Someone who didn't trust Captain John McElroy, Commander of the Seventh Precinct, to get the job done."

Wittstein started to respond, but Donnelly waved him off. "All right, Sarge, you're holding all the cards. Me and Wittstein, we're just following orders. The lieutenant asked us to come over and knock on the door. We didn't expect to find anyone, because the lieutenant also told us the suspect was long gone. That's how come we didn't bring backup. Now, me and Wittstein, we're goin' back up to Midtown North and tell the lieutenant that Sergeant Allen Epstein put the suspect under arrest before we arrived on the scene. And you could forget about draggin' us down to the Seventh. Unless you plan to shoot us in the back."

Epstein waited until the two detectives were out of sight, then closed the door and walked over to the window.

"Hey, Sarge," Moodrow said, "how 'bout takin' off these cuffs?"

"Wait a second, Stanley, I wanna see them drive away." He stared down at the street for a moment. "They're going. We got a little time." He turned back to find a grinning Stanley Moodrow.

"You're in it now, Sarge. You're in it up to your neck."

"Unless I actually make the arrest, Stanley. If I make the arrest, I'm a hero." Epstein was already turning the key in the handcuffs. "Jesus, what am I gonna tell the captain?"

"Tell him I escaped. Tell him you cuffed me with my own cuffs and I must have had a key."

"That's another charge against you, Stanley. And a black mark on my record. Plus, it still doesn't explain what I was doing here in the first place."

"Then tell him the truth. Tell him that *we*—meaning me and you—are gonna bring a murderer before the bar of justice." The look of disbelief on Epstein's face brought Moodrow up short. "Take a seat, Sarge. There's a few things you need to know. When you hear what I got to say, you're gonna feel a lot better."

Moodrow took his time, detailing O'Neill's statement and the contents of the complaint signed by Samuelson and Lieutenant Rosten. As he described Sal Patero's confession, Epstein's eyes began to widen. By the time Moodrow finished, the sergeant's mouth was hanging open.

"Holy shit. Patero *admitted* to covering up a homicide?"

"Well, I did ask him real nice."

"Don't give me that crap. You must've halfway killed him."

"Actually, he wasn't that tough. He didn't last as long as the Playtex Burglar."

Epstein took a minute to think about it. "How come you didn't tell me about this before?" he finally asked.

"I didn't trust you, Sarge. It's that simple."

"You're a smart kid, Stanley. With that blank face, you look like a big dumb flatfoot, but you're smarter than hell. Why don't you tell me what you think I should do? Being as you already know."

"First, I take you down to my neighbor's apartment and let you look at the evidence. Then, you go back to the house and find the captain. Tell him you're a go-between, a negotiator. Describe the evidence. Make sure he understands that *he's* not involved. Tell him that I threatened to go to the papers if you brought me in. All you did was act in the best interests of the Department. Which interests would be well served by allowing Stanley Moodrow to make a case against Jake Leibowitz."

"I don't know, Stanley. The captain's got all ten fingers in Patero's pie."

"That's the whole point. McElroy's on the take. The last thing he wants is for me to go public. I've been thinking about this for a long time. About what I want and what I don't. You tell McElroy that I'm not out to fuck the Department. That's not my intention at all. I have two goals here. I wanna put Luis Melenguez's killer in the electric chair and I want to keep my job. Look, Sarge, what I'm trying for is a little offense. Pat Cohan claims to run lower Manhattan. He brags about it. So why hasn't McElroy sent half the precinct after me? Why does Cohan have to send out detectives from Midtown North?"

"The guys are refusing, Stanley. That's why Cohan's reaching into other precincts."

"Yeah? So, why didn't McElroy assemble a squad and directly order the men to cooperate? Why didn't he jump on their heads with both feet which is what precinct commanders *always* do when the boys get out of hand? I got a funny feeling that McElroy didn't know about the coverup. I also have a feeling that McElroy has no interest in helping Pat Cohan. Look, Sarge, you make sure McElroy understands that *he's* not implicated. Maybe we can isolate Cohan. Maybe McElroy will go over Cohan's head. Whatever happens, I don't see how we can lose. You came here to talk me into surrendering, but when you saw what I had and realized it was enough to make headlines, you decided to back off and consult your superiors. They'll give you a fucking commendation."

Epstein, smiling, held his hands up. "Okay, I surrender."

"Not yet, Sarge. Because I got one more favor to ask. I was hoping you'd take the prints home with you and make the comparison yourself. Because I have to get up to see Pearse O'Malley. Before someone decides to kill him."

Twenty-six

IT WAS nearly midnight as Pat Cohan drove along the Belt Parkway near Idlewild Airport in southern Queens. He could plainly hear the roar of landing airplanes. He could hear the planes a quarter of a mile away, but he could barely see the car in front of him. The warm air and the rain had had a predictable effect on the icy waters of nearby Jamaica Bay. The fog was so thick you could taste it.

Maybe that was why Joe Faci had chosen Howard Beach for their meeting. Because you couldn't be followed in this fog. A tail would have to work in your trunk to keep up. It was definitely a night for murder. Which is exactly what Pat Cohan wanted to talk about.

Or, better, he wanted to talk about murders. Murders past, murders present and murders future. The past was two pimps and a spic named Luis Melenguez who forgot to mind his own business. The present was Steppy Accacio, dead in his own home. The future was a Jew named Leibowitz. And maybe an Irishman named O'Malley. And a cop named Moodrow.

It was unthinkable, really. Or, at least, it always *had* been. Killing a cop, the ultimate crime in the eyes of the NYPD. Hell, you could shoot the mayor and half the force would go out and have a beer to celebrate. But let a cop get killed and it didn't matter if he was the dirtiest lowlife on the force. Two thousand uniformed patrolmen, accompanied by the Emerald Society bagpipers, would turn out for his funeral. The killer would not live to see a jail cell.

Pat Cohan drew a deep breath. His whole life was falling apart. There was no use pretending things were under control. His life was falling apart and he wasn't going to get any help from the Department. From *his* Department. From the Department that his father and his father's father had helped to build.

Maybe it would have been easier if the word had come from an Irishman. From someone whose family had known the pain of the Five Points and the Fourth Ward. Someone whose family had lived through cholera, diphtheria, smallpox, tuberculosis. Nobody came to help you when you needed help. Not in 1847 when his grandfather had arrived in New York. And you didn't send for the doctor when Granny got sick. No, you nursed your own as best you could and when they died you tossed the corpse out in the street. The morgue wagon came through every morning, just before dawn, to collect the bodies.

What it made you was strong enough to fight your way out. Strong enough to elect your own mayors and councilmen. Politicians who made sure *you* got the best jobs. Who gave you a shot at an education. Who gave you the New York Police Department as your one special jewel.

That was why it came so hard. So hard to be summoned to the office of Deputy Chief Milton Morton. Summoned all the way from Bayside by a hook-nosed sheeny with a collection of degrees that covered the wall behind his desk like flypaper. So hard to be told, in no uncertain terms, to back off, to let Stanley Moodrow pursue his investigation unimpeded.

"Do not hinder," Morton had said. "Do not help. Do not do anything at all."

Then he'd leaned on the desk, forming a little tent with his fingers and palms as if he was about to pray. "I'm not jumping to any conclusions here, Pat," he'd continued. "But from everything I can gather, Stanley Moodrow is a good cop."

"There's a warrant out for Stanley Moodrow. He assaulted a police officer."

"Well, there seems to be two sides to that question." Milton Morton had gotten up and crossed the room. "At least, that's what I'm hearing from the commander of the Seventh Precinct. McElroy thinks we should, as they say, let sleeping dogs lie. Eventually, the pieces will sort themselves out." He'd opened the door and waited, a wet smile pasted to his narrow pock-marked face.

"Have you spoken to Chief Rooney?"

"Chief Rooney and I are in perfect sync on this, Pat. The Chief, as you know, is a big fight fan. He admires Stanley. Always has."

Pat Cohan took the exit for Cross Bay Boulevard, made a left at the light and headed south. His destination wasn't really Howard Beach. It was a neighborhood with no name, a small island suspended between Far Rockaway and the Queens mainland.

Cross Bay Boulevard, at 197th Avenue, was lined with touristy restaurants and closed real estate offices. A cluster of houses sat far back in the shadows. They were summer homes for the most part, escapes from the broiling city, and the overwhelming majority were dark. An occasional lit window, glowing dimly in the fog, announced the presence of souls hardy enough to brave the cold relentless winds that ordinarily blew off Jamaica Bay.

But there was no wind tonight. And it wasn't cold, either. Tonight the fog curled around the streetlamps like cotton candy. It slithered down telephone poles to fall on already glistening sidewalks.

Pat drove along the Boulevard, peering through the fog at the various neon signs until he found the one he was looking for—Sharkey's Seafood Palace. He took a deep breath and turned into the parking lot. It was time, now. Time to do or die.

The restaurant, on first inspection, seemed to be deserted. Pat Cohan, standing just inside the still-open door, had to resist an urge to flee. Then he saw Joe Faci sitting in the shadows at the end of the bar. Faci was smiling and waving him over.

"Good to see ya," Faci said as Pat approached. He offered his hand and waited until Cohan took it. "I thought maybe ya would'a found it tough goin'. What with the fog and all. Cross Bay's a bitch for fog."

"I guess I got used to it, Joe. Being as I've been out in every kind of weather."

"Them was the old days. You been sittin' behind a desk for a long time."

Pat Cohan stiffened momentarily. Was he being insulted? Faci's tone was friendly, but you could never be sure with these people. They'd feed you for hours before stabbing you in the back. Sausages and switchblades. That was their way.

"Who would'a believed a Jew could cause so much trouble?" Faci continued. "Who would'a believed that a Jew could kill Steppy Accacio?"

"You don't seem too upset," Pat Cohan observed. He sat on the barstool next to Faci and looked around for the bartender.

"We're havin' a private party here, Pat. Whatta ya want?"

"A Scotch would be nice. I don't suppose you've got Irish whiskey."

"Hey, Carmine," Faci called. "We got Irish whiskey?"

A door behind Joe Faci opened and a short, thick man emerged. "Irish whiskey? You got the wrong neighborhood, pal."

"Pat," Joe Faci said, "this here is Carmine Stettecase. He's takin' over for Steppy."

Pat Cohan grinned. "Now, I was thinking that job would fall to you, Joe. I was thinking you'd get yourself a promotion."

"It ain't in the cards," Joe Faci said, his face composed. "The family wants me to take a vacation. See the old country. I got relatives in Palermo."

"The family?" Cohan was still smiling.

"The bosses," Carmine interrupted. "They figure this bullshit ain't good for business. Bodies flyin' everywhere. Hey, America's the Land of Progress, right? So how come we're goin' back to the old days?"

"Does that mean you intend to let this Leibowitz off the hook, Joe?" Pat Cohan pushed the question at Joe Faci. "After what he did to your boss?"

"Life is like that," Faci said calmly. "Especially the life we live."

"Nobody said nothin' about Leibowitz comin' outta this in one piece." Carmine took a bottle of Johnnie Walker off the shelf. He half-filled a tumbler, then set it in front of Pat Cohan. "But what with Steppy dead and Joe goin' across the ocean, there ain't much the sheeny can do to hurt us. If we find him first, that'll be the end of it. If he gets busted, he'll most likely get the chair. What we don't want is more bodies lyin' around where people could find 'em."

"What about O'Malley?" Pat sipped at his drink. He could feel the bad news coming.

"O'Malley ain't a problem for us," Faci said, "because the only mug he saw belongs to the Jew and the Jew ain't family. Leibowitz is hired help and we don't have no obligation to protect him."

"And Moodrow? The cop who made all the trouble in the first place?"

Carmine shook his head. "Stanley ain't doin' nothin' to *us*. I mean, when ya think about it, the Jew made it easy when he knocked Steppy off. He could'a maybe traded Steppy for a life sentence. Now, Stanley's gonna put him in the hot seat. That's why we don't gotta do nothin' drastic. Stanley's gonna fry the punk."

"That's the second time you said 'Stanley.' Is Moodrow a friend of yours?"

"I wouldn't exactly say we was friends," Carmine said, grinning, "but we was schoolmates at St. Stephen's."

Pat Cohan felt disoriented, almost dizzy. "Are you telling me that Stanley Moodrow's working with *you*?"

"Ya gotta be kiddin' me. Stanley's the fuckin' Lone Ranger. I got about as much chance of gettin' to Stanley as gettin' to heaven. Even Pius XII couldn't fix *that* one."

Pat Cohan watched the two men, Stettecase and Faci, as they enjoyed Carmine's joke. He understood that they were laughing at him, at what they perceived to be his foolishness. But there really wasn't anything he could do about it. His life was falling apart. What had seemed like a gentle slide into the oblivion of retirement had become a runaway locomotive flying down the side of a mountain.

"What's the point of this meeting, Joe?" he asked. "If all we're going to do is sit on our hands?"

Joe Faci glanced at Carmine. To Pat Cohan, the puzzled look on his face seemed absolutely genuine.

"Pat," Faci said, "we gotta get back to business. I'm talkin' about the gambling business and the whore business and the drug business. That's why I wanted ya to meet Carmine."

Carmine Stettecase nodded agreement. "All we want is things should get back to normal. Normal has been very good for you, Pat. Very good."

Pat Cohan leaned forward, "Listen, you stupid wop, there is no normal with '*Stanley*' on the loose. Patero's already running scared. He's given '*Stanley*' some kind of a statement. If *I* go and *Sal* goes, you end up with nothing. No protection, no contacts." Pat Cohan took a deep breath. "Let me tell you how it works. In case you don't know. The first thing they'll do is eliminate ninety percent of the ranking officers in the Seventh Precinct. Captains, lieutenants, sergeants—they transfer them out or ask them to retire. The new captain knows that his job is to double the arrest rate in the first year. That covers the department's royal behind. Now, where do you suppose, boyo, that all these arrests are going to be made? Who do you think is going to be arrested? The whores, the pimps, the runners, the bookies, the dealers . . . Need I continue?"

Carmine Stettecase's expression never changed. He stared at Pat Cohan with the calm neutrality of a chemist looking through a microscope. "I could see you're in a bad spot, Pat. Only there ain't nothin' we can do about it. I mean there ain't nothin' *I* could see. How 'bout you, Joe? Could ya see anything?"

Joe Faci shook his head and Pat Cohan suddenly felt much better. *Now* it was finally being spelled out. He was completely alone.

"Unless," Faci said, his face brightening, "he's askin' us to *kill* Stanley. Is that what ya want, Pat? Ya want we should knock Stanley off? And maybe Sal Patero, too?" He paused for a response, but got none. "Because if somethin' happens to Stanley, if he should like disappear without a trace, all that shit ya say he's got is gonna fall on *your* head. I mean what ya got here is a situation where ya can't win for losin'."

Pat Cohan got off the stool. He straightened his tie, then turned to Carmine. "Well, boyo, you've made yourself plain. And being as you're in the clear, I can't say as I blame you. Would I go out on a limb for Carmine Stettecase? Probably not. But here's something to put between the meatballs in your dago brain. Just suppose that I *do* survive. Suppose that a month from now I'm still running the show in southern Manhattan. Do ya think, boyo, that I might be lookin' to get even? To get even with *you*?"

Carmine sighed loudly, spreading his arms. "Pat, whatta ya want us to do?"

"I want you to kill the prick." Now it was out in the open. "After that, it's my word against Sal Patero's."

Pat Cohan started to walk out, but Carmine stopped him. "All right, ya want that Stanley should disappear. Maybe we could accommodate ya, but it ain't like turnin' off the radio. First, we gotta get permission. Then we gotta import the talent. Do ya think ya could hold out for a couple of days?"

"How many days is a 'couple'?"

"A week, maybe."

"Too long. And what happens if you *don't* get permission?"

"Look, Pat, I ain't gonna do it myself." Carmine was angry for the first time. "If that's what ya want, I'll loan you a cold piece and you could put it behind Stanley's ear and personally blow his fuckin' brains out."

Cohan, halfway to the door, turned to face the two men at the bar. "No, it has to be handled by a professional. But a week is too long. It'll be over in a week."

Joe Faci's face brightened. "I just thought of a happy ending. Tell me what ya think of this: Stanley finds Jake; Jake kills Stanley; Jake gets the chair; everybody lives happily ever after. Cause I'll tell ya one thing, Pat. This fuckin' Jew is as tough as they come. What me and Steppy done is take him too light. It could be that Stanley'll make the same mistake. I mean who would'a figured a *Jew* could be that tough?"

Dominick Favara waited until Pat Cohan pulled out of the parking lot before leaving the office to join his partner. Carmine, without asking, went behind the bar and poured Dominick a glass of red wine.

"Ya heard?" Carmine asked.

"Yeah, I heard."

"Whatta ya think?"

"I think cops are fairies. What they oughta do is a little hard time. That'd toughen 'em up."

"I don't know about that," Carmine said. "There's always Stanley."

The two men looked at each other and grinned.

"*Leave Stanley alone*," they shouted in unison.

"I don't get it," Faci said.

"Don't worry about it," Favara responded. "Let's worry about Santo Silesi instead. Santo's *real*, if ya take my meaning."

"I been tryin' to think of somethin' all night," Faci said. "But I keep comin' up blank. Santo wants to revenge his uncle. I don't see no way to stop him."

"He ain't Sicilian," Carmine grunted. "What does he know about revenge?"

"That's the whole point, Carmine. He *ain't* Sicilian. Nobody's gonna give him a job. Uncle Steppy was his only hope in life. His ticket to the big time. Now, he's got nothin'."

Dominick Favara handed his empty glass to Carmine. "Do that again." He waited until his glass was full, then took a sip before speaking. "Santo Silesi's got nothin' on *us*. Ditto for the Jew. Let 'em kill each other off. It ain't our business. What we gotta do is prepare in case the cops put the heat on. Now, I got an idea for the dope business. The way the bulls make themselves look good is by sweepin' up the guys on the street, right? I'm talkin' about the junkies and the dealers. Now, ask yaself why we gotta put Italian kids on streetcorners where the cops can get to 'em when there's a thousand spics out there who'd suck our dicks for a chance to take the risk. Steppy did a smart thing when he hired them Jews. It didn't work out, but it was a smart thing. What we gotta do is find the meanest street gang in the projects on Avenue D and teach 'em how to make money. Maybe our profits'll go down at first, but if things work out the way I think, we could move on every project in the city."

Favara raised his glass to Joe Faci. "Here's to a healthy vacation, Joe. You'll be home in six months. I guarantee it." He turned to Carmine. "And here's to the future, Carmine. As the nuns used to say: 'The Lord works in mysterious ways.' "

Twenty-seven

JANUARY 22

"IT WAS pretty amazing, Sarge," Moodrow said as he filled Allen Epstein's mug with steaming coffee. "I come walking down the hall, thinkin' about what I'm gonna do if the uniform gives me any trouble, when I see this old cop sleeping in a chair outside O'Malley's door. I swear, Sarge, he looks like he's been dead for twenty years, like somebody unwrapped the mummy and dressed him in a blue uniform. I don't know how these guys hang on, but this one's much too old to stay awake at night. So what I do is kick the chair out from under him, jab my shield in his face and start screaming about how he's endangering the life of a witness and I'm gonna have his pension for a midnight snack. By the time I finish, he's ready to polish my shoes with his tongue. He doesn't even ask for my name. Meanwhile, O'Malley turns out to be sharp as a tack. The first thing he wants to know is why he's being held prisoner.

" 'The filthy Brits have been abusing us for a thousand years. Tell me, now, copper, could it be I've come all the way to America only to arrive in Belfast? Do ya think maybe the captain had a wee bit of a nip and sailed himself a great circle back to Ireland?'

"What happened was the suits gave him a choice: sit in his apartment or be held as a material witness in the West Street jail."

Epstein grunted. "They wanted him where they could find him."

"Which makes sense from a police point of view, because O'Malley, in addition to being a witness to murder, also happens to be in this country illegally. According to him, the British are trying to nail him for a series of bombings and shootings in Belfast. I got his confidence by telling him about Pat Cohan and Steppy Accacio *before* I showed him Jake's mug shot."

"What'd he say?"

"He said, 'Do ya know of the troubles in Ireland, laddie? Do ya know the history of the poor unfortunates in that sad land? Do ya know how the sons and daughters of old Ireland have been driven to awful deeds in the name of freedom?' "

"You've got the accent down pat, Stanley, but does it *have* to be word for word?"

Moodrow stirred a teaspoon of sugar into his coffee. He was feeling too good to take offense. One of the latents found in O'Neill's office had matched Jake Leibowitz's left index finger. Add that to O'Malley's signed statement placing Jake in the hallway just after the O'Neill murders and it added up to a search warrant for Leibowitz's last known address, his mother's apartment, and an arrest warrant for Jake himself.

"What O'Malley's gonna do is take it on the lam as soon as he figures a way to get out of there. He'd be gone already if the fire escape outside his window wasn't hanging by a thread. Which means that we have to move fast. We've gotta get the DA's office to pull O'Malley off the street before he takes a hike. Or before someone kills him. Maybe Maguire'll help. I didn't wanna ask him to come out in the open, but if O'Malley disappears, the case against Leibowitz is thinner than Olive Oyl's butt."

Epstein held up a hand. "What you said about me being a hero for *not* busting you? It turned out to be a hundred percent accurate. I told McElroy that I went to your apartment to ask you to surrender. I was afraid of what you might do if someone else showed up. Then you gave me Patero's confession and the rest of the evidence. You said that you'd go to the papers if I tried to arrest you. What could I do? I'm only a sergeant. How could I make a decision like that? By the time I finished describing Patero's confession, the captain was ready to give me a medal. McElroy guarantees that you will *not* be arrested before Leibowitz goes down. He *begged* me to help keep the lid on. You don't need Maguire, Stanley. You can go to the DA's people for whatever you want."

Moodrow got up and walked over to the kitchen window. He pulled aside the curtain and looked down at the street below. It was six o'clock in the morning and he was anxious to get to work.

"Why did McElroy cave in so fast?"

"A couple of reasons. He kicked me out of his office at one point. Asked me to wait in the bullpen for a few minutes while he made some calls. I figure he phoned his rabbi, who has to be at *least* a deputy chief, and his rabbi ordered him to hold off. McElroy's only forty-five. He's a cinch to make inspector and he could go much higher. But not if he has a major scandal in his precinct. Think about it, Stanley. It's the precinct commander's job to keep things running smoothly. Business as usual is what it's all about. If the papers get their hands on Patero's confession, McElroy's career is *over.*"

Moodrow watched the raindrops bounce off the sidewalk. The temperature was down in the thirties and the few pedestrians were hunched beneath umbrellas as they hustled toward the subway. Some were actually running.

"There's a kid named Moretti in the DA's office. He's eager, real eager. I think I'm gonna use him for the warrants, Sarge. Make sure it's done right. The judges don't read the warrants before they sign them. It could be that Cohan has enough pull to get an ADA to blow the paperwork."

"That's stretching it, Stanley."

"I just wanna be sure." Moodrow dropped the curtain and walked back to the table. "Moretti comes in early to work on pending cases. I've gotta get to him before he goes to court. You wanna come along and keep an eye on me? Maybe they'll make you commissioner."

Santo Silesi was getting very tired of trailing Mama Leibowitz through the Essex Street Market. How could anyone, even a Jew, spend an hour choosing pickled tomatoes from a barrel? Why didn't the pickle man shove one of those tomatoes up her gargantuan butt? What the hell could they be talking about?

When Mama Leibowitz shifted her attention to a tub of double-sours, Santo emitted a groan of genuine pain. If there was any other way to get into Jake Leibowitz's apartment, any other way to trap his uncle's killer, he'd take it in a hot flash. Except, of course, simply kicking the door down, the only other way he could think of. Santo's hatred of Jake Leibowitz hadn't quite driven him over the edge. Not yet. Not while Mama Leibowitz was available to *lead* him through that door.

"You are having the pain, *señor*?"

Santo glanced down at the shoe salesman kneeling at his feet. You had to feel sorry for the little greaseball. Six pair of shoes and no hope of a sale. Not at *Paolo's Zapateria* with its two-dollar cardboard specials. The shoes were so goddamned pointy they looked more like deadly weapons than something you'd wear on your feet.

Puerto Rican Fence Climbers. That's what everybody called them. The perfect size for a chain-link fence in your neighbor's back yard.

"Don't you have any *brown* shoes?" Santo asked. He looked at his own Florsheim wing tips sitting next to one of Paolo's specials, two thoroughbreds next to a plow horse, and shook his head. Spics and sheenys—what had the world come to?

"This is disgusting," he said.

"You no like the shoes, *señor*?"

"Too greasy," Santo muttered, slipping his feet into his own shoes. The bitch was moving at last, sliding her blubber along the concrete floor. As she passed each stall, she shouted a greeting to the proprietor.

"Yoo-hoo, Solly, how's by you today? How's business?"

How's your son? Your daughter? Your wife? Your grandchildren? How's your heart? Your liver? Your second cousin's hairy butt? How's . . . Disgusting. But maybe not as disgusting as all the bullshit he'd taken from Jake Leibowitz. He could remember every episode. Word for word. The way Santo Silesi saw it, there were only two options and both of them spelled death. Death for Jake Leibowitz. Or death for Santo Silesi.

When Mama Leibowitz stopped at Moishe's Kosher Poultry, Santo ducked into the first available stall: B&B Foundation Garments.

"You want maybe a girdle?"

Santo stared down at the old lady who'd asked the question. She couldn't have been more than four feet tall and she was skinny as a rail. Meanwhile, there was no fear in her voice. None whatsoever.

"Sorry," Santo said, "wrong sewer." He crossed the aisle between stalls and began to sort through a tray of men's wallets. Mama Leibowitz showed no sign of moving on. She was busy examining a live chicken in a little wooden cage. Santo wondered what she was looking for. The cage was so small, the animal could barely move. As he watched, the proprietor, a tall skinny man with an adam's apple that bobbed up and down like a yo-yo, put the cage back and brought out another.

"This is a chicken?" Santo heard Mama Leibowitz cry out in disbelief. She sounded the way she would after he, Santo Silesi, blew the top of her son's head off. "This chicken is so old it's a *duck.*"

"Why should an old chicken be a duck?"

"Please, I didn't come off the boat this minute. I want a chicken that's a chicken for roasting, not a hen for stewing."

"Maybe you'd like to come around the counter and pick one for yourself? Before I get a hernia from carrying the cages?"

"That would be fine."

Santo watched the proprietor swing a section of the counter up. Even turned sideways, Mama Leibowitz could barely squeeze her fat gut through the opening. Then she was in the back, surrounded by squawking birds and the acrid stench of manure. The chickens, perhaps sensing her intentions, began to flutter in the cages, sending up a thick cloud of feathers that veiled her bulk.

Maybe she'll disappear, Santo thought. Maybe she'll pull a Houdini and vanish.

The chickens were squawking in near panic, but nobody in the market appeared to notice. It was everyday stuff to the shoppers and the shopkeepers. The chaos. The gossip. The dirty concrete floor and the ill-kept stalls piled with shoddy merchandise. All perfectly natural in this universe of sheenys and spics.

Well, the hell with it. The fat bitch didn't know him from Adam. Santo walked right past her to the hot dog wagon near the Delancey Street entrance to the market and ordered two franks and a beer. Naturally, he didn't get to finish the first frank, before she up and walked right past him. *Without* the chicken.

What I'm gonna do, Santo thought, as he imitated her slow-motion walk through the neighborhood, is make sure Jake looks me right in the eye before I kill him. He's gotta know who's pulling the trigger. Maybe I'll gut-shoot him first. So I could watch him flop around until he begs me to finish him off.

Mama Leibowitz seemed to know everybody on the Lower East Side, calling out greetings to passersby as she waddled the four blocks to her apartment. It'd finally stopped raining and the housewives were out in force, so she had plenty of company. The five-minute stroll took almost an hour. She'd shuffle forward a few yards, her body swaying like a metronome as she tried to pick her feet off the sidewalk, then it would begin: "Sadie, how's by you? Your husband's arthritis, it's better, maybe?" Santo thought he was going to go off his rocker.

Still, it wasn't all bad. Despite the stops and starts, Mama Leibowitz never turned around, not once, not even when Santo followed her through the entrance to her building, when he practically clipped her heels as she hauled herself up three flights of stairs. Not even when he yanked out his .44 and came up directly behind her as she turned the key in the lock.

Santo slammed the revolver into Mama Leibowitz's head with all the force at his command. He was *trying* to kill her. Actually *trying*. Not that there was time to check her out. He pushed her body through the door, then stepped across her blubbery butt as he swept the open space in front of him. He was standing in the living room. The kitchen was on his right. He could see most, but not all of it. On his left, a hallway led to the bedrooms.

He stepped out into the center of the living room, extending the revolver, holding it with both hands. The bitch fell without a sound, he reminded himself. There's no rush. Jake *can't* know you're here. Do it slow and do it right. Because the very worst thing that could happen is to die knowing you let the Jew off the hook.

The kitchen was empty. Santo crossed the living room, keeping his body close to the wall. The bathroom door at the far end of the apartment was open. It, too, was empty. Unless Jake was hiding in the tub. But Santo couldn't worry about that. You couldn't look in the closets until you covered the obvious places. Which meant the bedrooms, two *closed* doors on the left side of the hallway.

If I'm not afraid to die, Santo asked himself, then why am I sweating? Why's my hand shaking? This isn't the way it happens in the movies. It isn't the way it happened with Izzy Stein, either. Izzy went out like a man. He was tough and he made it easy. What if Jake was behind one of those doors? What if he was kneeling behind the bed with a .45 aimed at the very space Santo Silesi was sure to occupy?

A moment followed in which there were *no* thoughts. A dead space, a lost chunk of time when the world simply didn't exist. Wasn't there a thing in the Bible about time standing still? Or the sun standing still? There were objects in front of Santo's eyes, but he couldn't see them, couldn't focus. They were there and they weren't there. Like ghosts in a movie.

I'm not cut out for this, Santo thought. I'm not a pro. And if I don't get my act together, I never will be.

What he wanted to do was run from room to room, throwing open doors and closets, to scream Jake's name, calling him out to a fair fight. There's only room for one of us in this town, pardner. Come tomorrow at noon, that one is gonna be *me*.

In the end, when the world was solid again, when chairs and tables were chairs and tables, when the sofa didn't shimmer like a desert mirage, Santo took it very slowly. He tiptoed over to the first door and put his ear against the wood, reminding himself that Jake couldn't know there was anyone else in the apartment. The fact that all he, Santo, could hear was dead silence, didn't mean that Jake was inside with a .45 trained on the door.

Santo turned the knob carefully, almost rejoicing in its smooth motion, then pushed it open, careful to keep most of his body behind the frame. Still, his heart beat wildly as his eyes surveyed the empty room.

What I should've done, he thought, is wait somewhere for Jake to come to *me*. Because I can't control this shit.

He scanned the room quickly. It was a woman's room, Mama Leibowitz's most likely. There was no one under the neatly made bed, he could see that much, but the closet door was closed. Jake could be in that closet, squatting down, a shotgun cradled in his arms. He could be just about to kick it open, to come out blasting . . .

Santo closed the bedroom door. He *had* to close it. To get to that other room before he drowned in fear. Quickly and quietly, he moved to the next door, laying his ear against it as he had with the first. The cool wood felt somehow comforting and his first thought was to leave his face there, to rest it against the door as he would against a woman's breast. There was no sound on the other side.

Finally, as though he were under water and pushing against a tidal wave, Santo managed to turn the knob and shove the door open. The room was deserted.

He stepped inside, already beginning to feel like a cowardly fool. The closet door was mercifully open. A few suits and jackets hung inside, far too few to conceal Jake Leibowitz or anybody else. The truth, despite Santo's racing pulse, was that Jake Leibowitz had flown the coop. He'd taken it on the lam, which, under the circumstances, was the only thing he *could* have done.

You're a punk, Santo told himself, a miserable punk. And this don't mean you're off the hook, either. You *still* have to find the Jew and take care of him. Because if you don't revenge Steppy, you'll never be able to hold up your head in this town again. You might as well go out and buy yourself a lunchpail. You might as well get a *job*.

Santo shoved the .44 down into the waistband of his trousers. A few minutes ago, he'd been hoping that Mama Leibowitz was dead. Now, he saw her as his ticket to Jake. Of course, he couldn't be sure that she knew where Jake was hiding, but if she did, he, Santo Silesi, would find out.

"You're maybe looking for somebody?"

Santo spun on his heel to find a bloody Mama Leibowitz standing right behind him. She was holding the biggest handgun Santo had ever seen, holding it right up to his face. It was a vision beyond even his worst nightmare. The blood streamed down over her bloated face. It dripped onto her ratty fur coat, matting the long hairs.

"Where's your sword, you Cossack bastard? Where's your horse?"

"Wha, wha, wha . . ."

"Ha, so you're *plotzing*, already." She grinned, showing a full set of small bloody teeth. "You brought, maybe, a change of underwear?"

"I, I, I . . . I don't get it? I don't . . ."

"Don't worry about nothing, sonny. This you're gonna get."

The force of the slug blew Santo Silesi halfway across the room. It picked him up and tossed him backwards as carelessly as a superstitious housewife tossing spilled salt over her shoulder. Mama Leibowitz walked after him, holding the revolver in front of her, looking for any sign of life. She needn't have bothered. The hole in Santo's forehead was small and neat, but the back of his head was missing altogether.

"*Oy*," Mama Leibowitz groaned, "what a mess." She stepped over a small lump of wet gray brain and squatted next to Santo. Using just the tips of two fingers, she tugged at his .44 until it came free, then dropped it on the carpet next to his right hand. Finally satisfied, she walked back into the kitchen and called the police.

Twenty-eight

"PATIENCE, STANLEY," Allen Epstein said, "like I taught you in the ring."

"For Christ's sake, Sarge, the prick's spent half the morning bottled up in his room. Why can't he see us for ten minutes?"

"Because the '*prick*' happens to be a judge. Which means he doesn't have to answer to a couple of flatfoots like us. His '*room,*' by the way, is called his chambers. Which oughta give you an even better idea of where we stand in relation to *him*. Besides, there were five hundred homicides in New York last year. What's another killing to a big-time judge?"

"Three, Sarge," Moodrow said. "Three killings to a big-time judge. Jake's been a busy boy."

"Four, if you wanna get technical. Don't forget Steppy Accacio."

Moodrow snorted. "*That* was in New Jersey. It doesn't count."

They'd found out about Accacio's murder accidentally. Epstein, with Moodrow's permission, had called McElroy, filling the captain in on what they were doing and what they planned to do. McElroy had offered backup, been refused, then casually mentioned that Steppy Accacio had been gunned down in his New Jersey home. No, he had none of the details. It wasn't the 7th Precinct's business.

"Besides," Moodrow continued, "we don't know if Jake pulled that one off. What I'm trying to be here is accurate. I'm trying to be fair to the Honorable Judge Marone, because the last thing I wanna do is show contempt for the court. I'm sure he got himself elected fair and square. Even if he *was* nominated by Tammany Hall and ran without opposition."

They'd been sitting in a hallway of the Criminal Court Building on Centre Street for almost three hours. Tom Moretti, the ADA, had left the unsigned warrants with Judge Marone's clerk before nine o'clock, then gone off to a trial in another part of the building. The judge's signature, Moretti had insisted, was a mere formality. Now it was twelve o'clock and nearly time for the Honorable Judge Marone to go to lunch.

The plain truth was that Stanley Moodrow was afraid somebody, Santo Silesi or Joe Faci or Dominick Favara or Pat Cohan or Sal Patero or *somebody*, would get to Jake Leibowitz before he did. In fact, the idea terrified him. Not that he couldn't see the justice in it. The very real possibility that Jake's body would come floating up in the East River *had* to be seen as justice of a sort. Death was the ultimate penalty. A bullet or the electric chair—what difference did it make?

The difference was that it wouldn't be *him*. It wouldn't be Stanley Moodrow uttering the magic words: *You're under arrest for the murder of Luis Melenguez.* That pronouncement belonged to him and he intended to speak it, even if he had to do it over Jake's dead body. What was the point of hunting, of tracking your quarry down and bringing it to bay, if you had to turn over the rifle at the last minute?

And there was another point, too. McElroy and the rest of the brass might be cooperating, but it wasn't because they'd suddenly gotten religion. Right now, they were afraid of Stanley Moodrow. Later on, when Jake Leibowitz, Pat Cohan and Sal Patero were as meaningless as yesterday's news, there was every reason to believe the big shots would come for their revenge.

Pat Cohan had spelled it out best when he'd insisted that a cop's first loyalty is to the Department, not to the Constitution of the United States or the New York State Penal Code. McElroy was protecting the Department's fat butt. When that butt was no longer exposed, he (and the rest of the Department) would look for revenge. If, when the time came, Stanley Moodrow was the hero detective who'd arrested a quadruple murderer, it wouldn't hurt his case at all.

Moodrow stood up and walked over to Marone's office. "I'm goin' inside and find out what's happening. This is bullshit."

"Don't get crazy," Epstein said brusquely. "You can't put heat on a judge. If you try it, you'll lose him for the future. Assuming you don't intend to find another career, you're gonna need judges like you're gonna need stool pigeons. There's no way to work without 'em."

But Judge Marone didn't get sore when Moodrow barged into his chambers. He was apologetic.

"I'm sorry, Detective," he said, tapping his desk with a nervous forefinger, "I forgot all about it. I'm sentencing a convicted murderer tomorrow and I've got to decide whether he lives or dies. My problem is that I don't believe the death penalty has any effect on crime. If I had my way, I'd *never* send a man to his death no matter what he did. But there's the question of the law. I'm *obliged* to submit to the will of the legislature. The legislature is *obliged* to submit to the will of the people. If the people *want* the death penalty—and they most assuredly do, they yearn for it like vampires yearn for blood—who am I to oppose them?"

"And don't forget," Moodrow said brightly, "you're gonna have to go *back* to those vampires when you run for reelection."

Marone, much to Moodrow's surprise, laughed out loud. "Yes, there's that, too," he said. "That, too. But it doesn't matter, really. What matters is that I have to read one hundred and seventy-two letters from 'concerned citizens' before I pass sentence. So far, half of them are demanding that I let the kid off with life. That's what he is, by the way, a seventeen-year-old, semi-retarded, Puerto Rican *kid*. The other half want to fry *me* if I don't give him the chair. What happened to you is that you got lost in the shuffle. I apologize."

Moodrow watched the judge flip through the papers on his desk until he found the two sheets he was looking for. He scanned them quickly before scrawling his signature on the bottom. The whole process took thirty seconds.

"Thanks, Your Honor," Moodrow said, repressing a smile.

"Just doing my job, son. Don't forget, you're a voter, too. Come back whenever you need me."

Fifteen minutes later, Moodrow and Epstein were sitting in front of Jake Leibowitz's last known address. Or, rather, they were sitting half a block away which was as close as they could get. The rest of the block was packed with police cruisers and unmarked detectives' cars.

"It doesn't *have* to be related," Moodrow groaned. "But why do I know it *is*?"

"Cheer up, Stanley. If it's Jake Leibowitz, it's all over."

Moodrow looked at Epstein. "More likely it's the poor cop who came to arrest him."

But there was no point in speculating. Both men got out of the car and walked the half block to Jake's building. A knot of detectives and uniformed patrolman stood outside, Detective Lieutenant Michael Rosten among them. Moodrow, smiling now, flashed his badge.

"Detective Moodrow," he announced.

"What's that supposed to mean?" Rosten said, moving away from the pack. His expression was neutral, without a hint of the anger Moodrow assumed he must be feeling.

"Somebody get to Jake Leibowitz?" Moodrow ignored the question.

Rosten took his time before answering. His eyes remained blank as he recited the facts. "We've got an unidentified DOA in apartment 5C. We've got a fifty-five-year-old female perpetrator, one Sarah Leibowitz, who claims she killed the victim in self-defense. The perpetrator suffered a severe head injury, possibly at the hands of the DOA, and has been transported to Bellevue Hospital."

"*Transported?* That's a good one."

"Stanley, can I talk to you a minute?" Epstein pulled Moodrow to one side. He was smiling, but his voice was as sharp as a razor. "Listen, you asshole, I'd really appreciate it if you didn't flush *my* career down the toilet along with your own. You think you're gonna get any closer to Jake Leibowitz by insulting a lieutenant? Maybe you took too many shots to the head and you're losin' it."

"Look, Sarge, this *lieutenant* wanted to put me in jail. Remember? And he was willing to sign a false affidavit to do it. You expect me to kiss his ass?"

"Yeah, that sounds about right. In fact, that's *exactly* what I expect. And if you think it's too much for you, tell me right now. So I can walk away before I end up directing traffic in the Midtown Tunnel."

"Sarge . . ."

"I'm not joking, Stanley." Epstein's voice was much softer, but no less determined. "Right now, thanks to you, I'm a hero. I'm a neutral go-between, keeping you in line while protecting the Department's interests. If Rosten or McElroy come to the conclusion that I've taken sides, the black mark'll follow me for the next twenty years. Which is how long I expect to stick around."

Moodrow started to respond, but Epstein cut him off. "I'm gonna go back and talk to Rosten. You, on the other hand, are gonna stay here and keep your mouth shut. This is not a difficult thing, Stanley, but you might wanna take notes so you don't forget. We're looking for cooperation here and we're not gonna get it by making the lieutenant sore. Remember, the captain *ordered* him to back off."

Epstein spun around and marched back over to Rosten. "Look, lieutenant," he said, loud enough for Moodrow to hear, "we've got a warrant to search the Leibowitz apartment. What's the chance of getting in there?"

"Getting in there *when*?" Rosten answered. "The Medical Examiner won't be here for another two hours. He's working a multiple on East 72nd Street. *Nobody* goes in there until the M.E. clears the body. This you already know. After the M.E.'s finished, the lab boys take their turn. That's standard procedure, which you also know. What I'm telling you is to get in line, because after the lab boys clear the crime scene, the detective in charge, John Samuelson, will conduct a complete search of the premises."

"John Samuelson?"

"He was next up when the squeal came through. That's the way it's done, sergeant. Being a patrolman, I suppose you didn't know that."

"Yeah? Well, lieutenant, being a patrolman and not a detective, I *do* know where my first loyalties lie. Did the captain okay this?"

Rosten's composure broke for the first time. "It's not McElroy's business. He's not a detective."

"He's the precinct *commander*, lieutenant. In the Seventh Precinct, he's accountable for *everything*. Look, I know we can't enter the apartment before the M.E. and forensics finish up. Far be it from me to compromise a crime scene. But there's no way Samuelson's gonna go in there ahead of us. Not without the captain personally giving me his okay. Look at it like this. First, we're in the process of gathering evidence on a man suspected of having committed *four* murders. Second, you already know who killed your unidentified DOA. You've got a statement. Third, this case is so fucking dirty, if you had half a brain you wouldn't come within ten miles of it."

"What's that supposed to mean?"

"It means if you don't instruct Samuelson not to enter that apartment without Stanley or me looking over his shoulder, I'm gonna get McElroy down here to instruct him *for* you. Samuelson is completely compromised in this situation and you goddamned well know it."

Rosten shook visibly. "I'll tell you what, sergeant. Say the word and I'll hand the case over to the jerk standing behind you."

"No way," Moodrow said before Epstein could take Rosten up on his offer. "The jerk has two warrants in his pocket. Both drawn up by an assistant district attorney and signed by the Honorable Judge Marone. He intends to execute the both of 'em and he doesn't need any distractions. Maybe after the jerk gets that done, he'll have time to enjoy the vacation Sal Patero forced him to take."

Rosten turned away from them without another word and walked into the building. Moodrow started to follow, but Epstein held him back.

"Give it a couple of minutes, Stanley. Let him do what he's gotta do in private. Remember, there's still a warrant out for you."

Moodrow stopped, then grinned broadly. "By the way, Sarge, I wanna thank you for the lesson in self-control. You really showed me the smart way to get cooperation. And I want you to know that I took detailed notes, just like you asked me to. You want a copy to give to the rookies?"

Rosten came down five minutes later. An infuriated John Samuelson trailed behind him. "I decided to take your advice," Rosten said to Allen Epstein. "Paul Maguire's gonna handle this investigation. He's upstairs. I instructed him to cooperate and he agreed. That satisfactory?"

"Sure."

"But there *is* one thing, sergeant. I'm going to have to see those warrants with my own eyes. I'd be derelict in my duty if I didn't." His gaze moved from Epstein to Moodrow, a thin smile spreading across his face. "You don't hand them over, I'm going to bar you from entering the building." He paused again. "If you want to call McElroy, there's a phone booth in the candy store on the corner. I'll *lend* you the dime."

"Why should we get sore?" Moodrow said. He pulled the warrant from his pockets and carefully unfolded them. "Don't touch, lieutenant. Just read and remember." Moodrow knew what was coming. He also knew there wasn't a damn thing he could do about it.

"This warrant only mentions one victim, Luis Melenguez," Rosten said after a moment. "You claimed there were four murders."

"You can only fry a man once," Moodrow responded. "No matter how many times you throw the switch."

"You have a point there, Moodrow." Rosten stepped back and stared directly into Moodrow's eyes. "On the other hand, if you let the perpetrator live, you can hurt him every single day of his miserable fucking life. Now, what I'm gonna do is go back to the house and get an APB out on Leibowitz. And I'm gonna personally attend the next three roll calls so I can pass out Leibowitz's photo and spur the troops on with a rousing pep talk. Of course, I'll have to warn them, too. I'll have to say that Jake Leibowitz is suspected of having committed *four* murders and that he's *extremely* dangerous. Be quite a feather in the cap of the man who takes him down."

"Especially if he shoots him in the back, right?"

Rosten didn't bother to answer. He turned away and began to shout at the lounging patrolmen. "Let's get these cars out of here. I want everybody back to work. This isn't a holiday. There's criminals out there. Let's nab 'em."

"Just great," Moodrow muttered. "When you give your pep talk, do it just like that." He watched Rosten walk away for a moment, then shook his head admiringly. Rosten had prepared a trap and he'd blundered into it like a stupid lumbering bear. He was now obliged to stay on the scene until the Medical Examiner and the lab boys finished working. Meanwhile, every cop in the 7th would be looking for Jake Leibowitz.

"What are you thinking, Stanley?" Epstein asked. "I can see the little wheels turning in your head."

"Rosten thinks I'm after *his* ass. His and Pat Cohan's. But that's not the point at all. The Department is here to stay. If I want to keep on being a cop, I have to accept that. Which doesn't mean I'm not disappointed. I wanted to arrest Leibowitz myself. You know what I'm saying, Sarge. I wanted to put the cuffs on with my own hands and that doesn't seem too likely, now. On the other hand, before I came along . . ."

"It sounds like you're taking this personally," Epstein replied.

"Yeah, that's just the word I would've used. Personal. It's a good word, Sarge. Keeps you interested."

Twenty-nine

WHAT IT IS, is I've lost almost everything I value, Pat Cohan thought, and I don't want to lose the little I have left.

It was really that simple. He'd known the truth of it as he'd handed his retirement papers to Deputy Chief Morton. It'd sunk into him like droplets of rain sinking down between grains of desert sand. He could still feel it in every pore of his skin.

"Pat," Morton had said, "this isn't necessary."

But Morton hadn't refused to accept them. No, he'd dumped Inspector Pat Cohan's retirement papers in a desk drawer, then sucked on his pipe like the gutless fairy he was.

"How long have you been on the job, Pat?" Morton had asked.

"Thirty-seven years. Since January eighth, 1921. I've seen a lot over the decades, but I've never seen a deal as dirty as this. When the Department takes the word of a rookie detective with five years in the job over the word of a full inspector . . . let's just say the force I joined in 1921, the force my father joined in 1898, the force my grandfather joined in 1867, has changed too much to include the likes of *me.*"

Pat Cohan watched Morton hem and haw. The situation, pleasing as it may have been to the deputy chief's sheeny soul, had apparently taken him by surprise. "What makes you think we believe Stanley Moodrow?" he'd finally asked.

"I think you believe him, boyo, because you stepped all over my authority. Because you put the heel of your shoe on my head and ground me into the sidewalk like you were disposing of a cigarette butt."

"Aren't you being overly dramatic, Pat?" Morton's head had wobbled on his skinny neck as he denied Cohan's statement. "*Believing* Moodrow has nothing to do with the situation. In our best judgment, he has enough information, be it true or false, to make the Department very uncomfortable. What I'm trying to say is you don't have to protect your pension by retiring."

The little bastard may have been surprised, but it'd hadn't taken more than a few seconds to figure it out. If he, Pat Cohan, was dismissed from the force as the result of a departmental investigation, his pension would fly out the window like an escaped canary. If, on the other hand, he retired *before* the investigation, they'd have to get a court conviction to take his money away.

"Well, that's neither here nor there, Milton. I've handed in my papers and you've accepted them. The only thing left is for me to warn you about Stanley Moodrow, which I intend to do whether you've got the time or not."

Morton, resigned, had puffed out a little sigh, then settled back in his chair. "Go ahead, Pat. Tell me."

"Moodrow's a vicious dog. He deliberately seduced my daughter, then left her like you'd leave a prostitute on the street. He stalked her, waited until she was vulnerable, then took her innocence. I know this to be true because my daughter *told* me. When I confronted Stanley Moodrow, he invited me to come out behind the house and settle matters. When I refused, he swore he'd get even some other way. Sal Patero's statement was forced, Milton. It'll never stand up in court."

"Just a minute, Pat. We're under the impression that you pulled Sal Patero out of the Seventh Precinct *before* he, shall we say, *confessed.* By the way, I don't actually know what Patero said. The only one who's seen this so-called confession is a sergeant named Epstein. I did call Patero into the office, but he refused to talk to me. I might add that Lieutenant Patero seemed fit as a fiddle. There wasn't a mark on him."

"You don't have to leave bruises to get a confession, Milton. I realize you never had much street experience, but you ought to know that much. A cocked thirty-eight will do just fine."

But that'd been that. There was nothing more to be said. He'd left and come home to Bayside. To his house and his wife and his daughter. And to the money, of course. He'd done quite well over the years. That had to count for something in a man's life. He'd taken care of his family and put enough away for a comfortable old age. It had to count for *something*.

He was making himself a cup of tea when the front door opened. Quickly, while Kate was shrugging out of her coat and pulling off her galoshes, he added a shot of Bushmill's to the tea, then hid the bottle in a cabinet beneath the sink.

"That you, Kate?"

"Yes, Daddy, it's me." Kate bounced into the room, smiling.

"Yer a sight for sore eyes, darlin'. A sight for sore eyes." She'd always had that bounce. As far back as he could remember. A tomboy to her bones. "Kate, do ya remember the time I had to pull you out of the oak in the back yard?"

"Yes, Daddy. How can I forget when you remind me at least once a week?"

Pat Cohan ignored the comment. He'd begun knocking down shots the minute he'd walked through the door. Not that he was falling-down drunk or anything close to it. No, he was on the kind of jag that glues you to the barstool. That makes your thoughts spin through your mind until you have to reach out for an anchor. Or another shot, which is the same thing.

"You couldn't have been more than ten years old."

"I was eleven. And if you hadn't panicked, I'd have gotten down by myself." She walked over to the stove, lit the right front burner with a match, then hefted the teapot. "Is the water hot?"

"Almost. I just poured meself a cup." He raised the cup to his mouth, sipped a little, spilled more. "B'Jesus," he muttered. "Now I'm after foulin' meself."

"Daddy, have you been drinking? It's only three o'clock."

"I'm sober as a judge."

"Then why are you putting on that Irish accent? You only do that when you've been drinking."

"Well, I may have had a drop, darlin'. It's in the way of a celebration."

Kate turned back to him, smiling. "That's swell, Daddy. What's the event?"

"I've retired from the New York Police Department. Did it this afternoon. Just walked in and handed my papers over to the sheeny in charge . . ."

"Don't say that word." Kate turned back to the stove. The teapot was whistling madly. "You *must* be drunk. You know how much I hate that kind of talk."

"Now, darlin' . . ." He could see the gears turning in her head. The questions were going to fly and he didn't have any good answers.

Kate took her time, dipping the teabag, then pressing it dry against the spoon before tossing it into the garbage. "Daddy," she said, coming back to the table, "what made you decide to retire? Didn't you always say, 'They'll have to rip the uniform off my back'?"

Pat Cohan put his cup on the table, noting, with satisfaction, that he hadn't spilled a drop. "When the time comes, the time comes," he proclaimed. "You don't have to pull on the rope to hear the bell toll."

"And Stanley? Has Stanley been arrested?"

Damn, but she was persistent. There *had* to be some way to talk about Moodrow without looking like a criminal. There *had* to be. "You saw the warrant yourself, Kate."

"Has he been *arrested*, Daddy? Is Stanley in jail?"

"No, he hasn't been arrested and he's not in jail." He wanted to lie, but he couldn't take the chance that she'd call him and find out for herself.

Kate stirred a teaspoon of sugar into her tea, then blew the steam away before sipping delicately. "What are they waiting for?"

"They're trying to *find* him. The charge is simple assault, remember? That doesn't exactly make him public enemy number one. Eventually, he'll come in on his own."

"And Stanley had nothing to do with your retirement?"

Pat Cohan took a deep breath. It was 'do or die' time. "Kathleen, do you know when the first St. Patrick's Day parade was held in New York City?"

"What has that got to do with anything?"

"Please, darlin', indulge your father on the day of his retirement. If you don't know, give us a guess."

"All right, March seventeenth, 1892, that's my guess."

"You're off by a hundred and thirty years." He noted her surprise with satisfaction. "The first St. Patty's Day parade was held in 1762. Think about it, Kate. There were enough Irishmen in New York before the Revolutionary War to hold a parade. Do you know how they got here? They were indentured servants. They were brought here to serve the Brits and the Dutch. To wait on 'em like good Irish slaves. Well, we kept on coming, even though we didn't get anywhere. We came to work the railroads and the coal mines and the factories. We dug the tunnels, built the roads and the bridges. Our reward was to be treated like dogs for a hundred years. Have I ever spoken of the Five Points? Or the Fourth Ward? There were years when the cops didn't enter the Five Points at all. Whatever happened in the Five Points—murder, rape, robbery—the residents were on their own. Now, add cholera, flu, smallpox and the like . . ."

"You've made this speech before, Daddy. Many, many times. I don't get the point. What has this got to do with Stanley?"

Pat Cohan drained his cup. "We were talking about my retirement, were we not, darlin'?" He waited until she acknowledged his point with a resigned shrug. "It took us a long time to fight our way out, but we finally did it. We took over New York, made it our own. You wait and see, Kate. One day soon we'll have ourselves a president. Only, by the time it happens our day in New

York will be over. *That's* happening as we speak. Robert Wagner will be the last Irish mayor." He stopped for a moment, dropping his eyes to the tabletop. What he wanted was a stiff drink, but the timing was all wrong. "I'm a fossil, girl. It's not my Department anymore. The Jews and the Italians run the city now. That's why they brought in the Puerto Ricans. That's why they give them welfare and build projects. The Puerto Ricans would vote for a *communist* if he promised to increase the dole."

He was rambling now, and he knew it. It was time to cap his argument. Make that final point and hope for the best. He raised his eyes to meet his daughter's. "You were right, in a way, Kate. It *is* about Stanley Moodrow. There was a time in my life when I couldn't have made the mistake I made when I allowed him to court you. I was his *rabbi*, Kate. Do you know what that means?"

"Does it have something to do with the Department?"

"It has *everything* to do with the Department. A rabbi is a protector, a guardian angel, a mentor. Without a rabbi, there's no way to rise up in the job. And *that's* the point. In *my* Department, a man didn't turn on his rabbi. He didn't bite the hand that fed him. But it's not *my* Department anymore. No, it's gone over and it's time for me to go over with it. What I decided to do was count my blessings. I've my health and enough money so I won't be puttin' out my hand in my old age." He let his voice drop to a hoarse whisper. "I also have you, Kate. And the grandchildren you'll one day give me."

Pat Cohan wanted to examine his daughter's face the way he'd once, long ago, examined the faces of suspects in basement interrogation rooms. But he couldn't do that. It was a time for weakness, not strength. Besides, he wasn't the interrogator, here; he was the suspect. So what he did was let his eyes drop to his folded hands, a sad old man facing the loss of his power.

He stayed that way for a full minute before raising his eyes. When he did he found his daughter, hands on hips, staring down at him. "What happened to Sal Patero, Daddy? Why hasn't Sal been around? He used to be here every other day."

"That wop is exactly what I've been talking about. Guineas like him don't belong in the Department. Not *my* Department." It was out before he could put a brake on his mouth. He'd had no more control over what he'd said, than over the twin scarlet roses blossoming on his cheeks.

"Are you ever going to tell me what's going on, Daddy?" She was turning away from him, walking back into the foyer. "How long do you expect me to be the family pet? How long do you want me to be Lassie? Every time I talk to Stanley, he tells me to grow up. He doesn't tell me about his side of the story. He tells me to grow up."

Pat Cohan stared at the bottom of his empty cup, then looked back at his daughter. "Are you calling me a liar, Kate?" This time the whisper wasn't forced. His momentary anger had fled as suddenly as it had come. What he felt was close to terror.

"No, Daddy, not a liar. But I can't take your word for it, either. I have to go find out for myself."

It was nearly eleven o'clock, and Moodrow, walking up Allen Street toward his apartment, was trying to connect the events of the day. He was going to have to put the day into *some* kind of order if he hoped to find Jake Leibowitz. That was a given. It was funny, in a way. Initially, he'd been worried that somebody would get to Jake before he did. Now, he was afraid that Leibowitz had left the city altogether, that he might *never* be taken.

After four hours of cooling their heels in the hallway, he and Epstein, accompanied by Paul Maguire, had finally gotten into the Leibowitz apartment. Their search had taken almost two hours as they looked under beds, behind cabinets, inside the toilet tank. As they unrolled pairs of socks, fumbled in Jake's silk underpants, pulled out empty drawers and flipped them over.

In the end, Moodrow had found what he was looking for in a closet not ten feet from where he'd entered the apartment. A forest of hats rested on two shelves. Beneath them, a black cashmere overcoat hung on a wooden hangar. A spatter of dark spots was just barely visible on the hem of the overcoat.

Moodrow was sure it was blood, the blood of Al O'Neill or Betty O'Neill or both. They'd been killed with knives, butchered, and there was no way Jake Leibowitz could have kept himself entirely clean. There'd be traces of blood in the car, too. Assuming they found it.

Allen Epstein had been dubious, but Paul Maguire had put his years of experience on the line.

"It's blood, all right," he'd said. "I'd bet my pension on it."

"He couldn't be that stupid," Epstein had said.

"Maybe he didn't see it. The coat's *black*, for Christ's sake. Besides, if it wasn't for stupid, we wouldn't catch any of them. Stupid is what we count on." Maguire had carefully folded the coat before easing it into a paper bag. His movements were respectful, almost reverent, as if he was handling priestly vestments or folding the flag at sundown. "Congratulations, Stanley. Jake Leibowitz's fat is now officially fried."

Epstein had continued to be skeptical, even when they'd found more dark stains on the seam of the right arm, even when they'd found spatters on the brim of a black fedora. He'd refused to surrender his disbelief until they were standing in one of the M.E.'s labs and a white-coated technician officially pronounced the stains to be *blood*stains.

"We still don't know the blood came from Al or Betty O'Neill," he'd insisted.

By that time Moodrow had grown tired of it. Epstein, sergeant or not, was a patrolman, not a detective. He couldn't (or wouldn't) understand. There were times when you knew where it was going, when you could feel the energy racing through the wires and you either raced along with it or got left behind. Permanently.

"Sarge," he'd said, "what I'd like you to do is go back into the house and see how the search for Jake is being organized. I'd like to know what Rosten's doing, if anything. Paul and I will interview Sarah Leibowitz."

"Look, Stanley, you can't order me around. I know you like to have things your own way, but you're gonna have to wait until you pass the lieutenant's exam before you start telling me what to do."

Moodrow had grinned, holding up his hands defensively. "Easy, Sarge. I'm not trying to take anything away from you. But you have to admit that investigations are for detectives. Paul and I have legitimate reasons for questioning Sarah Leibowitz. Nobody'll challenge our authority. I'm afraid that Rosten's gonna try to fix it so Jake never sees the inside of a jail cell. You can talk to the beat cops in the Seventh. I don't know if we can do anything about it, but if there's an all-out hunt for Jake Leibowitz, it'd be nice if we knew about it."

Epstein had snorted his disapproval, then driven off to the precinct while Moodrow and Maguire headed up to Bellevue Hospital where Sarah Leibowitz, half her head covered with gauze, rested in a private room. She began to moan as soon as she saw the two detectives.

"Mrs. Leibowitz," Moodrow had begun, "I'm Detective . . ."

Coming over, he and Maguire had carefully worked out their strategy. Sarah Leibowitz was not going to be charged with any crime in connection with the death of Santo Silesi, so they had no leverage on that end. If they couldn't appeal to Sarah Leibowitz's conscience, they'd explain that the only certainty here was Jake's eventual capture. If he resisted, he'd be shot down like a dog. Plus (as Santo Silesi had ably demonstrated) the mob was after him and they'd have no mercy at all. The best thing Jake could do was surrender quietly.

It'd seemed like a decent approach to both detectives: prod the worried mother with promises of protection for her son, appeal to her motherly instincts. What could be simpler? In Sarah Leibowitz's presence, however, their strategy had evaporated like morning mist under an August sun. Before Moodrow could finish introducing himself, the Leibowitz moan had turned into a howl that brought doctors and nurses running. Sarah Leibowitz, having suffered a serious head injury, had to be kept quiet. She wasn't up to an interview, much less an interrogation. So sorry, but it would just have to wait.

Moodrow and Maguire had retreated to Maguire's car, then decided to separate. Maguire had to go into the precinct. The Silesi shooting was his responsibility and he wanted to make sure the paperwork was in order before he wrote his own reports. Moodrow had accepted a ride to Houston Street, then, in the time-honored tradition of stymied detectives everywhere, had begun to pound the pavement.

He'd made mental notes as he worked the bars and the small bookie joints, as he stopped numbers runners on the street and interrupted the shylocks working the lofts and factories. The message he'd projected had been the same to one and all: the heat was coming down. There would be no "business as usual," not while Jake Leibowitz was on the loose. Their best move was to give Jake up *before* the raids began.

"How come I never seen you before?" Sam Gelardi, a low-level bookie had asked.

Moodrow, ignoring the question, had jammed his index finger into Gelardi's chest. "Do yourself a favor," he'd hissed, "if ya *kill* the bastard, leave his body where it can be found. If he disappears, I'm gonna make it my personal business to run you off the Lower East Side."

Of course, he'd had no idea whether or not he could deliver on his various threats. That wasn't the point, anyway, because he was preparing for a time when Jake Leibowitz was long forgotten. As he went along, he began to create an internal file, matching names to reactions. So-and-so had examined the photo carefully. So-and-so had admitted knowing Jake Leibowitz. So-and-so had provided some tidbit of gossip concerning Jake's history. So-and-so had known nothing, but had shown *fear*.

It was all necessary, he told himself as he fumbled with his keys. It was necessary if he intended to own the Lower East Side, to make himself indispensable to the precinct brass, to build a protective wall between himself and the wrath of Pat Cohan. But that didn't mean he wasn't exhausted.

He stood in the lobby of his building for a moment, looking up at the stairs. He'd been climbing those stairs for a lot of years, had made it a habit to take them two at a time when he was in training. Now, they looked like Mt. Everest.

But there was nothing to be done about it. Not unless he wanted to sleep in the lobby. Wearily, lost in thought, he began to climb the four flights to his apartment. He was on the third floor landing when a familiar voice called out to him.

"Stanley, Stanley. Come here a minute."

"Greta, please, I don't . . ." He looked down the hallway and was stunned to see Kate Cohan standing in the hall next to Greta Bloom. His fatigue vanished in an instant. He'd been telling himself that he'd never see her again, that he could get along without her. That even if Pat Cohan vanished, along with his lies, their love could never overcome their differences. Not in the long run.

Now, as he stood with one foot on the stairs leading up to the next floor, his mouth hanging open, the "long run" had no meaning whatsoever. You *couldn't* dump the present because you were afraid of the future. His own father had squirreled away every extra penny, saving for an "old age" that never came.

"Stanley, say something," Greta demanded.

"Stanley?" Kate Cohan took a hesitant step forward. "Can I talk to you?"

"When did you get here?" It was the first coherent sentence that popped into Moodrow's mind.

"I got here a little after three."

"I went up to see you, Stanley," Greta interrupted, "and I found her standing by your door. She's a lovely girl. You should have brought her to meet me long ago."

"What's next, Greta?" Moodrow asked. "You gonna invite us in for coffee and homemade *rugelah?*"

"Such a fresh mouth," Greta said to Kate. "I don't see how you put up with such a fresh mouth. Stanley, you're too old to be a *bondit.*"

"A what?" Kate asked.

"There's no word in English," Greta said. "It means like the boy in the funny papers. The one with the blond hair."

"Oh," Kate said, "I get it. Dennis the Menace."

Thirty

THEY WERE in each other's arms before they made it to the fourth-floor landing. They held each other fiercely, mouths joined, eyes closed. As if they could live entirely in an animal present. As if they could live without regret for the past or fear of the future. As if they could rid themselves of the pain of their separation by squeezing it out like a tube of toothpaste.

Moodrow found himself beyond thought, beyond even the desire for thought. He could feel Kate's heart beating through their bulky overcoats. It seemed to beat inside his skull, driving away every other consideration. No more Jake Leibowitz or Pat Cohan. The concrete steps, the narrow steel railing, the freezing streets, the whores, the junkies and the jack rollers: the whole stinking miserable history of the Lower East Side of New York City vanished in an instant.

Minutes later, Moodrow heard a deep groan, an exhalation of equally mixed loss and gain. It took him another moment to realize that he was doing the groaning. And that Kate's hands were inside his jacket, her fingers cupping the long muscles running along his ribs, her lips pressed to his chest.

He was supposed to sweep her up in his arms and he knew it. He was supposed to carry her across the threshold, to lay her gently on his bed, to play the leading man. Instead, he pulled away from her and asked a question.

"Kate, are you sure?"

He wasn't asking just about Inspector Pat Cohan. He was asking about Father Ryan and Sacred Heart Church and a lifetime in suburbia. He was talking about every facet of her life.

"No," she admitted. "No. But it doesn't matter. I don't want to think about it. I've been thinking and thinking and thinking. It doesn't get me any place. You can't stay up in the air. You have to come down and do something."

They made their way to Moodrow's apartment in silence. The silence seemed right to Moodrow, but still, once inside, once their coats were off and draped over the back of the couch, he couldn't stop himself from speaking. Despite the fact that he knew he might be tossing away the finest moment of his life.

"Kate," he began. "Kate . . . do you, uh . . . do you want coffee or something?"

It was an astonishingly dumb thing to say and he knew it.

"Isn't it a little late for coffee?" Kate answered, without letting go of his hand. She looked up at him for a moment, then grinned and punched him in the stomach. "If you don't smile," she said, "I'm gonna cry."

Moodrow managed a quick grin. "Let's sit down."

"Yes, I guess we have to talk." Kate sat on the couch, pulling Moodrow down alongside her. "Your friend, Greta, is a pretty amazing person. Was your mother like her?"

"Greta has a lot in common with most of the women who live down here. Tough times, tough women."

Kate looked up at Moodrow for a moment. Her gaze was sharply speculative. "I guess I'm learning, Stanley. My father retired today."

"I didn't know that." Moodrow's surprise was evident. "Did he say why?"

"He gave me a speech about how hard it was for the Irish when they first came here. And about how they're losing what it took a hundred years to gain. 'It's not my Department anymore.' That's what he said. I didn't believe him, so I came down here to find out for myself. It was stupid not to call first."

"How did Greta happen to find you?"

"She was bringing you some food. Potato *something*. I didn't understand her when she told me. She repeated it, but I still didn't understand, so I let it drop."

"Potato *latkes*. It means 'pancakes.' "

"She makes pancakes out of potatoes?"

"Yeah. It just goes to prove there *are* things you can do with a potato besides boiling it. Being Irish, you wouldn't know that."

Kate giggled, then turned serious again. "I was a real sap, Stanley. I feel like a yokel who just bought the Brooklyn Bridge. Maybe I had some doubt when I got here, but after sitting in Greta's kitchen all night, I know the truth." She looked up at him. "You got sucked into this, didn't you? It wasn't something you wanted."

"That's for sure." Moodrow shook his head slowly. He could feel the tension beginning to ease. Kate was leaning against his chest; his arm was around her shoulder. "But sometimes you have to do what's right. Especially when Greta Bloom gets on your case. The job's pretty corrupt, Kate. Most of the guys are on the take, especially the brass. I don't wanna get too righteous about it, because as far as I can tell, it's always been that way. But homicide is something else. I couldn't let it go and neither could your father. It's been a war zone down here ever since Luis Melenguez was murdered. Your father had a lot to do with that."

"Well, he's out of it, now." She hesitated, letting her eyes drop to her lap. "I made a decision while I was sitting down at Greta's. I decided not to ask you this question and now I'm asking it anyway. What are you going to do to my father?"

"Probably nothing. I don't have the kind of evidence that can be used against your father in court and now that he's retired, it can't be used by the Department, either. That's probably why he handed in his papers." Moodrow slid his index finger beneath Kate's chin and pulled her head up gently. "I never went after him. I never deliberately went after your father, but I had to protect myself. What I'm talking about is survival, before and after Luis Melenguez's killer pays the price."

Kate nodded. "Are you going to get him? The killer?"

"His name's Jake Leibowitz and I'm right on top of him. It's just a matter of time. The whole precinct's after him. It seems that the Department brass, in their infinite wisdom, have decided that Jake Leibowitz must go. What they're doing is protecting themselves. They *say* they're protecting the Department, but it's their own butts they're worried about. I have to make them understand that they can best protect themselves by protecting me."

"That's going to be a neat trick." Kate laid her hand on his knee and drew a rough circle with her fingertips. "Have you given any thought to what you'll do with your life if you lose the Department?"

"None."

"Have you given any thought to what you'll do if you lose me?"

"That's the $64,000 Question, isn't it? Maybe I should have taken my shot ten minutes ago."

"Is that because you think the answer isn't something I want to hear?"

"It's because the answer doesn't make anybody happy, including me." Moodrow abruptly stopped speaking. He looked up at the ceiling for a moment, then turned back to Kate and drew a deep breath. "There are times in your life when you wake up for a moment and realize you're a big dope. That you've been a dope for so long it's as natural as combing your hair. That's part of what it's about. Somewhere along the line I decided that I wanted a *gold* shield. An ordinary badge wasn't good enough. It had to be gold for a big shot like me."

"It's not wrong to want to get ahead, Stanley. It's natural. It's what *everybody* wants."

"That's just it. I decided to become a detective, because I *didn't* want to be like everyone else. When I was in high school, all I could think about was becoming heavyweight champion of the world. I didn't think about the price. Not for one minute. The same thing happened when I joined the Department. I didn't give up the kid's dream. No, I decided I wanted to be a detective and I used my face to get it. These last few weeks? Every time I look in the mirror and see the scars, I think about what a dope I was. Let me tell you something, Kate, the price wasn't long in coming. Your father put me to work learning the price from day number one."

Kate put a finger to his mouth. She was smiling. "I bet I know what happened next."

"What?"

"Greta Bloom happened next."

Moodrow leaned forward and kissed her lightly. "You get a gold star."

Kate grabbed hold of his ear and held him in place while she explored his mouth with her own. "One star isn't enough for an ambitious young lady like myself. I want the whole galaxy."

"Are you sure, Kate?" What he wanted to do was run his finger down along her throat, to unbutton her blouse and press his head between her breasts. "My galaxy isn't very big. It runs south to Canal Street and north to Fourteenth. It's got the river on the east and the Bowery on the west. Like I said, it's not very big, but it's mine and I'm not gonna leave it. Not without a fight. See, the thing of it is I never meant for any of this to happen. Greta came up one morning and asked me to check on a homicide that'd happened while I was in training for the O'Grady fight. Her visit was step one in the process of learning that I was a dope and it was an innocent step. Nothing more than a favor for an old friend. After that, it just happened."

Kate stood up abruptly. "I guess I could say the same thing about myself. Everything I value just happened. Everything the nuns told me; everything my father told me. I bought the whole package, all nine yards. Of *course*, I wanted you to get ahead. I wanted you to come out to Bayside, to leave the slums and . . . It was a joke and the joke was on me. I really believed that an ordinary detective could afford to live in Bayside. Why shouldn't my father have a big house and a new car every two years? Why shouldn't we put down new carpeting before the old carpeting wore out? You want a piano? Go out and buy it. A mahogany bedroom set? A finished basement? A vacation in Havana?"

"I get the point, Kate, but the question is what do you want to do about it?"

She answered by walking toward the bedroom. "What I want to do is change. Hell, Stanley, I already *have* changed. When I think about that jerk, Father Ryan, and his sadistic penance, and that I actually went through with it, I want to throw up. I'm twenty-two years old and I'm tired of being a little girl."

It was late and, as in most New York tenements, the landlord wasn't sending up much heat. They huddled together beneath the blankets and Moodrow, determined to go slowly, let his finger drift over Kate's breasts, let them trail along the smooth, flat plane of her belly, let them caress the outside of her leg down to the knee, then crawl along the ribbon-smooth flesh of her inner thigh.

"Jesus, Kate," he whispered. "I never dreamed this would happen again."

Instead of answering, Kate swung up to straddle his hips. She leaned forward, the expression on her face at once determined and fierce. Holding him in her hand for a moment before sliding down to envelop him.

Moodrow's decision to go slowly was lost in a moment, as was the entire decision-making process. Thinking about it later, he decided that what they'd done was fuck. That the act was purely physical, despite the fact that afterwards, his breath coming in long deep heaves, he could literally feel the bond between them as it tightened. Their union, he realized, had been more elemental than love. It might even be stronger, though he couldn't be sure of that. Time would tell.

They hadn't slept very much when Moodrow glanced over at the clock, noted that it was 6:10, and rolled out of bed. He looked down at Kate for a moment, then gently shook her.

"Kate, Kate."

"Not again, Stanley," she muttered. "I'm too old."

Moodrow flipped on a bedside lamp and shook her more roughly. "It's six o'clock, Kate, and I have to get ready to leave. What are you gonna do about work? You want me to set the alarm?"

Kate sat up and Moodrow found his eyes drawn to her breasts the way a shopkeeper's eyes are drawn to the barrel of a shotgun. At that moment, her beauty was almost frightening. To lose her and gain her and then lose her again . . .

"I'll have coffee with you before you go," Kate said. "Just let me use the bathroom."

"As soon as I finish."

"Why should you go first?" Kate was smiling as she said it.

"Because I'm closer."

Fifteen minutes later, Moodrow poured out two cups of steaming coffee, setting one in front of Kate and sipping at the other.

"We haven't talked about what you want to do," he said.

"I want to stay here," Kate answered quickly. "If you'll have me."

"Well, I don't know, Kate. It seems to me like I already *had* you."

"You never change, Stanley." Kate shook her head. "Thank God."

"Actually, we've *both* changed. No matter what happens, neither of us can go back to your father. Not anymore. But that doesn't put Jake Leibowitz behind bars, does it? I've gotta get going. You know how it is, right?"

"I'm a cop's daughter, remember?"

Moodrow nodded solemnly. "All things considered, I don't think I'm likely to forget. What time do you have to be at work?"

"I'm going to call in sick today. I may call in sick permanently."

"Are you serious?"

Kate looked down at the table, her expression almost shy. "It's too far away. I thought I might find something on the Lower East Side."

"You sure you can live down here?"

"I don't know if 'sure' is the right word for it, but I was talking to Greta last night and she offered to show me around the neighborhood. Let me ask you something, Stanley. Does Greta tell the truth? Some of her stories are pretty unbelievable."

Moodrow walked around to Kate's side of the table. "Well, I've never caught her in a lie." He leaned over and kissed her on the lips, letting his hands slide down to cover her breasts, then abruptly stood up.

"Wait a minute, I just had an idea. I just had a *great* idea. Do me a favor, Kate. You tell Greta that I want to see her when I get back this afternoon. Tell her there's something I need to talk to her about."

"Stanley," Kate said, grabbing onto both of his hands, "she's harmless. She's an old lady."

"Huh? What are you talking about?"

"I thought you were angry because she's interfering in our lives."

Moodrow giggled, then covered his mouth with his hand. "Even if I was sore about that, I wouldn't waste my time trying to change her. Not Greta Bloom. I'd get better results waving a fan at a blizzard. No, I think I just came up with a way Greta can help me get to Jake Leibowitz. But don't tell her that. Just ask her if she can take a few minutes out of her busy schedule to talk to me. I wanna figure out exactly what I'm gonna say before she hears about it. *Capish?*"

"Is that Yiddish?"

"No, it's Italian. But it's good to see you're tryin'."

Thirty-one

JANUARY 23

IF YOU absolutely *have* to stand around outside, Moodrow thought as he took up a position on the north side of Houston Street near the East River, you couldn't pick a better day, not in the winter in New York.

It was seven o'clock in the morning and the temperature was already in the forties. There wasn't a cloud in the sky above the tenements to the west or the river to the east. The edge of a solid-gold sun was just visible over the factories and warehouses lining the Queens side of the river. Its sharply angled light sparkled on the red-brick facade of the nearly completed Baruch Houses across Houston Street. The Baruch Houses, when finished, were expected to provide a little over two thousand heavily subsidized apartments to as many worthy families. There was a fly in the proverbial ointment, however. According to the *Daily News*, the waiting list already held ten thousand names.

Moodrow was standing in front of another project, the Lillian Wald Houses, one of the known dealing addresses of Santo Silesi. It seemed as good a place to do random canvassing as anywhere else. He didn't expect much to come of his efforts, but that didn't mean he could allow himself to duck them. He held his badge in one hand and his quarry's photo in the other, approaching residents as they came out of the doorway.

"Can I talk to you a minute? You know this guy?"

Most hurried past with a quick glance and a quicker shake of the head. A few stopped for a closer look. Fewer still were known to Moodrow, some from school and some from his days in the gym. They were friendlier, more willing to consider the problem, but one and all, they professed ignorance.

Whenever possible, Moodrow filed away the names and faces of those who tried to help. He'd always had a prodigious memory. That was why he'd done so well at St. Stephen's where a premium was placed on the rote learning and eventual regurgitation of simple, unconnected facts. Moodrow fully intended to put that asset to work for him. Every detective in the NYPD had informants, but very few could count on ordinary citizens for a steady flow of information. Having grown up in the neighborhood, Moodrow knew from experience that Joe Citizen often lived cheek by jowl with some of the most vicious maggots on the Lower East Side. That, for instance, keeping *your* kids away from the bad apples usually made the difference between college and prison for the younger generation. If he could tap into their knowledge, gain their trust . . .

It was almost nine o'clock when a tall Spanish kid, his nose heavily bandaged, strolled through the project doorway. He wore the tightly pegged pants and the satin baseball jacket typical of teenage gang members. Moodrow approached him with caution.

"Excuse me, son." He flipped his shield in the kid's face. "You know this guy?"

The kid glanced at Moodrow's badge, then at Jake Leibowitz's photograph. He started to push by, muttering some proof of his impending manhood, then stopped in his tracks.

"You know this guy?" Moodrow repeated.

He looked up at Moodrow for a moment. "*Si*, I have seen this *blanco*. Selling *decata*. Say to me, *Señor Policia*, do you look for him to go to jail?"

"More like the electric chair."

"You goin' to catch him, *Señor Policia*?" The kid's voice dripped sarcasm.

Moodrow stepped forward, allowing his face to lose all expression. "Dig the wax out of your ears, punk, because I'm only gonna say this once. I may be asking for your help, but that don't mean I'm gonna take your shit. You keep running that smart mouth, you're not gonna have to worry about whether you did your homework. My name is Detective Moodrow. I *own* the Lower East Side. *Comprende*?"

"I am no your stool pigeon, Detective Moodrow. No matter wha' you own."

"Take it easy. Whatta ya think, I picked you out special? I've been standing here for two hours and I've been talkin' to *everybody*. Look, this guy has killed four people. I want him off the streets. What I think is that maybe *you* want him off the streets, too. If you know where he's holed up and you tell me, I won't forget it. I won't forget it and I won't ask why you told me."

The kid took his time, mulling it over for a few minutes before responding. "Thees *maricón*, someone seen him on Henry Street."

Henry Street was a half-mile and several hundred thousand people away from where Moodrow was standing.

"You looking for him, kid? You lookin' for Mister Leibowitz?" Moodrow already knew the answer. He could feel it. Poor old Jake. The cops, the mob, the Tenth Street Dragons—was there anyone who *didn't* want to kill him?

"Do me a big favor," Moodrow continued. "If *you* find him first, leave his carcass in the street. You'll be making life a lot easier for both of us."

In his own way, Jake Leibowitz was also enjoying the January thaw. He was lying in a short alleyway between two tenements on Thompson Street in Greenwich Village. Lying next to half a dozen garbage cans, dressed in rags, sucking on a wine bottle filled with grape juice. He'd been lying there all night.

It wasn't the way he wanted it, but Jake figured it was necessary. By this time Joe Faci must be staring over both shoulders and between his legs whenever he was on the street.

"The sap's head must look like a fuckin' pendulum," Jake said out loud.

It was eight o'clock in the morning and the sidewalks were crowded. Several people looked over at the sound of his voice, but then quickly turned away, that special disgust reserved for terminal drunks evident on their faces. Jake raised the bottle to his lips and kissed the side of the closest garbage can.

"Fuck 'em," he muttered. Ordinary citizens had never been more than prey to him and now that his *own* goose was cooked, they weren't even that. They meant nothing; they were irrelevant. Like telephone poles or fire hydrants. Pure scenery.

What next? Jake asked himself. What next after I do the deed on Joe Faci?

Santo Silesi was his best guess. He hadn't spoken to his mother in the last couple of days and knew nothing of Silesi's execution or the intense police scrutiny that had followed it. What he figured was that he'd take care of Joe Faci, then go after Santo. That'd wipe the slate clean. Once young Santo was resting on a slab in the morgue, he'd be free to run. Assuming that was what he wanted to do. He didn't know and he couldn't worry about it. Why should he?

His chances of getting past Silesi, who lived somewhere in Brooklyn, were slim to none.

The door to 1473 Thompson, directly across the street, opened suddenly and Jake slipped behind the cans. It was Joe Faci, accompanied by his wife and wearing his Sunday best. Joe was carrying two suitcases and his lumpy old lady was dragging a third bag along the ground. They hesitated for a fraction of a second, looking up and down the block, then made their way across the street to Faci's Cadillac.

Jake rose, his back to Faci, deliberately knocking over a half-filled garbage can. He shuffled down the alley, fell hard on the pavement, then slowly dragged himself to his feet again. Pulling his battered filthy hat over his face, he turned and stumbled forward.

Jake's plan was to touch Faci, to get Faci's attention by rubbing his greasy fingers on the sleeve of Faci's lambswool overcoat. He wanted to see Joe Faci's look of disgust slowly dissolve into pure terror.

He got his wish, though he didn't have to make contact with Faci. Faci's wife wrinkled her nose in disgust and pointed over her husband's shoulder at the advancing menace.

"Watch for the bum," she said.

Faci turned quickly, his features set into the hardest look in his repertoire. The glare didn't phase Jake. Not one bit. His eyes never left Joe Faci's hands, hands that remained empty too long.

"Hi, Joe, how's it hangin'?" Jake raised his eyes to meet Faci's. Abe Weinberg's .45, its barrel riveted on Faci's gut, nestled comfortably in his hand. Little Richard.

Joe Faci's expression jumped from disgust to fear to a half-assed smile in the space of an eyeblink.

"Hey, Jake, how ya doin'? Long time no see."

"If your old lady don't shut her mouth, you ain't gonna *see* another five seconds," Jake answered. He jerked his chin toward Faci's wife. Already whimpering, she looked like she was working herself up to a full-fledged scream.

"*Statti citta*," Joe Faci snapped. It came out 'stata geet,' a far cry from anything ever heard in Rome, but enough to shut his wife's mouth.

"I killed Steppy," Jake announced. He was starting to get excited, starting to work himself up toward a rush of pure pleasure that seemed to get more and more familiar as time went on. Now that he knew it was coming, like orgasm at the end of sex, he wanted to take his time, to enjoy the preliminaries as much as the inevitable result. Jake slid the gun back under his overcoat without taking the business end off Joe Faci's navel.

"Ya know what ya problem is?" Joe Faci asked calmly. "Ya problem is that ya crazy."

"Jeez," Jake returned, "a regular Siggy Freud. He was a Jew, too, ya know. Freud, I mean."

"All we asked ya to do is take a vacation and you turn it into this. What's the point, Jake? What does it get ya?"

"The point is that I done twelve years in the joint and I somehow got tired of people tellin' me what to do. When to get up. When to eat breakfast. When to go to work. When to go to sleep. When to take a fuckin' vacation."

"Okay, Jake, I get the picture. But how could I know ya felt like that? Look at me. Am I a gypsy fortune teller? Me and Steppy, we thought it was for your own good. If ya remember, the heat was on *you*, Jake. It was *you* the cops was tryin' to put in the electric chair."

"They're still tryin', as far as I know." Jake wanted to see that quick flash of fear return to Joe Faci's face, but Faci's voice remained calm.

"Ya know, it ain't too late to blow town. You could still get out. Maybe they ain't got a good case. Maybe if ya weren't goin' around knockin' guys off, the cops'd forget about ya."

Jake nodded thoughtfully. "Ya wanna live, don't ya, Joe? Ya wanna eat dinner tonight. Watch the *Honeymooners*. Give your old lady a chunk of the old salami before ya fall asleep." He paused, allowing a smile to spread across his face. "Maybe you could help me out with somethin', Joe. Do ya think ya could?"

"Anything's possible."

Jake's finger tightened on the trigger, pulling hard enough for the hammer to ease back a fraction of an inch. Not only had Joe Faci's voice not reflected the fear Jake expected, it was damn close to sarcastic.

"What's the matter, Joe? You had enough life? You wanna die?"

"No, I don't wanna die."

The sentence whistled out of Joe Faci's mouth and Jake took it for fear. Not that Faci was broken. No, Faci wasn't exactly pissing his pants, but he'd shown enough for Jake to offer him a little hope.

"I got a problem, Joe, and I was wonderin' if ya could help me out with it. Ya know, for old time's sake."

"Look, Jake, I think it would be good if ya took something into consideration. Sooner or later, you gotta take it on the lam. Whatta ya gonna do, kill every cop in New York? No, sooner or later ya gonna have to make like a bunny and hop outta town. How ya gonna live, Jake? Rob? Steal? You go into a strange town and start pullin' jobs, ya gonna end up back here in the electric chair. *You* know that as well as I do."

"Get to the point, Joe. It ain't like I got all day."

"Money, that's the point I'm makin' here. And not a couple of grand, either. I know you, Jake. I seen the way ya take care of yourself. I could get you the kind of dough that'd let ya live in *style*. Maybe you could buy youself a business somewhere. Jews are good at business."

Jake laughed out loud. "Ya got that dough in ya pocket? Maybe packed in one of them suitcases? Or do I gotta let ya go and meet ya somewhere? Like maybe under the Manhattan Bridge at midnight."

"It ain't like that. . . ."

"I said ya could help me out with something, but it ain't money. What I'm lookin' for is Santo Silesi. Me and Santo, we gotta have ourselves a little talk."

"Santo's dead." The words were out before Joe Faci could take them back.

"Whatta ya mean, dead? Who killed him?"

"Your mother."

"Watch ya fuckin' mouth, Joe."

"I mean it. Santo went lookin' for you and your mother shot him down. He's dead."

"And her?"

"Look, Jake, I wasn't there so I ain't exactly got the whole scoop. I heard she was taken to the hospital and the cops were talkin' to her. I'm sure you could figure out what they was askin'."

Jake sighed. So, this was the last one. Steppy Accacio, Santo Silesi and Joe Faci. That was gonna have to do it for Abe and Izzy.

"Get in the car," Jake said. "We're gonna take a little ride."

"What about my wife?"

"Don't worry, I ain't sunk so low as to kill a broad. Ya got ya keys in ya coat pocket?"

"Yeah."

"Okay, first ya take off your overcoat. Then ya get in the car and toss the coat on the back seat, bein' real careful that I should see ya hands every second. What I'm gonna do is get in the back and hand ya the keys. Then we're gonna drive somewhere to get that dough you was talkin' about. Don't make no mistakes, Joe. One more dead spaghetti-brain don't mean shit to me."

Carefully, one button at a time, Joe Faci peeled out of his overcoat. He opened the door, tossed the coat in the back, then slid onto the front seat. He kept both hands exposed all the time, finally dropping them onto the steering wheel as Jake closed the door.

"You ready, Jake?" Faci asked.

"Yeah. As Abe used to say, I'm 'Ready, ready, Teddy, to rock-n-roll.' "

Jake pulled the trigger three times. Once for Izzy. Once for Abe. Once for himself. The first shot killed Joe Faci. It blew his head apart, spattering blood and brains all over the side window. The mixture, as thick as oatmeal, covered the glass. In the momentary silence between the explosions and the screams of Joe Faci's wife, Jake, much to his satisfaction, could hear it dripping down onto the seat.

It was nearly ten o'clock by the time Moodrow finished his rounds. He'd spent most of the day on Henry Street and the surrounding neighborhood, the area where Jake Leibowitz had been spotted. Working the candy stores and lunch wagons, the lofts and warehouse by day; the bars and social clubs by night. The effort had proven fruitless, as such efforts usually did, and by the time

Moodrow decided to head back to Kate and Greta Bloom, his feet were swollen tight against the sides of his shoes. Trudging up Avenue B, he looked down at his almost-new wing tips and silently wished for the black brogans he'd worn as a patrolman.

Well, he thought, at least Jake Leibowitz hasn't skipped town. Moodrow had met Paul Maguire for dinner (taking the opportunity to phone Kate and make sure Greta was coming over) and heard the news about Joe Faci. While both had agreed that it couldn't have happened to a nicer guy, Faci's execution meant that two new elements would be added to the picture.

Now, Dominick Favara and his people would *have* to go after Jake Leibowitz. It was a matter of honor. The same principle, honor, apparently applied to the 6th Precinct as well. The crime had been committed on their turf. The manner in which it had been committed (in full view of witnesses; in full view of the victim's *wife*) guaranteed a vigorous investigation.

"You know the captain over there?" Maguire had asked.

"Bettino."

"Yeah, a hard-ass if there ever was one. He hates the word 'Mafia,' thinks they bring all Italians down. I went over to the Six around four o'clock and the suits wouldn't talk to me. The word is Bettino wants the bust for himself. He's decided that Jake Leibowitz compromised the honor of the Sixth Precinct. *His* precinct."

"Wait a second. What makes him so sure Jake Leibowitz was the shooter?"

"He's got witnesses, Stanley. It happened early this morning while people were going to work."

"Jesus, this guy is crazy. It's like he's jumping off the roof."

"That's right. It's just a matter of who's gonna play sidewalk."

Moodrow, within sight of home, felt his energy level rising. He was looking forward to this confrontation. Greta Bloom loved to function as Stanley Moodrow's conscience. Now, it was his turn.

He took the first steps two at a time, then reconsidered when his feet screamed in protest. Maybe, he thought, I can't afford to move out of the Lower East Side, but if I watch my pennies, I might be able to afford an elevator building.

The door to his apartment opened before he could turn the key in the lock. Moodrow looked down at Kate's smiling face and broke into a huge grin. He'd been preoccupied all day, but now that they were face to face, he could scarcely believe his good fortune.

"How'd it go today?" Kate asked.

"It went and it's gone." Moodrow, spotting Greta perched on his living room sofa like a bird of prey, settled for a chaste kiss instead of the somewhat more lusty greeting bouncing around in his imagination.

"Are you hungry?"

"Not really. But I'd take a cup of coffee. I'm gonna be up for a while."

"There's coffee on the stove. I'll warm it up."

"Thanks, Kate. My feet are killing me. I don't think I could make it to the kitchen."

"Stanley," Greta called, "for me you don't have a 'hello'?"

"For you I have much more than a 'hello.'" Moodrow dropped into an overstuffed chair and slowly removed his shoes. "I'm not takin' off the socks, because I don't wanna see the blood."

"If you take off the socks, we'll have to evacuate the premises." Greta, smiling, pinched her nose.

"Look at it as a genteel version of the third degree. You give me what I want, I'll wash 'em."

"*Nu*, so what is it you want? I don't mean to *kvetch*, but I'm an old lady and I need my sleep. It's ten o'clock, already."

They were interrupted by Kate returning with a mug of coffee for Moodrow and a cup of tea for Greta. "Am I allowed to stay for this?"

"Allowed?" Moodrow snorted. "We're not discussing the country's nuclear secrets here." He waited for Kate to sit down, before continuing. "Tell me something, Greta," he said mildly. "Do you know Sarah Leibowitz?"

"*Oy*," Greta moaned, "so *this* is what you want." She leaned back and folded her arms across her chest. "You're a bully is what you are. I'm glad your mother isn't here for this."

"Cut the crap, Greta."

"Stanley," Kate broke in, "is that necessary?"

"As a matter of fact, it *is* necessary. I'm tired and my feet hurt. I don't wanna be playing Ring-Around-The-Rosie until it's time to get up tomorrow morning."

"Stanley," Greta said, fingering a lace doily spread over the arm of the couch, "do you know your mother made this? She was a wonderful seamstress. She could make anything."

"Cut the crap, Greta. Do you know Sarah Leibowitz? A simple answer will do here. Yes or no?"

"I see her on the street, I recognize her. I see her in the *shul*, I nod hello. Is this *knowing*? Does this make us *landsleit*?"

"You belong to the same temple?"

"Yes."

"And when you nod to her, she nods back?"

"I'm not saying no."

"That's 'knowing,' Greta. It's enough for what I have in mind." Moodrow sipped at his coffee, turning away from Greta to wink at Kate. "You having fun?" he asked.

"I think I *will* be," Kate responded. "As soon as I figure out what's going on."

Moodrow turned back to Greta without commenting. "Did you know the rabbi went to see the police?" he asked.

"I heard. At the market someone mentioned this."

"The cops were going to hold her for the gun. They were going to charge her with a violation of the Sullivan Act and hold her as a material witness. The rabbi had a talk with the captain and now she's sitting in her own apartment. She won't talk to anybody. Won't even deny that she knows where her son is. As soon as a cop gets within ten feet of her, she starts screaming. Or she throws things. Or she grabs her head and moans in pain."

"It's not an act, Stanley. She's a very nervous woman."

"Greta, does she clean her house in the morning? Make her bed? Take a shower? Does she cook? Go to the market?" He paused for an answer, but Greta merely shrugged, her eyes widening. "I don't know why, Greta, but I'm convinced that if she can do all those things, she can answer a few questions."

Kate shifted her chair closer to Moodrow and Greta. They were staring at each other so intently, Kate felt like she was watching a movie. "I don't see what this has to do with anything? She's nervous. She's not nervous. What difference does it make?"

"He wants I should be a stool pigeon is the point," Greta huffed. "It's against my principles."

"What do you mean, 'a stool pigeon'? Do you know where Jake Leibowitz is hiding?"

"He wants me to convince my friend to inform on her own son. He should bite his tongue."

"Your *friend*?" Moodrow said. His face was blank, his small features immobile in his huge skull. "Sarah Leibowitz is your friend?"

"She's not a *friend* friend," Greta protested. "Stanley, please, I'm *begging* you. All my life I fought against the cops. I'm telling you we had *battles* with the police. Informing was the worst crime you could commit. It was worse than murder. I'm an old lady. I can't change."

Moodrow leaned back in the chair and managed a quick smile. "Greta, you run into Rosaura Pastoral lately?"

"This is not right."

"Does she still talk about her ex-boarder? She ever mention Luis Melenguez?" He leaned forward, slapping his palms on his knees. "Maybe now that Melenguez's widow has gone back to Puerto Rico, you don't give a shit anymore."

"This is not right."

"But why *should* you care? Sarah Leibowitz is Jewish. She belongs to your *shul*. Luis Melenguez was just another Puerto Rican immigrant. You have to have loyalties, right? You have to make choices. Isn't that what *you* told *me* when you sent me after Jake Leibowitz?"

Greta Bloom sighed. "What you are, Stanley, is a bully. A common neighborhood bully."

"Not a bully, Greta. A cop. Did you think I was going to pull Melenguez's killer out of a hat? If that's what you thought, you should have thought twice, because it turns out that you're the hat. Ain't life grand?"

Thirty-two

JANUARY 24

STANLEY MOODROW sat at his kitchen table, the *Daily News* in one hand, a cup of coffee in the other, and listened to the sound of water running in the shower. He hadn't heard that sound in a long time, not unless he was standing in the tub. He could remember a time when he and his parents had made do with a clawfoot bathtub, remember the weekend his father had decided to add a vertical pipe, a showerhead and a support for a plastic curtain. Max Moodrow had begun the job in a grouchy mood. He'd felt that, considering who actually *owned* the property, improvements were the landlord's responsibility. Unfortunately, when he'd brought it up while paying his rent, Ed Boyer had laughed in his face.

"You would maybe like to pay more rent, Max? Perhaps you will vote for a politician to repeal rent control?"

Max Moodrow had spent the whole day (a Sunday, his one day off) assembling a Rube Goldberg contraption of his own design. At the very end, he'd turned on the water with a great flourish only to discover that the valve designed to switch the flow of water from the tub to the showerhead wasn't working. No matter how hard he twisted the tiny lever, water continued to pour into the bathtub.

By the time he'd given up, it was after six and there was no chance of finding an open hardware store in New York City. Not even on the Lower East Side where Jewish merchants (who closed on Saturday for *Shabbes*) dared the politicians and the police to enforce the Blue Laws.

Initially, Max Moodrow's profane howls of frustration had filled the air in their apartment. But not for long. Accompanied by his son ("Stanley, from these things you learn how to be a man, not a bum."), he'd marched down the block to Igor Melenkov's apartment and confronted the shopowner in his own home. Melenkov had sold him the defective valve and Melenkov had to replace it. No, he couldn't come by the store tomorrow morning. He had to work tomorrow. And the next day and the next and the next. If he didn't get the shower going tonight, it'd have to wait the entire week.

Melenkov had shrugged into his coat and marched back to inspect Max Moodrow's plumbing.

"You are an idiot, Moodrow. Walve is upside-down. Please in future to stick with hammer and nails. Plumbing is for plumbers. Now, give me wrench and pour for me a wodka."

Stanley Moodrow recalled watching Malenkov unscrew the various fittings. Malenkov had crooked a finger into the freed valve, extracted a wad of soaked paper, then re-fitted the valve with the handle reversed.

The whole process had seemed magical to five-year-old Stanley Moodrow and it was years before he figured it out. He'd watched Malenkov through childhood eyes, absorbing the information without trying to understand it. The valve must have worked either way. All reversing did was move the handle from one side to the other. Malenkov had either left something inside the valve or failed to warn Max about something left by the manufacturer. His father hadn't done anything wrong.

Moodrow sipped at his coffee and glanced down at the day's headline: *HUGE DOPE RAID TIES IN LUCIANO*. The Feds had conducted simultaneous raids in Philly, New York and Washington, netting twenty-one criminals, thirty-five pounds of heroin and fifty-four pounds of opium. More than the total amount seized in the entire country in 1957.

But, of course, that was the point. There were new records every year. Dope seemed to be unstoppable, like a wall of lava flowing down the side of a volcano. The papers liked to blame it on corruption, but the truth was that no one, not the most ardent cop or social reformer, had the faintest idea what to do about it.

"Morning, Stanley, anything interesting happen last night?"

Moodrow looked up to find Kate, wrapped in a large blue towel, standing in the doorway. Her hair glistened in the harsh light of an unshielded ceiling fixture. The light illuminated the spray of freckles across her cheekbones. It sparkled in her small even teeth.

In an instant, before he could take a breath, twenty-one criminals, thirty-five pounds of heroin and fifty-four pounds of opium fled up to newspaper heaven. Moodrow, his attention riveted to the corner of the towel tucked beneath Kate's arm, lost all capacity to consider social problems.

"Damn," he whispered.

"Damn what?" Kate was giggling.

" 'Damn the torpedoes. Full speed ahead.' "

They made love in the living room, Kate on the couch and Moodrow kneeling in front of it. He held her by the hips as he thrust into her. As if she might fly away if he dared to let her go. He watched her closely, the twist of her mouth, the sharply indrawn breath, the tightly closed eyes. Now she was his. The thought came to him as suddenly as the opening credits in a Technicolor movie. The theatre was dark and then . . . magic.

Half an hour later, they were sitting across from each other at Moodrow's kitchen table. Moodrow was buttering a piece of toast as Kate ran a brush through her hair.

"Ya know, I heard the honeymoon suite at the Waldorf was overpriced, but I never expected *this*." He waved his toast at the four walls.

"What'd you say, Stanley?"

"I made a joke."

"I'm sorry, I wasn't listening. Would it still be funny if you said it again?"

"It wasn't funny the first time. You going to work today?"

"No, I'm not ready to go back. Maybe I'll stick around to comfort Greta after you get through brutalizing her."

"Don't feel sorry for Greta. She knows what she has to do. She knew it *before* I spelled it out last night. Ask yourself this: if she had such a problem with cops, why'd she come to me in the first place? People in this neighborhood don't go to the police. They handle their own problems whenever they can. And that includes revenge. Me, I'm a cop and I *need* cooperation. I get it by giving folks a reason to do what they already know is right."

"It seemed more like the Battle of the Bulge than gentle persuasion."

Moodrow reached behind his chair and opened the refrigerator door. He pulled a jar of Welch's Grape Jelly off the shelf, closing the door as he turned back to the table. "You have to do what you have to do, Kate. If there's another way to get to Jake Leibowitz, I haven't thought of it."

"Stanley, do you mind if I ask you a question?" Kate leaned forward, absently rolling the salt shaker between her palms.

"Does it matter?"

"Yes, it matters. It's very personal, but I'd like to know the answer."

"Let's hear it."

"From what you told me, it's obvious that somebody's going to get Jake Leibowitz. The cops, the mob, *somebody*. Why does it have to be you?"

"Jesus," Moodrow whispered.

"Jesus has nothing to do with this. Jesus *forgave* the thief, remember?"

"Yeah, I heard that somewhere. Look, I gotta get down to Greta's. As for your question, it's like asking Roy Campanella why he wants to hit a home run. There're plenty of cops, detectives, too, who'd spend their tours sleeping at their desks if they could. A paycheck and a pension, that's all they want. Me, I'm not one of them. It's my game and I want to play it. I want to be the best. Hall of Fame all the way."

Pat Cohan glanced at his reflection in the mirror and shuddered.

"This calls for a drink," he said out loud. The drink, a bottle of Bushmill's, was already in his hand. He looked at it for a second, then drank deeply before turning back to the mirror.

The alcohol had done nothing to improve the image that stared back at him. His mane was as wild as a *real* lion's mane. It stood almost straight out, a thin white halo that looked more ghostly than saintly.

But his mane wasn't the worst of it. His complexion was red, *bright* red. He resembled one of the heavily-rouged whores he used to roust when he was working Vice.

He thought about the whores for a moment. Thought about what they'd offered him to avoid an arrest. The memory was pleasant enough, though he wasn't aroused by the legs and breasts that flitted through his mind. No, what aroused him was the sudden thrust of an entirely different image. He saw his darlin' Kathleen lying on Stanley Moodrow's sheets. Her legs were wrapped around his hips and she was moaning as he rammed into her.

"Fuckmefuckmefuckmefuckmefuckmeeeeeeeeeeeeeeeee."

Now his face was *really* red. Flag red. Santa Claus red. Fire engine red. He shook the image out of his mind before they got to something even worse.

"Hair of the dog," he muttered, pulling at the bottle as he turned away from the mirror. "Now there's *something* you've got to do, boyo. And you know what it is."

Pat Cohan walked down the hallway, surprised by his steady gait. The door to his wife's room was closed, as usual. He could hear her moving inside, hear the monotonous drone as she pursued her various rituals.

"Are ya decent, Rose?" he called, pushing the door open. "Not that I give a damn."

He found her kneeling on the bare floor. Staring up at the serene smile of a five-foot plaster statue.

"Holy Mary, mother of God," she droned.

Did she even know he was there? He took a quick drink, then crossed the room and jerked her to her feet.

"A little talk, Rose. That's what we're after havin'."

She turned and looked up at him, a bony old woman in a shapeless black dress. Her gray eyes, he noted, were surprisingly sane. Did that make it harder? Or easier?

"A talk," she whispered. "Yes, a talk." She cocked her head and looked at him out of the corner of one eye. "Is it Jesus you've come to talk about, Matthew?"

Pat Cohan started. Matthew was his Confirmation name. It was the name she'd called him during the early days of their marriage.

"No, not Jesus, Rose. It's Stanley Moodrow. It's the devil himself I've come to discuss. He's ruined our lives and he must be punished. We can't be lettin' him have our darlin' Kathleen, can we? We can't be lettin' them fornicate like dumb animals. They're livin' in sin, Rose. That's what the pair of 'em are doin'. Ruttin' around like dogs in the road."

Rose Cohan turned back to her tiny altar, lips already moving.

"Not now, Rose. We've somethin' to discuss. After which I promise never to interrupt your prayers again."

He spun her around, once again struck by her lucid stare, and wondered if she'd been faking it all along. He, like everybody else, including the priests at Sacred Heart, had assumed that she was crazy. Was there a parish that didn't have its share of Rose Cohans? Of shriveled old ladies mumbling their way to the grave? They were tolerated, their piety never questioned. And if they were stable enough to mop the nunnery basement, so much the better.

"You shouldn't have made him go, Matthew. Why did you make him go? He wanted to be a priest. He was in the seminary; he didn't have to go."

Peter, always Peter. She'd taken that sissy and made him into a holy martyr. Why couldn't she understand? Everybody in the Department, lieutenants, captains, inspectors, *everybody* was packing his kid off to fight the war. Younger cops were resigning by the hundreds. They were *enlisting*.

Meanwhile, his own son played priest in his seminary room. His own son pissed his pants at the thought of Hitler's tanks.

Better a dead son to bring you honor than a live son to bring you shame. That's what he'd thought at the time and that's what he still believed.

"Pete was a hero and a patriot," Pat Cohan said. "He died like a man."

"Is that how a man dies? With thousands of other men in the waters off a beach? Is that a hero's funeral? A letter from the Department of the Army saying '*presumed lost*'?"

He snorted in disgust. "Maybe you're right. Hero *is* stretchin' it a bit. In fact, havin' known the little coward intimately, it wouldn't surprise me to learn he swam all the way to the North Pole. And ya can stop prayin' for him. Between all the prayers *he* said and all the prayers *you've* said, little Peter's sure to be floatin' around with the Big Prick himself."

Rose Cohan started at the epithet. "It's not Peter I pray for, Matthew. It's you."

She turned away, walking back to the little altar, blessing herself before kneeling.

"Well, I guess Baby Jesus hasn't been listenin', Rose, because I'm as unrepentant as ever."

He slid the worn .38 from his jacket pocket as he approached her. Thinking maybe the touch of it against her skull would bring her back to the present. But she continued to pray, her lips moving quickly over the words.

Well, he thought, Rose Cohan isn't the point anyway. The point is Kathleen, darlin' Kathleen. The point is what's mine and what I intend to keep.

He left Rose lying on her own altar, a gory sacrifice to a vindictive god, and strolled downstairs to his den. The telephone seemed to beckon. He raised the bottle of Bushmill's.

"Here's to the glories of modern life. Here's to the death of my lovely wife."

The alcohol slid down his throat as if it had a life of his own, as if it was *eager* to radiate its heat to his brain.

It's a question of last straws, he thought, laughing out loud. Of which last straw is the last last straw.

"The last last straw," he said, responding as if he'd been called on to recite, "is *your* last straw. The straw *you* pluck. The straw *you* play."

That's why Detective Lieutenant Irv Rosten's phone call hadn't been the climax it appeared to be. All it had done was bring the problem into focus. He'd been mulling over ways to bring Kate home, anyway. Had thought of nothing else since she'd walked out on him. Rosten's call had served to sharpen his resolve. Sharpen it by placing it firmly in the present.

"What kind of fucking game are you playing?" That was Rosten's idea of a greeting.

"Well, I . . ."

"Don't bother with the bullshit, Cohan. You figured you'd retire and leave me holding the bag. Well, it didn't work. Your papers are sitting in Chief Rooney's desk. They haven't been processed and they're not gonna be."

"Irv, look . . ."

"I said, don't bother. You brought me in and it was up to you to protect me. That's the way it works. You were my rabbi. You had a right to call in your markers, but not to put my head in the noose. I just came out of Chief Rooney's office and it's my pleasure to personally deliver the message. Rooney doesn't want *me*, Pat. He wants *you*. I don't know why, but I get the feeling it's personal. Rooney wants your ass and I'm gonna give it to him. You ordered me to arrest Stanley Moodrow and I'm willin' to say so. You were with Joe Faci and Santo Silesi the night Izzy Stein disappeared. I'm willing to say that, too. You shouldn't have run out on me, Pat. I figured you for a standup guy and you made me into a sap. Now the joke's on you."

Pat Cohan grabbed the phone and quickly dialed Moodrow's number. He had no idea what he'd say if Moodrow answered. Beg, probably. Beg to speak to his own daughter.

"Hello."

Cohan heaved a sigh at the sound of Kate's voice. It was going to be all right, now. It was going to be all right.

"Kathleen," he whispered, "darlin' Kathleen."

"Don't, Daddy. It won't work. I know the truth."

" 'And the truth shall set you free?' " He made it into a question. Not that he cared about her answer. The idea was to keep her talking, to make a link.

"Not free, Daddy, but freer. I used to be imprisoned by lies. From here on, I intend to make my own decisions based on the truth."

"Ah yes, lies." He put the bottle to his lips and drank deeply. "I won't bother to deny 'em, Kathleen. Nor are explanations in order. It's your mother I've called to talk about. She needs to see you. Needs you to dry her tears. 'First Peter, now Kathleen.' That's all she can say, Kate. She's been crying for the last twenty-four hours and I don't know how to stop it. Is it possible you could spare a few hours for your poor suffering mother?"

He paused for a moment, listening to the metallic hiss of his own heavy breathing through the receiver. "I love ya, Kathleen. I don't suppose that makes much difference, now. Why should it, considerin' the things I've been after doin' to ya? But that's over. You've found me out, girl, and I know it can never be like it was. I *know* this, but does what I've done to ya *have* to mean that your mother and myself are out of your life forever? For God's sake, Kathleen, come home for a visit. Talk to your mother. She thinks she's never going to see you again. I swear before the Almighty that I won't try to hold you."

"Okay, Daddy. I have to come back sooner or later, anyway. I need my clothes and I need to settle things between us. Just give me an hour to get myself together before I leave."

"Thank you, darlin'. Thank you."

Pat Cohan gently lowered the receiver. He looked down at the bottle in his hand for a moment, then heaved himself erect and slowly walked up the stairs to his wife's room.

"Top of the mornin', Rose," he said. "What's the matter? Cat got your tongue? You could at least be polite."

It'd been months, maybe years, since he'd felt this good. "The last last straw," he muttered, "is the last straw *you* play."

There was an upholstered chair next to his wife's bed. A useless ornament, really, because she never got up off her knees. He tucked the bottle under one arm, slid the chair across the room until it was facing the door, then sat heavily.

"Any regrets?" he asked himself.

"None," he answered, putting the barrel of his .38 into his mouth, cocking the hammer, splattering his brains all over the ceiling.

Thirty-three

STANLEY MOODROW, on his way down to Greta Bloom's apartment, knew that he had a problem. On the one hand, he felt that Greta had a better chance of penetrating Sarah Leibowitz's armor if she confronted Sarah without a cop (namely, himself) being present. On the other hand, he wasn't sure that given Greta's general reluctance, she'd push Mama Leibowitz very hard if Stanley Moodrow wasn't around to give *her* an occasional nudge.

It was Greta, herself, who finally enabled Stanley Moodrow to make up his mind. There were no blintzes waiting for him when he knocked on her door. Not even a cup of coffee. Greta, answering his soft knock, was dressed to go out.

"We'll talk on the way," she announced, pushing past him.

Moodrow was stunned. Not by her attitude, which he'd more or less expected; it was her outfit that left him openmouthed. She was encased from head to toe in a bright yellow slicker with a matching hat that swooped down in back to cover her collar. Moodrow didn't know who'd owned the raincoat before she'd gotten her hands on it, but he was positive that she hadn't bought it new. It was so big the bottom seam dropped to the tops of her galoshes. The sleeves, even rolled up, covered all but the tips of her fingers.

"Greta," Moodrow said, "could you please come back here for a minute."

Already halfway down the hall, Greta stopped and turned to face him. "If you don't mind, please, I'd like to get this over with," she said.

"Me, too, Greta. Which means we should go in there with some kind of a plan. Do you know what you're going to say?"

Amazed, he watched a shudder run through Greta Bloom's body. The situation was tearing her apart. He wondered, briefly, if she'd eventually forgive him. Greta had a reputation for holding a grudge to the bitter end.

"What you should think about," he said, "is how you'll feel if we *don't* find Jake Leibowitz at the end of this rainbow. If you go through with it and fail."

"Stanley," Greta declared, planting her fists on her hips, "you're nothing but a bully."

Moodrow shrugged. "You already said that, Greta. And it might actually bother me if I wasn't a hundred percent convinced that you'd never do this, not even if I put a gun to your head, unless you knew it was right. You wanna blame me, that's fine. But let's get Jake Leibowitz, okay?"

"We'll talk as we go," Greta insisted.

"Can we at least take our time about it? Do we have to run?" Moodrow, at that moment, knew he'd be going into the Leibowitz apartment with Greta. He knew he'd be doing some of the talking, too. Despite everything, Greta simply wasn't tough enough for the job. Well, he'd brought a little surprise with him. A kicker to sweeten the pot.

"We'll talk as we go," Greta repeated, turning away.

Moodrow hustled after her, following her down two flights and out into the street before she ran out of gas.

"All right, Stanley, I'm too old to run. Tell me your scheme, already. One thing I'm sure is that you got one."

"Ya know, Greta, it would've been nice to do this inside. Where it's dry."

The January thaw was definitely over. It was raining steadily and the temperature was in the high thirties. Moodrow watched the rain bounce off Greta's slicker for a moment, then launched himself into it.

"I spoke to the detectives who caught the Leibowitz case. I know it sounds unbelievable, but they suspect that Santo Silesi was shot deliberately. You understand what I'm saying, right? Not in self-defense, but deliberately. Now, I'm not the judge and jury here, but I have a real strong feeling that we're not gonna convince Sarah Leibowitz to give up her kid by appealing to her conscience. We're gonna have to offer her something, something she can understand. That something is gonna be her son's life."

"You're God, Stanley? You can give life?" Greta began to walk, staring down at her feet as she stamped through the puddles.

"You're gonna tell her that he knows too much, that the cops want to kill him as much as the mob. He's only got one chance at survival and that's to give himself up to the right man."

"Should I guess who that is?"

"It's not a joke, Greta. What I'm telling you is close to the truth. If the mob finds him first, Jake's dead. We'll be lucky to find the body. Now, maybe the cops haven't actually been told to gun him down, but if he puts up any resistance the neighbors'll think World War Three broke out. And if he runs, nobody's gonna bother with a warning shot. They'll kill him before he takes a step. Jake Leibowitz only has one chance at survival and that's to surrender."

"Surrender for what? So you can send him to the electric chair? Maybe I didn't have your education, but this I don't call survival."

Moodrow put a hand on Greta's shoulder, stopping her long enough to allow a milk truck to plow through an enormous puddle.

"Thank you, Stanley."

"You're welcome."

They crossed the street in silence, stepping onto the opposite curb before Greta spoke again.

"What makes you think you can protect him? If so many people are trying to kill him?"

"I can get him down to the precinct in one piece. That takes the cops out of it. Once he's booked, I'll go over to the DA's office and put myself on the record. I'll tell them I *know* Jake Leibowitz's life has been threatened by members of organized crime. If I'm on the record, the city'll have to protect him. Plus, the press is bound to get its hands on the story and that'll put even more pressure on the city. I . . ."

"Stanley, I'm against capital punishment. Did I ever tell you this?" Greta looked up at him for the first time. "It's decades, already, I've been against capital punishment. Since before the Rosenbergs. As far as I'm concerned, the death penalty is legalized murder."

Moodrow reached out and took Greta's hand. "I have to admit that when I first hatched this scheme I was looking forward to putting you on the spot. I thought the situation was funny. It's not funny, now. Look, Greta, you're about the only family I have left and I don't want Jake Leibowitz bad enough to lose you in the process. We can't be sure that Sarah Leibowitz knows where Jake's holed up. Or that she'll tell us if she does know. Let's forget about it. *Somebody's* gonna get Jake Leibowitz. It doesn't have to be me."

Greta continued to stare into Moodrow's eyes for a moment. "Is it true?" she finally whispered. "If I help you, will I be saving his life?"

"Jake Leibowitz has killed at least four people. Two of them were mobsters and two others were operating under mob protection. You've been living down here long enough to know what that means. Now add the fact that every cop on the Lower East Side has a photo of Jake Leibowitz in his pocket. They've all been told that he's wanted for multiple homicides and that he's armed and that he's *extremely* dangerous. Remember what I told you about Pat Cohan? He tried to cover up the murder of Luis Melenguez and he didn't work alone. You don't have to be a genius to figure out that Cohan and his buddies are as anxious as the mob to see Jake Leibowitz dead and gone. Look, Greta, all I'm really asking you to do is get Sarah Leibowitz to listen to me. And all *I'm* gonna do is offer her a simple proposition. If she tells me where he's hiding, I'll do everything I can to bring him in alive. If she can talk him into surrendering, I'll *guarantee* his safety."

"But, Stanley, the electric chair . . ."

"Between the trials and the appeals, it'll be two or three years before he has to take the last walk. You remember the old saying? Where there's life, there's hope? Maybe Jake'll get lucky and draw a judge who's against capital punishment. Maybe the governor will decide to commute his sentence. Maybe the legislature will abolish the death penalty altogether. But if he's dead, *maybe* doesn't enter into it. If he's dead, they put him in a box, dig a grave and lower him down."

Greta turned and began to walk again. The rain poured off her bright yellow hat. Moodrow watched it run down her back and drop onto the sidewalk. At least she wasn't heading for her own apartment.

"Let me go in alone," Greta said after a moment. "I think it would be better if I went in by myself."

"You sure you're up to it?"

"Sarah's a very nervous woman. If she sees you and decides to pitch a fit, I won't be able to get a word in edgewise. Me she'll talk to, because she doesn't know what I want."

"What are you gonna tell her?"

"The danger she already knows about. Sarah's husband was a gangster who ended up floating in the river. What I'll say is I've known you since you were a *pitseleh*. I'll tell her she can't trust the cops, but she can trust *you*. I don't know if she'll go for it, but I think it's the best approach. There's one thing, though. You've got to promise me that you'll keep your end of the bargain. What I'm doing is hard enough without also being a liar."

"I'm not a killer," Moodrow returned. "I'm a cop. I hunt, but I don't kill. On the other hand, if Jake Leibowitz decides to fight, there's nothing I can do about it."

They parted company in the small lobby of Sarah Leibowitz's tenement. Moodrow, standing by the mailboxes, watched Greta until she disappeared on the second-floor landing. He noted her straight back and firm step with satisfaction. Taking both as proof of her commitment.

He listened to her footsteps for another moment, then, with nothing to do but wait, let his mind drift over the events of the last two days. He had, he decided, meant what he'd said about allowing Greta to walk away. If she'd accepted, he would have let the matter drop without a word. But even as he'd made the offer, he'd been sure that she wouldn't take him up on it. Would he have been so generous if he'd thought she'd jump at the opportunity?

Moodrow was honest enough to admit that he didn't know the answer. There was no way he *could* know. But he was sure that what he'd actually done, no matter what his intentions had been, amounted to one more nail in Jake Leibowitz's coffin. Last night, he'd told Greta that she *had* to help him. That it was her duty. That by insisting on *his* obligation, she'd obliged herself. This morning, he'd told her it was all right to wash her hands of the whole affair. Both statements had served to advance him one step closer to his goal.

There *was*, he finally decided, one truth buried in his manipulation of Greta Bloom—he didn't want to lose her. He needed Greta in his life as much he needed Kate. Maybe more. For a time after the death of his mother, Moodrow had felt as if he was floating. As if he was a speck of dust at the mercy of the slightest breeze. Greta had been there constantly, ministering to him as she had to his mother. She'd been living proof that he wasn't alone. There were times, he recalled, when he'd resented her visits. When he'd felt it was his duty to be alone. Greta had ignored his sharp remarks, plying him with food and long stories until he'd come back down to earth.

"Stanley."

He looked up to find Greta standing at the top of the stairs. "So quick?" he asked as he climbed the steps.

"What could I say? Sarah claims that she doesn't know where her Jake's hiding, but she'll listen to you. In case he calls."

"You believe her?"

Greta didn't answer. She led Moodrow to a doorway on the fourth floor. Pushing the door open, she stepped back to let Moodrow enter the apartment.

"Good luck," she whispered.

Sarah Leibowitz, wrapped in a cheap fur coat, was sitting on an upholstered chair in the living room. The glare she tossed in Moodrow's direction convinced him to stick to a line he'd already decided to pursue. What he saw in her eyes was pure hate. It wasn't the first time he'd come across that reaction, but the intensity was something else again. By comparison, Carmine Stettecase's glare was caressing.

Moodrow drew his lips into a thin smile, but his eyes remained cold. He walked across the room, watching his shadow advance before him, until he was right on top of her.

"I'm not gonna fuck around," he said, "because I ain't got the time for it. No, I'm gonna make it real simple. Take a look at this."

He reached beneath his overcoat and took a glossy photograph from his jacket pocket. Unfolding it carefully, he dropped it into Sarah Leibowitz's lap. It was a forensic shot, taken at the crime scene, of Luis Melenguez's body. Melenguez was lying on his side with his back to the camera. His jawbone had been shot away and several glistening white teeth were clearly visible in the pool of blood surrounding the body.

"This is what's gonna happen to Jake if he doesn't give himself up. Ya wanna know what's gonna happen to *you*. You're gonna hear a knock on the door one day. There's gonna be a cop out there, a detective, like me. He's gonna take you down to the morgue to identify the body of your son. Jake's gonna look just like the body in this photograph. Except for one thing. The photo's in black and white. Jake's gonna be in living color. Or should I say *dying* color."

He retrieved the photo and carefully refolded it before shoving it back into his pocket. He could feel Greta behind him, feel her eyes boring into his back.

"I heard your husband was a floater. How many days was he in the river? Two? Three? A week? It's funny, you see a stiff after a couple of days in the river, you think it can't get any uglier. Then you see one after it's been down for a month. Who'd they get to identify your husband's body, Mrs. Leibowitz? They get you? They pull back the sheet for you? You wanna go through that again?"

"You bastard."

Despite the words, Moodrow could see the defiance seep out of Sarah Leibowitz's eyes. She looked frightened now, like a trapped animal.

"I won't argue the point," he said. "You say I'm a bastard, I'm a bastard. A bastard who's willing to save your kid when everybody else on the Lower East Side wants him dead. Look, why don't you get on the phone and give Jake a call? I'll go wherever he is, pick him up and get him into the station house before guys like Dominick Favara and Carmine Stettecase know what's happening."

"You think I'm a *schmuck*? You think I don't know they'll kill him in the jail?"

"I'll see that he's protected."

"Now you're the commissioner?"

"Jake's still in town, isn't he?" Moodrow abruptly changed the subject. "If he'd already skipped town, you wouldn't be talking to me at all."

"I'm not saying I know where he is."

Moodrow turned to face Greta. Ignoring the outrage in her eyes, he shook his head and shrugged. "I don't know why I bothered coming here," he said. "It's better this way. Dying in the street is too good for the prick. I hope the mob gets him and I hope they take their time. Let's go."

"Wait."

"Yeah?"

"Tell me how you'll protect my Jake."

Moodrow repeated the offer he'd made to Greta Bloom a few minutes earlier. "It's the best chance he's got. It's the *only* chance he's got."

"I couldn't call him. He'd just run out into the street. My Jake, he's stubborn like a rock."

Moodrow slowly turned around. Sarah Leibowitz was staring up at him. Her eyes held neither fear nor hate. They were as cold as glass.

"Jake buy you that coat?" he asked.

"What's it to you?"

"Where is he, Mrs. Leibowitz?"

"He's in the project on Madison Street."

"Which one? The La Guardia Houses?"

"No, the Vladeck. Building A, apartment 678. It's where my sister used to live before she went into the hospital. I been holding onto it in case she got better."

Moodrow repressed a smile. The Vladeck Houses were a block from Henry Street.

"You did the smart thing, Mrs. Leibowitz," he intoned piously. "You won't regret it."

Thirty-four

WHEN THE phone rang, Jake Leibowitz was having the time of his life. He was in the bathroom, trimming his mustache, a mustache he could actually *see* for a change. One of the first things he'd done upon arriving at his Aunt Golda's apartment was rummage through the drawers and closets. He'd done it more out of habit than anything else (after all, what in the world could he possibly find that'd help him out of *this* pickle), discovering an ancient pair of wire-rimmed spectacles in a night table drawer. The glasses were so thick, Jake'd had to put his face right up against the mirror in order to see anything, but, still, once he'd done that, his mustache had leaped into sharp focus.

It'd been amazing. Like being down at the track with a good pair of binoculars. Just spin the little knob and . . . Pow! Individual black hairs had jumped out at Jake Leibowitz like neatly stacked prison bars. He hadn't minded the fact that he could barely get the scissors between his face and the mirror. Nor the fact that the scissors were so dull they refused to cut, pressing down on the hairs like a tiny curling iron. *Seeing* was enough to keep him happy.

What he'd done was sharpen the scissors against the concrete sill outside the bathroom window. It'd been a slow process, but he had nothing, but time, anyway. Besides, the work had reminded him of the old days in Leavenworth.

How many shivs had he made? Only to have them eventually confiscated? Only to make another?

"I must'a made a hundred of 'em," he'd said out loud. "I must'a made a thousand. One for every day I done in the hole. What's the old saying? 'Better the man should catch me with it, than the boys should catch me without it.' I don't know who made that up, but he must'a been a fuckin' genius."

Once he'd gotten the mustache looking halfway decent, he'd gone to his teeth. Taking them one at a time. Polishing each tooth as if he was washing windows in the Leavenworth administration building. Then he'd gone to the small hairs in his nose, then to his eyebrows, then to his ears.

When the telephone rang, he was so deeply engrossed that he jumped back as if he'd been slapped. Aunt Golda's glasses slipped off the bridge of his nose, crashing to the tile floor. He knelt quickly, ignoring the phone. Scooping up the glasses and holding them against his forehead as he anxiously peered into the mirror.

"Jeez," he said, "that was a close one."

But it was all right. Only a small crack up a corner of the right lens. Which was just as well, because he didn't have his mustache perfect yet. Not quite perfect.

The phone continued to ring and Jake continued to stare at his reflection. He wasn't in any hurry, because he already knew who it was. Anyone but his mother would've hung up a long time ago.

"Awright, aweady," he called, sliding the spectacles into his shirt pocket.

Mama Leibowitz had been calling every few hours. Detailing her adventure with Santo Silesi. Hadn't she ever heard of tapped phones? If the flatfoots were listening, she'd be a candidate for the electric chair. Despite the wound in her skull. Despite being a fat old lady with a heart condition.

But he couldn't discourage her, couldn't get through. She talked about killing Santo Silesi the way she'd talked about her new fur coat. Bragging about it.

"Jake, you should have seen the look on his face. Like he opened the closet and out came Dracula."

Jake strolled over to the phone and picked it up. "Yeah, ma," he sighed.

"*Jakeleh*, I told them where you are. The coppers. I told them."

"Jeez, ma, what'd ya do that for? I was thinkin' about skippin' town."

The *real* question was why he'd hung around with her all this time. That was the biggest mistake he'd ever made. Bigger than tryin' to get in with the guineas. Hangin' out with a crazy woman must've made him crazy, too.

"They *beat* me, Jake. They burned me with cigars. They kicked me when I fell on the floor. It was terrible, Jake. I could barely walk."

"Ya forgot the rubber hose."

"Pardon?"

"What I'm sayin' is ya sound pretty good for a cripple." Not that it mattered.

Crazy people did crazy things. Look at him. What he should've done was go out to Los Angeles. He should've done what Steppy Accacio told him to do. Hell, he should've done what that drill sergeant told him the day he'd stepped off the bus at Fort Dix. But the past didn't matter, either. The cops were coming and he was gonna die and that was that.

"Jake, *nu*, you should consider giving up."

"Good advice, ma. I'll be sure to take it."

Jake could see his mother arriving at Sing-Sing to witness the execution. Wearing a shapeless black dress beneath her fur coat. Stopping to pose for the cameras.

"My poor Jakeleh. He was such a good boy. Like an angel. With curls you wouldn't believe. I still have my Jakeleh's curls. I keep them in a locket."

"Awright, ma, I gotta go and get ready. I don't wanna die in my underwear."

Jake hung up and walked into the bedroom. He rummaged through his Aunt Golda's closet, pushing her dresses out of the way. What he wanted was his absolute best. Silk tie, silk shirt. His beautiful gray suit; his shiniest black shoes.

"Should I wear a hat?" he asked himself. A hat didn't make any sense, because he wasn't going anywhere. Only he didn't really feel dressed without a hat. Of course, maybe he shouldn't wear the suit, either. If the flatfoots shot up his good suit, he was gonna have to be buried in an off-the-rack from Macy's.

But, no, the suit didn't matter, either. There was no way he was gonna be buried like a *goy*. Jews didn't have wakes with the relatives coming to the coffin for a last look. Mama Leibowitz would jam his carcass into a pine box and dump him as soon as possible. Assuming the rabbi gave permission for a Jewish burial.

"What it is," he said, shrugging into his silk shirt, "is if I wear a hat, they'll say I was gettin' ready to run. They'll say I was a punk."

Finished dressing, Jake went back into the living room and made himself a barricade by turning a heavy oak table on its edge, then jamming it tight against the sofa. He wasn't worried about surprise. There was only one way into the apartment (or out of it, for that matter) and it was protected by a steel-covered fire door. What the cops would do is try to flush him out with tear gas. And they'd do it from the roof of the next building, because they couldn't reach him from the ground. And they'd have to stand up to make the toss. They'd have to become *targets*.

"I wonder how many cops I could take out?" Jake mused as he drew the shades. "Five? Ten?"

Why not? Wasn't he the mug who knocked off Steppy Accacio and Joe Faci?

Nobody would've believed that, either. Nobody would've believed a lotta things about Jake Leibowitz. Until they crossed him.

"If I was a wop," he said, "they woulda known about me a long time ago."

Moodrow stayed with Greta Bloom until they reached the front door of Sarah Leibowitz's apartment building. What he wanted to do was break into a dead run. To flag down the first cab he saw, rip the driver out and mash the pedal through the floorboards. The worst part was that he knew he could get away with it. Greta hadn't said a word, hadn't even turned to look at him.

"Tell me something, Greta," he finally said, holding himself in place with the sheer force of his will. "How do you think the horses felt?"

"What horses? What are you talking about?"

"The horses, Greta. The ones you say my mother jammed in the ass with a hatpin. How do you think the horses felt?"

She stared at him for a moment, her eyes narrowing, then dropped her gaze. "It was necessary," she admitted. "But I felt sorry for the horses. The cops were animals because they wanted to be animals. But the horses . . ."

"Now, I'm gonna tell you something so you'll understand. Right now, while we're out here talking, Sarah Leibowitz is calling her son."

"So maybe you should have acted like a *mensch* instead of a Nazi."

"I wasn't gonna sweet-talk her out of Jake's address and you know it. She was wearing a goddamned fur coat. In the house. What do ya wanna bet it came from her son? And that she knew where he got the money to buy it? Look, Greta, I have to go. Just think about the horses, all right?"

Moodrow stepped out into the street and waved down a passing cruiser. He had no room, now, for Greta. Or for anybody else except Jake Leibowitz.

"Hey, Stanley, whatta ya say?"

The cop driving the car was named Fred Stone. A boxing enthusiast, he and Moodrow had sparred in the department gym on several occasions.

"What's doin', Freddy. You still droppin' the left?" Moodrow crouched slightly, making eye contact with the cop riding shotgun. "Butch, how's it goin'?" Butch Buccarelli was neither friend nor foe. A ten-year veteran, he'd already passed the sergeant's exam and was just killing time while he waited for his appointment.

"Tell me somethin', Moodrow," Buccarelli said evenly, "you a bad guy or a good guy these days? I can't keep track. You change costumes faster than Superman."

Moodrow smiled agreeably. "I haven't checked in with the captain this morning, but I think I'm a good guy. Look, I got a line on Jake Leibowitz. You boys interested? I could use some backup."

Buccarelli's eyes widened. "This a serious tip? Or a bullshit guess?"

Moodrow answered by getting into the back of the cruiser. "It's decent," he answered, closing the door. "Head for the Vladeck Houses. Building A."

The problem was that he had no right to order these men around. If a detective needed help, he was expected to go through the sergeant. The line blurred in emergency situations, but the exact degree of cooperation varied with the mood of the patrolman. Moodrow was counting on a cop's natural desire to be there for a big arrest. Jake Leibowitz was a star and the cops who took him down would bathe in his light.

"You want me to call it in?" Buccarelli asked. "Because what I'm thinking is the captain'll wanna be present. I'm thinkin' he's gonna be *mucho* pissed if he doesn't get an invite to this particular party."

"Relax, Butch. What I got is a *tip*. It's not like I spoke to Jake on the phone and traced back the number. What you oughta think about is what the captain's gonna say if the whole precinct turns out for a false alarm." Moodrow leaned back in the seat. "Of course, if you just wanna drop me off and go back on patrol, I promise I won't hold a grudge."

They drove the rest of the way in silence. Heavy rain continued to fall, pooling up on the East River Drive, forcing traffic to standstill. Fred Stone flipped on the roof light and worked his way onto the shoulder of the road. They weren't going far, but the ride seemed endless to Moodrow. By the time they pulled up in front of the Vladeck Houses, he was half-convinced that Jake Leibowitz had packed his bags and gone.

"Who's supervising in the field today?" he asked.

"Epstein."

"All right, Butch. Get on the horn. Leibowitz is up in 678. I want the building surrounded. And tell Epstein to bring the tear gas. All the apartments have steel-covered fire doors and if I can't talk him out, we're gonna have a hell of a time getting inside."

"Wait a second, Moodrow. Ten minutes ago, you told me to stay off the radio. Now you want the National Guard down here. What you're doin' is makin' me look like an asshole."

Moodrow put his hand on Butch Buccarelli's shoulder and squeezed hard. "Tell ya what, Butch," he said. "You wanna sit on your hands, it's okay by me. But if Leibowitz goes out the side door while you're jerkin' off in the cruiser, you could forget about those sergeant's stripes. Something else, too. A forty-five, like the one Leibowitz packs, can punch holes right through the side of this car. What're you carrying? A six-shot thirty-eight? Do yourself a favor, Butch. Call it in to the sergeant. Let Epstein make the decisions." He released Buccarelli's shoulder and turned to Fred Stone. "You wanna come up with me, Freddy? You wanna play cops and robbers?"

"Just call me Dick Tracy."

Fred Stone was twenty-three years old and looked seventeen. He had a heartbreaker smile and bedroom eyes to match. Both, Moodrow knew, masked a reckless attitude.

"Freddy," Moodrow put his arm around the young patrolman's shoulder as they walked away from the cruiser, "I'm gonna put you at the head of the stairs. Your first job is to keep citizens off the sixth floor. Your second job is to keep Jake Leibowitz *on* the sixth floor. I don't care what happens to me. I don't care if I'm shot or if I disappear or if I scream for help. You don't leave your post until the sergeant relieves you. *Capish?*"

"Yeah, sure. But what about you, Stanley? You gonna play Superman? You gonna crash through the door?"

"We're talking about a steel-covered fire door, remember? It'd take me five minutes to get through it with a sledgehammer. No, Freddy, what I'm gonna try to do is talk him out. I'm gonna give him a chance."

But what, Moodrow thought as they began to climb the stairs, am I gonna do if nobody answers my knock on the door? How will I know whether or not he's in there? Do I kick the door down and walk into an ambush? Or do I wait for Epstein and let someone else do it?

Jake Leibowitz looked at the two mattresses covering the living-room windows and shook his head. What he needed was a hammer and nails, but a quick search of the apartment had failed to turn up so much as a screwdriver. The way he had them propped up on tables, the mattresses would most likely turn back a canister of tear gas. But if the cops opened up with shotguns . . .

"The old bitch lived poor," Jake said to himself. "She didn't have nothin'."

And that was putting it mildly. If he had a china cabinet or a couple of bookcases or a triple dresser, he could wedge those mattresses in good. But, no, his Aunt Golda never had two nickels to rub together. That's why she was in Bellevue Hospital instead of Mount Sinai. That's why she was lying in her own shit instead of on starched white sheets.

"Well, whatta ya gonna do?" Jake asked. "Whatta ya gonna do?"

He strolled down the short hallway to the bathroom and stepped inside. The single opaque window was shoulder height, exactly the way he wanted it. Jake raised the window a few inches, then drew Little Richard from his belt and aimed him at the neighboring rooftop forty feet away. The foot-high ledge wouldn't offer much protection unless you were lying right against it. Which was also the way he wanted it.

Jake took a moment to imagine the rooftop covered with fat New York City cops. He imagined shooting them down. Bing! Bing! Bing! Like ducks in a shooting gallery. By the time the flatfoots zeroed in on *his* location, there'd be enough bodies to make it worthwhile. And that's what it was all about. Because once Jake Leibowitz set Little Richard to singing his song, there was no turning back. Cop killers weren't taken alive. That's one of the reasons they became neighborhood legends.

Jake grabbed a couple of towels off the rack and tossed them over his shoulder. Later on, if they fired tear gas into the bedrooms, he'd stuff the towels under the doors. On a whim, he wedged Aunt Golda's spectacles onto the bridge of his nose and peered at his mustache in the mirror.

"Not bad," he decided. "Not perfect, but not bad."

He strolled into the bedroom and yanked his aunt's box spring off its metal frame, revealing five wooden cross-slats. He grabbed two of them and headed back to the living room where he knelt and jammed them under the doorknob.

"Maybe they'll blow out the lock," he said, "and try to bust through the door. How many could I get before they figure it out? Two? Three?"

He aimed Little Richard at the door, imagining the cops' fear, imagining his .45 blasting away. Imagining the screams.

There hadn't been any screams when he'd done poor Abe Weinberg. When he'd done his fucking *buddy*. Maybe that's was the *real* reason he hadn't gone out to Los Angeles like Steppy told him. The wops had asked him to sacrifice Abe and he'd done it. It was like a promise they'd made to him, a promise they didn't bother to keep.

"Joe Faci told me that Abe would be the end of it."

They could've skipped town right after they'd done the spic. All of them—Jake, Izzy and Abe. But Joe Faci said, "Take care of Abe. He's got a screw loose somewhere. Y'understand? Take care of Abe and we'll take care of you."

Jake walked across the living room and opened an end table drawer. He took out his second gun and slipped it beneath his belt. Six spare clips, all full, lay in plain view on a small pile of old magazines. Sighing, he scooped them up and slipped three into each pocket of his jacket. Despite the fact that he *knew* they'd make his pockets bulge. That he'd look like a Jew pedlar from the old days instead of a successful gangster.

"Whatta ya gonna do?" he said, shaking his head sadly. "Whatta ya gonna fuckin' do?"

As he and Fred Stone climbed toward the sixth floor, Stanley Moodrow found himself looking for Jake Leibowitz at every turning of the stairs. He recalled his earliest fights and the way his heart had punched at his ribs as he waited for the opening bell. What had he been afraid of back then? A broken nose? A swollen lip? It seemed like a joke, now. A joke in comparison with facing a Colt .45. Talk about a punch in the ribs. A .45 would turn your ribs into dominoes.

Moodrow pulled his .38 and slid it into the pocket of his overcoat. His already thin mouth tightened into a bloodless white line. For a moment, as they approached the door to the sixth-floor corridor, Moodrow felt something near to panic. His legs seemed to belong to someone else. They barely lifted him from one step to the next.

"Hold it a second, Fred." Moodrow became aware of his hoarse whisper only after he'd spoken. "What we're gonna do is prop the door open so you can stay here and still cover the apartment. Now, look, there's only one way out of there. If he decides to use it, *don't* shoot me."

"C'mon, Stanley," Stone said, smiling his sunniest, little-brother smile. "It's just a tip. Besides, he can't shoot through the wall, can he?"

"Not through these walls," Moodrow admitted. The Vladeck Houses, completed in 1940, had one thing in common with the most modern skyscrapers. They had steel fire-shields in the walls between apartments and the walls running along the common corridor. There were no fire escapes on the outside of the buildings, because the whole idea was to seal yourself in your apartment in case of fire. Unless, of course, the fire was *in* your apartment. Then, you ran like hell.

The net effect was to turn every apartment into a little fortress. If Jake refused to surrender, there was no easy way to get to him. In the tenements, a few blows with a sixteen-pound sledgehammer would bust through any wall. Here, you'd need a welder's torch.

"I think you oughta take this seriously," Moodrow said, surprised to find his voice much stronger. The simple fact was that he only had a few minutes before Epstein showed up and became the ranking officer on the scene. The captain would follow Epstein, along with several lieutenants. If the siege took any kind of time, the inspectors and the deputy chiefs would arrive with the reporters. By then, Stanley Moodrow would be little more than an innocent bystander.

"I *am* taking it seriously," Stone insisted. "But that doesn't mean it can't be fun." He twirled his .38 on his index finger, still grinning madly.

Moodrow turned away in disgust. The trick, he knew, was to turn the fear into power, to aim the wasted energy at your opponent. He'd promised Greta that he'd try to talk Jake Leibowitz into surrendering. That didn't mean he was obliged to go crashing through the door. It didn't, as far as he was concerned, mean that he was obliged to take any risk at all. He was going to give Jake a chance at life, but if Jake refused, Mama Leibowitz would get her trip to the morgue after all.

He walked past the door to apartment 678 and stationed himself alongside it. Fred Stone, across the hall and twenty feet away, held his thumb up and winked.

"Go get him, Stanley. And don't forget to jab."

Moodrow shook his head. "After we take Mr. Leibowitz, I think I'm gonna celebrate by slapping your ass from here to Central Park."

Moodrow pounded the door with the side of his fist, then quickly yanked his hand away. A second later, Jake Leibowitz emptied half a clip through the door. Moodrow watched five small mushrooms appear, one at a time, on the door's steel sheath. He saw the mushrooms burst, saw tiny sharp points blossom on the ruptured metal, saw five clouds of plaster explode from the opposite wall.

He saw all of it before he heard the sound of the shots. Or rather, the sound of the *shot*. Because what he heard was a single sharp crack, like the sound of Mickey Mantle's bat hitting a Don Newcombe fastball. The echo was surprisingly short, but the emptiness that followed seemed to last forever.

Moodrow looked over at Freddy Stone. The young cop wasn't smiling anymore. His mouth was agape, his eyes so wide his lashes merged with his eyebrows. The sight was comical, but Moodrow didn't bother to smile.

"Hey, Jake," he shouted through the door. "Does this mean you're not gonna surrender?"

"Why don't ya come in and find out for yourself? I was just settin' up for tea and crumpets."

Moodrow reached out, carefully twisted the doorknob, then gave a gentle push. The door was locked.

"I can't join you unless you open the door, Jake," he said calmly. "Your mother was much more hospitable."

"How'd ya talk her into rattin' on me? She told me ya gave her the third degree."

"You believe that?" Moodrow paused for a moment, then continued. "What I did was show her a picture of Luis Melenguez's body. I told her that's what you're gonna look like if you don't give yourself up."

A second volley of shots roared through the door. Moodrow felt a sharp pain on the left side of his cheek. His first thought was that he'd somehow been shot, but that was clearly impossible. He looked at the pock-marked wall across the corridor as if it might hold the answer, then reached up and touched a thin steel splinter protruding from his face.

"Damn," he whispered, pulling it out. Now that he knew it wasn't serious, it hurt all the more.

"Stanley, you're bleedin'."

Moodrow looked over at Freddy Stone. "Keep your mind on business, Freddy."

"You talkin' to me?" Jake Leibowitz asked. "Cause I can't hear ya."

"Say, Jake," Moodrow called. "Do you want me to go through the deal about how you're surrounded? About how there's a hundred cops out here? About how they've got submachine guns and shotguns and tear gas?"

"Don't bother. I could'a run when my old lady called, but I didn't. What I want is that you should try to take me. I don't care how many cops ya got out there, ya could only come through that door one at a time. Ya listenin', flatfoot? I don't care if ya got a fuckin' army out there. Ya gotta come through one at a time."

Moodrow saw the door behind Freddy Stone open wide. A dozen uniformed cops poured through. Half of them took up stations near the stairs. The other half ran past him to the far end of the hall. Moodrow closed his eyes as they came abreast of Jake Leibowitz's door.

"Stanley. Come over here."

Moodrow looked up to find Allen Epstein beckoning to him. "Whatta ya want, Sarge?" He wasn't about to cross that doorway.

"C'mere, for Christ's sake."

Jake Leibowitz chose that moment to send another volley through the door. Moodrow watched Epstein's eyes squeeze shut. The uniforms in the hallway dropped to one knee and aimed their service revolvers in his direction. As if, in the absence of a preferred target, they'd decided to shoot *him*. It wasn't until Captain McElroy appeared in the doorway that he was sure they wouldn't open fire.

"Any bodies out there?" Jake called.

"Not yet," Moodrow answered. "But I'm glad to see you're interested."

McElroy tiptoed up to the doorway. "Can you keep him talking?" he whispered. "Keep him distracted? We need about fifteen minutes to evacuate the floor and set up on the rooftops."

"I'm not gonna stay here another fifteen *seconds* unless you get these assholes to point their weapons at the floor."

McElroy looked down the hallway as if seeing it for the first time. "Whatta you plan to do," he roared, "shoot *me*? Lower your weapons."

The cops complied instantly, their fear of authority considerably greater than their fear of Jake Leibowitz. Jake, on the other hand, responded by firing several shots through the door. McElroy didn't even blink. He'd come up in the days when social workers and bleeding-heart liberals had about as much influence in city politics as the toilet bowls in Tammany Hall. When Hell's Kitchen was still called the Tenth Ward and breaking heads was the answer to every problem.

"Fifteen minutes," McElroy repeated. "I'm not gonna let this drag out. I want Leibowitz before the reporters show up."

"Look, captain, I think if we let him sit for a while, he'll come out of there. I guarantee he can cover the roofs from inside. If you put an army of cops up there . . ."

"Shut up, Moodrow." McElroy jammed his fists into his hips. "I've had enough of your bullshit to last a lifetime. I'm ordering you to submit. Do you understand what I'm saying? You are *not* the fucking commissioner. You do *not* set policy in my precinct. You're a piece-of-crap detective, third grade. A monkey in a suit. When I play my accordion, the monkey always dances. *Always.*"

"I understand." There wasn't anything else Moodrow could say. Jake Leibowitz had fifteen minutes and that was that. "Do you bring any tools with you?"

"What?" McElroy's posture hadn't changed. He was still livid.

"I could use a four-pound hammer. To hold his attention while you get ready to kill him."

Jake Leibowitz, peering through his bathroom window, couldn't help but smile. The six-story buildings making up the Vladeck Houses were joined to each other in rows. Only, instead of laying the buildings end-to-end, the architect had connected the buildings at forty-five degree angles, giving the project a weird, saw-toothed appearance. It was stupid, really, because the arrangement left half the windows in permanent shadow. Maybe the builder was trying to save money. Just the way he'd saved money by letting one stairwell serve an entire line of roofs.

Whatever the reason, that last part was good for Jake Leibowitz and he knew it. The small brick tower that housed the stairwell would have provided excellent cover if it hadn't been more than eighty feet away from the roof that overlooked his apartment. Not that it would actually be *impossible* to shoot from behind the stairwell, but the angle was wrong. Even a sharpshooter with a telescopic sight wouldn't be able to cover more than a tiny part of Jake's window.

"They gotta come to me," Jake laughed. "They *gotta*."

And they did. Picking their way along the tar-covered roofs as if they were tiptoeing over hot coals. God, but it was stupid. Big, blue-uniformed men carrying Thompsons and shotguns and rifles. Dancing like ballerinas. Wishing they were *anywhere* but where they were.

Jake raised Little Richard and aimed carefully. The army-issue Colt .45 was a notoriously inaccurate weapon, especially when fired rapidly. It weighed a ton and kicked like a mule. What he was going to get, he knew, was one decent shot. The rest of the clip, which he fully intended to empty, was more likely to kill pigeons than cops.

Boom! Boom!

It took Jake a moment to realize that something was wrong. That there'd been *two* reports when he'd only pressed the trigger once. He looked at the gun, then out across the roofs. Thinking maybe one of the cops was shooting back. What he saw drove that second explosion right out of his mind. Two uniformed cops were dragging the limp body of a third cop. They were heading for the stairwell as fast as they could go, which is not to say they were moving as fast as their unburdened buddies. The rest of the cops were *running*.

Boom! Boom! Boom!

"What the fuck is goin' on here?"

Then he knew what it was. They were coming through the front door.

Jake flew out of the bathroom. He began firing through the door as soon as he could see it and continued firing until the clip was empty. Then he leaped behind his makeshift barricade, expecting some kind of volley in return. But there was nothing. Just the echo of dying gunfire and the calm voice of the cop in the hallway.

"You back, Jake? I was gettin' lonely out here with no one to talk to. That's why I decided to knock on the door. You know, to get your attention."

Jake peered over the back of the couch. The door was still in one piece. The lock had broken out—that's most likely where the cops had aimed—but the bolt a foot above the knob was still intact and the bed slats hadn't budged an inch.

"Jesus, that was close," Jake muttered.

He replaced the empty clip, then walked over to the window and pushed one of the mattresses a few inches to the side. The roof directly across from the window was empty. A few cops were crouched behind the stairwell tower eighty feet away. He punched out the glass and aimed Little Richard in their general direction. They weren't giving him much target, but if he waited long enough . . .

Boom! Boom!

"For Christ's sake, stop doin' that." Jake fired through the door again. Just a single shot, this time. He didn't want to run out of ammo before the cops made their charge.

"What do you think, Jake? You think I'm standing in front of this door? You're doin' a nice job on the wall out here, but you're not doin' shit to *me*."

"Yeah? Well, sooner or later, somebody's gotta come *through* that door. If your balls are as big as your mouth, maybe you'll be leadin' the parade."

"If that's the way you feel about it, why don't you just unlock the damn thing and get it over with? This hammer's gettin' heavy."

Jake took a quick look out the window. There were more cops out there, now, but they weren't moving toward his building. They were hanging their heads while some big-shot officer chewed them out. He laid Little Richard on the windowsill and carefully sighted down the barrel.

Boom! Boom! Boom! Boom!

Somewhere along the line, Jake knew, he must have pulled the trigger. Because he could see smoke curling from the business end of the .45. Only, the cops on the roof were still talking. Even as he watched, one of them leveled his rifle and fired a shot. The bullet thumped into the mattress above Jake's head.

Jake turned back to the door. The deadbolt was definitely bent, now. Once it let go, the bed slats would have to take the heat. They wouldn't last long.

"You still in there?"

"Yeah," Jake shouted. "Me and my aunt. She's sittin' right in front of the door."

"That's funny, your mama told me your aunt was in the hospital. She told me the apartment was empty."

"Mama's got a big mouth. What else did she tell ya?" Jake wasn't exactly in the mood for conversation, but on the other hand, he didn't want the cop pounding on the door, either. Yeah, he was gonna die—that much was obvious—but there was no sense in rushing it.

"She told me your father was a gangster."

"Bullshit, Mama never talks about him. *Never*."

"Whatta ya think, I'm making this up? Your father was a gangster. They found him floating in the river. Which is exactly what the mob'll do to you, if they ever get their hands on you. Of course, that's not likely to happen, considering the only way you're gonna get out of here alive is to surrender and you're much too tough to do anything like *that*."

"It's too late. I nailed one of the cops on the roof. From what I could see, the scumbag wasn't movin'."

"Look, Jake, the thing is I told your mother if you gave yourself up, I'd protect you. She wants to see you alive. That's why she told me where you were."

"How many cops ya got out there? Fifty? A hundred? I never got much education, but I ain't so stupid I think a hundred cops are here to keep me alive."

Boom!

"Hey, whatta ya doin'? I'm talkin', ain't I?"

"What'd I tell you, Jake? Didn't I say I promised your mother? Now you're making me out a liar and I don't like it. I gave my word and I don't welsh. Why don't you open the door? Why don't you toss the gun and come on out?"

Jake shook his head slowly. He looked down at Little Richard. Thinking about how he should just put the gun in his mouth and get it over with.

"What's ya name, cop?"

"Moodrow. Detective Stanley Moodrow."

"Stanley? What kinda pansy name is *Stanley*?"

"You know how it is, Jake. You don't get to pick your name. Just like you don't get to pick your parents. Some things in life you gotta learn to overcome."

"Like the electric chair? How do ya *overcome* the hot seat?"

"With a lawyer, Jake, like everybody else. We made almost four hundred arrests for murder last year. Four hundred arrests, but how many executions? Two? Three? I can hear the social worker testifying. Giving the judge an earful about how your father corrupted you and your mother's crazy and you never caught a break in your life."

Suddenly, Jake got an idea. An idea that might keep him alive for a few more hours.

"A few hours ain't a long time," he muttered. "Unless ya lookin' at a few minutes."

"I can't hear you, Jake? If you're talking to me, I can't hear a word you're sayin'."

"Ya want me to surrender, Stanley?"

"I wouldn't complain."

"Then get me a lawyer. *Before* I come out. Get me a lawyer named Irving Blumstein. He's got an office on Broadway, near the courthouse. Ya put him out in that hall, where he can see what's happening, and I'll give myself up."

Silence. Dead silence. Which was about what Jake expected. Well, let them take their time. Let 'em take all the time in the world. *He* wasn't going anywhere.

When the cops on the rooftop opened fire, it sounded, as Moodrow had predicted, like WWIII had broken out. They opened up with submachine guns, shotguns and rifles. Thirty of them, firing as rapidly as possible. They concentrated their fire on the covered living-room windows, blowing the mattresses out with the first volley. Filling the room with deadly, dancing lead.

Stanley Moodrow stood, unflinching, through the two-minute volley, his eyes fixed to those of Captain John McElroy. McElroy, for his part, returned Moodrow's stare. The two of them might have been alone in the hallway. Despite the presence of twenty crouching patrolmen, all of whom had their eyes tightly closed.

The silence, when it came, was worse than the shooting. *Dead* silence was the phrase that popped into Moodrow's mind.

"Detective," McElroy finally said. "Take the door down."

Moodrow lowered the four-pound hammer to the floor. He dropped it gently, avoiding any sound, then picked up a sixteen-pound, long-handled sledge and drove it into the door. The crash was obscenely loud, a clear violation of the collective silence. As if a flasher had wandered into a crowd of mourners gathered around an open grave.

It wasn't until the door gave way, suddenly flying open to smash against the inner wall, that Moodrow considered the possibility that Jake Leibowitz was alive and waiting. He dropped the sledgehammer, drew his weapon, then glanced up at McElroy.

"You got anything special in mind?" he asked.

McElroy didn't bother to respond. He stepped into the doorway, leaving Moodrow no choice except to follow.

They found Jake Leibowitz's body in a pool of blood and glass. He was lying face-down, the dozen wounds on his back clearly entrance wounds. The shotguns had done their job on the barricaded windows, but it was the rifles and the Thompsons that'd killed Jake Leibowitz. The single shotgun wound on his body hadn't been fatal, although it must have been extremely painful. The pellets had ripped into the back of his head, tearing through his scalp and flipping it over his face.

Captain John McElroy stared down at Jake Leibowitz's bloody skull for a moment, a thin smile pulling at his lips, then turned to face the young detective standing next to him.

"Looks like they started the autopsy without us," he said.

Thirty-five

JANUARY 29

"I CHICKENED out, Greta," Moodrow explained. "I chickened out twice. There's no other way to look at it. When I left you and got in that car, I was determined to arrest Jake Leibowitz by myself. I wanted to drag him into the Seventh and toss him to the captain. Jake was gonna be my trophy. Proof that I was right all along. Only, I kept thinking about what might happen if he got past me. I mean he killed four men that we know about. I couldn't take a chance, so I called in the troops. If I'd been there alone, I think I might've talked him out."

He watched Greta reach into the oven and remove two sliced bagels. She dropped them onto a plate, then licked her fingers.

"Hot," she said without turning around.

"You should use a fork."

"One more thing to wash." She unwrapped a bar of Philadelphia Cream Cheese and began to spread it over the bagels.

Moodrow watched her for another moment. He'd been postponing this talk for the last five days. Knowing it had to take place, despite his preoccupation with Kate and the swirl of events following her father's suicide.

He'd come home that night to find a note: *Gone to Bayside. Back this evening. Much love.* The only problem was that "this evening" had already come and gone. Between a dead Jake Leibowitz, a dead cop named Strauss, more than five hundred rounds of police fire and fifty reports to be filed by fifty patrolmen, Moodrow, the only detective on the scene, hadn't left the 7th Precinct until well after midnight.

What he'd assumed was that Kate had decided to spend the night in Bayside. The only question was whether she'd somehow fallen back under her father's spell. But that hadn't seemed possible. Not even to a thoroughly shell-shocked Stanley Moodrow. No, most likely Kate had called a half-dozen times and gotten no answer. Maybe she'd even called Greta. There'd been no way of knowing, because it was nearly one o'clock and he couldn't make it into an emergency no matter how many scenarios he concocted.

He'd awakened the next morning to find Pat Cohan on the radio, on television, on the front page of every newspaper in New York City. The murder-suicide had transformed Jake Leibowitz and the rooftop shootout from a banner headline to an item on page fifteen.

The first phone call had come at ten o'clock in the morning: "John Hughes, from the *Journal-American*. You were Kate Cohan's fiancé. Could you . . . ?"

Could you? Would you? Do you? It'd gone on for days. Despite his muttered, "No comment." Despite hanging up again and again and again. It was *still* going on, though the volume of calls had slowed now that the funeral was over.

The sad part was that he'd answered every call, each time hoping to hear Kate's voice. His own calls out to Bayside had been fielded by any number of unidentified friends and relatives. Most had been firm, but polite. A few had called him a bastard. One, a woman, had fairly hissed at him.

"Haven't you done enoughhhhhhhhhh?"

Desperate, he'd driven out to St. John's Cemetery in Flushing and watched the funeral procession pass through the cemetery gates. He'd seen Kate in the back of the limousine following the casket, a small veiled figure encircled by men in black overcoats. Were they relatives or cops? And where were the women? The helpful aunts? The trusted friends?

The questions were making him crazy. He'd sought Greta's advice, then Allen Epstein's. Both had delivered the same message: give her time to sort it out. Time was the *only* cure.

He should, he knew later, have taken their advice, because when he'd finally driven out to Bayside, the trip had made him even crazier. Kate's Uncle Bill, her mother's brother, had answered the door. An elderly man, he'd looked embarrassed at first. Then he'd invited Moodrow inside.

"She's not here, lad," he'd said. "You can look if you want."

Moodrow, a cop to his bones, had taken the old man up on the offer, wandering from room to room. He'd found a lot of empty space and a single locked door. It led, he knew, to Rose Cohan's bedroom.

"It hasn't been cleaned," Bill Brannigan had said apologetically. "It'll have to be cleaned soon, I suppose. If we're to put the house on the market."

Moodrow had responded by kicking the door off the hinges. Only to find that Bill Brannigan hadn't been lying. The room was covered with dried blood. The furniture, the floors, the walls, the ceiling. Brannigan, staring helplessly at the carnage, had begun to cry.

"Take as long as you have to, Bill. I'm not leaving until you tell me where she is."

"She's on retreat." Brannigan had peered at him through bewildered eyes. "Holy Mother Church has taken Kate to her sacred bosom."

"Stanley, you want lox on your bagel?"

Moodrow looked up quickly. Telling himself to stop drifting off. Willing himself to remain in the present. Reminding himself that his career was on the line, that he had to be in Deputy Chief Milton Morton's office in less than two hours and that he'd better be ready.

"Yeah, fine." He sipped at his coffee and ran his fingers over his newly shaven face. "What was I saying?"

"About chickening out. Which only a *meshugganer* could believe you'd do."

"Yeah, right." Moodrow watched Greta set the plate down in front of him. "I guess 'chickening out' is a kid's way of putting it, but I had choices and I made them. I didn't have to call in the troops, but I did. And I didn't have to obey the captain, either. When he so much as *told* me that he wasn't gonna give Jake a chance, I didn't have to help him create a diversion. I could have taken the gold shield and rammed it up his ass. Why not, Greta? If my mother could use a hatpin, why couldn't I use a badge?"

"*Nu*, because a captain is not a horse."

Moodrow bit off a chunk of bagel and began to chew thoughtfully. "I loved the hunt," he said after a moment. "You know, the investigation. Tracking Jake down. Boxing him into a corner. That's the way I fought in the ring. The way I *had* to fight. I was too slow to catch anybody on the run."

"Stanley, please. Life is difficult enough. Only a *shlemiel* goes through life making things more difficult. A man is killed; a killer is dead. *Nu*?"

"Yeah? Well, it wasn't '*nu*' for Al and Betty O'Neill. Maybe they were a couple of pimps, but they didn't deserve the death penalty."

"This was your fault?"

"And then there's Rose Cohan. And Kate."

It was Greta's turn to fidget. She brushed a small pile of crumbs into the palm of her hand and dumped them on the edge of her plate. "She'll come around, Stanley. It's only been five days."

"You do one thing and ten things happen. There's no way to control it." He shook his head. "It's like throwing a punch at your opponent and hitting a spectator."

"Stanley, could I tell you a story?"

Moodrow smiled for the first time in days. "Please," he answered.

"This happened in nineteen thirty-three. A strike at Goldman Furs. At the time, I was pregnant with my second and I wasn't even working. But Yussel Mittman, from the union, came to me and begged me to help out. 'It's a *mitzvah*, a *mitzvah*. Please, we need a woman and there's nobody else.'"

Greta drew a deep breath, then let it out in a long sigh. She looked up at Moodrow and shrugged. "So, what could I do? I went and I made speeches and I walked with the pickets. The morale was good, the workers inspired, but the strike went on and on. Goldman wouldn't budge. He was a rich man, Stanley, a millionaire, but also a skinflint. Instead of bargaining, he offered to *lower* the wages. Five months we stood out there, all through the winter. 'He can't hold out forever.' That's what we told ourselves and we were right. Spring came around and Goldman's two sons took over the business. I remember the celebration when they settled with the union. This was in the middle of the Depression and there were no jobs to be had, so you can imagine how the workers felt. But for me, it wasn't such fun. I was at the party when the pains started. The doctors called it a 'spontaneous abortion,' which was probably the truth, but I blamed myself. I still do. You know how it is, *nu*? The head says one thing and the heart says another. Eventually, you live with the past and keep on going."

An hour and a half later, Moodrow found himself in the waiting room of Deputy Chief Milton Morton's Centre Street office. Morton's secretary, a very grizzled, very male sergeant named Goldfarb, hadn't even bothered with the customary, "Chief Morton will be right with you." He'd checked Moodrow's i.d. carefully, then nodded him into a seat.

Moodrow picked at his nails for a moment, then grabbed the *Daily News* off a low table and glanced at the headline: CAMPY FIGHTS PARALYSIS.

"Jesus Christ."

"What's that?" Sergeant Goldfarb peered over his reading glasses to nail Moodrow with his hardest stare.

"Nothing."

Moodrow edged closer to the light and examined the newspaper closely. There were two photos on the front page. The one on the right showed Roy Campanella's wife holding a telephone to her ear. The one on the left showed a man lying face-down on a stretcher. Oddly, the man was still wearing his hat.

Moodrow turned the pages quickly, scanning the headline as he searched for the main story. *Principal Dies In Leap, Faced HS Crime Quiz; 6 Wined-Up Teeners Knife Two Girls on Stairs of Subway; 200 Police Hunt Nebraska Teen Lovers Who Killed 7; Sketch Put Out in Hunt For Knifer of UN Sec'y; 2 Ganglings Seized In Murder of Youth; Crime Rises 25% In State; Police Budget Up $13,519,136.*

He got all the way to the classifieds before he realized that he'd passed over the Campanella story. Thumbing quickly, he worked his way back through the pages until he found the story on page three. Roy Campanella, the veteran Dodger catcher, had been on his way home (the old J. P. Morgan estate on East Island) at three in the morning. He was within a mile of his house when his car had skidded off the road and slammed into a light pole. Now, his neck was broken. Not only would he never play baseball again, the doctors felt he'd spend the rest of his life in a wheelchair.

Moodrow let the paper drop to his knees. Roy Campanella, the second Negro player in the major leagues, had come to the Brooklyn Dodgers in 1948, a year after Jackie Robinson. Short and squat, always smiling, life seemed to roll off his broad shoulders. Jackie may have paved the way, but Campy was the steamroller who'd held everything in place. In the ten years since he'd come to Ebbets Field, Campanella had been named National League MVP three times.

"*Damn*," Moodrow said aloud, "God*damn*."

"What's the matter, you got a twitch or somethin'?"

Moodrow looked up at a scowling Sergeant Goldfarb. "You hear about Campy?" he asked.

"Yeah, I heard he missed a curve on Long Island and now he's a loaf of bread." Goldfarb leaned forward, grinning wildly. "That's *one* nigger who ain't gonna play in Los *fucking* Angeles."

The intercom on Goldfarb's desk buzzed once, a sharp jolt that brought the sergeant up short. He waved toward the door behind him. "Batter up, kid."

Moodrow crossed the room quickly, took a deep breath and opened the door. Deputy Chief Milton Morton was seated behind an enormous wooden desk. The dark wood gleamed with polish. A gold fountain pen lay on a square of black marble. It, too, gleamed, drawing Moodrow's attention. As, he understood, it was meant to do.

"Sit down, detective," Morton said.

Moodrow obeyed. Just as he'd obeyed Captain John McElroy in that hallway. What he'd come to understand over the past month was that he wanted two incompatible things. He wanted to be independent and he wanted to be a cop. That couldn't happen. Somewhere along the line, he was going to have to pay for his independence. Milton Morton's job, as Moodrow understood it, was to name the price.

"You did well, detective," Morton said.

Thin and sallow, Deputy Chief Morton looked like anything but a cop. The story, among the rank-and-file, was that his lofty position was a gift to the Jews of New York. Pure politics, from beginning to end. Moodrow had gotten another story from Allen Epstein. According to Epstein, Morton had been a decent patrolman, as willing as any to wade into a bar brawl or mediate a violent family dispute. Not that he stayed a patrolman very long. Within twelve years, he'd passed the sergeant's, lieutenant's and captain's exams. At age thirty-six, he'd been appointed deputy inspector. Then full Inspector. At each stage, he'd demonstrated an ability to command.

"The point is," Epstein had explained, "that whenever Morton was in charge, things went smoothly. He controlled his cops. Kept his statistics up. Never went on the take. Never made a complaint against anyone who did. The guys walking a beat think you have to break heads to be a good cop. That's why they stay patrolman. Morton was smart enough to know that the New York Police Department is one giant headache waiting for an aspirin. He dedicated himself to being that aspirin."

Moodrow looked over at Chief Morton, noting the folded arms and the patient expression. "Did well at *what*?" he asked. "I thought I was here to walk the plank."

Morton smiled. "I'm talking about Pat Cohan. The reporters have been in touch with you, right?"

"Yeah."

"And you must have been tempted, at some point or other, to put the whole thing on the table. Patero, Accacio, Jake Leibowitz—the whole thing. Yes?"

"Yes."

"But you didn't. You held it back. You protected the Department instead of protecting yourself. You did well."

"Thanks." There wasn't anything else for Moodrow to say. He settled his bulk in the chair and let his hands drop into his lap.

"You have a package, I believe," Morton said.

"A package?"

"Patero's statement, the Leibowitz case file, the other evidence against Pat Cohan. A package." Morton paused, his eyes fixed on Moodrow, obviously waiting for a response.

"Yeah," Moodrow finally said. "I've got your 'package.' "

"Well, I want it. I want you to give it to me." Morton fished a cigarette out of his shirt pocket and tapped it on the desk a few times before lighting it. "Coffin nails," he said, blowing out a thin stream of smoke. "Now, I've told you what I want. Which also happens to be what the Department wants. The only question is what do *you* want?"

"You don't waste much time."

Morton managed a quick smile. "I don't have much time to waste." He gestured at the neat stack of paperwork on his desk.

"What if I don't give you the 'package'? What if I decide to hold onto it?"

"I believe we're here to negotiate, detective," Morton answered without blinking an eye. "But let me take it a step further. Pat Cohan is dead. The murder of Rose Cohan has been solved. Salvatore Patero has decided to seek employment elsewhere. As has Lieutenant Rosten. A year down the line, your evidence will be about as useful to you as five pounds of cat shit. If you're going to survive, you're going to need friends. You're going to need a rabbi to protect you. I want the evidence you've accumulated. I want it dead and buried, just like the man it implicates. The only question, as I said before, is what *you* want."

"I want to stay where I am. I want to stay in the Seventh Precinct and be left alone to do my job." Now that it was out in the open, the request seemed modest enough.

"Is that it?" Even Morton seemed surprised. "No promotion? No transfer to Homicide or Narcotics?"

"Look, Chief." Moodrow, suddenly annoyed, leaned forward. "I never set out to get Pat Cohan. Whatever I did, I did to survive."

"I know all that. Believe me, I know everything that happened."

"Then maybe you also know that what I hear you saying is that you can't trust me. You're afraid I'll call in the reporters, that I'll embarrass the Department. Let me ask you this, why should I trust a man who doesn't trust *me*?"

"A good question." Morton tapped the gray ash at the end of his cigarette into a glass ashtray. "Would you be willing to give me a copy of the evidence? To show good faith."

"Done."

"Good. Now tell me, Detective, do you understand the traditional relationship between a rabbi and his protégé?"

"I'm sure you'll tell me."

Once again, Morton failed to respond to a verbal jab. "The protégé," he said, "functions as the rabbi's eyes and ears. He does favors for his rabbi and expects favors in return. A protégé's favors usually involve an advantageous transfer or an out-and-out promotion, but in your case, I suspect that you'll be more interested in protection. Am I right?"

Moodrow sat back in the chair. No matter what you did, it always came back to the same thing. The politics of the job reached into every cop's working life. There was no way to get around it. What you had to do was find a way to satisfy the Department. And there was no magic formula. One day the tightrope would be as wide as the Brooklyn Bridge and the next it would be a single strand of wire suspended over the Grand Canyon.

"There're no rules, are there?" he asked.

"There are nothing *but* rules," Morton responded. "Pages and pages and pages of rules. The only question is which of them apply to what situation."

"All right. You can call in your marker whenever you want. Only I'm not a trained poodle so don't expect blind obedience. You ask and I'll check the rules to see which ones apply to the *situation*. In the meanwhile, I expect to do my job."

Morton puffed on the cigarette, sucking the smoke deep into his lungs before slowly exhaling. "Did I tell you that Captain McElroy is being transferred out of the Seventh?"

"No."

"You might be surprised to hear this, but he's not being transferred because he's an incompetent moron who lost control of his command. Nor is he being transferred because I want to put my own man in charge of the Seventh. McElroy, who will soon retire, is being transferred because he let a cop die unnecessarily. Keep it in mind, detective. The first rule is to succeed. If McElroy had handled Jake Leibowitz without incident, he would have been a hero. Especially if he did it before the reporters arrived. But he didn't and now he's out."

"Bad for him, good for me," Moodrow said. "We weren't the best of friends."

"As a matter of fact, he blamed you for all his troubles." Morton ground out the cigarette. "Is something wrong, detective?"

Moodrow snorted. If he started naming all the things that were *wrong*, he'd be sitting in Milton Morton's office until he retired. Maybe, he thought, I oughta start with what's right. The list'll be a lot shorter.

"Because," Morton continued, "you don't seem very happy, detective. Which I find somewhat surprising. You did get what you wanted, didn't you? You did get yourself a piece of the action."

NEW HANOVER COUNTY PUBLIC LIBRARY

3 4200 00287 8151

NEW HANOVER COUNTY PUBLIC LIBRARY
201 Chestnut Street
Wilmington, NC 28401